PLAYING A GAME

OF

GHOST STORIES

A COLLECTION

FIRST VOLUME OF TWO PARTS

I saw the Pale Student
of the Unhallowed Arts
Kneeling beside the thing
He had put together.
I saw the hideous phantasm
Of a man stretched out,
And then, on the working
Of some powerful engine.
Show signs of life, and stir with an
Uneasy, half vital motion——
MARY SHELLEY

London:
PRINTED FOR
ROBERT DWIGHT BROWN & ALLONYMOUS BOOKS
2025

ALLONYMOUS BOOKS

A Division of Chi Xi Stigma Publishing Company, LLC

ISBN 13: 978-1-931608-70-1 — *Playing a Game of Ghost Stories*
ISBN 13: 978-1-931608-72-5 — *A Strange Birth to Frankenstein*
ISBN 13: 978-1-931608-73-2 — *A Strange Birth to Frankenstein (Omnibus)*
ISBN 13: 978-1-931608-75-6 — *A Strange Birth to Frankenstein (Omnibus)*

Includes the following Novels and Short Stories (Complete):
FRANKENSTEIN;
   or, The Modern Prometheus – Vol. 1 by Mary Shelley, 1818
THE BURIAL a Fragment by Lord Byron, 1819
ERNESTUS BERCHTOLD; or, The Modern Œdipus – Part 2
   by Dr. John Polidori, 1819
THE DEATH BRIDE by Friedrich Laun,1813
   xs(English translation by Sarah Elizabeth Utterson, 1813)

Includes the following Poems (Complete or Partial):
CHRISTABEL by Samuel Taylor Coleridge, 1816
THE PRISONER OF CHILLON by Lord Byron, 1816
PROMETHEUS by Lord Byron 1816
PROMETHEUS UNBOUND by Percy Bysshe Shelley, 1820

We acknowledge the corrections made to *Ernestus Berchhold* made by D.L. Macdon-
ald and Kathleen Scherf in their University of Toronto Press edition.

Table of Contents

Preface

At first blush, these two volumes are merely a collection of classic Gothic Horror tales from the 1810's, over two hundred years ago. One is extraordinarily famous: *Frankenstein; or The Modern Prometheus*, the first science-fiction novel. One is ordinarily famous (in vampire circles): *The Vampyre*, the first novel featuring a suave, seductive member of the undead. The remaining works: 'The Burial: A Fragment', *Ernestus Berchtold; or The Modern Œdipus*, and "The Death-Bride" are so obscure they are barely known out of academic circles. If these volumes had been published by a university press, they would a 'merely' be a collection of stories, perhaps with annotations from scholars, but a collection nonetheless.

The unique factor linking these stories together they were all conceived and/or written in 1816: "The Year Without Summer". After reading "The Death-Bride", from a French translation of German ghost stories titled *Fantasmagoriana*, Lord Byron proposed playing a game of ghost stories. During this game, he wrote "The Burial: A Fragment", his personal physician Dr John Polidori wrote both *Ernestus Berchtold* and his plagiarism, *The Vampyre*, and Mary Shelley, the step-sister of his lover, wrote *Frankenstein*. This now becomes a special collection of stories linked in both time and space.

What you hold in your hands is not 'merely' a collection of these inextricably linked stories, it is *the* story of that long, cold, lightning-fuelled volcanic winter at the Villa Diodati on the shore of Lake Geneva. This is *the* story which I am telling in my own Gothic Horror-styled ghost story, interwoven throughout the rest. Mary Shelley, Lord Bryon, Dr John Polidori are *Playing a Game of Ghost Stories*, which gave *A Strange Birth To Frankenstein*!

A conceit in historical fiction, whether the medium is literature or cinema, is that liberties must be taken. These liberties include, but are certainly not limited to, combining multiple characters into one and contracting the timeframe and/or locations the story takes place in. The story of the haunting of the Villa Diodati includes only five people (six if you count the toddler, William), so one could easily have been tempted to turn one character into two or three, but I have not chosen that exercise that obscene option. The second liberty is the contraction of time. Through journals, diaries, and letters written during these three months, we know when certain stories and poems were begun and when or if they were completed during their stay at the Villa. I have taken the liberty of contracting the timeline of the writings into a little over two weeks (for the *Playing a Game of Ghost Stories* volume), instead of the three months and beyond that the actual writings took. And while Percy Shelley rent-

Table of Contents

Preface

At first blush, these two volumes are merely a collection of classic Gothic Horror tales from the 1810's, over two hundred years ago. One is extraordinarily famous: *Frankenstein; or The Modern Prometheus*, the first science-fiction novel. One is ordinarily famous (in vampire circles): *The Vampyre*, the first novel featuring a suave, seductive member of the undead. The remaining works: 'The Burial: A Fragment', *Ernestus Berchtold; or The Modern Œdipus*, and "The Death-Bride" are so obscure they are barely known out of academic circles. If these volumes had been published by a university press, they would a 'merely' be a collection of stories, perhaps with annotations from scholars, but a collection nonetheless.

The unique factor linking these stories together they were all conceived and/or written in 1816: "The Year Without Summer". After reading "The Death-Bride", from a French translation of German ghost stories titled *Fantasmagoriana*, Lord Byron proposed playing a game of ghost stories. During this game, he wrote "The Burial: A Fragment", his personal physician Dr John Polidori wrote both *Ernestus Berchtold* and his plagiarism, *The Vampyre*, and Mary Shelley, the step-sister of his lover, wrote *Frankenstein*. This now becomes a special collection of stories linked in both time and space.

What you hold in your hands is not 'merely' a collection of these inextricably linked stories, it is *the* story of that long, cold, lightning-fuelled volcanic winter at the Villa Diodati on the shore of Lake Geneva. This is *the* story which I am telling in my own Gothic Horror-styled ghost story, interwoven throughout the rest. Mary Shelley, Lord Bryon, Dr John Polidori are *Playing a Game of Ghost Stories*, which gave *A Strange Birth To Frankenstein*!

A conceit in historical fiction, whether the medium is literature or cinema, is that liberties must be taken. These liberties include, but are certainly not limited to, combining multiple characters into one and contracting the timeframe and/or locations the story takes place in. The story of the haunting of the Villa Diodati includes only five people (six if you count the toddler, William), so one could easily have been tempted to turn one character into two or three, but I have not chosen that exercise that obscene option. The second liberty is the contraction of time. Through journals, diaries, and letters written during these three months, we know when certain stories and poems were begun and when or if they were completed during their stay at the Villa. I have taken the liberty of contracting the timeline of the writings into a little over two weeks (for the *Playing a Game of Ghost Stories* volume), instead of the three months and beyond that the actual writings took. And while Percy Shelley rented a nearby home, I have Percy, Mary, and Claire stay in the Villa Diodati for the entirety of their visit. I have also taken a fourth liberty common in historical fiction: creative licence to fudge the facts and outright lie. Sorry... not sorry (well, kinda actually).

A NOTE ON QUOTING SOURCES: I have included footnotes noting the sources that I have utilized to produce this book, including the full (and partial) texts written during, shortly after, or at very least inspired by the "Year Without Summer". During the debate between Percy Bysshe Shelley and Lord Byron about galvanism, I have the characters quote many contemporary (to them) and near contemporary sources. While strict rules to counter plagiarism are to utilize quotation marks, I have chosen not to. My reasoning is simple. As this is a novel of historical fiction, I feel these quotation marks in the character's dialogue distracts from the readability of the prose. When we naturally speak quotation marks are implied, so I imply the quotation marks by changing the font to the Century Old Style typeface.

A NOTE ON MODERN SOURCES: I have attempted to include sources as contemporary to the events of 1816 when humanely possible. In the modern age of the Internet, I have been amazed at the sheer number of contemporary or near contemporary sources available on the World Wide Web, whether from Project Gutenberg, Wikisource, the Internet Archive, Google Books, etc. Thankfully, many of these sources have long since fallen into the public domain, which permits me to use them freely. When this fails, I have used more modern sources and have cited them accordingly.

1816: A "Year Without A Summer" Classics Collection

Death-Bride

In the introduction to *Frankenstein*, Mary Shelley mentions the ghost story that inspired Lord Byron's game of ghost stories. The story she remembers being called 'The History of the Inconstant Lover', but is probably "La Morte Fiancée", written by Friedrich Laun. The 'Death-Bride' is one of eight German ghost stories included *Fantasmagoriana: Recueil d'histoires, d'apparitions, de spectres, revenans, fantômes, etc.; Traduit de l'allemand, par un Amateur*, published in 1813. The edition found in the library of the Villa Diodati was a French translation of the German ghost stories. Sarah Elizabeth Utterson translated the stories into English in her *Tales of the Dead*, also published in 1813. I have included this ghost story because it was the impetus for Lord Byron's game of ghost stories which gave a strange birth to Frankenstein.

The Burial: A Fragment of a Novel

Lord Byron's contribution to the game of ghost stories he proposed is *The Burial: A Fragment of a Novel*, an unfinished vampire horror novel. Along with Dr John Polidori's *The Vampyre*, *The Burial* is one of the earliest (if not the earliest) to explore vampire themes. He abandoned the tale to never be completed. Dr Polidori explained later 'that though the groundwork is certainly Lord Byron's, its development is mine'. Plagiarism surely be damned.

Christabel

'The Death-Bride' is not the only recitation of other authors' works that summer. Dr John Polidori records in his diary on June 18, 1816: 'My leg much worse. Shelley and party here. Mrs. S[helley] called me her brother (younger). Began my ghost-story after tea. Twelve o'clock, really began to talk ghostly. L[ord] B[yron] repeated some verses of Coleridge's *Christabel*, of the witch's breast; when silence ensued, and Shelley, suddenly shrieking and putting his hands to his head, ran out of the room with a candle. Threw water in his face, and after gave him ether. He was looking at Mrs. S[helley], and suddenly thought of a woman he had heard of who had eyes instead of nipples, which, taking hold of his mind, horrified him.'

Prometheus & Prometheus (Unbound)

Lord Bryon wrote and published 'Prometheus' in 1816. I am including it in this collection, not only because it was probably written during his stay at the Villa Diodati, but because Mary Shelley's alternate title to *Frankenstein* is *The Modern Prometheus*. It does not stretch credulity that the writing and recitation of Lord Byron's poem may have served as the inspiration for the alternate title of *Frankenstein*. Percy Bysshe Shelly also wrote and published a four-act lyrical drama based on the Greek myth, *Prometheus (Unbound)*, first published in 1820. There is no reason to believe that any of *Prometheus (Unbound)* was composed during the 'Year Without a Summer', but I have included the first lines because they fit the narrative.

Frankenstein

There is no question why I have included *Frankenstein; or The Modern Prometheus* in his collection of stories written during the 'Year Without a Summer'. It is by far the greatest contribution to Lord Byron's game of ghost stories. Lord Byron's own contribution is largely forgotten outside of Romantic circles. In Dr Polidori's own words, *The Vampyre* was not his contribution to the game, but instead was *Ernestus Berchtold; or The Modern Oedipus*, a most obscure work that is not readily available even on the Internet. Percy Bysshe Shelley seemingly contributed nothing to the game. But Mary's contribution gave birth to the modern concept of science-fiction. An eighteen-year-old girl is solely responsible for putting the 'science' in science-fiction. The work has never been out of print in the 200-plus years since its publication. While I have consider the 1818 text the best choice for this collection (being the most contemporary text to the 'Year Without Summer'), I have utilized certain passages from the 1831 edition when I feel they are the most appropriate.

The Prisoner of Chillon

This chapter includes a couple sources written in 1816. Lord Byron penned the poem, 'The Prisoner of Chillon' during a week-long excursion along Lake Geneva. There was a brief respite in the thunderstorms. His poem was inspired by a visit to the *Château de Chillon*, a medieval castle located on Lake Geneva, south of Veytaux. Percy Bysshe Shelley records this expedition in *History of a Six Weeks' Tour through a part of France, Switzerland, Germany, and Holland; with Letters Descriptive of a Sail Round the Lake of Geneva and of the Glaciers of Chamouni*, a collection of travelogues written by himself and Mary. I have included both the travelogue and the poem in this chapter.

Ernestus Berchtold

History records that Dr John Polidori's contribution to the game of ghost stories was *The Vampyre*, a blatant plagiarism of Lord Byron's *The Burial: A Fragment of a Novel*. But the doctor insists that the ghost story he began that summer was *Erenestus Berchtold; or a Modern Oedipus*. William Micheal Rossetti, the editor of *The Diary of Dr John William Polidori* comments, 'Polidori, after tea, began his ghost-story. This, according to Mrs. Shelley, was a tale about "a skull-headed lady, who was so punished for peeping through a keyhole—what to see, I forget; something very shocking and wrong, of course." So says Mrs. Shelley: but Polidori's own statement is that the tale which he at first began was the one published under the title of *Ernestus Berchtold*, which contains nothing about a skull-headed lady... Afterwards he took up the notion of a vampyre, when relinquished by Byron. The original story, *Ernestus Berchtold*, may possibly have been completed in 1816: at any rate it was completed at some time, and published in 1819, soon after *The Vampyre*.' Written in four parts, the story was influenced by Lord Byron's own incestuous relationship with his half-sister with whom he produced a child. I have chosen to include only the second part in the main text of my collection because of the length of the novella. Parts one, three, and four are included in the appendices for completionist's sake.

Memoir of Stamford Raffles

Prologues typically serve the purpose of establishing a element of the story that takes place before or separate from the novel's primary storyline. In my book, a specific selection from the *Memoir of the life and public services of Sir Thomas Stamford Raffles, F.R.S. &c., particularly in the government of Java 1811–1816, and of Bencoolen and its dependencies 1817–1824: with details of the commerce and resources of the eastern archipelago, and selections from his correspondence* serves this purpose to a 't'. The inciting incident of the 'Year Without a Summer' began a year before when Mount Tambora exploded (not merely erupted) in Indonesia. Raffles' contemporary reports from that time set the stage for weather disruptions that would trap Mary and Percy Shelley, Lord Byron, Dr Polidori, and Claire Clairmont in the Villa Diodati.

History of a Six Weeks' Tour

Mary Shelley and Percy Bysshe Shelley would publish a travelogue of two journeys, one across Europe in 1814 and the other, of most importance to this collection, one to Lake Geneva in 1816, the very save "year without summer". This collection's mission statement is to collect the writings made during this summer, whether they are stories, poems, letters, or even a travelogue. By including these letters and diary entries, I can flesh out the events prior to their arrival at the Villa Diodati.

Mary Shelley, Lord Byron & Dr. Polidori Are

Playing a Game of
GhostStories

June 1816

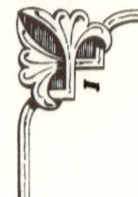

June 1816

1		

| **2** | **3** | **4** |
| | | |

| **5** | **6** | **7** |
| | | |

| **8** | | |
| | | |

| **9** | **10** | **11** |
| | | |

| **12** | **13** | **14** |
| | | |

| **15** | | |
| *P. sprains his ankle.* | | |

| **16** | **17** | **18** |
| *Byron proposes the Game of Ghost Stories.* | *P. has dinner w/ Madame Odier's. Byron completes his fragment.* | *S. conniption over "Christabel". P. begins writing Ernestus. The Sun burns hot.* |

| **19** | **20** | **21** |
| *Teasing of Mary begins every morning.* | | *P. & B. have their Spirited Debate. M. has her nightmare!* |

| **22** | | |
| *The Pale Student begins his tale of the Birth of the Creature.* | | |

| **23** | **24** | **25** |
| *Party leaves on eight-day tour of Lake Geneva.* | | |

| **26** | **27** | **28** |
| | | *B., M., P.S., & C. Visit Château de Chillon. B. writes "Prisoner" & presents at hotel.* |

| **29** | | |
| | | |

| **30** | | |
| *Party returns from their tour of Lake Geneva.* | | |

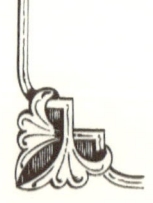

Prologue[1]

r. Raffles gives the following account of the eruption from the Tomboro Mountain, in the Island of Sambawa, which took place at this time, (the 11th and 12th of April, 1815,) one of the most violent and extraordinary of such explosions yet known.

To preserve an authentic account of the violent and extraordinary eruption of the Tomboro Mountain on Sambawa, in April last, I required from the several Residents of districts on this Island a statement of the circumstances that occurred within their knowledge, and from their replies, the following narrative is collected; it is, perhaps, incomplete until some further accounts are received of the immediate effects upon the mountain itself; but the progress is sufficiently known to render interesting a present account of a phenomenon which exceeds any one of a similar description on record. The first explosions were heard on this Island in the evening of the 5th of April, they were noticed in every quarter, and continued at intervals until the following day. The noise was, in the first instance, almost universally attributed to distant cannon; so much so, that a detachment of troops were marched from *Djocjocarta*, in the expectation that a neighbouring post was attacked, and along the coast boats were in two instances dispatched in quest of a supposed ship in distress.

On the following morning, however, a slight fall of ashes removed all doubt as to the cause of the sound, and it is worthy of remark, that as the eruption continued, the sound appeared to be so close, that in each district it seemed near at hand; it was attributed to an emption from the Marapi, the Gunung Kloot or the Gunung Bromo.

From the 6th, the sun became obscured: it had every appearance of being enveloped in fog, the weather was sultry, and the atmosphere close and still; the sun seemed shorn of its rays, and the general stillness and pressure of the atmosphe0re foreboded an earthquake. This lasted several days, the explosions continued occasionally, but less violently, and less frequently than at first. Volcanic ashes also began to fall, but in small quantities; and so slightly as to be hardly perceptible in the western districts.

---

1 From the *Memoir of the life and public services of Sir Thomas Stamford Raffles, F.R.S. &c., particularly in the government of Java 1811–1816, and of Bencoolen and its dependencies 1817–1824: with details of the commerce and resources of the eastern archipelago, and selections from his correspondence* by his widow, Sophia (Hull) Raffles, published by John Murray, 1830

This appearance of the atmosphere remained with little variation, until the 10th of April, and till then it does not appear that the volcano attracted much observation, or was considered of greater importance than those which have occasionally burst forth in Java. But on the evening of the 10th, the emptions were heard more loud, and more frequent from Cheribon eastward; the air became darkened by the quantity of falling ashes, and in several situations, particularly at Solo and Rembang, many said that they felt a tremulous motion of the earth. It is universally remarked in the more eastern districts, that the explosions were tremendous, continuing frequently during the 11th, and of such violence as to shake the houses perceptibly; an unusually thick darkness was remarked all the following night, and the greater part of the next day. At Solo, on the 12th, at four P.M., objects were not visible at 300 yards distance. At Gresie, and other districts more eastward, it was dark as night the greater part of the 12th of April, and this saturated state of the atmosphere lessened as the cloud of ashes passed along and discharged itself on its way. Thus the ashes, which were eight inches deep at Banyuwangi, were but two in depth at Sumanap, and still less in Gresie; and the sun does not seem to have been actually obscured in any district westward of Samarang.

No description of mine, however, can so well express what happened, as the extracts from the reports at several places; the remarks there made are applicable also to all the other districts, only in a lesser degree, as the same became more distant from the cause of the phenomena.

Extract of a Letter from Gresie.

I woke on the morning of the 12th, after what seemed to be a very longnight, and taking my watch to the lamp, found it to be half-past eight o'clock; I immediately went out, and found a cloud of ashes descending; at nine o'clock no day-light; the layer of ashes on the terrace before my door at the Kradenan measures one line in thickness; ten A. INI. a faint glimmering of light can now be perceived over-head: half-past ten, can distinguish objects fifty yards distant; eleven, A.M. breakfasted by candle-light, the birds begin to chirrup as at the approach of day; half-past eleven, can discover the situation of the sun through a thick cloud of ashes; one, P.M. found the layer of ashes one line and a half thick, and measured in several places with the same results; three, P.M. the ashes have increased one-eighth of a line more; five, P.M. it is now lighter, but still I can neither read nor write without candle. In travelling through the district on the 13th, the appearances were described with very little variation from my account, and I am universally told that no one remembers, nor does their tradition record so tremendous an eruption. Some look upon it as typical of a change, of the re-establishment of the former government; others account for it in an easy way, by reference to the superstitious notions of their legendary tales, and say that the celebrated Nyai Loroh Kidul has been marrying one of her children, on which occasion she has been firing salutes from her supernatural artillery. They call the ashes the dregs of her ammunition.

Extract of a Letter from Sumanap.

On the evening of the 10th the explosions became very loud; one in particular shook the town, and they were excessively quick, resembling a heavy cannonade. Towards evening, next day, the atmosphere thickened so much, that by four o'clock it was necessary to light candles. At about seven, P.M., of the 11th, the tide being about ebb, a rush of water from the bay occasioned the river to rise four feet, and it subsided again in about forty minutes; the bay was much agitated about this time, and was illuminated from a northerly direction. On the Island of Sahotie, fire was seen distinctly at a short distance to the south-east. The uncommon darkness of this night did not break till ten and eleven, A.M. of the 12th, and it could hardly be called day-light all day. Volcanic ashes fell in abundance, and covered the earth about two inches thick, the trees also were loaded with them.'

Extract of a Letter from Banyuwangi.

At ten, P.M. of the first of April, we heard a noise resembling a cannonade, which lasted, at intervals, till nine o'clock next day; it continued at times loud, at others resembling distant thunder; but on the night of the 10th, the explosions became truly tremendous, frequently shaking the earth and sea violently. Towards morning they again slackened, and continued to lessen gradually till the 14th, when they ceased altogether. On the morning of the 3d of April, ashes began to fall like fine snow; and in the course of the day they were half-an-inch deep on the ground. From that time till the 11th the air was constantly impregnated with them to such a degree, that it was unpleasant to stir out of doors. On the morning of the 11th, the opposite shore of Bah was completely obscured in a dense cloud, which gradually approached the Java shore, and was dreary and terrific. By one, P.M. candles were necessary; by four, P.M. it was pitch-dark; and so it continued until two o'clock of the afternoon of the 12th, ashes continuing to fall abundantly: they were eight inches in depth at this time. After two o'clock it began to clear up; but the sun was not visible till the 14th, and during this time it was extremely cold. The ashes continued to fall, but less violently, and the greatest depth, on the 15th of April, was nine inches.

All reports concur in stating, that so violent and extensive an eruption has not happened within the memory of the oldest inhabitants, nor within tradition. They speak of similar effects in a lesser degree, when an eruption took place from the volcano of Carang Assum, in Bah, about seven years ago; and it was at first supposed that this mountain w^as the seat of eruption in the present instance. The Balinese attributed the event to a recent dispute between the two Rajahs of Bah Baliling, which terminated in the death of the younger Rajah, by order of his brother.

The haziness and heat of the atmosphere, and occasional fall of volcanic ashes, continued until the 14th, or, in some parts of the Island, until the 17th of April; they were cleared away universally by a heavy fall of rain, after which the atmosphere became clear and more cool; and it would seem that this seasonable relief prevented much injury to the crops, and removed an appearance of epidemic disease, which w'as beginning to prevail. This was especially the case at Batavia, where, for the two or three days preceding the rain, many persons where attacked with fever. As it was, however, no material injury was felt beyond the districts of Banjniw'angi. The cultivators every where took the precaution to shake off the ashes from the growing paddy as they fell, and the timely rain removed an apprehension very generally entertained, that insects would have been generated by the long continuance of the ashes at the root of the plant. At Rembang, where the rain did not fall till the 17th, and the ashes had been considerable, the crops were somewhat injured. In Gresie the injury was less; but in Banymvangi and the adjacent part of the Island, on which the cloud of ashes spent its force, the injury was more extensive: 126 horses and eighty-six head of cattle also perished, chiefly from want of forage during a month from the time of the eruption.

The local effects of this emption have been ascertained by Lieutenant Owen Phillips, who proceeded to Sumbawa for this purpose, and was charged to distribute to the sufferers a supply of rice, dispatched by this government on hearing of the extreme distress to which the inhabitants of Sumbawa had been reduced.

The Noquedah of a Malay prow from Timor had reported that on the 11th of April, while at sea, far distant from Sumbawa, he was in utter darkness; that on his passing the Tomboro mountain at a distance of five miles, the lower part of it was in flames, and the upper part covered with clouds; he went on shore for water, and found the ground covered with ashes to the depth of three feet, several large prows thrown on the land by a concussion of the sea, and many of the inhabitants dead from famine. On leaving Sumbawa, he experienced a strong current to the westward, and fell in with great quantities of cinders floating on the sea, through which he with difficulty forced his way; he was surrounded by them the whole of the night of the 12th, and says they formed a mass of two feet thick, and several miles in extent. This person states that the volcano of Carang Assam in Bali, was in commotion at the same time; and it appears from the several reports, that a greater rumbling than usual was heard in the mountains in the Rembang district, as well as in the Gunnug Gede in the Preanger Regencies, but after a strict enquiry, it does not appear that any simultaneous movement or connection could be traced on this occasion along the chain of Volcanic Mountains running east and west in Java.'

The Honourable Company's cruzier Benares, was at this time at Macasar, and the following official report, received from the Commander of this vessel, confirms the circumstances already related.

'On the 5th of April, a firing of cannon was heard at Macasar, continuing at intervals all the afternoon, and apparently coming from the southward: — towards sun-set the reports seemed to have approached much nearer, and sounded hke hea\y guns, with occasional slight reports between. Supposing it to be occasioned by pirates, a detachment of troops was embarked on board the Honourable Company's cruzier Benares, and sent in search of them, but after examining the neighbouring Islands, returned to Macasar on the 8th, without having found any cause of the alarm. During the night of the 11th, the firing was again heard, but much lower, and towards morning the reports were in quick succession, sometimes like three or four guns fired together, and so heavy that they shook the ship, as they did also the houses in Fort Rotterdam. Some of them seemed so near, that I sent people to the mast-heads to look out for the flashes, and weighed at day-dawn, proceeding to the southward to ascertain the cause. The morning of the 12th was extremely dark and lowering, particularly to the southward, and S.W., the wind light, and from the eastward. At eight A.M. it was apparent that some extraordinary occurrence had taken place; the face of the heavens to the southward and westward had assumed a dark aspect, and it was much darker than before the sun rose; as it came nearer it assumed a dusky red appearance, and spread fast over every part of the heavens; by ten it was so dark that a ship could hardly be seen a mile distant; by eleven the whole of the heavens were obscured, except a small space near the horizon to the eastward, the quarter from which the wind came. The ashes now began to fall in showers, and the appearance was altogether truly awful and alarming. By noon the light that had remained in the eastern part of the horizon disappeared, and complete darkness covered the face of day. This continued so profound during the remainder of the day, that I never saw any thing to equal it in the darkest night; it was impossible to see your hand when held up close to your eyes. The ashes fell without intermission throughout the night, and were so light and subtle, that not withstanding the precaution of spreading awnings fore and aft as much as possible, they pervaded every part of the ship.

'At six o'clock the next morning it continued as dark as ever, but began to clear about half-past seven; and about eight o'clock objects could be faintly discerned upon deck. From this time it began to get lighter very fast.

'The appearance of the ship when day-light returned was most singular; every part being covered with the falling matter: it had the appearance of calcined pumice stone, nearly the colour of wood-ashes; it lay in heaps of a foot in depth in many parts of the deck, and several tons weight of it must have been thrown overboard; for though an impalpable powder or dust when it fell, it was, when compressed, of considerable weight; a pint measure of it weighed twelve ounces and three-quarters, it was perfectly tasteless, and did not affect the eyes with painful sensation, had a faint burnt smell, but nothing like sulphur; when mixed with water it formed a tenacious mud difficult to be washed off.

'By noon of the 12th, the sun made his appearance again, hut very faintly, through the dusky atmosphere; the air being still charged with ashes, which continued to fall lightly all day.

'From the 12th to the 15th, the atmosphere remained thick and dusky, the rays of the sun scarce able to penetrate through it, with little or no wind the whole time.

'On the morning of the 13th left Macasar, and on the 18th made Sumbawa; on approaching the coast passed through great quantities of pumice-stone floating on the sea, which had at first strongly the appearance of shoals, so much so that I sent a boat to examine one, which, at the distance of less than a mile, I took for a dry sand-bank, upwards of three miles in length, with black rocks in several parts of it. It proved to be a complete mass of pumice-stone floating on the sea, some inches in depth, with great numbers of trees and logs, that appeared to be burnt and shivered as if by lightning. The boat had much difficulty in pulling through it, and until we reached the entrance of Bima Bay, the sea was literally covered with shoals of pumice and floating timber.

'On the 19th arrived in Bima Bay, in coming to an anchor grounded on the bank of Bima Town, shoaling suddenly from eight fathoms; hove off again as the tide was rising. The anchorage at Bima must have altered considerably, as where we grounded the Ternate cruiser lay at anchor in six fathoms a few months before. The shores of the bay had a most dreary appearance, being entirely covered with ashes.'

From the account of the Resident of Bima, it appears that the eruption proceeded from the Tomboro mountain, situated about forty miles to the westward of Bima. On the night of the 11th, the explosions he represents to have been most terrific, and compares them to the report of a heavy mortar close to his ear. The darkness commenced about seven in the morning, and continued twelve hours longer than it did at Macasar. The fall of ashes was so heavy as to break the Resident's house in many places, and render it uninhabitable, as well as many other houses in the town. The wind was still during the whole time, but the sea greatly agitated, its waves rolled in upon the shore, and filled the lower parts of the houses with water a foot deep. Every prow and boat was forced from the anchorage and driven on shore, and several large prows are now lying a considerable distance above high-water-mark.

'On the 22d, the Dispatch country ship arrived in the bay from Amboyna. It appears that this vessel had mistaken a bay to the westward, called Sampo or Sangin Bay, for Bima, and had gone into it; the Rajah of this place informed the officer that the whole of the country was entirely desolated, and the crops destroyed. The town of Sangin is situated about four or five leagues to the S. E. of the Tomboro mountain; the officer found great difficulty in landing in the bay, a considerable distance from the shore being completely filled up with pumice-stones, ashes, and logs of timber; the houses appeared beaten down and covered with ashes.

'Understanding that messengers had been sent into the interior, I waited till the evening of the 22d, and as they had not then returned, owing, as was supposed, to having found the country impassable, I left the bay at eleven o'clock that night, and the next day was off the Tomboro mountain; in passing it at the distance of six miles the summit was not visible, being enveloped in clouds of smoke and ashes. The sides were smoking in several places, apparently from lava which had flown down them not being cooled, several streams had reached the sea; a very considerable one to the N.N.W. of the mountain, the course of which was plainly discernible, both from the black colour of the lava contrasted with the ashes on each side of it, and the smoke arising from every part of it. The Tomboro Mountain in a direct line from Macasar is about 217 nautical miles distance.'

It has been ascertained that these eruptions of the Tomboro Mountain were heard through the whole chain of the Molucca Islands. The Honourable Company's cruiser Teignmouth was lying at anchor at Ternate on the 5th April; between six and eight, P.M., several very distinct reports like heavy cannon were heard in the S.W. quarter, which was supposed to be a ship in the offing, in consequence of which the Resident sent a boat round the Island to ascertain if it was so. The next morning, however, the boat returned without seeing any vessel in the offing, and the conclusion then drawn was that it might be occasioned by the bursting of some volcanic mountain in that quarter. Ternate Island 5° 0'N. 127° 30'E.

The easterly monsoon, however, had at this time distinctly set in, and consequently the sounds would not be heard so loudly and distinctly in the Moluccas, as from the relative distance would otherwise have happened. They extended, in the opposite direction, to Fort Marlbro', and several parts of Sumatra, as appears from the following extract from thence.

It is an extraordinary fact, that precisely the same noise (taken by all who heard it to be a cannonade) occurred at several stations along this coast at the same time, viz. the morning of the 11th April several gentlemen heard it in Marlbro', the people from the interior came down with accounts of it, and those from the higher Dusuns spoke of a kind of ash-dust which had covered the herbage and the leaves of the trees. Reports to the same effect, (not mentioning any fall of ashes however,) were received from Moco-moco, Laye, Salumah, Manna, Padang Guchee, Croee, and Semanka. From some of these stations the hill-people came down armed, to assist against attacks which they imagined might be made upon the head factories.'

It has not appeared that any noise of this kind was heard at Padang, or much further north than Moco-moco. I have since heard that the same noise was heard at Trumon in about 2'40'N. lat. and at Aver Bungi in about 0'15'N. lat. at aU on or about the 11th April last.

From Sumbawa to the port of Sumatra, where the sound was noticed, is about 970 geographical miles in a direct line; from Sumbawa to Ternate is a distance of 720 miles; and the existence of the S. E. monsoon at the time may account for the difference of distance to which the sound was heard in the westerly and easterly directions; the distance also, to which the cloud of ashes was carried, so thickly as to produce utter darkness, is clearly pointed out to have been the Island of Celebes, and the districts of Gresie on Java. The former is 217 nautical miles distant from the seat of the volcano — the latter in a direct line more than 300 geographical miles distant.

I shall conclude this account with an extract of a letter from Lieutenant Owen Phillips, written from Bima on the 23d ultimo. It has been mentioned in a former part, that on receiving intelligence of the extreme distress that had been occasioned by this extraordinary event, I dispatched a supply of rice to their relief, and Lieutenant Phillips was desired to proceed and adjust the delivery thereof, with instructions, at the same time, to ascertain, as nearly as possible, the local effects of the volcano. His report is as follows:

'On my trip towards the western part of the Island, I passed through nearly the whole of Dompo, and a considerable part of Bima. The extreme misery to which the inhabitants have been reduced, is shocking to behold; there were still on the road side the remains of several corjises, and the marks of where many others had been interred; the villages almost entirely deserted, and the houses fallen down, the surviving inhabitants having dispersed in search of food.

'In Dompo, the sole subsistence of the inhabitants for some time past has been the heads of the different species of palm, and the stalks of the papaya and plantain.

'Since the eruption, a violent diarrhoea has prevailed in Bima, Dompo, and Saugar, which has carried off a great number of people. It is supposed by the natives to have been caused by drinking water which has been impregnated with the ashes; and horses have also died, in great numbers, from a similar complaint.

'The Rajah of Saugar came to wait on me at Dompo on the 3d inst. The sufferings of the people there appear, from his account, to be still greater than in Dompo. The famine has been so severe, that even one of his own daughters died from hunger. I presented him with three coyangs of rice in your name, for which he appeared to be truly grateful.

'As the Rajah was himself a spectator of the late eruption, the following account which he gave me, is, perhaps, more to be depended upon than any other I can possibly obtain:

'About seven, P.M. on the 10th of April, three distinct columns of flame burst forth, near the top of Tomboro mountain, all of them apparently within the verge of the crater; and after ascending separately to a very great height, their tops united in the air in a troubled confused manner. In a short time the whole mountain next Saugar appeared like a body of liquid fire extending itself in every direction.

'The fire and columns of flame continued to rage with unabated fury, until the darkness caused by the quantity of falling matter obscured it at about eight, P.M. Stones at this time fell very thick at Saugar; some of them as large as two fists, but generally not larger than walnuts. Between nine and ten, P.M. ashes began to fall, and soon after a violent whirlwind ensued, which blew down nearly every house in the village of Saugar, carrying the tops and high parts along with it. In the part of Saugar adjoining Tomboro, its effects were much more violent, tearing up by the roots the largest trees, and carrying them into the air, together with men, houses, cattle, and whatever else came within its influence (this will account for the immense number of floating trees seen at sea.) The sea rose nearly twelve feet higher than it had ever been known to be before, and completely spoiled the only small spots of rice-lands in Saugar, sweeping away houses and every thing within its reach.

The whirlwind lasted about an hour. No explosions were heard till the whirlwind had ceased, at about eleven, A.M. From midnight till the evening of the 11th, they continued without intermission; after that, their violence moderated, and they were only heard at intervals; but the explosions did not cease entirely until the 15th of July. The mountain still throws out immense volumes of smoke, and the natives are apprehensive of another eruption during the ensuing rainy season.

'Of the whole of the villages of Tomboro, Jempo, containing about forty inhabitants, is the only one remaining. In Precate, no vestige of a house is left. Twenty-six of the people who were at Sambawa at the time are the whole of the population who have escaped.

'From the most particular inquiries I have been able to make, there were certainly not fewer than 12,000 individuals in Tomboro and Precate at the time of the eruption.

The trees and herbage of every description along the whole of the north and west sides of the Peninsula, have been completely destroyed, with the exception of a high point of land near the spot where the village of Tomboro stood; on it a few trees still remain. In the night of the eruption, two men and two women, I am informed, escaped to this point, and were saved. I have sent in search of them, but have not yet been able to get hold of them; no person has yet been along the eastern side of the hill.

'A messenger who returned yesterday from Sambawa, relates that the fall of ashes has been heavier at Sambawa than on this side the Gulf, and that an immense number of people have been starved: they are now parting with their horses and buffaloes for a half or quarter rupee's worth of rice or corn. The distress has, however, I trust, been alleviated by this time, as the brig, with sixty-three coyangs of rice, from Java, arrived there the day he was leaving it.'

—Batavia, September 28, 1815.

Second Prologue[2]

Letter 1.

Hôtel de Secheron, Geneva,
May 17, 1816.

We arrived at Paris on the 8th of this month, and were detained two days for the purpose of obtaining the various signatures necessary to our passports, the French government having become much more circumspect since the escape of Lavalette. We had no letters of introduction, or any friend in that city, and were therefore confined to our hotel, where we were obliged to hire apartments for the week, although when we first arrived we expected to be detained one night only; for in Paris there are no houses where you can be accommodated with apartments by the day.

The manners of the French are interesting, although less attractive, at least to Englishmen, than before the last invasion of the Allies: the discontent and sullenness of their minds perpetually betrays itself. Nor is it wonderful that they should regard the subjects of a government which fills their country with hostile garrisons, and sustains a detested dynasty on the throne, with an acrimony and indignation of which that government alone is the proper object. This feeling is honourable to the French, and encouraging to all those of every nation in Europe who have a fellow feeling with the oppressed, and who cherish an unconquerable hope that the cause of liberty must at length prevail.

Our route after Paris, as far as Troyes, lay through the same uninteresting tract of country which we had traversed on foot nearly two years before, but on quitting Troyes we left the road leading to Neufchâtel, to follow that which was to conduct us to Geneva. We entered Dijon on the third evening after our departure from Paris, and passing through Dôle, arrived at Poligny. This town is built at the foot of Jura, which rises abruptly from a plain of vast extent. The rocks of the mountain overhang the houses. Some difficulty in procuring horses detained us here until the evening closed in, when we proceeded, by the light of a stormy moon, to Champagnolles, a little village situated in the depth of the mountains. The road was serpentine and exceedingly steep, and was overhung on one side by half distinguished precipices, whilst the other was a gulph,

---

2 From *History of a Six Weeks Tour* by Mary Wollstonecraft Shelley and Percy Bysshe Shelley, published by T Thomas Hookham, Jr. and Charles and James Ollier, 1817

filled by the darkness of the driving clouds. The dashing of the invisible mountain streams announced to us that we had quitted the plains of France, as we slowly ascended, amidst a violent storm of wind and rain, to Champagnolles, where we arrived at twelve o'clock, the fourth night after our departure from Paris.

The next morning we proceeded, still ascending among the ravines and vallies of the mountain. The scenery perpetually grows more wonderful and sublime: pine forests of impenetrable thickness, and untrodden, nay, inaccessible expanse spread on every side. Sometimes the dark woods descending, follow the route into the vallies, the distorted trees struggling with knotted roots between the most barren clefts; sometimes the road winds high into the regions of frost, and then the forests become scattered, and the branches of the trees are loaded with snow, and half of the enormous pines themselves buried in the wavy drifts. The spring, as the inhabitants informed us, was unusually late, and indeed the cold was excessive; as we ascended the mountains, the same clouds which rained on us in the vallies poured forth large flakes of snow thick and fast. The sun occasionally shone through these showers, and illuminated the magnificent ravines of the mountains, whose gigantic pines were some laden with snow, some wreathed round by the lines of scattered and lingering vapour; others darting their dark spires into the sunny sky, brilliantly clear and azure.

As the evening advanced, and we ascended higher, the snow, which we had beheld whitening the overhanging rocks, now encroached upon our road, and it snowed fast as we entered the village of Les Rousses, where we were threatened by the apparent necessity of passing the night in a bad inn and dirty beds. For from that place there are two roads to Geneva; one by Nion, in the Swiss territory, where the mountain route is shorter, and comparatively easy at that time of the year, when the road is for several leagues covered with snow of an enormous depth; the other road lay through Gex, and was too circuitous and dangerous to be attempted at so late an hour in the day. Our passport, however, was for Gex, and we were told that we could not change its destination; but all these police laws, so severe in themselves, are to be softened by bribery, and this difficulty was at length overcome. We hired four horses, and ten men to support the carriage, and departed from Les Rousses at six in the evening, when the sun had already far descended, and the snow pelting against the windows of our carriage, assisted the coming darkness to deprive us of the view of the lake of Geneva and the far distant Alps.

The prospect around, however, was sufficiently sublime to command our attention—never was scene more awfully desolate. The trees in these regions are incredibly large, and stand in scattered clumps over the white wilderness; the vast expanse of snow was chequered only by these gigantic pines, and the poles that marked our road: no river or rock-encircled lawn relieved the eye, by adding the picturesque to the sublime. The natural silence of that uninhabited desert contrasted strangely with the voices of the men who conducted us, who, with animated tones and gestures, called to one another in a patois composed of French and Italian, creating disturbance, where but for them, there was none.

To what a different scene are we now arrived! To the warm sunshine and to the humming of sun-loving insects. From the windows of our hotel we see the lovely lake, blue as the heavens which it reflects, and sparkling with golden beams. The opposite shore is sloping, and covered with vines, which however do not so early in the season add to the beauty of the prospect. Gentlemens' seats are scattered over these banks, behind which rise the various ridges of black mountains, and towering far above, in the midst of its snowy Alps, the majestic Mont Blanc, highest and queen of all. Such is the view reflected by the lake; it is a bright summer scene without any of that sacred solitude and deep seclusion that delighted us at Lucerne.

We have not yet found out any very agreeable walks, but you know our attachment to water excursions. We have hired a boat, and every evening at about six o'clock we sail on the lake, which is delightful, whether we glide over a glassy surface or are speeded along by a strong wind. The waves of this lake never afflict me with that sickness that deprives me of all enjoyment in a sea voyage; on the contrary, the tossing of our boat raises my spirits and inspires me with unusual hilarity. Twilight here is of short duration, but we at present enjoy the benefit of an increasing moon, and seldom return until ten o'clock, when, as we approach the shore, we are saluted by the delightful scent of flowers and new mown grass, and the chirp of the grasshoppers, and the song of the evening birds.

We do not enter into society here, yet our time passes swiftly and delightfully. We read Latin and Italian during the heats of noon, and when the sun declines we walk in the garden of the hotel, looking at the rabbits, relieving fallen cockchafers, and watching the motions of a myriad of lizards, who inhabit a southern wall of the garden. You know that we have just escaped from the gloom of winter and of London; and coming to this delightful spot during this divine weather, I feel as happy as a new-fledged bird, and hardly care what twig I fly to, so that I may try my new-found wings. A more experienced bird may be more difficult in its choice of a bower; but in my present temper of mind, the budding flowers, the fresh grass of spring, and the happy creatures about me that live and enjoy these pleasures, are quite enough to afford me exquisite delight, even though clouds should shut out Mont Blanc from my sight. Adieu!

M.

Letter II.

Campagne Chapuis near Coligny,
1st June.

You will perceive from my date that we have changed our residence since my last letter. We now inhabit a little cottage on the opposite shore of the lake, and have exchanged the view of Mont Blanc and her snowy aiguilles for the dark frowning Jura, behind whose range we every evening see the sun sink, and darkness approaches our valley from behind the Alps, which are then tinged by that glowing rose-like hue which is observed in England to attend on the clouds of an autumnal sky when day-light is almost gone. The lake is at our feet, and a little harbour contains our boat, in which we still enjoy our evening excursions on the water. Unfortunately we do not now enjoy those brilliant skies that hailed us on our first arrival to this country. An almost perpetual rain confines us principally to the house; but when the sun bursts forth it is with a splendour and heat unknown in England. The thunder storms that visit us are grander and more terrific than I have ever seen before. We watch them as they approach from the opposite side of the lake, observing the lightning play among the clouds in various parts of the heavens, and dart in jagged figures upon the piny heights of Jura, dark with the shadow of the overhanging cloud, while perhaps the sun is shining cheerily upon us. One night we enjoyed a finer storm than I had ever before beheld. The lake was lit up—the pines on Jura made visible, and all the scene illuminated for an instant, when a pitchy blackness succeeded, and the thunder came in frightful bursts over our heads amid the darkness.

But while I still dwell on the country around Geneva, you will expect me to say something of the town itself: there is nothing, however, in it that can repay you for the trouble of walking over its rough stones. The houses are high, the streets narrow, many of them on the ascent, and no public building of any beauty to attract your eye, or any architecture to gratify your taste. The town is surrounded by a wall, the three gates of which are shut exactly at ten o'clock, when no bribery (as in France) can open them. To the south of the town is the promenade of the Genevese, a grassy plain planted with a few trees, and called Plainpalais. Here a small obelisk is erected to the glory of Rousseau, and here (such is the mutability of human life) the magistrates, the successors of those who exiled him from his native country, were shot by the populace during that revolution, which his writings mainly contributed to mature, and which, notwithstanding the temporary bloodshed and injustice with which it was polluted, has produced enduring benefits to mankind, which all the chicanery of statesmen, nor even the great conspiracy of kings, can entirely render vain. From respect to the memory of their predecessors, none of the present magistrates ever walk in Plainpalais. Another Sunday recreation for the citizens is an excursion to the top of Mont Salève. This hill is within a league of the town, and rises perpendicularly from the cultivated plain. It is ascended on the other side, and I should judge from its situation that your toil is rewarded by a delightful view of the course of the Rhone and Arve, and of the shores of the lake. We have not yet visited it.

There is more equality of classes here than in England. This occasions a greater freedom and refinement of manners among the lower orders than we meet with in our own country. I fancy the haughty English ladies are greatly disgusted with this consequence of republican institutions, for the Genevese servants complain very much of their scolding, an exercise of the tongue, I believe, perfectly unknown here. The peasants of Switzerland may not however emulate the vivacity and grace of the French. They are more cleanly, but they are slow and inapt. I know a girl of twenty, who although she had lived all her life among vineyards, could not inform me during what month the vintage took place, and I discovered she was utterly ignorant of the order in which the months succeed to one another. She would not have been surprised if I had talked of the burning sun and delicious fruits of December, or of the frosts of July. Yet she is by no means deficient in understanding.

The Genevese are also much inclined to puritanism. It is true that from habit they dance on a Sunday, but as soon as the French government was abolished in the town, the magistrates ordered the theatre to be closed, and measures were taken to pull down the building.

We have latterly enjoyed fine weather, and nothing is more pleasant than to listen to the evening song of the vine-dressers. They are all women, and most of them have harmonious although masculine voices. The theme of their ballads consists of shepherds, love, flocks, and the sons of kings who fall in love with beautiful shepherdesses. Their tunes are monotonous, but it is sweet to hear them in the stillness of evening, while we are enjoying the sight of the setting sun, either from the hill behind our house or from the lake.

Such are our pleasures here, which would be greatly increased if the season had been more favourable, for they chiefly consist in such enjoyments as sunshine and gentle breezes bestow. We have not yet made any excursion in the environs of the town, but we have planned several, when you shall again hear of us; and we will endeavour, by the magic of words, to transport the ethereal part of you to the neighbourhood of the Alps, and mountain streams, and forests, which, while they clothe the former, darken the latter with their vast shadows. Adieu!

M.

Chapter One
An Introduction

29 August, in the Year of our Lord Eighteen-Hundred-and-Frozen-to-Death, Lake Geneva— Preparing to leave the most haunted Villa Diodoti and the company of Lord Byron after a long, cold, lightning-fuelled, and wintery summer on the shore of Lake Geneva. Despite the completeness of my journal over the course of the winter of 1816— correction, 'summer'— I'll allow myself to briefly summarize while the memories are fresh. The journey back to England and the prison of my father is long, but not nearly long enough.

At first we spent our pleasant hours on the lake, or wandering on its shores; and Lord Byron, who was writing the third canto of *Childe Harold*, was the first among us who put his thoughts upon paper. These, as he brought them successively to us, clothed in all the light and harmony of poetry, seemed to stamp as divine the glories of heaven and earth, whose influences we partook with him.

But it proved a wet, ungenial summer, and incessant rain often confined us for days to the house. Some volumes of ghost stories, translated from the German into French, fell into our hands. There was the *History of the Inconstant Lover*, who, when he thought to clasp the bride to whom he had pledged his vows, found himself in the arms of the pale ghost of her whom he had deserted. There was the tale of *The Sinful Founder of His Race*, whose miserable doom it was to bestow the kiss of death on all the younger sons of his fated house, just when they reached the age of promise. His gigantic, shadowy form, clothed like the ghost in *Hamlet*, in complete armour, but with the beaver up, was seen at midnight, by the moon's fitful beams, to advance slowly along the gloomy avenue. The shape was lost beneath the shadow of the castle walls; but soon a gate swung back, a step was heard, the door of the chamber opened, and he advanced to the couch of the blooming youths, cradled in healthy sleep. Eternal sorrow sat upon his face as he bent down and kissed the forehead of the boys, who from that hour withered like flowers snapt upon the stalk. I have not seen these stories since then; but their incidents are as fresh in my mind as if I had read them yesterday.

'We will each write a ghost story,' said Lord George Gordon Byron; and his proposition was acceded to. There were four of us. The noble author began a tale, a fragment. Shelley, more apt to embody ideas and sentiments in the radiance of brilliant imagery, commenced one founded on the experiences of his early life. Poor Polidori had some terrible idea about a modern OEdipus, a queer overblown ghost story, something very shocking and wrong of course; but overtly inspired by George's scandalous and incestuous relationship with Augusta Leigh, the daughter of John 'Mad Jack' Byron, his own disgraced father. Was Elizabeth Medora Leigh, born 15 April 1814, the lovechild of Lord Byron and his half-sister as gossiping hens suppose? Who knows! But clearly poor Polidori felt so inspired to quite queerly write his OEdipal ghost story. The illustrious poets also, annoyed by the platitude of prose, speedily relinquished the uncongenial task.

I busied myself to think of a story, — a story to rival those which had excited us to this task. One which would speak to the mysterious fears of our nature, and awaken thrilling horror— one to make the reader dread to look round, to curdle the blood, and quicken the beatings of the heart. If I did not accomplish these things, my ghost story would be unworthy of its name. I thought and pondered— vainly. I felt that blank incapability of invention which is the greatest misery of authorship, when dull Nothing replies to our anxious invocations. Have you thought of a story? I was asked each morning, and each morning I was forced to reply with a mortifying negative.

Every thing must have a beginning, to speak in Sanchean phrase; and that beginning must be linked to something that went before. The Hindoos give the world an elephant to support it, but they make the elephant stand upon a tortoise. Invention, it must be humbly admitted, does not consist in creating out of void, but out of chaos; the materials must, in the first place, be afforded: it can give form to dark, shapeless substances, but cannot bring into being the substance itself. In all matters of discovery and invention, even of those that appertain to the imagination, we are continually reminded of the story of Columbus and his egg. Invention consists in the capacity of seizing on the capabilities of a subject, and in the power of moulding and fashioning ideas suggested to it.

Many and long were the conversations between Lord Byron and Shelley, to which I was a devout but nearly silent listener. During one of these, various philosophical doctrines were discussed, and among others the nature of the principle of life, and whether there was any probability of its ever being discovered and communicated. They talked of the experiments of Dr Darwin, (I speak not of what the Doctor really did, or said that he did, but, as more to my purpose, of what was then spoken of as having been done by him,) who preserved a piece of vermicelli in a glass case, till by some extraordinary means it began to move with voluntary motion. Not thus, after all, would life be given. Perhaps a corpse would be re-animated; galvanism had given token of such things: perhaps the component parts of a creature might be manufactured, brought together, and endued with vital warmth.

Night waned upon this talk, and even the witching hour had gone by, before we retired to rest. When I placed my head on my pillow, I did not sleep, nor could I be said to think. My imagination, unbidden, possessed and guided me, gifting the successive images that arose in my mind with a vividness far beyond the usual bounds of reverie. I saw— with shut eyes, but acute mental vision, — I saw the pale student of unhallowed arts kneeling beside the thing he had put together. I saw the hideous phantasm of a man stretched out, and then, on the working of some powerful engine, show signs of life, and stir with an uneasy, half vital motion. Frightful must it be; for supremely frightful would be the effect of any human endeavour to mock the stupendous mechanism of the Creator of the world. His success would terrify the artist; he would rush away from his odious handywork, horror-stricken. He would hope that, left to itself, the slight spark of life which he had communicated would fade; that this thing, which had received such imperfect animation, would subside into dead matter; and he might sleep in the belief that the silence of the grave would quench for ever the transient existence of the hideous corpse which he had looked upon as the cradle of life. He sleeps; but he is awakened; he opens his eyes; behold the horrid thing stands at his bedside, opening his curtains, and looking on him with yellow, watery, but speculative eyes.

I opened mine in terror. The idea so possessed my mind, that a thrill of fear ran through me, and I wished to exchange the ghastly image of my fancy for the realities around. I see them still; the very room, the dark parquet, the closed shutters, with the moonlight struggling through, and the sense I had that the glassy lake and white high Alps were beyond. I could not so easily get rid of my hideous phantom; still it haunted me. I must try to think of something else. I recurred to my ghost story, my tiresome unlucky ghost story! O! if I could only contrive one which would frighten my reader as I myself had been frightened that night!

Swift as light and as cheering was the idea that broke in upon me. 'I have found it! What terrified me will terrify others; and I need only describe the spectre which had haunted my midnight pillow.' On the morrow I announced that I had thought of a story. I began that day with the words, It was on a dreary night of November, making only a transcript of the grim terrors of my waking dream.

At first I thought but of a few pages of a short tale; but my Beloved urged me to develope the idea at greater length. I certainly did not owe the suggestion of one incident, nor scarcely of one train of feeling, to my husband, and yet but for his incitement, it would never have taken the form in which it was presented. From this declaration I must except the preface. As far as I can recollect, it was entirely written by him.

And now, once again, I bid my hideous progeny go forth and prosper. I have an affection for it, for it was the offspring of happy days, when death and grief were but words, which found no true echo in my heart. Its several pages speak of many a walk, many a drive, and many a conversation, when I was not alone; and my companion was one who, in this world, I shall never see more. But this is for myself; my readers have nothing to do with these associations.[1]

TWO-AND-A-HALF MONTHS EARLIER

10 June. Lake Geneva— Lord Byron welcomed us to his villa with the warmest of welcomes despite— nay, in spite of— the frigid mixture of lightning filled thunderstorms and wintry squalls. If my upbringing had been any less atheistic and anarchistic, my mind may have turned to the small comforts of the apocalyptic. How would my intellect have been twisted and distorted if my father had been a devoutly religious man, a parson? Would he have seen the scripture in Daniel chapter eight, verse fourteen: *'Unto two thousand and three hundred days; then shall the sanctuary be cleansed'* as a warning that the End Times were nigh? Would Father, a student of mathematics, have calculated the end of our age having come two thousand and three hundred 'years of days' from 457 BC with the decree to rebuild Jerusalem by Artaxerxes I of Persia? Would Father have preached that this 'sanctuary' to be 'cleansed' as the Earth's purification in a hell-fiery Second Coming of Jesus the Christ? But Father is not a man of religious superstition but scientific supposition: therefore the answer is a simple, unequivocal no. Hell no!

But this weather we encountered on our travels across the channel, through France, and into the Swiss Alps certainly wasn't hell-fiery as is captured in the common imagination. But then Dante Alighieri viewed Judecca, the fourth division of Cocytus, so named for Judas Iscariot, as a glacial prison that bound the traitors to their lords and benefactors in a lake of ice.

---

1 From the Introduction to the 1831 Edition of *Frankenstein; or, The Modern Prometheus*, published by Henry Colburn & Richard Bentley.

When we were down within the darksome well,
Beneath the giant's feet, but lower far,
And I was scanning still the lofty wall,
I heard it said to me: "Look how thou steppest!
Take heed thou do not trample with thy feet
The heads of the tired, miserable brothers!"
Whereat I turned me round, and saw before me
And underfoot a lake, that from the frost
The semblance had of glass, and not of water.

What once perceived idyllic summer when we first set out from England were we to likely to experience trapped inside while lightning flashes, thunder crashes, and a blizzard clashes with very notion of summer? Purchasing a boat and rowing the mirror-glassed lake, while wasting away a pleasant summer, would likely prove impossible given the improbable reversal of the seasons. What was the source of Mother Nature's sudden and sullen retraction of that idyllic summer we dreamed of? My father, being atheistic and anarchistic, invited into our home a radical student of the weather for a rather formal lecture, as he is wont to do quite often, on both the meteorological and the historical significance of the volcanic eruption in the Dutch East Indies. The most probable solution, according to this student of science, and by extension by father, is seen through the lens of history, not the insinuations of superstition. There are no acts of God. The geological has proven much more likely to affect the meteorological than dances to the spirit-gods ever can. In certain circles, whether they be religious or scientific, this may either be blasphemy or pseudoscience. Remember, he reminded us, the Minoan eruption of Thera would be documented on the distant Egyptian Tempest Stele and in the far more distant Chinese Bamboo Annals as a volcanic winter of yellow skies and summer frost.

A network of travellers, whether they be merchants, pilgrims, or those on holiday, told us of tales of weather corruptions and crop destructions, and from the farthest corner of the world as far east as east goes came the reports from the Dutch East Indies as published in the newspapers. The hungered, we heard, had protested their dire straits in markets and in front of bakeries, having taken much affront at the inflation of prices of common necessaries. Would riots, arson, and looting swept utter and fiery destruction through the great cities of Europe only now beginning to recover from the Napoleonic wars? Sir Stamford Raffles, the Governor-General of the Dutch East Indies, when artillery fire was heard seemingly comings from the island of Java, Raffles scrambled the Royal Navy to rebuff an impending invasion to retake control of the Indies from the British. This artillery fire proved to be the rumblings of a volcanic eruption; but this first eruption on 5 April 1815 would prove to be mere musket shot compared to the thunderous cannon fire that would come in five days' time. A mountain named Tambora, on the island of Sumbawa, not known to the locals to be a volcano, indeed erupted with a volcanic fury only known in the far distance of ancient history.

> 'On my trip towards the western part of the island, I passed through nearly the whole of Dompo and a considerable part of Bima. The extreme misery to which the inhabitants have been reduced is shocking to behold. There were still on the road side the remains of several corpses, and the marks of where many others had been interred: the villages almost entirely deserted and the houses fallen down, the surviving inhabitants having dispersed in search of food... Since the eruption, a violent diarrhoea has prevailed in Bima, Dompo, and Sang'ir, which has carried off a great number of people. It is supposed by the natives to have been caused by drinking water which has been impregnated with ashes; and horses have also died, in great numbers, from a similar complaint.'
>
> — Lt. Philips, ordered by Raffles to go to Sumbawa.

The Villa Diodati, to which Lord Byron had rented for the anticipated idyllic summer, proved to be dourly grey, though quite handsome, remarkably square, but reasonably modern enough. My always operational writer's imagination invented a note written by the architect upon completion of the villa, 'North-east of the city limits of Geneva, along the southern shore of Lake Léman, extends the district of Cologny. In a superb location on the Cologny heights stands a modest, square, stucco house. From the balustraded balcony encircling its exterior on all but the south side (where the front entrance opens directly upon a small courtyard) a marvellous panorama of Nature lies visible. Beyond a foreground of vineyards and large trees, sloping steeply to the wooded bank, stretches both east and west a lake of crystalline blue; in the distance, across the water, rise the jagged, often snowcapped peaks of the magnificent Jura range.'[2] Why cannot I simply take in the splendour without such foolishness.

But the house would prove a pleasant place to waste away a summer in exile. My Beloved and I could no longer enjoy our privacy in London for the scandal set upon us because of love. I am no longer

---

2 From an essay 'Milton and the Villa Diodati' by William S. Clark.

content to be sent, by fatherly decree, here or there, wither and thither for protect his name. Our love was found in my father's home during many a dinner party and lecture. My Beloved says often my father enchanted him with his anarchistic politics and atheistic rationales; the ghost of my mother enchanted him with her feminist philosophies; and I enchanted him with my entire being. I come from good stock being the daughter of William Godwin and Mary Wollstonecraft. Therefore, we should take our flight due to an unfortunate lack of legal (and religious) marital contract.

But scandal would be content to follow us to the continent for we both fled away from it and toward it. If a woman were a nation-state, our own host would be more akin to Napoleon Bonaparte, exiled to Lake Geneva (instead of Elba) for having waged war with the entire continent of Europe. He is beset on all sides by scandal. How can a single man be so hated and loved, despised and admired, often in but a single breath? Including the breaths in our own party.

In his letter of invitation to Claire Clairemont, Lord Byron made it a point to reference John Milton having vacationed here in the summer of 1639. He proudly exclaimed in a letter written to sweetest Claire— one could audibly hear him while reading— that the landlord let slip a 'secret':

> '... while examining which place was best to lease, the landlord of the Villa Diodati let slip a secret. Giovanni Diodati, the original owner, who commissioned its construction, was the uncle of Charles Diodati. Sweetest Claire, you may be forgiven in asking, "Who?" because I most certainly had. The landlord explained he was a close and dear childhood friend to John Milton. Yes! That John Milton! had spent part of 1639 with said uncle during his "grand tour" of Europe at this very villa. What theorists and intellectuals guested with him for him to display his poetic mastery? What works of his were written within these walls? So, I purchased my lease without a moment's hesitation. If even the smallest fragment the ghost of John Milton still lingers in this villa— haunting it with such unbridled creativity— then what works could I write over course of the summer!'
> — Letter from Lord Byron to Claire Clairmont

But unfortunately for our overly and overtly romantic little Lord, Milton *may* never have vacationed in this house— physically. Not because of certain monetary concerns of the poet given the inherent familial relations, but the concerns of the temporal. Our carriage-driver, when my Beloved mentioned our hopes of being haunted by John Milton's spirit, chuckled. He regretted to inform us of an unfortunate truth. The villa had not been constructed until (in his words) 'the year of our Lord and Saviour 1710'. Slightly over seventy years is quite the temporal error one cannot easily dismiss as typographical. Why then is there a bronze plaque affixed to the wall of the caretaker's house proclaiming, '*John Milton, poéte anglaise, Secrétaire d'Etat d'Olivier Cromwell, auteur du* Paradis perdu, *vélcut ici l'hôte de Jean Diodati en 1639.*' Given Byron's anticipation for his own ceaseless creativity over the course of this summer, hopefully future generations of landlords will not set a bronze plaque declaring '*Lord Byron, poéte anglaise, auteur de* Child Harold, *habita la villa Diodati en* **1917**'. What else could explain such a wild discrepancy? My Beloved preferred this story, whether factual or not, because it amuses him and could precipitate an enjoyable argument with Lord Byron. As for me? I dismissed it as the idle-talking gossip of a layman. History— even such recent history— cannot possess a seven-decade discrepancy. Modern and enlightened theologians dispute the birth of Jesus in 1AD by a mere four to six years. Seventy-one? Amusing.

The Diary of Dr. John William Polidori

15June. Up late; began my letters. Fell madly, deeply, passionately in love with Mary Wollstonecraft Godwin. Percy Shelley presented her to us as his wife, though I believe she is merely his fiancée, or she is at worse a scarlet woman. If the situation is the former, then I must respect Percy's right to his wife; if she is the latter, then I am honour-bond to free Mary from such a strain... stain; if she is the centre, then I am free to woo for no marriage contract has been entered into either the registry of the state or the Church. George— Lord Byron to others— saw the restless fire of passion in my eyes when I look upon the fair Mary and mocked me relentlessly for my foolishness.

What is there not to love? Her porcelain skin; her straight nose; her high cheekbones; roselike lips; dainty hands; ink-stained, delicate fingers. The soft ringlets of her brunette hair. Her breasts supple with milk. Her hips shapely for childbearing. Her voice strong and sultry. Her laugh; her gorgeous laugh; a laugh at once joyous and vicious. Nightingales are jealous of that melodious song. If I but possessed a whit of wit, I could make that song ring out continuously. But her own eviscerating wit splits open my belly and spills my bowels upon my shined shoes. Her razor-sharp tongue is circumcising; she infantizes a professional, educated man back into being a snot-nosed boy toddling around his father's writing desk. If these barbs her tongue and lips willingly form, I wonder and ponder the dangers that creak under the floorboards in her haunted mind.

Or what of her pedigree? William Godwin, the renowned Utilitarianist and Anarchist, is a great stallion to be bred from. If I could expose the privileges of the aristocracy which are fuelled the abuses of power by a tyrannical and monarchist government with the skill of *Things as They Are; or The Adventures of Caleb Williams*, I could die a happy and justified author. My own prose is verbose compared to his skill with capturing the world in word. Oh! How can such vitriol and scorn fall upon the great man for his marriage to the overly loud (to the conflicting circles of society) and overtly proud (to all circles especially her own) advocate for women's rights, Mary Wollstonecraft? The marriage lasted but the length of a pregnancy! Mary Wollstonecraft Godwin's. Oh! How loss in childbirth haunts poor Mary to this very day. Her mother, the radical feminist author of *A Vindication of the Rights of Woman*, died mere days after young Mary's birth, leaving the child motherless. And then poor Mary lost her own unchristened and nameless daughter mere days after she gave birth, leaving the mother childless.'

But madly, deeply in love I found myself to be. And Lord Byron chose mockery and scorn over brotherly support. For days I withstood his pointed slings and arrows of derision at the passion that fuelled by heart and fired my blood, for the lovely Mary. But this morning, I believed he had turned another leaf as the idiom says. As lovely Mary came walking up the towards the Villa, George (I refuse to honour his Lordship in this entry for he lacks in all civility) proffered a quick lesson in chivalry that I should offer my arm to lovely Mary lest she fall on the dew-slicked stones that had turned to frost. His devilish tongue painted me, in with Arthurian analogies, as Tristan and Mary as Iseult. Leaping off the wall, I slipped on the dew-slicked frozen stones (for of course I did) and strained my left ankle (for of course I did). My spirits were suddenly fallen because my leap was certainly pratfallen. George, the lovely Mary, and the rivalrous Percy guffawed as if I were nothing more than a *zanni* in *commedia dell'arte*. Why cannot I be for once cast as a lover instead of a typecast the clown?

Shelley etc. came down in the evening. Lovely Mary presented herself to Lord Byron and myself in our parlour. She honoured me by not looking down upon me in my hobbled, wobbled state; she smiled a polite smile and took her seat by the fire. In spite of my tumble that same morning, there was precious little we could accomplish given the oxymoronic summer we all five were encountering at the shore of Lake

Geneva. They were as hobbled by the rained-in-weather as I was hobbled by my strained ankle. The antsy sought an activity to occupy the evening for our occupation of the Villa Diodati proved to be more a captivity. Lord Byron began to talk of my play, to which the Shelley etc. agreed to disguss by play— future readers of a future publication, this is not a clerical error— I will speak nothing of my play here for it is nothing to talk about. They entreated me to give them a one-man reading of a scene and I obliged them, though I should not have. Laughter during a dramatic reading is demeaning. How would The Bard have reacted to laughter during the readthrough of *Titus Andronicus*? Now I understand the emotions of an actor standing upon the stage when the audience pelts them with rotten tomatoes and cabbages. They did not pelt me with rotten corn or onions but scorn and derision. How could have I have written in the months previous this line, "Tis thus the goter'd idiot of the Alps.' How could I have been so prescient to foresee my own strained ankle while on holiday on the shore of Lake Geneva. The French astrologer Nostradamus holds no candle to Dr John William Polidori. Is this evening an oxymoron? Or am I simply a moron?

Mary Wollstonecraft Godwin's Journal

15 June. Lord Bryon's Doctor presented us a scene from a play he had written, in which he possessed no title. This brief little scene, which could have been briefer and could have been littler, contained within it an unfortunate line, unfortunate in its timing, unfortunate that it elicited in his friends some laugher. There is not-a-thing so memorable in the work that I can transcribe (or remember) of the scene with the notable exception of the unfortunate line: "Tis thus the goter'd idiot of the Alps.' The Doctor sat in a comfortable chair with his unfortunate and uncomfortable script drifting down, like the snow sleeting down the windows, to his bandaged foot. A foot had been bandaged, not due to a foolish slip on the frozen stones, but due to a foolish passion for me. However, he possesses foolish fancies of even more foolish polyamorous love between the five of us. As if Percy, George, Clair, or I would ever be so foolish. We each love whom we love and do not love those whom we do not love, as unfortunate as this is for the scorned. The Doctor may scorn at such words as honest as they are, but this is why he is, by the very definition of the verb and noun, the 'scorned'.

Lord Byron attempted to comfort the suddenly sullen-temperamented Doctor that 'worse playscripts were often submitted to Drury Lane.' Our laughter had been unfortunate. This is the beauty, and in

the Doctor's case the horror, of the expression. One does not intention-
ally laugh. An intentional laugh is the height of condescension or perchance even condemnation. A clown whether on the stage or the street
may intend to evoke laughter, but he has no control over the evocation
of that laugh. If the joke is not humorous, then no laughter will be
evoked. But counter to this, the dramatic line, written to evoke tears,
gasps, or shrieks, may just evoke laugher. Both of his imaginings are
the worst horror a playwright can experience. To reiterate: our laughter
was not our intention. The Doctor's line: "Tis thus the goter'd idiot of
the Alps,' when sitting with a bandaged foot— as if goitered— caused
such uproarious laugher as to make the clown envious. But no words
of support could draw the Doctor out of his being 'worth nothing'.
While he may have felt worth nothing, as he repeated to himself, his
unfortunate line has been forever imprinted on my mind that I cannot
stop saying over and over again: "Tis thus the goter'd idiot of the Alps'.
Should these journals of mine be published, the line will be imprinted
on the mind of my reader. Is this not the wish of the playwright? To
have written a line memorable enough to last for time immemorial?

Chapter Two
The Death-Bride[3]

Mary Wollstonecraft Godwin's Journal

16 June.— Lord Byron had, in his brief residency at the Villa Diodati, found a peculiar French translation of German ghost stories absentmindedly left on a miscellaneous table in the parlour by a previous guest. The book had been titled, tantalizingly, *Fantasmagoriana, ou Recueil d'histoires, d'apparitions, de spectres, revenans, fantômes.* Was the ghost of John Milton playing games with us by presenting a scandalous book in the presence of a cabal of creatives as a present?

Lord Byron selected the second of the volumes and chose the first story in the table of contents (a most suitable selection given we know nothing of these tales other than their titles). What would we find reading the stories this anthology? Apparitions of spectres? Obviously. Revenants? Certainly. Phantoms? One can only hope. The story Byron chose was titled *La Morte Fiancée* in French, *Die Todtenbraut* in the original German, and *The Death-Bride* in the King's English.

Lord Byron began the evening's narration, *'L'été étoit superbe; aussi, de mémoire d'homme, jamais on n'avoit ru tant de monde aux caux. Mais les salons de réunion avoient beau se remplir, la gaité ne sy trouvoit pas. La noblesse se tenoit à part, le militaire en faisoit autant, et la bour-geoisie médisoit de tous les deux. Tant de réunions partielles devoient nécessaire-ment obstacle à une réunion générale. Les bals publics même ne produ-isoient pas plus de rapprochement parmi les personnes du beau monde, parce que le propriétaire des eaux y paroissoit chamarré de cordons, et que cet éclat, joint à la roîdeur des manières de la famille de ce seigneur, et au grand nombre de laquai, vêtus de riches livrées, qui les suivoient, forçoit la plupart des personnes présentes a se renfermer silencieusement dans les bornes fixées par la diversité des rangs.'* Four us were fluent in French so to need no translation, with the exception of the Doctor, poor thing, who was familiar *enough* to understand and enjoy. Though I saw his brow furrow with the struggle of his mind's eye to promptly translate as

---

3 From *Fantasmagoriana, ou Recueil d'histoires, d'apparitions, de spectres, revenans, fantômes,* published by F. Schoell in 1812. 'The Death-Bride' was written by Friedrich Laun, translated into English by Sarah Elizabeth Utterson in *Tales of the Dead,* published in 1813 by White, Cochrane and Co.

Bryon hastily read. But for you dear Reader of my journal, rest assured here is the translation as I remember the story:

'The summer had been uncommonly fine,' a strange beginning for a ghost story. Byron stopped to note our own has been uncommonly awful. We all hear-heared. Then he continued the story, 'and the baths crowded with company beyond all comparison: but still the public rooms were scarce ever filled, and never gay. The nobility and military associated only with those of their own rank, and the citizens contented themselves by slandering both parties. So many partial divisions necessarily proved an obstacle to a general and united assembly.'

'Certainly a true statement in any nation or age,' my Beloved observed.

'Even the public balls did not draw the beau-monde together, because the proprietor of the baths appeared there bedizened with insignia of knighthood; and this glitter, added to the stiff manners of this great man's family, and the tribe of lackeys in splendid liveries who constantly attended him, compelled the greater part of the company assembled, silently to observe the rules prescribed to them according to their different ranks.'

'As true in England as anywhere else,' my Beloved bemoaned and he was not alone.

'For these reasons the balls became gradually less numerously attended. Private parties were formed, in which it was endeavoured to preserve the charms that were daily diminishing in the public assemblies.

'One of these societies met generally twice a week in a room which at that time was usually unoccupied. There they supped, and afterwards enjoyed, either in a walk abroad, or remaining in the room, the charms of unrestrained conversation.

'The members of this society were already acquainted, at least by name; but an Italian marquis, who had lately joined their party, was unknown to them, and indeed to every one assembled at the baths.

'The title of Italian marquis appeared the more singular, as his name, according to the entry of it in the general list, seemed to denote him of Northern extraction, and was composed of so great a number of consonants, that no one could pronounce it without difficulty.'

'I wonder and ponder if we will be provided his name, or will it prove too difficult for the author to transcribe,' my Beloved said.

'His physiognomy and manners likewise presented many singularities. His long and wan visage, his black eyes, his imperious look, had so little of attraction in them, that every one would certainly have avoided him, had he not possessed a fund of entertaining stories, the relation of which proved an excellent antidote to ennui: the only drawback against them was, that in general they required rather too great a share of credulity on the part of his auditors.

The party had one day just risen from table, and found themselves but ill inclined for gaiety. They were still too much fatigued from the ball of the preceding evening to enjoy the recreation of walking, although invited so to do by the bright light of the moon. They were even unable to keep up any conversation; therefore it is not to be wondered at, that they were more than usually anxious for the marquis to arrive.

' "Where can he be?" exclaimed the countess in an impatient tone.

' "Doubtless still at the faro-table, to the no small grief of the bankers," replied Florentine. "This very morning, he has occasioned the sudden departure of two of these gentlemen."

' "No great loss," answered another.

' "To us— ," replied Florentine; "but it is to the proprietor of the baths, who only prohibited gambling, that it might be pursued with greater avidity."

' "The marquis ought to abstain from such achievements," said the chevalier with an air of mystery. "Gamblers are revengeful, and have generally advantageous connections. If what is whispered be correct, that the marquis is unfortunately implicated in political affairs— ."

' "But," demanded the countess, "what then has the marquis done to the bankers of the gaming-table?"

' "Nothing; except that he betted on cards which almost invariably won. And what renders it rather singular, he scarcely derived any advantage from it himself, for he always adhered to the weakest party. But the other punters were not so scrupulous; for they charged their cards in such a manner that the bank broke before the deal had gone round."

' "Bankers"? "Punters"? Is he playing *Baccarat Banque?*'

'Aye, my sweet Claire,' poor Polidori answers, 'it is a ruinously French game. A blight and a stain upon the psyche.'

The countess was on the point of asking other questions, when the marquis coming in changed the conversation.

' "Here you are at last!" exclaimed several persons at the same moment.

' "We have," said the countess, "been most anxious for your society; and just on this day you have been longer than usual absent."

' "I have projected an important expedition; and it has succeeded to my wishes. I hope by to-morrow there will not be a single gaming-table left here. I have been from one gambling-room to another; and there are not sufficient post-horses to carry off the ruined bankers."

' "And cannot you," asked the countess, "teach us your wonderful art of always winning?"

'Ha! Has no one ever studied the mathematics on such games of gambling? It is the ruin of many a good man,' Polidori protested.

' "It would be a difficult task, my fair lady; and in order to do it, one must ensure a fortunate hand, for without that nothing could be done."

'Sensible man, this marquis, to divert their attention and fortunes away from such a future,' my Beloved observed.

' "Nay," replied the chevalier, laughing, "never did I see so fortunate an one as yours."

' "As you are still very young, my dear chevalier, you have many novelties to witness."

'Saying these words, the marquis threw on the chevalier so piercing a look that the latter cried: "Will you then cast my nativity?"

' "Provided that it is not done to-day," said the countess; "for who knows whether your future destiny will afford us so amusing a history as that which the marquis two days since promised we should enjoy?"

' "I did not exactly say amusing."

' "But at least full of extraordinary events: and we require some such, to draw us from the lethargy which has overwhelmed us all day."

' "Most willingly: but first I am anxious to learn whether any of you know aught of the surprising things related of the Death-Bride."

'Ah! Ho-ho!', my Beloved exclaimed, 'The titular character comes anon!'

'No one remembered to have heard speak of her.

'The marquis appeared anxious to add something more by way of preface; but the countess and the rest of the party so openly manifested their impatience, that the marquis began his narration as follows:—

' "I had for a long time projected a visit to the count Lieppa, at his estates in Bohemia. We had met each other in almost every country in Europe: attracted hither by the frivolity of youth to partake of every pleasure which presented itself, but led thither when years of discretion had rendered us more sedate and steady.— At length, in our more advanced age, we ardently desired, ere the close of life, once again to enjoy, by the charms of recollection, the moments of delight which we had passed together. For my part, I was anxious to see the castle of my friend, which was, according to his description, in an extremely romantic district. It was built some hundred years back by his ancestors; and their successors had preserved it with so much care, that it still maintained its imposing appearance, at the same time it afforded a comfortable abode. The count generally passed the greater part of the year at it with his family, and only returned to the capital at the approach of winter. Being well acquainted with his movements, I did not think it needful to announce my visit; and I arrived at the castle one evening precisely at the time when I knew he would be there; and as I approached it, could not but admire the variety and beauty of the scenery which surrounded it.

' "The hearty welcome which I received could not, however, entirely conceal from my observation the secret grief depicted on the countenances of the count, his wife, and their daughter, the lovely Ida. In a short time, I discovered that they still mourned the loss of Ida's twin-sister, who had died about a year before. Ida and Hildegarde resembled each other so much, that they were only to be distinguished from each other by a slight mark of a strawberry visible on Hildegarde's neck. Her room, and every thing in it, was left precisely in the same state as when she was alive, and the family were in the habit of visiting it whenever they wished to indulge the sad satisfaction of meditating on the loss of this beloved child. The two sisters had but one heart, one mind: and the parents could not but apprehend that their separation would be but of short duration; they dreaded lest Ida should also be taken from them.' I cast my eyes down to my little William sleeping in his bassinet. My mind flashed back to my poor little nameless daughter lost to me. The very thought of losing an elder child proved to be as painful, if not more, than losing a mere babe in her crib, a child you loved but had yet to truly bond with.

' "I did everything in my power to amuse this excellent family, by entertaining them with laughable anecdotes of my younger days, and by directing their thoughts to less melancholy subjects than that which now wholly occupied them. I had the satisfaction of discovering that my efforts were not ineffectual. Sometimes we walked in the canton round the castle, which was decked with all the beauties of summer; at other times we took a survey of the different apartments of the castle, and were astonished at their wonderful state of preservation, whilst we amused ourselves by talking over the actions of the past generation, whose portraits hung in a long gallery.

' "One evening the count had been speaking to me in confidence, on the subject of his future plans: among other subjects he expressed his anxiety, that Ida (who had already, though only in her sixteenth year, refused several offers) should be happily married; when suddenly the gardener, quite out of breath, came to tell us he had seen the ghost (as he believed, the old chaplain belonging to the castle), who had appeared a century back. Several of the servants followed the gardener, and their pallid countenances confirmed the alarming tidings he had brought.

'A-ha!' my Beloved interrupted again, 'finally a ghost for this ghost story! I have experienced far too many words and far too few frights for a book threateningly called *Fantasmagoriana.'*

'Be patient, my Beloved,' I said, "Surely we will meet the titular "Death-Bride" as soon as the bathers do. It is the marquis' ghost story after all.'

'I'd have drowned in waters of the bathes waiting for the "Death-Bride' to appear,' my Beloved countered.

' "'I believe you will shortly be afraid of your own shadow,' said the count to them. He then sent them off, desiring them not again to trouble him with the like fooleries.

' "'It is really terrible,' said he to me, 'to see to what lengths superstition will carry persons of that rank of life; and it is impossible wholly to undeceive them. From one generation to another an absurd report has from time to time been spread abroad, of an old chaplain's ghost wandering in the environs of the castle; and that he says mass in the chapel, with other idle stories of a similar nature. This report has greatly died away since I came into possession of the castle; but it now appears to me, it will never be altogether forgotten.'

'I've always considered it queer,' the poor doctor said, 'that others in these ghost stories never tend to believe the superstitiously enchanted servants when they claim to have seen a ghost. Why must the practically arrogant nobility, in that moment, see with their own eyes the spectre and not heed the word of men who serve them well?'

'Would you believe me, Doctor,' my dearest sister said, 'if I claimed to see a spectre walking the halls of the Villa Diodati. Would you dismiss my observations as appearing when the lightning flashes and vanishing when the thunder crashes? Would you believe me if you hadn't seen its form. Would you disbelieve my account when you hadn't heard its chains and its moans. My dear Doctor, what if I was so afraid as to not leave my apartment out of perilous fear.'

'Claire,' Polidori cooed, 'I would stalk these very halls with you to find the spectre and drive it away from ever concerning you again.' He winked quickly in her direction so that I would not see, but I saw, and I kicked his chair. The doctor coughed and straightened his hair. He then turned his attention back to our little Lord who was not amused with the doctor's enthused flirtations. Claire, my sweet sister, was flattered by the doctor's flirtation solely because the object of her affection has continuously over the course of the dismal summer objected to her affections.

Lord Byron, irritated at these constant interrupts to his telling of this ghost story, huffed one long exhale that could have been mistaken for a rumbling thunderclap. Once he was satisfied with our silence, only then would he continue. ' "At this moment the duke de Marino was announced. The count did not recollect ever having heard of him.

' "I told him that I was tolerably well acquainted with his family; and that I had lately been present, in Venice, at the betrothing of a young man of that name.

' "The very same young man came in while I was speaking. I should have felt very glad at seeing him, had I not perceived that my presence caused him evident uneasiness.

' "'Ah,' said he in a tolerably gay tone, after the customary forms of politeness had passed between us; 'the finding you here, my dear marquis, explains to me an occurrence, which with shame I own caused me a sensation of fear. To my no small surprise, they knew my name in the adjacent district; and as I came up the hill which leads to the castle, I heard it pronounced three times in a voice wholly unknown to me: and in a still more audible tone this strange voice bade me welcome. I now, however, conclude it was yours.'

' "I assured him, (and with truth,) that till his name was announced the minute before, I was ignorant of his arrival, and that none of my servants knew him; for that the valet who accompanied me into Italy was not now with me.

' "'And above all,' added I, 'it would be impossible to discover any equipage, however well known to one, in so dark an evening.'

' "'That is what astonishes me,' exclaimed the duke, a little amazed.

' "The incredulous count very politely added, 'that the voice which had told the duke he was welcome, had at least expressed the sentiments of all the family.'

My Beloved said a single word, 'Curious!'

' "Marino, ere he said a word relative to the motive of his visit, asked a private audience of me; and confided in me, by telling me that he was come with the intention of obtaining the lovely Ida's hand; and that if he was able to procure her consent, he should demand her of her father.

' "'The countess Apollonia, your bride elect, is then no longer living?' asked I.

' "'We will talk on that subject hereafter,' answered he.

' "The deep sigh which accompanied these words led me to conclude that Apollonia had been guilty of infidelity or some other crime towards the duke; and consequently I thought that I ought to abstain from any further questions, which appeared to rend his heart, already so sensibly wounded.

' "Yet, as he begged me to become his mediator with the count, in order to obtain from him his consent to the match, I painted in glowing colours the danger of an alliance, which he had no other motive for contracting, than the wish to obliterate the remembrance of a dearly, and without doubt, still more tenderly, beloved object. But he assured me that he was far from thinking of the lovely Ida from so blameable a motive, and that he should be the happiest of men if she but proved propitious to his wishes.

' "His expressive and penetrating tone of voice, while he said this, lulled the uneasiness that I was beginning to feel; and I promised him I would prepare the count Lieppa to listen to his entreaties, and would give him the necessary information relative to the fortune and family of Marino. But I declared to him at the same time, that I should by no means hurry the conclusion of the affair by my advice, as I was not in the habit of taking upon myself so great a charge as the uncertain issue of a marriage.

' "The duke signified his satisfaction at what I said, and made me give (what then appeared to me of no consequence) a promise, that I would not make mention of the former marriage he was on the point of contracting, as it would necessarily bring on a train of unpleasant explanations.

' "The duke's views succeeded with a promptitude beyond his most sanguine hopes. His well-proportioned form and sparkling eyes smoothed the paths of love, and introduced him to the heart of Ida. His agreeable conversation promised to the mother an amiable son-in-law; and the knowledge in rural economy, which he evinced as occasions offered, made the count hope for an useful helpmate in his usual occupations; for since the first day of the duke's arrival he had been prevented from pursuing them.

' "Marino followed up these advantages with great ardour; and I was one evening much surprised by the intelligence of his being betrothed, as I did not dream of matters drawing so near a conclusion. They spoke at table of some bridal preparations of which I had made mention just before the duke's arrival at the castle; and the countess asked me whether that young Marino was a near relation of the one who was that very day betrothed to her daughter.'

' "'Near enough,' I answered, recollecting my promise.— Marino looked at me with an air of embarrassment.

' "'But, my dear duke,' continued I, 'tell me who mentioned the amiable Ida to you; or was it a portrait, or what else, which caused you to think of looking for a beauty, the selection of whom does so much honour to your taste, in this remote corner; for, if I am not mistaken, you said but yesterday that you had purposed travelling about for another six months; when all at once (I believe while in Paris) you changed your plan, and projected a journey wholly and solely to see the charming Ida?'

' "'Yes, it was at Paris,' replied the duke; 'you are very rightly informed. I went there to see and admire the superb gallery of pictures at the Museum; but I had scarcely entered it, when my eyes turned from the inanimate beauties, and were riveted on a lady whose incomparable features were heightened by an air of melancholy. With fear and trembling I approached her, and only ventured to follow without speaking to her. I still followed her after she quitted the gallery; and I drew her servant aside to learn the name of his mistress. He told it me: but when I expressed a wish to become acquainted with the father of this beauty, he said that was next to impossible while at Paris, as the family were on the point of quitting that city; nay, of quitting France altogether.

' "'Possibly, however,' said I, 'some opportunity may present itself.' And I looked everywhere for the lady: but she, probably imagining that her servant was following her closely, had continued to walk on, and was entirely out of sight. While I was looking around for her, the servant had likewise vanished from my view.'

' "'Who was this beautiful lady?' asked Ida, in a tone of astonishment.

' "'What! you really did not then perceive me in the gallery?'

' "'Me!'— — 'My daughter— — !' exclaimed at the same moment Ida and her parents.

' "'Yes, you yourself, mademoiselle. The servant, whom fortunately for me you left at Paris, and whom I met the same evening unexpectedly, as my guardian angel, informed me of all; so that after a short rest at home, I was able to come straight hither.'

' "'What a fable!' said the count to his daughter, who was mute with astonishment.

' "'Ida,' he added, turning to me, 'has never yet been out of her native country; and for myself, I have not been in Paris these seventeen years.'

' "The duke looked at the count and his daughter with similar marks of astonishment visible in their countenances; and conversation would have been entirely at an end, if I had not taken care to introduce other topics: but I had it nearly all to myself.

' "The repast was no sooner over, than the count took the duke into the recess of a window; and although I was at a considerable distance, and appeared wholly to fix my attention on a new chandelier, I overheard all their conversation.

' "'What motive,' demanded the count with a serious and dissatisfied air, 'could have induced you to invent that singular scene in the gallery of the Museum at Paris? for according to my judgment, it could in no way benefit you. Since you are anxious to conceal the cause which brought you to ask my daughter in marriage, at least you might have plainly said as much; and though possibly you might have felt repugnance at making such a declaration, there were a thousand ways of framing your answer, without its being needful thus to offend probability.'

'I have it. I have it,' Claire said, 'I know who the woman in the museum is!' As did we all, for the foreshadowing cast no shadow at all over the story. The title of the story and the twin-sisters cliché all but clinched the outcome of this plot. I'm sure the four of us writers prayed for a twist in this very predictable plot.

' "Monsieur le comte,' replied the duke much piqued; 'I held my peace at table, thinking that possibly you had reasons for wishing to keep secret your and your daughter's journey to Paris. I was silent merely from motives of discretion; but the singularity of your reproaches compels me to maintain what I have said; and, notwithstanding your reluctance to believe the truth, to declare before all the world, that the capital of France was the spot where I first saw your daughter Ida.'

' "But what if I prove to you, not only by the witness of my servants, but also by that of all my tenants, that my daughter has never quitted her native place?'—

' "I shall still believe the evidence of my own eyes and ears, which have as great authority over me.'

' "What you say is really enigmatical,' answered the count in a graver tone: 'your serious manner convinces me you have been the dupe of some illusion; and that you have seen some other person, whom you have taken for my daughter. Excuse me, therefore, for having taken up the thing so warmly.'

' "Another person! What then, I not only mistook another person for your daughter; but the very servant of whom I made mention, and who gave me so exact a description of this castle, was, according to what you say, some other person!'

' "My dear Marino, that servant was some cheat who knew this castle, and who, God only knows for what motive, spoke to you of my daughter as resembling the lady.'

' "Tis certainly no wish of mine to contradict you; but Ida's features are precisely the same as those which made so deep an impression on me at Paris, and which my imagination has preserved with such scrupulous fidelity.'

' "The count shook his head; and Marino continued:—

' "What is still more— (but pray pardon me for mentioning a little particularity, which nothing short of necessity would have drawn from me)— while in the gallery, I was standing behind the lady, and the handkerchief that covered her neck was a little disarranged, which occasioned me distinctly to perceive the mark of a small strawberry.'

' "Another strange mystery!' exclaimed the count, turning pale: 'it appears you are determined to make me believe wonderful stories.'

' "'I have only one question to ask:— Has Ida such a mark on her neck?'

' "'No, monsieur,' replied the count, looking steadfastly at Marino.

' "'No!' exclaimed the latter, in the utmost astonishment.

' "'No, I tell you: but Ida's twin-sister, who resembled her in the most surprising manner, had the mark you mention on her neck, and a year since carried it with her into the grave.'

' "'And yet 'tis only within the last few months that I saw this person in Paris!'

' "At this moment the countess and Ida, who had kept aside, a prey to uneasiness, not knowing what to think of the conversation, which appeared of so very important a nature, approached; but the count in a commanding tone ordered them to retire immediately. He then led the duke entirely away into a retired corner of the window, and continued the conversation in so low a voice that I could hear nothing further.

' "My astonishment was extreme when, that very same evening, the count gave orders to have Hildegarde's tomb opened in his presence: but he beforehand related briefly what I have just told you, and proposed my assisting the duke and him in opening the grave. The duke excused himself, by saying that the very idea made him tremble with horror; for he could not overcome, especially at night, his fear of a corpse.

' "The count begged he would not mention the gallery scene to any one; and above all, to spare the extreme sensibility of the affianced bride from a recital of the conversation they had just had, even if she should request to be informed of it.

' "In the mean time the sexton arrived with his lantern. The count and I followed him.

' "'It is morally impossible,' said the count to me, as we walked together, 'that any trick can have been played respecting my daughter's death: the circumstances attendant thereon are but too well known to me. You may readily believe also, that the affection we bore our poor girl would prevent our running any risk of burying her too soon: but suppose even the possibility of that, and that the tomb had been opened by some avaricious persons, who found, on opening the coffin, that the body became re-animated; no one can believe for a moment that my daughter would not have instantly returned to her parents, who doted on her, rather than have fled to a distant country. This last circumstance puts the matter beyond doubt: for even should it be admitted as a truth, that she was carried by force to some distant part of the world, she would have found a thousand ways of returning. My eyes are, however, about to be convinced, that the sacred remains of my Hildegarde really repose in the grave.

' "'To convince myself!' cried he again, in a tone of voice so melancholy yet loud that the sexton turned his head.

' "This movement rendered the count more circumspect; and he continued in a lower tone of voice:

' "'How should I for a moment believe it possible that the slightest trace of my daughter's features should be still in existence, or that the destructive hand of time should have spared her beauty? Let us return, marquis; for who could tell, even were I to see the skeleton, that I should know it from that of an entire stranger, whom they may have placed in the tomb to fill her place?'

' "He was even about to give orders not to open the door of the chapel, (at which we were just arrived,) when I represented to him, that were I in his place I should have found it extremely difficult to determine on such a measure; but that having gone thus far, it was requisite to complete the task, by examining whether some of the jewels buried with Hildegarde's corpse were not wanting. I added, that judging by a number of well-known facts, all bodies were not destroyed equally soon.

' "My representations had the desired effect: the count squeezed my hand; and we followed the sexton, who, by his pallid countenance and trembling limbs, evidently shewed that he was unaccustomed to nocturnal employments of this nature.

' "I know not whether any of this present company were ever in a chapel at midnight, before the iron doors of a vault, about to examine the succession of leaden coffins enclosing the remains of an illustrious family. Certain it is, that at such a moment the noise of bolts and bars produces such a remarkable sensation, that one is led to dread the sound of the door grating on its hinges; and when the vault is opened, one cannot help hesitating for an instant to enter it.

'Oh, the sound of those doors opening,' Claire said, 'are sending bolts of lightning up my spine.'

' "The count was evidently seized with these sensations of terror, which I discovered by a stifled sigh; but he concealed his feelings: notwithstanding, I remarked that he dared not trust himself to look on any other coffin than the one containing his daughter's remains. He opened it himself.

' "'Did I not say so?' cried he, seeing that the features of the corpse bore a perfect resemblance to those of Ida. I was obliged to prevent the count, who was seized with astonishment, from kissing the forehead of the inanimate body.

' "'Do not,' I added, 'disturb the peace of those who repose in death.' And I used my utmost efforts to withdraw the count immediately from this dismal abode.

'So is she merely a ghost in this ghost story and not a revenant stolen from her grave?' Claire inquired.

'Naïve little girl,' Polidori said, 'this is a collection of ghost stories.'

'Oh, no little doctor,' I corrected him in defence of my dear sister. Having punctuated the *little*, Polidori's expression turned pained. 'Have you forgotten or are you ignorant of the subtitle to these volumes, "*Recueil d'histoires, d'apparitions, de spectres, revenans, fantômes, etc.*". Revenants, *little* doctor. Clearly Claire would be correct in assuming Ida's sister was a revenant.'

'Except for the fact,' Polidori countered, 'the body is still interred in the mausoleum! A revenant by its very definition is a reanimated corpse. Nothing in science can reanimate a corpse. This is left to the superstitions of the peasantry of the rural countryside. They cage gravesites and place blades over the necks of the corpse, lest it should arise in the night to stalk the bereaved families of the recently deceased. As a man of science, there is no cause to say that I have any fear of the reanimation of a corpse. For it is an impossibility, my sweet Mary. Nothing in the history of natural philosophy, the sciences, gives me cause to fear any corpse! And yes, by the subtitle, we can expect this poor girl to be a revenant, but having seen the corpse, she must be a ghost.'

'Can we,' Lord Byron said frustrated, 'Can we return to our ghost story?' To which we all acquiesced.

' "On our return to the castle, we found those persons whom we had left there, in an anxious state of suspense. The two ladies had closely questioned the duke on what had passed; and would not admit as a valid excuse, the promise he had made of secrecy. They entreated us also, but in vain, to satisfy their curiosity.

' "They succeeded better the following day with the sexton, whom they sent for privately, and who told them all he knew: but it only tended to excite their anxious wish to learn the subject of the conversation which had occasioned this nocturnal visit to the sepulchral vault.

' "As for myself, I dreamt the whole of the following night of the apparition Marino had seen at Paris; I conjectured many things which I did not think fit to communicate to the count, because he absolutely questioned the connection of a superior world with ours. At this juncture of affairs, I with pleasure saw that this singular circumstance, if not entirely forgotten, was at least but rarely and slightly mentioned.

' "But I now began to find another cause for anxious solicitude. The duke constantly persisted in refusing to explain himself on the subject of his previous engagement, even when we were alone: and the embarrassment he could not conceal, whenever I made mention of the good qualities that I believed his intended to have possessed, as well as several other little singularities, led me to conclude that Marino's attachment for Apollonia had been first shaken at the picture gallery, at sight of the lovely incognita; and that Apollonia had been forsaken, owing to his yielding to temptations; and that doubtless she could never have been guilty of breaking off an alliance so solemnly contracted.

'Foreseeing from this that the charming Ida could never hope to find much happiness in an union with Marino, and knowing that the wedding-day was nigh at hand, I resolved to unmask the perfidious deceiver as quickly as possible, and to make him repent his infidelity. An excellent occasion presented itself one day for me to accomplish my designs. Having finished supper, we were still sitting at table; and some one said that iniquity is frequently punished in this world: upon which I observed, that I myself had witnessed striking proofs of the truth of this remark;—when Ida and her mother entreated me to name one of these examples.

' "Under these circumstances, ladies,' answered I, 'permit me to relate a history to you, which, according to my opinion, will particularly interest you.'

' "Us!' they both exclaimed. At the same time I fixed my eyes on the duke, who for several days past had evidently distrusted me; and I saw that his conscience had rendered him pale.

' "That at least is my opinion,' replied I: 'But, my dear count, will you pardon me, if the supernatural is sometimes interwoven with my narration?'

' "Very willingly,' answered he smiling: 'and I will content myself with expressing my surprise at so many things of this sort having happened to you, as I have never experienced any of them myself.'

' "I plainly perceived that the duke made signs of approval at what he said: but I took no notice of it, and answered the count by saying,

' "That all the world have not probably the use of their eyes.

' "That may be,' replied he, still smiling.

' "But,' said I to him in a low and expressive voice, 'think you an uncorrupted body in the vault is a common phænomenon?'

' "He appeared staggered: and I thus continued in an under tone of voice:—

' "For that matter, 'tis very possible to account for it naturally, and therefore it would be useless to contest the subject with you.'

' "We are wandering from the point,' said the countess a little angrily; and she made me a sign to begin, which I accordingly did, in the following words:—

' "The scene of my anecdote lies in Venice.'

' "I possibly then may know something of it,' cried the duke, who entertained some suspicions.

' "'Possibly so,' replied I; 'but there were reasons for keeping the event secret: it happened somewhere about eighteen months since, at the period you first set out on your travels.

' "The son of an extremely wealthy nobleman, whom I shall designate by the name of Filippo, being attracted to Leghorn by the affairs consequent on his succession to an inheritance, had won the heart of an amiable and lovely girl, called Clara. He promised her, as well as her parents, that ere his return to Venice he would come back and marry her. The moment for his departure was preceded by certain ceremonies, which in their termination were terrible: for after the two lovers had exhausted every protestation of reciprocal affection, Filippo invoked the aid of the spirit of vengeance, in case of infidelity: they prayed even that whichever of the lovers should prove faithful might not be permitted to repose quietly in the grave, but should haunt the perjured one, and force the inconstant party to come amongst the dead, and to share in the grave those sentiments which on earth had been forgotten."'

'This is a quite queerly constructed story,' said I, 'Lord Byron is telling us a story that begins with a story being told to a collection of bathers in a bathhouse and now continues with another story being told to the count and his family within the confines of the first story. This is a confounding Russian nesting doll! Inverted commas within inverted commas within inverted commas. The typesetter of this tale must have been driven mad!' My Beloved, Polidori, and Claire all hear-heared, but our little Lord continued reading this story unabated, as if he did not even see the unnatural levels of nesting as he read. But I'll see them in my nightmares!

' "The parents, who were seated by them at table, remembered their youthful days, and permitted the overheated and romantic imagination of the young people to take its free course. The lovers finished by making punctures in their arms, and letting their blood run into a glass filled with white champaigne.

' " "Our souls shall be inseparable as our blood!" exclaimed Filippo; and drinking half the contents of the glass, he gave the rest to Clara.

' "At this moment the duke experienced a violent degree of agitation, and from time to time darted such menacing looks at me, that I was led to conclude, that in his adventure some scene of a similar nature had taken place. I can however affirm, that I related the details respecting Filippo's departure, as they were represented in a letter written by the mother of Clara.

' "Who," continued I, "after so many demonstrations of such a violent passion, could have expected the denouement? Filippo's return to Venice happened precisely at the period at which a young beauty, hitherto educated in a distant convent, made her first appearance in the great world: she on a sudden exhibited herself as an angel whom a cloud had till then concealed, and excited universal admiration. Filippo's parents had heard frequent mention of Clara, and of the projected alliance between her and their son; but they thought that this alliance was like many others, contracted one day without the parties knowing why, and broken off the next with equal want of thought; and influenced by this idea, they presented their son to the parents of Camilla, (which was the name of the young beauty,) whose family were of the highest rank.

' "They represented to Filippo the great advantages he would obtain by an alliance with her. The Carnival happening just at this period completed the business, by affording him so many favourable opportunities of being with Camilla; and in the end, the remembrance of Leghorn held but very little place in his mind. His letters became colder and colder each succeeding day; and on Clara expressing how sensibly she felt the change, he ceased writing to her altogether, and did every thing in his power to hasten his union with Camilla, who was, without compare, much the handsomer and more wealthy. The agonies poor Clara endured were manifest in her illegible writing, and by the tears which were but too evidently shed over her letters: but neither the one nor the other had any more influence over the fickle heart of Filippo, than the prayers of the unfortunate girl. Even the menace of coming, according to their solemn agreement, from the tomb to haunt him, and carry him with her to that grave which threatened so soon to enclose her, had but little effect on his mind, which was entirely engrossed by the idea of the happiness he should enjoy in the arms of Camilla.

' "The father of the latter (who was my intimate friend) invited me before hand to the wedding. And although numerous affairs detained him that summer in the city, so that he could not as usual enjoy the pleasures of the country, yet we sometimes went to his pretty villa, situated on the banks of the Brenta; where his daughter's marriage was to be celebrated with all possible splendour.

' "A particular circumstance, however, occasioned the ceremony to be deferred for some weeks. The parents of Camilla having been very happy in their own union, were anxious that the same priest who married them, should pronounce the nuptial benediction on their daughter. This priest, who, notwithstanding his great age, had the appearance of vigorous health, was seized with a slow fever which confined him to his bed: however, in time it abated, he became gradually better and better, and the wedding-day was at length fixed. But, as if some secret power was at work to prevent this union, the worthy priest was, on the very day destined for the celebration of their marriage, seized with a feverish shivering of so alarming a nature, that he dared not stir out of the house, and he strongly advised the young couple to select another priest to marry them.

' "The parents still persisted in their design of the nuptial benediction being given to their children by the respectable old man who had married them.— They would have certainly spared themselves a great deal of grief, if they had never swerved from their determination.— Very grand preparations had been made in honour of the day; and as they could no longer be deferred, it was decided that they should consider it as a ceremony of solemn affiance. At noon the bargemen attired in their splendid garb awaited the company's arrival on the banks of the canal: their joyous song was soon distinguished, while conducting to the villa, now decorated with flowers, the numerous gondolas containing parties of the best company.

' "During the dinner, which lasted till evening, the betrothed couple exchanged rings. At the very moment of their so doing, a piercing shriek was heard, which struck terror into the breasts of all the company, and absolutely struck Filippo with horror. Every one ran to the windows: for although it was becoming dark, each object was visible; but no one was to be seen."

' "Stop an instant," said the duke to me, with a fierce smile— His countenance, which had frequently changed colour during the recital, evinced strong marks of the torments of a wicked conscience. "I am also acquainted with that story, of a voice being heard in the air; it is borrowed from the 'Memoirs of Mademoiselle Clairon;' a deceased lover tormented her in this completely original manner. The shriek in her case was followed by a clapping of hands: I hope, *monsieur le marquis*, that you will not omit that particular in your story."

' "And why," replied I, "should you imagine that nothing of a similar nature could occur to any one besides that actress? Your incredulity appears to me so much the more extraordinary, as it seems to rest on facts which may lay claim to belief."

' "The countess made me a sign to continue; and I pursued my narrative as follows:

' "A short time after they had heard this inexplicable shriek, I begged Camilla, facing whom I was sitting, to permit me to look at her ring once more, the exquisite workmanship of which had already been much admired. But it was not on her finger: a general search was made, but not the slightest trace of the ring could be discovered. The company even rose from their seats to look for it, but all in vain.

' "Meanwhile, the time for the evening's amusements approached: fire-works were exhibited on the Brenta preceding the ball; the company were masked and got into the gondolas; but nothing was so striking as the silence which reigned during this fête; no one seemed inclined to open their mouth; and scarcely was heard a faint exclamation of Bravo, at sight of the fire-works.

' "The ball was one of the most brilliant I ever witnessed: the precious stones and jewels with which the ladies of the party were covered, reflected the lights in the chandeliers with redoubled lustre. The most splendidly attired of the whole was Camilla. Her father, who was fond of pomp, rejoiced in the idea that no one in the assembly was equal to his daughter in splendour or beauty.

' "Possibly to satisfy himself of this fact, he made a tour of the room; and returned loudly expressing his surprise, at having perceived on another lady precisely the same jewels which adorned Camilla. He was even weak enough to express a slight degree of chagrin. However, he consoled himself with the idea, that a bouquet of diamonds which was destined for Camilla to wear at supper, would alone in value be greater than all she then had on.

' "But as they were on the point of sitting down to table, and the anxious father again threw a look around him, he discovered that the same lady had also a bouquet which appeared to the full as valuable as Camilla's.

' "My friend's curiosity could no longer be restrained; he approached, and asked whether it would be too great a liberty to learn the name of the fair mask? But to his great surprise, the lady shook her head, and turned away from him.

' "At the same instant the steward came in, to ask whether since dinner there had been any addition to the party, as the covers were not sufficient.

' "His master answered, with rather a dissatisfied air, that there were only the same number, and accused his servants of negligence; but the steward still persisted in what he had said.

' "An additional cover was placed: the master counted them himself, and discovered that there really was one more in number than he had invited. As he had recently, on account of some inconsiderate expressions, had a dispute with government, he was apprehensive that some spy had contrived to slip in with the company: but as he had no reason to believe, that on such a day as that, any thing of a suspicious nature would be uttered, he resolved, in order to be satisfied respecting so indiscreet a procedure as the introduction of such a person in a family fête, to beg every one present to unmask; but in order to avoid the inconvenience likely to arise from such a request, he determined not to propose it till the very last thing.

' "Every one present expressed their surprise at the luxuries and delicacies of the table, for it far surpassed every thing of the sort seen in that country, especially with respect to the wines. Still, however, the father of Camilla was not satisfied, and loudly lamented that an accident had happened to his capital red champaigne, which prevented his being able to offer his guests a single glass of it.

' "The company seemed anxious to become gay, for the whole of the day nothing like gaiety had been visible among them; but no one around where I sat, partook of this inclination, for curiosity alone appeared to occupy their whole attention. I was sitting near the lady who was so splendidly attired; and I remarked that she neither ate nor drank any thing; that she neither addressed nor answered a word to her neighbours, and that she appeared to have her eyes constantly fixed on the affianced couple.

' "The rumour of this singularity gradually spread round the room, and again disturbed the mirth which had become pretty general. Each whispered to the other a thousand conjectures on this mysterious personage. But the general opinion was, that some unhappy passion for Filippo was the cause of this extaordinary conduct. Those sitting next the unknown, were the first to rise from table, in order to find more cheerful associates, and their places were filled by others who hoped to discover some acquaintance in this silent lady, and obtain from her a more welcome reception; but their hopes were equally futile.

' "At the time the champaigne was handed round, Filippo also brought a chair and sat by the unknown. She then became somewhat more animated, and turned towards Filippo, which was more than she had done to any one else; and she offered him her glass, as if wishing him to drink out of it.

' "A violent trembling seized Filippo, when she looked at him steadfastly.

' " "The wine is red!" cried he, holding up the glass; "I thought there had been no red champaigne."

' " "Red!" said the father of Camilla, with an air of extreme surprise, approaching him from curiosity.

' " "Look at the lady's glass," replied Filippo.

' " "The wine in it is as white as all the rest," answered Camilla's father; and he called all present to witness it. They every one unanimously declared that the wine was white.

' "Filippo drank it not, but quitted his seat; for a second look from his neighbour had caused him extreme agitation. He took the father of Camilla aside, and whispered something to him. The latter returned to the company, saying,

' "" "Ladies and gentlemen, I entreat you, for reasons which I will tell you presently, instantly to unmask."

' "'As in this request he but expressed in a degree the general wish, every one's mask was off as quick as thought, and each face uncovered, excepting that of the silent lady, on whom every look was fixed, and whose face they were the most anxious to see.

' "" "You alone keep on your mask," said Camilla's father to her, after a short silence: "May I hope you will also remove yours?"

' "'She obstinately persisted in her determination of remaining unknown.

' "'This strange conduct affected the father of Camilla the more sensibly, as he recognised in the others all those whom he had invited to the fête, and found beyond doubt that the mute lady was the one exceeding the number invited. He was, however, unwilling to force her to unmask; because the uncommon splendour of her dress did not permit him any longer to harbour the idea that this additional guest was a spy; and thinking her also a person of distinction, he did not wish to be deficient in good manners. He thought possibly she might be some friend of the family, who, not residing at Venice, but finding on her arrival in that city that he was to give this fête, had conceived this innocent frolic.

' "'It was thought right, however, at all events to obtain all the information that could be gained from the servants: but none of them knew any thing of this lady; there were no servants of hers there; and those belonging to Camilla's father did not recollect having seen any who appeared to appertain to her.

' "'What rendered this circumstance doubly strange was, that, as I before mentioned, this lady only put the magnificent bouquet into her bosom the instant previous to her sitting down to supper.

' "'The whispering, which had generally usurped the place of all conversation, gained each moment more and more ascendancy; when on a sudden the masked lady arose, and walking towards the door, beckoned Filippo to follow her; but Camilla hindered him from obeying her signal, for she had a long time observed with what fixed attention the mysterious lady looked at her intended husband; and she had also remarked, that the latter had quitted the stranger in violent agitation; and from all this she apprehended that love had caused him to be guilty of some folly or other. The master of the house, turning a deaf ear to all his daughter's remonstrances, and a prey to the most terrible fears, followed the unknown (at a distance, it is true); but she was no sooner out of the room than he returned. At this moment, the shriek which they had heard at noon was repeated, but seemed louder from the silence of night, and communicated anew affright to all present. By the time the father of

Camilla had returned from the first movement which his fear had occasioned him to make, the unknown was no where to be found.

' "The servants in waiting outside the house had no knowledge whatever of the masked lady. In every direction around there were crowds of persons; the river was lined with gondolas; and yet not an individual among them had seen the mysterious female.

' "All these circumstances had occasioned so much uneasiness to the whole party, that every one was anxious to return home; and the master of the house was obliged to permit the departure of the gondolas much earlier than he had intended.

' "The return home was, as might naturally be expected, very melancholy.

' "On the following day the betrothed couple were, however, pretty composed. Filippo had even adopted Camilla's idea of the unknown being some one whom love had deprived of reason; and as for the horrible shriek twice repeated, they were willing to attribute it to some people who were diverting themselves; and they decided, that inattention on the part of the servants was the sole cause of the unknown absenting herself without being perceived; and they even at last persuaded themselves, that the sudden disappearance of the ring, which they had not been able to find, was owing to the malice of some one of the servants who had pilfered it.

' "In a word, they banished every thing that could tend to weaken these explanations; and only one thing remained to harass them. The old priest, who was to bestow on them the nuptial benediction, had yielded up his last breath; and the friendship which had so intimately subsisted between him and the parents of Camilla, did not permit them in decency to think of marriage and amusements the week following his death.

' "The day this venerable priest was buried, Filippo's gaiety received a severe shock; for he learned, in a letter from Clara's mother, the death of that lovely girl. Sinking under the grief occasioned her by the infidelity of the man she had never ceased to love, she died: but to her latest hour she declared she should never rest quietly in her grave, until the perjured man had fulfilled the promise he had made to her.'"

'He broke his engagement with Clara?' Claire said. 'The rogue. The scoundrel. The thief.'

' "This circumstance produced a stronger effect on him than all the imprecations of the unhappy mother; for he recollected that the first shriek (the cause of which they had never been able to ascertain) was heard at the precise moment of Clara's death; which convinced him that the unknown mask could only have been the spirit of Clara.

' "This idea deprived him at intervals of his senses.

' "'He constantly carried this letter about him; and with an air of wandering would sometimes draw it from his pocket, in order to reconsider it attentively: even Camilla's presence did not deter him.

' "'As it was natural to conclude this letter contained the cause of the extraordinary change which had taken place in Filippo, she one day gladly seized the opportunity of reading it, when in one of his absent fits he let it fall from his hands.

' "'Filippo, struck by the death-like paleness and faintness which overcame Camilla, as she returned him the letter, knew instantly that she had read it. In the deepest affliction he threw himself at her feet, and conjured her to tell him how he must act.

' "' "Love me with greater constancy than you did her,"— replied Camilla mournfully.

' "'With transport he promised to do so. But his agitation became greater and greater, and increased to a most extraordinary pitch the morning of the day fixed for the wedding. As he was going to the house of Camilla's father before it became dark, (from whence he was to take his bride at dawn of day to the church, according to the custom of the country,) he fancied he saw Clara's spirit walking constantly at his side.

' "'Never was seen a couple about to receive the nuptial benediction, with so mournful an aspect. I accompanied the parents of Camilla, who had requested me to be a witness: and the sequel has made an indelible impression on my mind of the events of that dismal morning.

' "'We were proceeding silently to the church of the Salutation; when Filippo, in our way thither, frequently requested me to remove the stranger from Camilla's side, for she had evil designs against her.

' "' "What stranger?" I asked him.

' "' "In God's name, don't speak so loud," replied he; "for you cannot but see how anxious she is to force herself between Camilla and me."

' "' "Mere chimera, my friend; there are none but yourself and Camilla."

' "' "Would to Heaven my eyes did not deceive me!— Take care that she does not enter the church," added he, as we arrived at the door.

' "' "She will not enter it, rest assured," said I: and to the great astonishment of Camilla's parents I made a motion as if to drive some one away.

' "'We found Filippo's father already in the church; and as soon as his son perceived him, he took leave of him as if he was going to die. Camilla sobbed; and Filippo exclaimed:—

' "' "There's the stranger; she has then got in."

' "'The parents of Camilla doubted whether under such circumstances the marriage ceremony ought to be begun.

' "But Camilla, entirely devoted to her love, cried:— 'These chimeras of fancy render my care and attention the more necessary.'

' "They approached the altar. At that moment a sudden gust of wind blew out the wax-tapers. The priest appeared displeased at their not having shut the windows more securely; but Filippo exclaimed: 'The windows! See you not, then, that there is one here who blew out the wax-tapers purposely?'

' "Every one looked astonished: and Filippo cried, as he hastily disengaged his hand from that of Camilla,— 'Don't you see, also, that she is tearing me away from my intended bride?'

' "Camilla fell fainting into the arms of her parents; and the priest declared, that under such peculiar circumstances it was impossible to proceed with the ceremony.

' "The parents of both attributed Filippo's state to mental derangement. They even supposed he had been poisoned; for an instant after, the unfortunate man expired in most violent convulsions. The surgeons who opened his body could not, however, discover any grounds for this suspicion.

' "The parents, who as well as myself were informed by Camilla of the subject of these supposed horrors of Filippo, did every thing in their power to conceal this adventure: yet, on talking over all the circumstances, they could never satisfactorily explain the apparition of the mysterious mask at the time of the wedding fête. And what still appeared very surprising was, that the ring lost at the country villa was found amongst Camilla's other jewels, at the time of their return from church.'"

' "This is, indeed, a wonderful history!' said the count. His wife uttered a deep sigh: and Ida exclaimed,—

' "It has really made me shudder.'

'Are we in another nestling doll or has the previous doll been nested over us?' I inquired.

' "That is precisely what every betrothed person ought to feel who listens to such recitals,' answered I, looking steadfastly at the duke, who, while I was talking, had risen and sat down again several times; and who, from his troubled look, plainly shewed that he feared I should counteract his wishes.

' "A word with you!' he whispered me, as we were retiring to rest: and he accompanied me to my room. 'I plainly perceive your generous intentions; this history invented for the occasion— "

' "Hold!' said I to him in an irritated tone of voice: 'I was eye-witness to what you have just heard. How then can you doubt its authenticity, without accusing a man of honour of uttering a falsehood?'

' "We will talk on this subject presently,' replied he in a tone of raillery. 'But tell me truly from whence you learnt the anecdote relative to mixing the blood with wine?— I know the person from whose life you borrowed this idea.'

' "I do assure you that I have taken it from no one's life but Filippo's; and yet there may be similar stories— as of the shriek, for instance. But even this singular manner of irrevocably affiancing themselves may have presented itself to any two lovers.'

' "Perhaps so! Yet one could trace in your narration many traits resembling another history.'

' "That is very possible: all love-stories are founded on the same stock, and cannot deny their parentage.'

' "No matter,' replied Marino; 'but I desire that from henceforth you do not permit yourself to make any allusion to my past life; and still less that you relate certain anecdotes to the count. On these conditions, and only on these conditions, do I pardon your former very ingenious fiction.'

' "Conditions!— — forgiveness!— — And do you dare thus to talk to me?— — This is rather too much. Now take my answer: To-morrow morning the count shall know that you have been already affianced, and what you now exact.'

' "Marquis, if you dare— — '

' "Oh! oh!— yes, I dare do it; and I owe it to an old friend. The impostor who dares accuse me of falsehood shall no longer wear his deceitful mask in this house.'

' "Passion had, spite of my endeavours, carried me so far, that a duel became inevitable. The duke challenged me. And we agreed, at parting, to meet the following morning in a neighbouring wood with pistols.

' "In effect, before day-light we each took our servant and went into the forest. Marino, remarking that I had not given any orders in case of my being killed, undertook to do so for me; and accordingly he told my servant what to do with my body, as if every thing was already decided. He again addressed me ere we shook hands;—

' "For,' said he, 'the combat between us must be very unequal. I am young,' added he; 'but in many instances my hand has proved a steady one. I have not, it is true, absolutely killed any man; but I have invariably hit my adversary precisely on the part I intended. In this instance, however, I must, for the first time, kill my man, as it is the only effectual method of preventing your annoying me further; unless you will give me your word of honour not to discover any occurrences of my past life to the count, in which case I consent to consider the affair as terminated here.'

' "As you may naturally believe, I rejected his proposition.

' "'As it must be so,' replied he, 'recommend your soul to God.' We prepared accordingly.

' "'It is your first fire,' he said to me.

' "'I yield it to you,' answered I.

' "He refused to fire first. I then drew the trigger, and caused the pistol to drop from his hand. He appeared surprised: but his astonishment was great indeed, when, after taking up another pistol, he found he had missed me. He pretended to have aimed at my heart; and had not even the possibility of an excuse; for he could not but acknowledge that no sensation of fear on my part had induced me to move, and baulk his aim.

' "At his request I fired a second time; and again aimed at his pistol which he held in his left hand: and to his great astonishment it dropped also; but the ball had passed so near his hand, that it was a good deal bruised.

' "His second fire having passed me, I told him I would not fire again; but that, as it was possible the extreme agitation of his mind had occasioned him to miss me twice, I proposed adjusting matters.

' "Before he had time to refuse my offer, the count, who had suspicions that all was not right, was between us, with his daughter. He complained loudly of such conduct on the part of his guests; and demanded some explanation on the cause of our dispute. I then developed the whole business in presence of Marino, whose evident embarrassment convinced the count and Ida of the truth of the reproaches his conscience made him.

' "But the duke soon availed himself of Ida's affection, and created an entire change in the count's mind; who that very evening said to me,—

' "'You are right; I certainly ought to take some decided step, and send the duke from my house: but what could win the Apollonia whom he has abandoned, and whom he will never see again? Added to which, he is the only man for whom my daughter has ever felt a sincere attachment. Let us leave the young people to follow their own inclinations: the countess perfectly coincides in this opinion; and adds, that it would hurt her much were this handsome Venetian to be driven from our house. How many little infidelities and indiscretions are committed in the world and excused, owing to particular circumstances?'"

'Quite peculiar these particular circumstances,' my Beloved said, again bemused.

' "'But it appears to me, that in the case in point, these particular circumstances are wanting,' answered I. However, finding the count persisted in his opinion, I said no more.

' "The marriage took place without any interruption: but still there was very little of gaiety at the feast, which usually on these occasions is of so splendid and jocund a nature. The ball in the evening was dull; and Marino alone danced with most extraordinary glee.

' "Fortunately, *monsieur le marquis*,' said he in my ear, quitting the dance for an instant and laughing aloud, "there are no ghosts or spirits here, as at your Venetian wedding.'

' "Don't,' I answered, putting up my finger to him, 'rejoice too soon: misery is slow in its operations; and often is not perceived by us blind mortals till it treads on our heels.'

' "Contrary to my intention, this conversation rendered him quite silent; and what convinced me the more strongly of the effect it had made on him, was, the redoubled vehemence with which the duke again began dancing.

' "The countess in vain entreated him to be careful of his health: and all Ida's supplications were able to obtain was, a few minutes' rest to take breath when he could no longer go on.

' "A few minutes after, I saw Ida in tears, which did not appear as if occasioned by joy; and she quitted the ball-room. I was standing as close to the door as I am to you at this moment; so that I could not for an instant doubt its being really Ida: but what appeared to me very strange was, that in a few seconds I saw her come in again with a countenance as calm as possible. I followed her, and remarked that she asked the duke to dance; and was so far from moderating his violence, that she partook of and even increased it by her own example. I also remarked, that as soon as the dance was over the duke took leave of the parents of Ida, and with her vanished through a small door leading to the nuptial apartment.

' "While I was endeavouring to account in my own mind how it was possible for Ida so suddenly to change her sentiments, a conference in an under tone took place at the door of the room, between the count and his valet.

' "The subject was evidently a very important one, as the greatly incensed looks of the count towards his gardener evinced, while he confirmed, as it appeared, what the valet had before said.

' "I drew near the trio, and heard, that at a particular time the church organ was heard to play, and that the whole edifice had been illuminated within, until twelve o'clock, which had just struck.

' "The count was very angry at their troubling him with so silly a tale, and asked why they did not sooner inform him of it. They answered, that every one was anxious to see how it would end. The gardener added, that the old chaplain had been seen again; and the peasantry who lived near the forest, even pretended that they had seen the summit of the mountain which overhung their valley illuminated, and spirits dance around it.

' "'Very well!' exclaimed the count with a gloomy air; 'so all the old idle trash is resumed: the Death-Bride is also, I hope, going to play her part.'

' "The valet having pushed aside the gardener, that he might not still further enrage the count, I put in my word; and said to the count, 'You might at least listen to what they have to say, and learn what it is they pretend to have seen.'

' "'What is said about the Death-Bride?' said I to the gardener.

' "He shrugged up his shoulders.

' "'Was I not right?' cried the count: 'here we are then, and must listen to this ridiculous tale. All these things are treasured in the memory of these people, and constantly afford subjects and phantoms to their imaginations.— — Is it permitted to ask under what form?'— —

' "'Pray pardon me,' replied the gardener; 'but it resembled the deceased mademoiselle Hildegarde. She passed close to me in the garden, and then came into the castle."

' "'O!' said the count to him, 'I beg, in future you will be a little more circumspect in your fancies, and leave my daughter to rest quietly in the tomb— — 'Tis well— '

' "He then made a signal to his servants, who went out.

' "'Well! my dear marquis!' said he to me.

' "'Well?'

' "'Your belief in stories will not, surely, carry you so far as to give credence to my Hildegarde's spirit appearing?'"'

'The twin sister,' Claire squeeled.

' "'At least it may have appeared to the gardener only— — Do you recollect the adventure in the Museum at Paris?'

' "'You are right: that again was a pretty invention, which to this moment I cannot fathom. Believe me, I should sooner have refused my daughter to the duke for his having been the fabricator of so gross a story, than for his having forsaken his first love.'

' "'I see very plainly that we shall not easily accord on this point; for if my ready belief appears strange to you, your doubts seem to me incomprehensible.'

' "The company assembled at the castle, retired by degrees; and I alone was left with the count and his lady, when Ida came to the room-door, clothed in her ball-dress, and appeared astonished at finding the company had left.

' "'What can this mean?' demanded the countess. Her husband could not find words to express his astonishment.

' "'Where is Marino?' exclaimed Ida.

' "'Do you ask us where he is?' replied her mother; 'did we not see you go out with him through that small door?'

' "'That could not be;— you mistake.'

' "'No, no; my dear child! A very short time since you were dancing with singular vehemence; and then you both went out together.'

' "'Me! my mother?'

' "'Yes, my dear Ida: how is it possible you should have forgotten all this?'

' "'I have forgotten nothing, believe me.'

' "'Where then have you been all this time?'

' "'In my sister's chamber,' said Ida.

' "I remarked that at these words the count became somewhat pale; and his fearful eye caught mine: he however said nothing. The countess, fearing that her daughter was deceiving her, said to her in an afflicted tone of voice:—

' "'How could so singular a fancy possess you on a day like this?'

' "'I cannot account for it; and only know, that all on a sudden I felt an oppression at my heart, and fancied that all I wanted was Hildegarde. At the same time I felt a firm belief that I should find her in her room playing on her guitar; for which reason I crept thither softly.'

' "'And did you find her there?'

' "'Alas! no: but the eager desire that I felt to see her, added to the fatigue of dancing, so entirely overpowered me, that I seated myself on a chair, where I fell fast asleep.'

' "'How long since did you quit the room?'

' "'The clock in the tower struck the three-quarters past eleven just as I entered my sister's room.'

' "'What does all this mean?' said the countess to her husband in a low voice: 'she talks in a connected manner; and yet I know, that as the clock struck three-quarters past eleven, I entreated Ida on this very spot to dance more moderately.'

' "'And Marino?'— asked the count.

' "'I thought, as I before said, that I should find him here.'

' "'Good God!' exclaimed the mother, 'she raves: but the duke— Where is he then?'

' "'What then, my good mother?' said Ida with an air of great disquiet, while leaning on the countess.

' "Meanwhile the count took a wax-taper, and made a sign for me to follow him. A horrible spectacle awaited us in the bridal-chamber, whither he conducted me. We there found the duke extended on the floor. There did not appear the slightest signs of life in him; and his features were distorted in the most frightful manner.

' "Imagine the extreme affliction Ida endured when she heard this recital, and found that all the resources of the medical attendants were employed in vain.

' "The count and his family could not be roused from the deep consternation which threatened to overwhelm them. A short time after this event, some business of importance occasioned me to quit their castle; and certainly I was not sorry for the excuse to get away.

' "But ere I left that county, I did not fail to collect in the village every possible information relative to the Death-Bride; whose history unfortunately, in passing from one mouth to another, experienced many alterations. It appeared to me, however, upon the whole, that this affianced bride lived in this district, about the fourteenth or fifteenth century. She was a young lady of noble family, and she had conducted herself with so much perfidy and ingratitude towards her lover, that he died of grief; but afterwards, when she was about to marry, he appeared to her the night of her intended wedding, and she died in consequence. And it is said, that since that time, the spirit of this unfortunate creature wanders on earth in every possible shape; particularly in that of lovely females, to render their lovers inconstant.

' "As it was not permitted for her to appear in the form of any living being, she always chose amongst the dead those who the most strongly resembled them. It was for this reason she voluntarily frequented the galleries in which were hung family portraits. It is even reported that she has been seen in galleries of pictures open to public inspection. Finally, it is said, that, as a punishment for her perfidy, she will wander till she finds a man whom she will in vain endeavour to make swerve from his engagement; and it appears, they added, that as yet she had not succeeded.

' "Having inquired what connection subsisted between this spirit and the old chaplain (of whom also I had heard mention), they informed me, that the fate of the last depended on the young lady, because he had assisted her in her criminal conduct. But no one was able to give me any satisfactory information concerning the voice which had called the duke by his name, nor on the meaning of the church being illuminated at night; and why the grand mass was chanted. No one either knows how to account for the dance on the mountain's top in the forest.

' "For the rest," added the marquis, "you will own, that the traditions are admirably adapted to my story, and may, to a certain degree, serve to fill up the gaps; but I am not enabled to give a more satisfactory explanation. I reserve for another time a second history of this same Death-Bride; I only heard it a few weeks since: it appears to me interesting; but it is too late to begin to-day, and indeed, even now, I fear that I have intruded too long on the leisure of the company present by my narrative."

'He had just finished these words, and some of his auditors (though all thanked him for the trouble he had taken) were expressing their disbelief of the story, when a person of his acquaintance came into the room in a hurried manner, and whispered something in his ear. Nothing could be more striking than the contrast presented by the bustling and uneasy air of the newly arrived person while speaking to the marquis, and the calm air of the latter while listening to him.

' "Haste, I pray you," said the first (who appeared quite out of patience at the marquis's sang-froid): "In a few moments you will have cause to repent this delay."

' "I am obliged to you for your affecting solicitude," replied the marquis; who in taking up his hat, appeared more to do, as all the rest of the party were doing, in preparing to return home, than from any anxiety of hastening away.

' "You are lost," said the other, as he saw an officer enter the room at the head of a detachment of military, who inquired for the marquis. The latter instantly made himself known to him.

' "You are my prisoner," said the officer. The marquis followed him, after saying Adieu with a smiling air to all the party, and begging they would not feel any anxiety concerning him.

' "Not feel anxiety!" replied he whose advice he had neglected. "I must inform you, that they have discovered that the marquis has been detected in a connection with very suspicious characters; and his death-warrant may be considered as signed. I came in pity to warn him of his danger, for possibly he might then have escaped; but from his conduct since, I can scarely imagine he is in his proper senses."

The party, who were singularly affected by this event, were conjecturing a thousand things, when the officer returned, and again asked for the marquis.

' "He just now left the room with you," answered some one of the company.

' "But he came in again."

' "We have seen no one."

' "He has then disappeared," replied the officer, smiling: he searched every corner for the marquis, but in vain. The house was thoroughly examined, but without success; and the following day the officer quitted the baths with his soldiers, without his prisoner, and very much dissatisfied.'

The tale hangs in the air like the Death-Bride was present in this very room. I looked at Claire who was weeping. Polidoir seemed bored. My Beloved quite enjoyed the tale. And Lord Byron sat deep in thought. We remained in silence for a long while, as the lightning flashed and the thunder crashed in a collateral-damage cacophony of a natural-rage symphony. My mind did wander away from the tale of the Death-Bride to these unfortunates sitting in this parlour of the Villa Diodati, who have been forced by our circumstances to listen to a rather awful ghost story in a volume of, no doubt, further awful ghost stories. Is this our lot for the remaining days of the constantly raining days of summer?

We occupy this villa during this quite queer summer of rivers freezing, plains flooding, and dear personal friends plotting each other's murder. I plot to kill my Beloved as does Polidori, but for opposite reasons. There is the possibility one of us is going to murder all of the others in their sleep, then turn the pistol upon themselves. This act of passion the London newspapers would report as poets of Romance are wont to do; or we would prove the guests at the surrounding hotels correct of their rumourmongering of our Bohemian decadence by engaging in an ill-fated and ill-inducing orgy.

Who would be the first to take a pistol from the case, stalk the hallways of the Villa, entering into each bedchamber and with a feathered-pillow to muffle the sound snuffing out each life like our humanity was nothing more than a candle. The summer has transformed this pleasant lakeside mansion into a sanatorium. We are no longer free to jaunt on the lake or hike the rolling hills. We are imprisoned in the Villa Diodoti, and if we see not the sun warm our faces soon, we will continue to slip into madness. Though we are in great company, we are likewise ever so alone. Too much loneliness. Too much company. I love my Beloved as my lover; I love Claire as my sister; I love Lord Byron as our host; I even love Dr Polidori in a faint way, as shameful as that may sound. But they are slowly driving me slowly, ever so slowly, mad! And I am no doubt a cause of their own madness, because they each love me whether as family, as a friend, or as a lover. Love and madness are two sides of the same coin. When you look upon one face of the coin, you see only true love betwixt your lover and you, while those closest to you sees the other face and utter madness. And what of looking upon the face of the coin and you seeing utter madness, why then does the entire world believe this is surely a sign of true love? Love and madness? A paradox.

Or who would be the first to seduce one and then all in a free-love Bohemian orgy? The madlove of poor innocent Claire for Lord Byron could be the spark of the tinderbox that would light an orgy on fire; but one initiated by escape. Lord Byron would, no doubt, flee the childlike and childish advances of my young sister into the bedchamber shared by my Beloved and me. While I am not predisposed to sapphic love, I know by Beloved and the Lord have been tempted by strong callused hands and hard-pressing kisses. While that serpent of the garden of Eden is cursed to burrow into the crotch of Man to strike at the flower of a women with its bite and swell her belly with its milky venom to produce the rushing, gushing, putrid birth of birthwaters, like a festering boil bursting, Lucifer is not ashamed of borrowing in the dank and stank and rank sewers of the arse. Or perchance the impetus would be the unrequited love of Dr Polidori for me; he who pines away the hours with deep sighs and lusting eyes. Of his quickly diverting gaze, Noah Webster could easily assign such a look in his *A Compendious Dictionary of the English Language* under the definition of 'rape'. Would I contract a sickness as if his feverish love for me were typhoid? And would I fall ill and be so delirious with fever that my breath would be laboured and my brow would be sweating and my passions would be inflamed? Would I then in my delirium pass the fever to my Beloved with a kiss, a bite, the very act of love? Would our bedchamber be transformed into a ward in a hospital? Oh, but Lord Byron would consider it height of rudeness if we three then did not invite our host to join us in feverish decadence, if only to escape the lovesick Claire.

Murder and then suicide, or an orgy. These are the threads of fate that the Moirai weave: Clotho's feet rapidly pumping the treadle, spinning the drive wheel, and spinning together two distinct yarns this summer; which one will Lachesis select to weave into the tapestry of our lives; and which will Atropos snip and knot lest our mortal lives unravel? Murder and then suicide, or an orgy... or...

'Let us play a game. Not games of mine men's morris, troll-my-dames, Edward Shovel board, nor shall we a put each other on a wild-goose chase due to inclement weather, nor shall we implement a game of hoodman-blind. In-their-stead, I propose a game of ghost stories,' Lord Byron puts foward to his quieted and disquieted guests, 'We will each write a ghost story! There are five of us and in us five ghosts haunting the hallways and apartments of the Villa Diodati. Let the reading of this little volume be a séance that has lured lurid ghosts into haunting the Villa Diodoti. We will then under spells and signs force these ghosts, against their angered will, to tell us the story of their lives. Those trifles contained in his volume,' he said discarding and dismissing the book onto the floor, 'are a little too sleight in importance, while we five stand at the height of brilliance. These are at once too French in language and too German in origin. They do not arise above being fairy stories told by Irish servants to frighten the children of the households they serve. But we are not Irish servants bound by superstition and fear, but we are British gentry bound by reason and passion. If poets are not meant to commune with the ghosts of the dead, then why are the religious so fearful of our supposed Satanic rituals and rites. Why then not draw upon the wood of the flooring with a pentagram in human blood and place a lit candle at each point and intersection? We will then write the names of our ghosts in crude Hebrew; crude because none of us are possessed of the knowledge of that language and would write nothing but childish gibberish. For the demons of the Pit care not for readability; they, like the angels of Heaven and perhaps God Himself, hear our very thoughts and intentions as if we are bellowing. Why must I confess my supposed sins to a priest when God is both omniscient and omnipotent. Nay, I say. God is impotent, but the lusts of the incubuses and succubae are potent!'

'Nay, faith, my Lord Byron,' Claire shrieks, 'if we partake in such a Satanic ritual and rite and tempt the spirit-world through the mocking of the dead with imagined ghost stories this wintry summer, we will be punished by the malevolent God of the Old Testament— not the benevolent God of the New Testament— for witchcraft! God does not suffer a witch to live! Will our men be cursed with short lives'— her wild eyes suddenly stand vacant, staring across the veil that separates the realms of Living and the Dead. What does she see? Ghosts of the Past? The Present? The Yet To Come? What journey has she undertaken to see that which should not be seen— 'due to bloodletting or drowning or suicide?!' I look upon the Lord; he appears pale. I look upon my Beloved; he appears blue. I look upon the Doctor; he appears green. What affliction has been set upon my eyes to see these men with tinted-and-tainted-glasses? Claire then shrieks again, 'Why should we women risk dead children?!'

This cut me like a rusted back-alley surgeon's scalpel. I glance at my little William cooing quietly in the corner of the parlour and I fear for this immortal soul. Will I be immoral for participating in the proposed game of ghost stories that have set fire to my mind in this weary, deary wintry summer? O! My memories of my lost little nameless daughter born two months premature flood my mind as tears well in my eye. I only had possession of her for nine days! O! how I wept and wailed and wrote to Thomas Jefferson Hogg, who had struck up a great friendship with my Beloved:

> 'My dearest Hogg my baby is dead— will you come to see me as soon as you can. I wish to see you— It was perfectly well when I went to bed— I awoke in the night to give it suck it appeared to be sleeping so quietly that I would not awake it. It was dead then, but we did not find that out till morning— from its appearance it evidently died of convulsions— Will you come— you are so calm

a creature & Shelley is afraid of a fever from the milk— for I am no longer a mother now.'[4]

Lord Byron rips me out of the painful memory and back into the present when he continues suddenly, having given Claire's warning of dancing too close to the spirit-world only the slightest hesitation, 'Therefore, my dear friends, I invite the fiends into haunting the Villa Diodoti this summer... winter... whatever.'

---

4 From a letter 6 March, 1815 to Thomas Jefferson Hogg

Chapter Three
The Burial: A Fragment of a Novel[5]
The Diary of Dr John William Polidori

17 June. Went into the town; dined with Shelley etc. here. Went after dinner to a ball at Madamn Oldier's. There I was introduced to Princess Something-or-other and Countess Gräfin Potocka. The countess belonged to the highest Polish nobility, grand-niece of Stanislaus Augustus Poniatowski, who had been King of Poland up to 1798 when died of a stroke on 12 February 1798, while virtually imprisoned St. Petersburg's Marble Palace, there writing his memoirs. Another guest gossiped she was the daughter of Count Tyskiewicz, and married Count Potocki, and afterwards Count Wonsowicz. She was born in 1776, the same year the treasonous colonial Americans launched their 'revolutionary', but civil war against the crown of George III, but I digress. This strikingly handsome young woman, with dark eyes of singular brilliancy and sentiment gathered around herself a small confab of myself, Princess Something, and a couple of other hangers-on. Having danced (I should say *attempted* to dance; due to the horrid pain was forced to stop) and having glanced in her direction over the course of the evening, we all were soon entranced by Countess Potocka. There, in the centre of a ring of this confab, her beauteous voice would soon sing as she spun a most wonderous tapestry of a dinner with Napoleon, the failed Emperor of France himself:

'The emperor declared that, as there was to be no fighting, he wanted us to enjoy ourselves. The time was propitious, for the carnival had just begun. There was an impediment, however. The *liberators* were occupying all our houses; everywhere the proprietors were reduced, just like ourselves, to a few small rooms, where some sort of crowding in was possible, but where it was out of the question to think of entertaining.

'Prince Poniatowski, who alone could have invited a large company to the palace, was hampered by the presence of the emperor. After much discussion, it was decided to give the first ball at M. de Talleyrand's, Grand Chamberlain and Minister of Foreign Affairs.

'The emperor, as well as all the princes, were to be there. The assurance was given that there would be no more than fifty ladies, but such a

---

5 An unfinished 1819 vampire horror story written by Lord Byron, published under the title 'A Fragment' in the 1819 collection *Mazeppa: A Poem*, published by John Murray in London.

severe regulation could not hold out against the thousand and one little intrigues in vogue on similar occasions. It was certainly one of those parties which must not be missed for anything in the world.

'Everybody's vanity and curiosity were stretched to the ut-most. As for me, I was possessed of the liveliest desire to see the host at close quarters, who was reported to be the most affable and cleverest man of his time. To say the truth, he took little trouble to appear so to us. The intimates asserted that no one joined such dexterity to such brilliancy; but if I were to judge him according to the impression he then made upon me, I should say he was thoroughly satiated and bored with everything — greedy for fame and fortune, jealous of the favours of a master he detested, without either character or principles, and, in a word, as unhealthy in mind as in appearance.

'I can scarcely convey the surprise I experienced when I saw him advance laboriously to the middle of the drawing-room, a napkin folded under his arm, a gilt tray in his hand, and offer a glass of lemonade to the monarch whom he in private considered an upstart.

'In his youth M. de Talleyrand was said to have counted many successes among the ladies, and I have since seen him in the midst of his old seraglio. It was really very comical: all those dames, to whom he had in turn played lover, tyrant, or friend, vainly tried to amuse him. His rudeness defeated all their efforts. He yawned at one, was curt to another, and made fools of them all, maliciously recurring to reminiscences and dates.

'To return to the ball. It was one of the most remark-able that it was ever my privilege to attend. The emperor took part in a square dance, which paved the way for his affair with Madame Walewska.

' "How do you think I dance?" he asked me, smiling. "I suspect you have been laughing at me."

' "In truth, sire," I replied, "for a great man your dancing is perfect."

'A little before that Napoleon had seated himself between the future favourite and myself. After talking for a few minutes he asked me who his other neighbour was. As soon as I had mentioned her name, he turned to her as if no one knew more about her than he.

'We learnt afterward that M. de Talleyrand had extended his labours as far as managing this first interview and smoothing the preliminary obstacles. Napoleon, having expressed a wish to count a Pole among his conquests, one of the right kind was chosen — lovely and dull. Some pretended to have noticed that, after the quadrille, the emperor had shaken hands with her, which was equivalent, they said, to an appointment; and it did take place, in fact, the next evening. It was rumoured that a great dignitary had gone to fetch the fair one; quick and undeserved promotion for a good-for-nothing brother was spoken of, and a diamond ornament, which was said to have been refused. People said a great many things they perhaps did not know and invented at pleasure. They even went so far as to assert that Rustan, the Mameluke, had acted as lady's maid! What is certain, however, is that we were all distressed that a person admitted to society had shown such facility, and had defended herself as little as the fortress of Ulm.

'But time, which colours everything, gave this connection, so lightly contracted, a tinge of constancy and disinterestedness which partly effaced the irregularity of its origin, and ended in placing Madame Walewska among the notable personages of her period. Exquisitely pretty, she was a realization of Greuze's faces; her eyes, her mouth, and her teeth were beautiful. Her laugh was so fresh, her gaze so soft, her face so seductive, as a whole, that it was never apparent that anything was wanting to the complete regularity of her features.

'Married at sixteen to an octogenarian who never appeared in public, in society she had the position of a young widow. Her extreme youth, combined with such convenient circumstances, gave room to all sorts of surmises, and if Napoleon was her last lover, it was asserted that he had not been the first.

'After the emperor had made his choice the princes of the family wanted to follow suit. It was difficult, as there was more than glory involved in this audacious enterprise.

'One morning M. Janvier, Prince Murat's private secretary, was announced. He entered, a key in his hand, much embarrassed at his undertaking. Not knowing how to begin, he remained mute, and turned his key over and over without venturing to look at me, whilst I, on my side, racked my brain to guess what he wanted.

'In order that this anecdote may be understood, I must say a word about the arrangements of the palace. Between the story occupied by my mother-in-law and the ground floor, where the large apartment was situated which I had surrendered to Prince Murat, there were tiny mezzanine rooms, of which my mother-in-law never made use except in the coldest weather, because they communicated the heat thoroughly by way of a *secret staircase*.

'This charming retreat, furnished and decorated in Louis XV. style, was looked upon as a part of the large apartment. The key of it had been given to Prince Murat's servants when he had come to live in our house, and nobody had thought of it since. That was the key M. Janvier had been ordered to bring to me.

'Being a man of sense, he felt fully the impropriety of his mission, and was doubly confused when he perceived that I did not understand, and that I persisted in refusing the key as a useless object; because, inhabiting the same floor as my mother-in-law, her private stairs were all that concerned me. Seeing me utterly at a loss, he took the liberty to say, that His Highness, not caring to propose large parties, had thought I might perhaps be pleased to take tea occasionally in these charming nooks. I began to comprehend, and I got angry ! He must have read it in my eyes, for I thought he would fall from his chair. He rose, stumbling, and going to a bracket deposited there the miserable key, and made a profound bow, preparatory to his exit.

'I could scarce contain myself — indignation inspired me. Smiling as disdainfully as I was able, I begged M. Janvier to tell the prince that my mother-in-law would certainly be sensible to his attention, that at her age large parties were found objectionable, and that she might avail herself of His Highness' obliging offer; that, in any case, since he was leaving the key, I should hand it to my mother-in-law. And, bestowing my haughtiest salute on the poor secretary, who stood petrified by the door, I left the room.

'M. de Talleyrand's ball was followed by two others: one given by Prince Borghese, the other by Prince Murat. I was indisposed, and did not attend the first; it was my mother-in-law's opinion that I ought to be at the second, so as to sustain the part I had adopted towards M. Janvier, and not in any way change the relationship of frigid politeness existing between our guest and ourselves. The weather continuing to render the roads impassable, the emperor did not leave town, and his regular outings were limited to the parade which took place in Saxon Square. Although this was an almost daily drill, people flocked there in crowds whenever Napoleon showed himself. He was accompanied back to the palace with spontaneous shouts and hurrahs, which showed him how his fame and our hopes had endeared him to the nation. He did not seem in the least put out by these demonstrations, although sometimes the enthusiasm resulted in blocking his way.

'Besides the balls, there was a court reception once a week. The evening began with a splendid concert and ended with a game of whist. There was never any dancing at the palace.

'The emperor had a complete orchestra in his train, under the direction of the celebrated composer Paer. It was always Italian music. Napoleon seemed to be passionately devoted to it. He listened attentively, applauded with discrimination, and the sounds of harmony appeared to seize strongly upon his moral faculties. A proof was given us at one of the entertainments.

'He had just received information that General Victor, the bearer of a despatch of the highest importance, had allowed the Prussians to catch him! This piece of news put him beside himself. If not a case of treason

— so it was noised about — it was at least one of unpardonable care-lessness. Now, that very day a Dutch deputation, come to congratulate the emperor upon his victory at Jena, was to be admitted to audience immediately before the reception. It was near ten o'clock, we had been waiting a long time, and were beginning to suspect something extraordi-nary might be happening, when, the door being noisily thrown open, we saw the fat Dutchmen, in their scarlet clothes, roll rather than walk in. The emperor was prodding them, exclaiming in somewhat loud tones: "Go on ! Go on !"

'No doubt a number of people had accumulated at the door the mo-ment that Napoleon made his appearance, for he walked very quickly, as was his habit. The poor envoys lost their heads, and tumbled all over each other.

"At any other time this comical scene would have raised a laugh, but the master's voice and the expression of his face were not reassuring, and, to say truth, we should have preferred not to witness this episode. We were wrong. The music soothed the emperor quickly; towards the end of the concert he resumed his gracious smile, addressing pleasant words to the ladies he liked best, before sitting down to his whist table. The emperor always named the ladies in the morning who were to play with him in the evening. His choice habitually fell upon one of the oldest and two of the youngest. I was taught to play an indifferent game, and the first time the coveted distinction was mine I let slip a too hasty answer, which was apparently not taken amiss, seeing that from that day I was a fixture at the card table.

"At the moment when the cards were drawn, Napoleon, turning in my direction, inquired: 'What shall the stake be?'

' "Oh, sire,' I answered, 'some town, some province, some kingdom !"

'He laughed.

' "And supposing you should lose?" he asked, with a particularly sly look.

' "Your Majesty is in funds, and will perhaps deign to pay for me"

This speech won me favour which was never withdrawn. Whether in Poland or in Paris, Napoleon never failed to accord me a distinguished welcome, and to treat me with endless consideration.

'It was remarked that Madame Walewska never played cards, and this regard for propriety was universally commended.

'A really funny thing it was to see all the little German princes, who, under various pretexts remaining at headquarters, danced attendance at the emperor's game of cards. Among others there was the heir pre-sumptive to the throne of Bavaria, who respectfully kissed Napoleon's hand whenever he managed to get it. But he had the impudence to be in love with Madame Walewska! Napoleon's peace was not in the least disturbed by this rivalry, which was even supposed to amuse him. The prince, much maltreated by nature, was, besides, deaf and a stutterer.

'The foreign ministers apart and some of the high functionaries settled down at play, no one sat down in the emperor's presence, not even his brothers-in-law. This did not seem to displease Prince Murat, who did not lose the opportunity to pose, and to strike attitudes which he judged appropriate to show off the beauty of his figure. But little Borghese was enraged, and still had not the courage to sit down.

'After cards came supper. Napoleon never took a seat at table, but walked about, so as to chat with the ladies, diverting himself with asking a thousand questions, which sometimes were embarrassing, considering the extremely precise answers he exacted. He wanted to know what you did, what you read, what you thought about most, what you liked best.

'One day, or one evening rather, when, leaning on the back of my chair, he amused himself with examining me in this way as to my reading, he talked novels, and told me that of all which had come into his hands, the *'Comte de Comminges" had interested him by far the most. He had read it twice, and each time had been moved to tears.

'I did not know the book, and it may well be imagined that, no sooner had I reached home, I ransacked my fatherinlaw's library. Unfortunately, this novel was not there. Only a long time after that conversation did I succeed in getting a copy, and I too shed tears!

'My mother-in-law, being the only lady of Warsaw who had kept up a salon, found herself obliged to give drawingroom teas and dances. A host of strangers who had come with the diplomatic body asked nothing better than to be entertained. The princes, of the blood so-called, missed none of these parties, without, however, compromising their dignity, for they only danced at *court balls*!

'Prince Murat, little discountenanced by the failure of his absurd enterprise, seized this opportunity to talk to me, and overwhelmed me with insipid compliments. I scarcely made an effort to prevent his seeing how he wearied me. He finally, though somewhat late, did perceive it. Then, assuming a melodramatic air, he said this very ridiculous phrase — rendered more so by his Gascon accent — which has made my friends laugh so much: "Madame Alexandre! you are not ambitious; you do not care for princes!"

'At Paris I heard a companion anecdote. The day that Murat was proclaimed King of Naples, a fair one, touched by his greatness, accorded him a private interview. As the cares of his empire were not yet taking up much of his time, he arrived too early, and, impatient of waiting, he carried his hand to his forehead, exclaiming: "Was an unhappier monarch ever known?"

'When I reflect how petty and absurd all those princes of Napoleon's family seemed to us by the side of the colossus who overshadowed them, I repeat the maxim proved true by the ages, that in the eyes of mankind only a great character or great deeds can justify sudden elevation.'[6]

The party soon ended and the storms threatened, I retreated by to the Villa Diodati only to find the Shelleys, Lord Byron and Claire awaiting my arrival. Until I stepped foot over the threshold of the palour, I did not realize the importance of my absence. Lord Byron had completed his ghost-story. I quickly and silently took my seat, not entreating them to accept an apology I wasn't willing to offer. My absence, though an annoyance to them, was not inappropriate. I will not accept being a prisoner of the Villa Diodati.

Mary Wollstonecraft Godwin's Journal

18June, the Small Hours.— Lord Byron, the first to complete his ghost-story with the fever of a dream, stood before us all, all before the fire. Even poor Polidori who arrived tardy, though he was unaware of the Lord's sudden abrupt invitation, sat at the ready to hear what ghost had possessed our little Lord in this most haunted of houses to write so feverishly throughout the night into the next day until now. He came not down to breakfast, nor for lunch or tea. But now with the backdrop of a roaring fire as the pouring freezing rain pelts the high windows, he stood with ink-stained hands. If I knew not the familiar stain, I may have mistaken the ink for blood. Given the slight gasp from Claire, she may have.

My.

Lord Byron began, 'In the year 17— , having for some time determined on a journey through countries not hitherto much frequented by travellers, I set out, accompanied by a friend, whom I shall designate by the name of Augustus Darvell. He was a few years my elder, and a man of considerable fortune and ancient family— advantages which an extensive capacity prevented him alike from undervaluing or overrating. Some peculiar circumstances in his private history had rendered him to me an object of attention, of interest, and even of regard, which neither the reserve of his manners, nor occasional indications of an inquietude at times nearly approaching to alienation of mind, could extinguish.

---

6 From *Memoirs of Countess Potocka*, edited by Casimir Stryienski, Authorized Translation by Lionel Strachey, published by Doubleday & McClure Co., 1901

'I was yet young in life, which I had begun early; but my intimacy with him was of a recent date: we had been educated at the same schools and university; but his progress through these had preceded mine, and he had been deeply initiated into what is called the world, while I was yet in my noviciate. While thus engaged, I had heard much both of his past and present life; and although in these accounts there were many and irreconcileable contradictions, I could still gather from the whole that he was a being of no common order, and one who, whatever pains he might take to avoid remark, would still be remarkable. I had cultivated his acquaintance subsequently, and endeavoured to obtain his friendship, but this last appeared to be unattainable; whatever affections he might have possessed seemed now, some to have been extinguished, and others to be concentred: that his feelings were acute, I had sufficient opportunities of observing; for, although he could control, he could not altogether disguise them: still he had a power of giving to one passion the appearance of another in such a manner that it was difficult to define the nature of what was working within him; and the expressions of his features would vary so rapidly, though slightly, that it was useless to trace them to their sources. It was evident that he was a prey to some cureless disquiet; but whether it arose from ambition, love, remorse, grief, from one or all of these, or merely from a morbid temperament akin to disease, I could not discover: there were circumstances alleged, which might have justified the application to each of these causes; but, as I have before said, these were so contradictory and contradicted, that none could be fixed upon with accuracy. Where there is mystery, it is generally supposed that there must also be evil: I know not how this may be, but in him there certainly was the one, though I could not ascertain the extent of the other— and felt loth, as far as regarded himself, to believe in its existence. My advances were received with sufficient coldness; but I was young, and not easily discouraged, and at length succeeded in obtaining, to a certain degree, that common-place intercourse and moderate confidence of common and every day concerns, created and cemented by similarity of pursuit and frequency of meeting, which is called intimacy, or friendship, according to the ideas of him who uses those words to express them.

'Darvell had already travelled extensively; and to him I had applied for information with regard to the conduct of my intended journey. It was my secret wish that he might be prevailed on to accompany me: it was also a probable hope, founded upon the shadowy restlessness which I had observed in him, and to which the animation which he appeared to feel on such subjects, and his apparent indifference to all by which he was more immediately surrounded, gave fresh strength. This wish I first hinted, and then expressed: his answer, though I had partly expected it, gave me all the pleasure of surprise— he consented; and, after the requisite arrangements, we commenced our voyages. After journeying through various countries of the south of Europe, our attention was turned towards the East, according to our original destination; and it was in my progress through those regions that the incident occurred upon which will turn what I may have to relate.

'The constitution of Darvell, which must from his appearance have been in early life more than usually robust, had been for some time gradually giving way, without the intervention of any apparent disease: he had neither cough nor hectic, yet he became daily more enfeebled: his habits were temperate, and he neither declined nor complained of fatigue, yet he was evidently wasting away: he became more and more silent and sleepless, and at length so seriously altered, that my alarm grew proportionate to what I conceived to be his danger.

'We had determined, on our arrival at Smyrna, on an excursion to the ruins of Ephesus and Sardis, from which I endeavoured to dissuade him in his present state of indisposition— but in vain: there appeared to be an oppression on his mind, and a solemnity in his manner, which ill corresponded with his eagerness to proceed on what I regarded as a mere party of pleasure, little suited to a valetudinarian; but I opposed him no longer— and in a few days we set off together, accompanied only by a serrugee and a single janizary.

'We had passed halfway towards the remains of Ephesus, leaving behind us the more fertile environs of Smyrna, and were entering upon that wild and tenantless track through the marshes and defiles which lead to the few huts yet lingering over the broken columns of Diana— the roofless walls of expelled Christianity, and the still more recent but complete desolation of abandoned mosques— when the sudden and rapid illness of my companion obliged us to halt at a Turkish cemetery, the turbaned tombstones of which were the sole indication that human life had ever been a sojourner in this wilderness. The only caravansera we had seen was left some hours behind us, not a vestige of a town or even cottage was within sight or hope, and this "city of the dead" appeared to be the sole refuge for my unfortunate friend, who seemed on the verge of becoming the last of its inhabitants.

'In this situation, I looked round for a place where he might most conveniently repose:— contrary to the usual aspect of Mahometan burial-grounds, the cypresses were in this few in number, and these thinly scattered over its extent: the tombstones were mostly fallen, and worn with age:— upon one of the most considerable of these, and beneath one of the most spreading trees, Darvell supported himself, in a half-reclining posture, with great difficulty. He asked for water. I had some doubts of our being able to find any, and prepared to go in search of it with hesitating despondency— but he desired me to remain; and turning to Suleiman, our janizary, who stood by us smoking with great tranquillity, he said, "Suleiman, verbana su," (i. e. bring some water,) and went on describing the spot where it was to be found with great minuteness, at a small well for camels, a few hundred yards to the right: the janizary obeyed. I said to Darvell, "How did you know this?"— He replied, "From our situation; you must perceive that this place was once inhabited, and could not have been so without springs: I have also been here before."

' "You have been here before!— How came you never to mention this to me? and what could you be doing in a place where no one would remain a moment longer than they could help it?"

'To this question I received no answer. In the mean time Suleiman returned with the water, leaving the serrugee and the horses at the fountain. The quenching of his thirst had the appearance of reviving him for a moment; and I conceived hopes of his being able to proceed, or at least to return, and I urged the attempt. He was silent— and appeared to be collecting his spirits for an effort to speak. He began.

' "This is the end of my journey, and of my life— I came here to die: but I have a request to make, a command— for such my last words must be— You will observe it?"

' "Most certainly; but have better hopes."

' "I have no hopes, nor wishes, but this— conceal my death from every human being."

' "I hope there will be no occasion; that you will recover, and— — "

' "Peace!— it must be so: promise this."

' "I do."

' "Swear it, by all that"— — He here dictated an oath of great solemnity.

' "There is no occasion for this— I will observe your request; and to doubt me is— — "

' "It cannot be helped,— you must swear."

'I took the oath: it appeared to relieve him. He removed a seal ring from his finger, on which were some Arabic characters, and presented it to me. He proceeded—

' "On the ninth day of the month, at noon precisely (what month you please, but this must be the day), you must fling this ring into the salt springs which run into the Bay of Eleusis: the day after, at the same hour, you must repair to the ruins of the temple of Ceres, and wait one hour."

' "Why?"

' "You will see."

' "The ninth day of the month, you say?"

' "The ninth."

'As I observed that the present was the ninth day of the month, his countenance changed, and he paused. As he sate, evidently becoming more feeble, a stork, with a snake in her beak, perched upon a tombstone near us; and, without devouring her prey, appeared to be stedfastly regarding us. I know not what impelled me to drive it away, but the attempt was useless; she made a few circles in the air, and returned exactly to the same spot. Darvell pointed to it, and smiled: he spoke— I know not whether to himself or to me— but the words were only, "'Tis well!"

' "What is well? what do you mean?"

' "No matter: you must bury me here this evening, and exactly where that bird is now perched. You know the rest of my injunctions."

'He then proceeded to give me several directions as to the manner in which his death might be best concealed. After these were finished, he exclaimed, "You perceive that bird?"

' "Certainly."

' "And the serpent writhing in her beak?"

' "Doubtless: there is nothing uncommon in it; it is her natural prey. But it is odd that she does not devour it."

'He smiled in a ghastly manner, and said, faintly, "It is not yet time!" As he spoke, the stork flew away. My eyes followed it for a moment, it could hardly be longer than ten might be counted. I felt Darvell's weight, as it were, increase upon my shoulder, and, turning to look upon his face, perceived that he was dead!

'I was shocked with the sudden certainty which could not be mistaken— his countenance in a few minutes became nearly black. I should have attributed so rapid a change to poison, had I not been aware that he had no opportunity of receiving it unperceived. The day was declining, the body was rapidly altering, and nothing remained but to fulfil his request. With the aid of Suleiman's ataghan and my own sabre, we scooped a shallow grave upon the spot which Darvell had indicated: the earth easily gave way, having already received some Mahometan tenant. We dug as deeply as the time permitted us, and throwing the dry earth upon all that remained of the singular being so lately departed, we cut a few sods of greener turf from the less withered soil around us, and laid them upon his sepulchre.

'Between astonishment and grief, I was tearless.'

The Diary of Dr John William Polidori

17 June.— The Shelleys and Claire had retired to their apartments to the night was waning fast. Lord Byron and myself as around the fire with fine glasses of absinthe, mixed in its accustomed fashion with a square of sugar and drops of laudanum, and our mood this evening had certainly not soured. Lord Byron was pained that this was only a fragment of a novel; one which he intended on finishing, but the spirit had for now passed from his mind. He had such a fever upon the brain having written this 'fragment' in only a day that he sat exhausted. He told me of the story he desired to tell: that Darvell would reappear, alive again, as a vampire! While the spirit may have passed from his mind, the spirit did not pass far beyond the walls of the Villa Diodati. In fact, the spirit did not even pass out of this very parlour before the fire. Abandoning Lord Bryon, the spirit possessed me!

Chapter Four
Christabel[7]

The Diary of Dr John William Polidori

18 June.— My leg grows much much worse. Why was I cursed by the barbed shaft of Eros to have fallen in love with the betrothed of Percy Shelley? If not for my chivalry, I would not be possessed a sprained ankle. Dispossessed of my mobility! The nobility of my profession is lost! The shame of doctor to be seen bandaged and wearing a splint for simply and foolishly jumping from a minor height is more akin to knight being stabbed by his own sword on the battlefield after tripping over a corpse.

Shelley and his party of sisters came down for breakfast. Mrs Shelley (though I know truly not if she is legally married, merely betrothed, or perhaps a scarlet woman) called me her brother (younger).

Again.

Began my ghost story after tea. I don't yet have a proper title for the work, but I have a brilliant subtitle: 'the Modern Oedipus'. Such a brilliant concept. Why haven't more caretakers of insane asylums studied one's desire to have sexual relations with one's mother while desiring to kill one's father? Not that I suppose one who possesses such desires is by very necessity insane, but that such specialized hospitals are more fertile grounds to study such subjects. Shame is not a hindrance when probing lunatics. This subject proved not to be a foreign concept in ancient times as scene in the legend of King Oedipus and the drama of the same name by Sophocles. Surely, it is not a foreign concept in the modern age. Taking the classical and exposing it as modern!

Now, I'll just have to write my story worthy of Sophocles.

Doable.

Twelve o'clock, the Five really began to talk ghostly again. This game of ghost stories has been quite fun, though I know not if there will truly be a winner awarded. Nor what the reward will be. The others were quite haughty and dismissive of my own contributions. They were so naughty! I was not born with a silver tongue like Lord Byron, nor the genius of Shelley, nor the beauty of Mary. The latter of these three has not shown herself to be quick with a pen, though her wit is quick

---

7 Extract from an unfinished long narrative ballad by Samuel Taylor Coleridge, published in a pamphlet in 1816, alongside *Kubla Khan* and *The Pains of Sleep*.

and her tongue sharp as a quill. I will continue to harangue her every morning until the time she produces her ghost story. Cut me? I'll fillet her, my love.

Lord Byron repeated some verses of Coleridge's *Christabel*, of the witch's breast, which would pleasant away the afternoon since jaunting around and about the lake is nigh impossible with the inclement weather. Why bother with our holiday if we're stuck inside reading rhymes and exchanging niceties. I could be stuck inside in equally dour weather in London. Yes, I admit my mood is foul. It is my mood and I'll possess it in any manner I so choose.

> *Tis the middle of night by the castle clock,*
> *And the owls have awakened the crowing cock;*
> *Tu— whit! Tu— whoo!*
> *And hark, again! the crowing cock,*
> *How drowsily it crew.*
> *Sir Leoline, the Baron rich,*
> *Hath a toothless mastiff bitch;*
> *From her kennel beneath the rock*
> *She maketh answer to the clock,*
> *Four for the quarters, and twelve for the hour;*
> *Ever and aye, by shine and shower,*
> *Sixteen short howls, not over loud;*
> *Some say, she sees my lady's shroud.*
>
> *Is the night chilly and dark?*
> *The night is chilly, but not dark.*
> *The thin gray cloud is spread on high,*
> *It covers but not hides the sky.*
> *The moon is behind, and at the full;*
> *And yet she looks both small and dull.*
> *The night is chill, the cloud is gray:*
> *'Tis a month before the month of May,*
> *And the Spring comes slowly up this way.*
>
> *The lovely lady, Christabel,*
> *Whom her father loves so well,*
> *What makes her in the wood so late,*
> *A furlong from the castle gate?*
> *She had dreams all yesternight*
> *Of her own betrothèd knight;*
> *And she in the midnight wood will pray*

For the weal of her lover that's far away.

She stole along, she nothing spoke,
The sighs she heaved were soft and low,
And naught was green upon the oak
But moss and rarest misletoe:
She kneels beneath the huge oak tree,
And in silence prayeth she.

The lady sprang up suddenly,
The lovely lady Christabel!
It moaned as near, as near can be,
But what it is she cannot tell.—
On the other side it seems to be,
Of the huge, broad-breasted, old oak tree.

The night is chill; the forest bare;
Is it the wind that moaneth bleak?
There is not wind enough in the air
To move away the ringlet curl
From the lovely lady's cheek—
There is not wind enough to twirl
The one red leaf, the last of its clan,
That dances as often as dance it can,
Hanging so light, and hanging so high,
On the topmost twig that looks up at the sky.

Hush, beating heart of Christabel!
Jesu, Maria, shield her well!
She folded her arms beneath her cloak,
And stole to the other side of the oak.
What sees she there?

There she sees a damsel bright,
Drest in a silken robe of white,
That shadowy in the moonlight shone:
The neck that made that white robe wan,
Her stately neck, and arms were bare;
Her blue-veined feet unsandl'd were,
And wildly glittered here and there
The gems entangled in her hair.
I guess, 'twas frightful there to see

A lady so richly clad as she—
Beautiful exceedingly!

Mary mother, save me now!
(Said Christabel) And who art thou?

The lady strange made answer meet,
And her voice was faint and sweet:—
Have pity on my sore distress,
I scarce can speak for weariness:
Stretch forth thy hand, and have no fear!
Said Christabel, How camest thou here?
And the lady, whose voice was faint and sweet,
Did thus pursue her answer meet:—

My sire is of a noble line,
And my name is Geraldine:
Five warriors seized me yestermorn,
Me, even me, a maid forlorn:
They choked my cries with force and fright,
And tied me on a palfrey white.
The palfrey was as fleet as wind,
And they rode furiously behind.
They spurred amain, their steeds were white:
And once we crossed the shade of night.
As sure as Heaven shall rescue me,
I have no thought what men they be;
Nor do I know how long it is
(For I have lain entranced I wis)
Since one, the tallest of the five,
Took me from the palfrey's back,
A weary woman, scarce alive.
Some muttered words his comrades spoke:
He placed me underneath this oak;
He swore they would return with haste;
Whither they went I cannot tell—
I thought I heard, some minutes past,
Sounds as of a castle bell.
Stretch forth thy hand (thus ended she).
And help a wretched maid to flee.

Then Christabel stretched forth her hand,

And comforted fair Geraldine:
O well, bright dame! may you command
The service of Sir Leoline;
And gladly our stout chivalry
Will he send forth and friends withal
To guide and guard you safe and free
Home to your noble father's hall.

She rose: and forth with steps they passed
That strove to be, and were not, fast.
Her gracious stars the lady blest,
And thus spake on sweet Christabel:
All our household are at rest,
The hall as silent as the cell;
Sir Leoline is weak in health,
And may not well awakened be,
But we will move as if in stealth,
And I beseech your courtesy,
This night, to share your couch with me.

They crossed the moat, and Christabel
Took the key that fitted well;
A little door she opened straight,
All in the middle of the gate;
The gate that was ironed within and without,
Where an army in battle array had marched out.
The lady sank, belike through pain,
And Christabel with might and main
Lifted her up, a weary weight,
Over the threshold of the gate:
Then the lady rose again,
And moved, as she were not in pain.

So free from danger, free from fear,
They crossed the court: right glad they were.
And Christabel devoutly cried
To the lady by her side,
Praise we the Virgin all divine
Who hath rescued thee from thy distress!
Alas, alas! said Geraldine,
I cannot speak for weariness.
So free from danger, free from fear,

They crossed the court: right glad they were.

Outside her kennel, the mastiff old
Lay fast asleep, in moonshine cold.
The mastiff old did not awake,
Yet she an angry moan did make!
And what can ail the mastiff bitch?
Never till now she uttered yell
Beneath the eye of Christabel.
Perhaps it is the owlet's scritch:
For what can ail the mastiff bitch?

They passed the hall, that echoes still,
Pass as lightly as you will!
The brands were flat, the brands were dying,
Amid their own white ashes lying;
But when the lady passed, there came
A tongue of light, a fit of flame;
And Christabel saw the lady's eye,
And nothing else saw she thereby,
Save the boss of the shield of Sir Leoline tall,
Which hung in a murky old niche in the wall.
O softly tread, said Christabel,
My father seldom sleepeth well.

Sweet Christabel her feet doth bare,
And jealous of the listening air
They steal their way from stair to stair,
Now in glimmer, and now in gloom,
And now they pass the Baron's room,
As still as death, with stifled breath!
And now have reached her chamber door;
And now doth Geraldine press down
The rushes of the chamber floor.

The moon shines dim in the open air,
And not a moonbeam enters here.
But they without its light can see
The chamber carved so curiously,
Carved with figures strange and sweet,
All made out of the carver's brain,
For a lady's chamber meet:

The lamp with twofold silver chain
Is fastened to an angel's feet.

The silver lamp burns dead and dim;
But Christabel the lamp will trim.
She trimmed the lamp, and made it bright,
And left it swinging to and fro,
While Geraldine, in wretched plight,
Sank down upon the floor below.

O weary lady, Geraldine,
I pray you, drink this cordial wine!
It is a wine of virtuous powers;
My mother made it of wild flowers.

And will your mother pity me,
Who am a maiden most forlorn?
Christabel answered— Woe is me!
She died the hour that I was born.
I have heard the grey-haired friar tell
How on her death-bed she did say,
That she should hear the castle-bell
Strike twelve upon my wedding-day.
O mother dear! that thou wert here!
I would, said Geraldine, she were!

But soon with altered voice, said she—
'Off, wandering mother! Peak and pine!
I have power to bid thee flee.'
Alas! what ails poor Geraldine?
Why stares she with unsettled eye?
Can she the bodiless dead espy?

And why with hollow voice cries she,
'Off, woman, off! this hour is mine—
Though thou her guardian spirit be,
Off, woman, off! 'tis given to me.'

Then Christabel knelt by the lady's side,
And raised to heaven her eyes so blue—
Alas! said she, this ghastly ride—
Dear lady! it hath wildered you!

The lady wiped her moist cold brow,
And faintly said, ' 'tis over now!'

Again the wild-flower wine she drank:
Her fair large eyes 'gan glitter bright,
And from the floor whereon she sank,
The lofty lady stood upright:
She was most beautiful to see,
Like a lady of a far countrèe.

And thus the lofty lady spake—
'All they who live in the upper sky,
Do love you, holy Christabel!
And you love them, and for their sake
And for the good which me befel,
Even I in my degree will try,
Fair maiden, to requite you well.
But now unrobe yourself; for I
Must pray, ere yet in bed I lie.'

Quoth Christabel, So let it be!
And as the lady bade, did she.
Her gentle limbs did she undress,
And lay down in her loveliness.

But through her brain of weal and woe
So many thoughts moved to and fro,
That vain it were her lids to close;
So half-way from the bed she rose,
And on her elbow did recline
To look at the lady Geraldine.

Beneath the lamp the lady bowed,
And slowly rolled her eyes around;
Then drawing in her breath aloud,
Like one that shuddered, she unbound
The cincture from beneath her breast:
Her silken robe, and inner vest,
Dropt to her feet, and full in view,
Behold! her bosom and half her side—
A sight to dream of, not to tell!
O shield her! shield sweet Christabel!

Lord Bryon paused to take a sip of water from the glass on the round table beside him, when a brief silence ensued. Shelley suddenly shrieked. We all turned to Shelley and found his eyes so white with fear that his iris and pupils were devoid of all colour. His hands clutched his head with such ferocity that he was squeezing his head with the intensity of a vice. Crimson stained his philtrum (the scientific name for that crease under your nose, for those reading this diary when published at a later date), dripping down onto his upper lip. His teeth then clenched in such fearfulness and with such ferociousness I feared his teeth would bite off his tongue or shatter. He ran out of the room wielding a candle as if it were a short sword. He swung the candle-sword so wildly that the flame was snuffed out by the passing breeze. Percy bolted into his room and attempted to bolt the door, but my poor ruined foot was caught between the door and the jamb. I screamed with the sharp pain like a birthing woman. Shelley shrieked again and again as he forced the door closed on my foot! We both shouted at the other to either close or open the door. Then Lord Byron threw his shoulder into stout wooden door, knocking Shelley off his feet. Having collapsed onto the ground, I removed my belt and forced in between his upper and lower sets of teeth so that he did not bite off his tongue. He struggled with the viciousness of a patient in need of, not science, but an exorcist. His hands clawed at me like raptor talons (and I wasn't fucking wearing my hawking gloves). Lovely Mary threw water in his face. Claire, without any instruction, ran into my apartment to retrieve my satchel that contained all my medical instruments. These tools were intended for use on Lord Byron, as I am his personal physician. But the Hippocratic oath, which I swore before the Christian God and not the pagan Olympians, required my intercession whether or not Shelley was a dear friend or not. I held a bottle of ether under his nose and in his fear, he inhaled deeply and soon peace washed over him. Why does a medical doctor need an exorcist when he possesses a bottle of ether to exorcise the possessed?

Shelley, as his breath smoothed, was looking of at Mrs Shelley confessed the cause of his sudden fright. He thought of a woman he had heard of from superstitious women who had eyes instead of nipples. In his mind's eye, he saw Christabel with such queer nipples. This remained me of the stories of the early explorers in the Americas believing manatees were mermaids, giants lived in South America, and headless men who possessed faces in their chests. Where had Percy heard such a tale that a woman had eyes instead of nipples. He apologized for the thought having taken hold of his mind and horrified his mind.

Although the reading of Coleridge had ended for the evening and was not taken up again for the remainder of our time at the Villa Diodati, for posterities sake, Diary, I will include the remainder of the poem.

Yet Geraldine nor speaks nor stirs;
Ah! what a stricken look was hers!
Deep from within she seems half-way
To lift some weight with sick assay,
And eyes the maid and seeks delay;
Then suddenly, as one defied,
Collects herself in scorn and pride,
And lay down by the Maiden's side!—
And in her arms the maid she took,
Ah wel-a-day!
And with low voice and doleful look
These words did say:
'In the touch of this bosom there worketh a spell,
Which is lord of thy utterance, Christabel!
Thou knowest to-night, and wilt know to-morrow,
This mark of my shame, this seal of my sorrow;
But vainly thou warrest,
For this is alone in
Thy power to declare,
That in the dim forest
Thou heard'st a low moaning,
And found'st a bright lady, surpassingly fair;
And didst bring her home with thee in love and in charity,
To shield her and shelter her from the damp air.'

THE CONCLUSION TO PART I

It was a lovely sight to see
The lady Christabel, when she
Was praying at the old oak tree.
Amid the jaggèd shadows
Of mossy leafless boughs,
Kneeling in the moonlight,
To make her gentle vows;
Her slender palms together prest,
Heaving sometimes on her breast;
Her face resigned to bliss or bale—
Her face, oh call it fair not pale,

And both blue eyes more bright than clear,
Each about to have a tear.

With open eyes (ah woe is me!)
Asleep, and dreaming fearfully,
Fearfully dreaming, yet, I wis,
Dreaming that alone, which is—
O sorrow and shame! Can this be she,
The lady, who knelt at the old oak tree?
And lo! the worker of these harms,
That holds the maiden in her arms,
Seems to slumber still and mild,
As a mother with her child.

A star hath set, a star hath risen,
O Geraldine! since arms of thine
Have been the lovely lady's prison.
O Geraldine! one hour was thine—
Thou'st had thy will! By tairn and rill,
The night-birds all that hour were still.
But now they are jubilant anew,
From cliff and tower, tu— whoo! tu— whoo!
Tu— whoo! tu— whoo! from wood and fell!

And see! the lady Christabel
Gathers herself from out her trance;
Her limbs relax, her countenance
Grows sad and soft; the smooth thin lids
Close o'er her eyes; and tears she sheds—
Large tears that leave the lashes bright!
And oft the while she seems to smile
As infants at a sudden light!

Yea, she doth smile, and she doth weep,
Like a youthful hermitess,
Beauteous in a wilderness,
Who, praying always, prays in sleep.
And, if she move unquietly,
Perchance, 'tis but the blood so free
Comes back and tingles in her feet.
No doubt, she hath a vision sweet.
What if her guardian spirit 'twere,

What if she knew her mother near?
But this she knows, in joys and woes,
That saints will aid if men will call:
For the blue sky bends over all!

The Diary of Dr John William Polidori

18 June.— My jealousy seethes. Lord Byron is a unbridged genius. Not because the societal ladies swoon over his poetry. Not like the gentlemen of society are jealous of wealth, his title, or striking looks. It is his creative soul that I am most jealous of. He plucked a charming and sophisticated vampyre to jaunt among society out of the alarming and superstitious vampryes that haunt the peasantry. Who can take a hungry, decaying revenant out of the rural legends and transubstantiate the vampyre into a suave, sophisticated resident of high society? How I wish to tell this story! Every fibre of my being needs to write this story. The unholy spirit that entered me yesternight counts itself amongst common thieves. As I breathe, I cannot betray my benefactor by plagiarising his vampire story, as much as the desire to complete his novel washes over me. Drowning me in a sea of despair! How I wish to come up for air! The very nature of plagiarism is vampiric, unholy, unnatural. It requires the drinking of the creative blood of another fellow passenger to the grave to give us unholy fame and unnatural wealth. This theft is as abnormal in modern society as it is unseemly. There is no lure enticing enough to cause me to invite this thieving spirit to possess my intellect again. The exorcising of this spirit proved to be soul rending. Though my intentions were pure— no! there is no defending my plagiaristic ambitions! Yesternight, the spirit had complete possession of my psyche! The fiend would not release my mind to peace without, at least, the intercession of a priest! The foul spirit whispered in my ear that no one, not even Lord Bryon, would ever be aware of my thievery. This was the knavery of the evil spirit! But through shear will and out of fear of ending my relationship with Lord Byron, I cast the demon out! Once I had finally sent the spirit descending to the pit of Hell everlasting, I sat in the parlour exhausted from my intellectual warfare with plagiarism.

As the lightning dances across the sky, I wish the architect of the Villa Diodati had installed eaves on this window to give me a moment of peace. But as I sit here before the fire, the thunder thankfully off in the distance, the spirit of a new story has possessed me and intoxicated my brain. Like the Pentecostals, will I pick up snakes and speak in tongues as commanded by the Christ? The tale boils in my brain.

The entire story, from first sentence ('Upon the left side of the lake of Thun lies the small village of Beatenberg, which, under the care of a simple pastor contains no individual above the rank of a peasant: it was in this village that I was born. Misfortune seemed to be anxious at my very birth to stamp me for its own.') to the very last words ("But you married; I dreamt of happiness, on Louisa's birth-day accompanied you to your room, and the demon's threat I found had indeed been fulfilled. Your mother's portrait was Matilda's. Olivieri had seduced, you married a daughter of Matilda, of Matilda's husband, and I was the murderer of her father.") have already fully formed in my skull. All I must do is transcribe the words written upon the dural folds of my brain down onto the page. My dearest friends will believe I have the fever upon my brain, that I may have eaten a bad bit of beef, a spoiled blot of mustard, a mouldy crumb of cheese, a fragment of underdone potato. But I am perfectly healthy, as healthy as author can be when so feverish with story. The only cure for this creative encephalitis is to begin writing my contribution to our game of ghost stories this very night!

Mary Wollstonecraft Godwin's Journal

19 June.— Dr Polidori came down to breakfast like a cock of the walk. There was an ungentlemanly strut to his gate; he truly was a rooster who believed he ruled the roost. He triumphantly boasted that he had found his ghost story. When he inquired if I had a ghost story of my own for Lord Byron's game of ghost stories, I was forced to admit I had not yet found my story. He began to roast me for my lack of creative spark. He proudly and quite loudly proclaimed that he not only had the first line to his ghost story and not only had the last line, but the entire story in between fully formed in his head. He even recited these lines which I will not disgrace my journal by including them here for posterity. As I hanged my head, he harangued me and taunted me, flaunting the fire of creativity that had set his psyche ablaze. The doctor has no shame to make me that object of ridicule in his game of mockery. My Beloved sat in stone-cold silence when he should have joined me in an alliance against the good doctor. I sat in defiance when Lord Byron joined Polidori in his cruel game. My two so-called friends were positively ghoulish wallowing in their cesspool of keen mockery. But I would not be their fool. I abandoned my breakfast and questioned my friendship!

20June. The 'good' doctor came down to breakfast with a number of pages gripped in his covetous little hands. I sat with my head beginning to hang because I knew the harangue was eminent. These pages were, no doubt, the first pages written in Polidori's ghost story. He held them out reverently like a priest holding the Holy Writ during Easter Mass. He spoke of them like he had been God-breathed, that his ghost story had been *given to him by inspiration of God, and is profitable for doctrine, for reproof, for correction, for instruction in righteousness: that the man of God may be perfect, thoroughly furnished unto all good works*[8].His cruel ridicule continued for a second straight day. If I do not come up with a ghost story soon there will be no end to this keen mockery born. This very morning, I made it my sworn mission to find my ghost story that would trump anything that the 'good' doctor had composed, but I knew in the bottom of my heart— my very soul— that one simply does not order the Muses to provide me with such a story. Calliope will refuse to gift any epic poem or, in the modern day, any novel to a soul who dares command them. Their reprimand would be to utterly snuff out the creative spark. This silence is deafening. I seek their guidance to grant me the license to enter Lord Byron's game of ghost stories, but as of my writing this words into my journal, the Muses are still silent. Deafening!

21June. I record these words in mourning because this very morning, my 'Beloved' joined the 'good' doctor and 'Lord' Byron in this game of cruel mockery. I have nothing but contempt for their attempts to shame me for having not written a single blessed word onto the page. My rage no longer knows any bounds. The productivity and prolificacy of the 'good' doctor is simultaneously astounding and confounding. Why has Calliope bequeathed unto the 'good' doctor this cornucopia of creativity. That for the second straight morning, he produces proof of his nightly conquest. I continue to request— nay! pray!— to the Muses to grant me the rewards at the end of the quest Lord Byron has set us out on. But the doctor continues to flout this drought in my creativity. Where is my ghost story?

22June. Noon— There is no point in relating the cruel ridicule suffered by me at the hands of the good doctor, Lord Byron, and my Beloved this very morning for the third day in a row, they continue their scorn. I will no longer record for posterity any more keen mockery born from 'good' doctor, 'Lord' Byron, and my supposed 'Beloved'! The bell tolls midnight. To Hell with them all!

---

8 From 2 Timoth 3: 16-17 from the Authorized King James Bible.

22 June. Evening— Oh, how cruel this 'good' doctor is with is keen mockery. He is relentless and I am restless. Lord Byron and my Beloved have grown past this game with me, but the boy delights in toying with me. I will find a ghost to haunt me in the Villa Diodati this cruel year without a summer! And I will write that ghost's story down as part of our game of ghost stories. Shall I take dictation? Dedicatedly will I! I don't even care if my game story is born of my creativity, I will accept another's story, as long as I best Polidori in this game of ghost stories. If the Gospels and the Epistles could be written by mortal hands yet be inspired by a purely spiritual being in the Holy Ghost, then I will welcome such inspiration of God. Whether the ghost story is born out of my own perspiration or a markedly unholy ghost's inspiration, I will accept it. Am I tempted to offer my soul to Francis Dashwood's Order of the Friars of St. Francis of Wycombe; Beloved, am I willing to part with my very soul like Faust did before me?

23 June. Morning— Yesternight waned upon this talk, and even the witching hour had gone by, before we retired to rest. When I placed my head on my pillow, I did not sleep, nor could I be said to think. My imagination, unbidden, possessed and guided me, gifting the successive images that arose in my mind with a vividness far beyond the usual bounds of reverie. I saw— with shut eyes, but acute mental vision,— I saw the pale student of unhallowed arts kneeling beside the thing he had put together. I saw the hideous phantasm of a man stretched out, and then, on the working of some powerful engine, show signs of life, and stir with an uneasy, half vital motion. Frightful must it be; for supremely frightful would be the effect of any human endeavour to mock the stupendous mechanism of the Creator of the world. His success would terrify the artist; he would rush away from his odious handywork, horror-stricken. He would hope that, left to itself, the slight spark of life which he had communicated would fade; that this thing, which had received such imperfect animation, would subside into dead matter; and he might sleep in the belief that the silence of the grave would quench for ever the transient existence of the hideous corpse which he had looked upon as the cradle of life. He sleeps; but he is awakened; he opens his eyes; behold the horrid thing stands at his bedside, opening his curtains, and looking on him with yellow, watery, but speculative eyes.

I opened mine in terror. The idea so possessed my mind, that a thrill of fear ran through me, and I wished to exchange the ghastly image of my fancy for the realities around. I see them still; the very room, the dark parquet, the closed shutters, with the moonlight struggling through, and the sense I had that the glassy lake and white high Alps were beyond.

I could not so easily get rid of my hideous phantom; still it haunted me. I must try to think of something else. I recurred to my ghost story,— my tiresome unlucky ghost story! O! if I could only contrive one which would frighten my reader as I myself had been frightened that night!

Swift as light and as cheering was the idea that broke in upon me. 'I have found it! What terrified me will terrify others; and I need only describe the spectre which had haunted my midnight pillow.' On the morrow I announced that I had thought of a story. I began that day with the words, *It was on a dreary night of November*, making only a transcript of the grim terrors of my waking dream.[9]

23 June, Evening— I had burst into the kitchen this morning, exclaiming, 'I have found it!' My Beloved, poor Polidori, and our little Lord already sat for breakfast, with my helping of bacon and sausage still sizzling in the iron pan. 'Found what, my dove,' my love inquired. 'I found my ghost story!' I beamed. Then the doctor said, 'About time.' I nearly screamed in frustration. How I have grown tired of this man! My hands desired to wring his neck, for every morning for days he inquired if I had found my ghost story yet; every morning for days I had *not* found my ghost story yet; yet on the day that I find my ghost story, I find him unimpressed.

---

9 From the Introduction to the 1831 Edition of *Frankenstein; or, The Modern Prometheus*, published by Henry Colburn & Richard Bentley.

Chapter Five
A Galvanising Debate[10]

Mary Wollstonecraft Godwin's Journal

21 June. Lake Geneva— Many and long are the conversations between Lord Byron and Shelley, to which I am a devout but nearly silent listener. During one of these, various philosophical doctrines are discussed, and among others the nature of the principle of life, and whether there was any probability of its ever being discovered and communicated. They talk of the experiments of Dr Darwin, (I speak not of what the Doctor really did, or said that he did, but, as more to my purpose, of what was then spoken of as having been done by him,) who preserved a piece of vermicelli in a glass case, till by some extraordinary means it began to move with voluntary motion. Not thus, after all, would life be given. Perhaps a corpse would be re-animated; galvanism had given token of such things: perhaps the component parts of a creature might be manufactured, brought together, and endued with vital warmth.[11]

'I myself am a student of Luigi Galvani, the discoverer of the natural philosophy of animal electricity,' my Beloved boasted to Lord Byron who sits in the armchair opposite him by the hearth. Lord Byron heard the boast but, feared the cold seeping through the edges in the windowpanes of glass more, fed the flames an extra log from the metal basket. A heavenly battle waged as violent as any battlefield in the Napoleonic wars. Lightning incessantly flashed. Thunder violently crashed. Rain torrentially dashed any hope of expeditions outside the villa. Trapped in our opulent prison, my Beloved Percy and Lord Byron sought to make a game not of ghost stories, but of natural philosophical debate.

---

10 'All of the other chapters of this book (and its sequel) are myopically focused on collecting <u>all</u> the creative works written during, shortly after, or at very least inspired by the "Year Without Summer". This chapter on the other hand is a debate between Percy Shelley, Byron, and Polidori (with Mary and Claire as voyeurs) as it concerns the science of galvanism. This is THE VERY debate that precipitated Mary's "waking dream" which would inspire her novel *Frankenstein*. This is such a key scene, the penultimate scene. Therefore, I am drawing on quotations from contemporary scientific sources (or near contemporary) that Shelley, Bryon, and Polidori often literally and liberally quote to prove this point or that point in their debate, giving the fertile material to feed Mary' Shelley's dream.'— R.D.B.

11 From the Introduction to the 1831 Edition of *Frankenstein; or, The Modern Prometheus*, published by Henry Colburn & Richard Bentley.

'A student? Before the age of ten?' Lord Byron said mocking his friend. 'My. You were quite learned as a youth to be studying at the teat of the founder of galvanism.'

'Correction then. Perhaps I was more inspired by the experiments of Giovanni Aldini, his nephew, who continued Galvani's great work in animal electricity after his death.'

'Speak precisely then if you have any hope of winning our debate.'

'Very well. It is Galvani, professor of anatomy in Bologna, who in 1780 discovered the new electrical phenomena. By chance he noticed that a recently killed frog, put near an electric machine, produced lively contractions when sparks were drawn from the machine. It was a simple phenomenon. It was nothing else than the effect of a return shock, and a physicist would have given no importance to it.

'Unfortunately, Galvani,' Lord Byron countered, 'a clever anatomist, was poorly versed in electric knowledge.'

'Oh, no, Lord Byron! He varied his experiments in thousands of ways to find out the explanation of the phenomenon. Eventually, looking for what a physicist would have not have deemed worthy of investigation, he made one of those discoveries which— '

'— As properly said' Lord Byron said, 'come from a shaking ignorance than from a resting knowledge.'

'One day,' my Beloved electrically exclaimed, 'he saw a dead frog suspended from a copper hook on the railings of a balcony, and noticed violent muscular contractions whenever the wind blew the lower extremities again the iron bards of the balcony. This was a strange, inexplicable fact, because there was no intervention of any external electricity, with no electric machine or return stroke.'[12]

'So, I purchased the prerequisite equipment from a laboratory. I paid a young chap to catch some frogs and bring them to me. Why had I sent the urchin to the Thames (that dark and dismal river, the dirty one, and a river that smells to heaven) for merely catching frogs for a measly experiment? Towering warehouses, devouring factories, and glowering apartments built by the preposterously prosperous upon one shore and ramshackle shacks and embattled shanties housing the impoverished upon the demolished other. Into stinking back eddies, he dove sinking knee deep in the muck and mire; all to earn my shillings, he stroved... strived,' my Beloved quickly corrected himself. 'With a sack of leaping frogs, he returned and in turn I paid him his shillings.

'I was not alone in my desire to repeat Galvani's experiment. In the later years of the 18th century the poor little froggies in their ponds and pools must have believe the Biblical Apocalypse had been trumpeted.

---

12 From *Cours de Physique* by Adolphe Ganot, published by Chex, l'auteur in 1859.

The experiment was easily set up and easily replicated. Having cut off
the frog's head, I suspended the hind half of the body in a copper hook
passed between the back bone and the nerve filaments s which run on
each side of it; then holding a small plate of zinc in one hand, I brought
one end of it in contact with the copper stem that holds the hook, then
touch the legs of the frog with the other end. At every contact I saw the
legs bending and shaking, thus reproducing all the motion of life. To
account for this phenomenon, Galvani assumed the existence of an electricity proper to the animal tissues, which, passing from the nerves to the
muscle through the metals through the metallic arc, produced the contracts. Under the phrase *animal electricity* or *vital fluid* this theory was
adopted especially by physicians and physiologists, who supposed that
the secret of life had been discovered.[13] Lord Byron, I witnessed with
my mortal eyes the spark of life causing the frog's legs to dance. Instantly, I had been handed the primordial fire from Prometheus himself!'

'I have no doubt, my friend, you felt so inspired to compare yourself
with Prometheus. Hubris is not a common trait amongst our company,
but I must contest that by developing his contact theory Volta went on
to invent that wonderful instrument which won him an immortal fame,
known also nowadays as the *pile of Volta*. Wishes to multiply the contacts
and sum up together the electricity produced by every one of them, the
celebrated physicist contrived to put together one above the other, a zinc
disk, a copper disk, and afterwards a small piece of cloth moistened with
acidulated water; and again a zinc disk, a copper disk, and a small piece
of cloth, and again in the same way, with the caution of never inverting
the order. What could be expected from such an arrangement. Indeed
one should not hesitate in saying it, this apparently inert stuff, this *pile*
so many different metallic couples separated by a tiny liquid, is, as far as
the effects are concerned, the most wonderful instrument ever invented
with no exception, not even that of the steam engine and the telescope.'[14]

'Oh ho!' my Beloved bellowed quite mellowly, 'how by chance Volta invents the battery! Out of pure spite to prove the experiments of
Galvani insufficient.'

'Chance? Chance, you say? Why did Galvani possess the jumping
frogs?' Lord Byron protested, 'It certainly was not premeditated to investigate the role of electricity in violent muscular contractions. Oh!
no! Perchance Giovani or his servant or a waitress acquired the frog to
prepare as a delicacy to stimulate— no pun intended my dear friend,
at least not entirely— his beloved wife, Lucia's, appetite, who was of a
frail constitution. Was it merely to be prepared as a *bouillon* or perhaps

13 Ibid.
14 Ibid.

a more delicate preparation of *Cuisses de Grenouille à la Provençale?*' History never recorded the answer, because the frog gave birth to an entire new natural philosophy a science of animal electricity!

'As did an apple falling upon the head of natural *philosopher* Sir Isaac Newton,' my Beloved says, 'Your argument is faulty at its core. How many discoveries were made by mere chance? Many more than those sought by hypothesis and subsequent experimentation. Did not Archimedes of Syracuse, an original natural *philosopher*, exclaim, "Eureka! Eureka!", when sitting down to bath and perceived the water level rise and attributed this rise to the displacement of water equal to the volume of the submerged portion of his body? Chance, my dear little Lord, is in the very definition of a eureka moment, which I argue the nascent natural *philosopher* Galvani experienced first-hand.'

'Might I interject a brief tangent?' Dr Polidori said.

'Of course, doctor,' my Beloved said acquiescing his point momentarily.

'The tendency of the sciences has long been an increasing proclivity to separation and dismemberment ...The mathematician turns away from the chemist; the chemist from the naturalist; the mathematician, left to himself, divides himself into a pure mathematician and a mixed mathematician, who soon part company; the chemist is perhaps a chemist of electro-chemistry; if so, he leaves common chemical analysis to others; between the mathematician and the chemist is to be interpolated a *"physician"* (we have no English name for him), who studies heat, moisture, and the like. And thus science, even mere physical science, loses all traces of unity. A curious illustration of this result may be observed in the want of any name by which we can designate the students of the knowledge of the material world collectively. We are informed that this difficulty was felt very oppressively by the members of the British Association for the Advancement of Science, in their meetings at York, Oxford, and Cambridge, in the last three summers. There was no general term by which these gentlemen could describe themselves with reference to their pursuits. *Philosophers* was felt to be too wide and too lofty a term, and was very properly forbidden them by Mr Coleridge, both in his capacity of philologer and metaphysician; *savans* was rather assuming, besides being French instead of English; some ingenious gentleman [apparently William Whewell himself] proposed that, by analogy with *artist*, they might form *scientist*, and added that there could be no scruple in making free with this termination when we have such words as *sciolist*, *economist* and *atheist*— but this was not generally palatable. Perhaps we should use the new coinage, lest the term fall out of fashion.[15]

---

15 From an unsigned book review authored by William Whewell in *The Quarterly Review*, vol. 51 (March

'Of course, Doctor, from this point hence we will say *scientist*,' my Beloved says and Lord Byron, with a slight nod, agreed. Dr Polidori smiled, pleased with himself. My Beloved then continued his argument, 'What was the point I was arguing before the doctor's etymological tangent?' he paused to collect his thoughts, 'Ah! Yes! I have it. Luigi Galvani was both revered in certain scientific circles for his revolutionary experiments on the frogs and rivalled in a quite specific circle much to his reputation's detriment and never did these sets intersect with commonality. Scientists, to use the doctor's coinage, delight in thumbing their academic noses at the religious by claiming the sciences are uniquely adaptable to new evidences while the religious are stagnant in their archaic beliefs. The scientist, they claim, embraces new evidences while the religious dismiss the new evidences holding firm to spurious superstitions. But, I argue, scientists often find themselves mired in their own scientific dogmas when new evidences present themselves. In this stagnant swamp of scientific progress, one Alessandro Volta finds himself so mired. But I am not quite ready to debate concerning him yet. Luigi Galvani is where this debate begins, and I shall begin with his beginning.'

'Then hurry along, my dear friend,' Lord Byron said, needling his friend. 'The night wanes fast and our audience of young women may grow weary of our galvanising debate.' I take umbrage at the little Lord's insinuation. I find myself as enraptured by my three companions as I was as a child dropping eaves on my father's parlour! Why should my age or my gender play any part in my audience? How my mother would loathe this little Lord for his ignorance and my father would chastise him for his insult.

'Let us back up a bit in time. Did not the Joseph Priestly, an esteemed naturalist and a great populariser of science conclude that electrical experiments are, of all other, the cleanest and most elegant that the compass of philosophy exhibits. They are performed with the least trouble, there is an amazing variety in them, they furnish the most pleasing and surprising appearances from the entertainment of one's friends, and the expense of instruments may well be supplied, by a proportional deduction from the purchase of books, which are generally read and laid aside, without yielding half the entertainment.[16]

'Was not the society of the Enlightenment enraptured with great fascination over this new field of the scientific study and discovery of electricity? One can easily conclude that if we only consider what it is in objects that makes them capable of exciting the pleasing astonishment,

& June, 1834), pp. 58-59
16 From *History and Present State of Electricity* by Joseph Priestly

which has such charms for all mankind, we shall not wonder at the eagerness with which persons of both sexes, and of every age and condition, run to see electrical experiments. Here we see the course of nature, to all appearance, entirely reversed, in its most fundamental laws, and by causes seemingly the slightest imaginable. And not only are the greatest effects, and by causes which seem to be inconsiderable, but by those with which they seem to have no connection. Here, contrary to the principle of gravitation, we see bodies attracted, repelled, and held suspended by others, which are seen to have acquired that power by nothing but a very slight friction; while another body, with the very same friction, reverses all its effects. Here we see a piece of cold metal, or even water, or ice emitting strong sparks of fire, so as to kindle many inflammable substances, and *in vacuo* its light is prodigiously diffused and copious, so as exactly to resemble what is really is, the lightning of heaven.[17]

'Do you not, Lord Byron, question what can seem more miraculous than to find, that a common glass phial or jar, should, after a littler preparation (which, however, leaves no visible effect, whereby it can be distinguished from other phials or jars) be capable of giving a person such a violent sensation as nothing else in nature can give, and even of destroying animal life; and this shock attended with an explosion like thunder, and a flash like that of lightning?[18]

And then as if on the cue of the stage manager at the Dreary Lane Theatre, the divine sound effects hand rattled a thinned sheet of metal and flashed limelight to signal to the audience in attendance that thunder and lightning could be produced outside of inclement weather and inside a building made of brick and mortar. But outside the parlour's window, the divine sound effects hand was the Creator of the Natural World, and the thinned sheet of metal was the ominous darkened clouds that hung low over the lake and the flashes of limelight were electricity. The crash of thunder and the clash of lightning accentuated my Beloved's argument as if the Creator concurred.

Lord Byron countered with affirmation of my Beloved's argument, though from a different point-of-view. 'It could easily be said that the further experiments and discoveries in electricity— of which Newton had seen only the principle— seem to reinforce the great Philosopher's doubts. The speed with which the electrical vapour moves, changes direction, stops and races forth again seem consistent with the speed and changes in animal sensations and motions. The single ease of its travel— in general, through electrical bodies by communication, and in particular, through the nervous and muscular parts of animals— is consistent

17 Ibid
18 Ibid

with the ease with which the mutations induced in organ by various objects are conveyed to the seat of sentience; it is also consistent with the agility with which other motions correspondingly ensue in the body. And the contractions and dilatations caused in the muscles by an electrical spark or electrical shock are arguments, perhaps, even decisive ones, for the above-mentioned conjecture.'[19]

Poor Polidori, itching with anticipation to enter into the argument between my Beloved and our little Lord, blurted out as soon as Lord Byron's final syllable was uttered, 'Was it not high time for John Welsh to acquaint Benjamin Franklin with the result of my experiments on the Isle de Ré and he must do it in a word if he mean to use in a letter. The vigour of the fresh-taken torpedoes there was not able to force the Torpedinal fluid across the most minute tract of air, not from one link of a small chain to another, not even thro' a separation made by the edge of a knife in a slip of tinfoil pasted on sealing wax. The spark therefore and snapping noise attending it were denied to all their attempts, either in the light or complete darkness. Walsh observed to Franklin in his last the singularity of the Torpedo being able when insulated to give to an insulated person a great number of successive shocks: In this circumstance he has taken no less than fifty shocks from him in the space of a minute and half. All their experiments confirmed that the Torpedinal fluid was concentrated in the very instant of it's explosion by a sudden energy of the animal; and as there was no gradual accumulation and retention of this elastick fluid as in the case of charged glass, it is not surprizing that there should be no effect on Canton's Balls of attraction or repulsion. In short, the Torpedinal shock appears to arise from a compressed elastick fluid restoring itself to its former state by the same conductors as the elastick fluid compressed in charged glass. The skin of the animal, bad conductor as it is, appears to be a better conductor of the Torpedinal elastick fluid than the least tract of the likewise elastick fluid air. Notwithstanding the weak spring of the Torpedinal fluid Walsh was able to convey it in the publick exhibitions at La Rochelle thro' two brass wires of twelve feet each and thro' four to eight persons, at different times, the wires and persons communicating with each other by the medium of water, in basins placed between each. The Torpedo laid on a wet napkin was placed on a table six feet distant from the table on which the basins stood. One end of one of the wires was wrapt in the wet napkin and the other end went into the first basin in which the first gentleman put a finger of one hand, with a finger of the other hand in the next Basin. The circuit was in this manner continued to the last basin. One end of the other wire was put into this last basin and with the other end he just touched the back of

---

19 From *Of Artificial and Natural Electricity* by Giambatista Beccaria, published in 1753.

the fish, when all the persons in the circuit were affected, but Walsh, the toucher, being out of it felt nothing. The effect in air, on many repeated experiments, is about four times as strong as it is in water.'[20]

The hyperbolic statement hung in the air like a balloon made of lead.

Polidori then barrelled on bloviating about some letter from one Sieur Seignette, Mayor of la Rochelle, and second perpetual Secretary of the Academy of that City, to the publisher of the *French Gazette*. He had written, "In the Gazette of the 14th August, the publisher mentioned the discovery made by Mr. Walsh, Member of the parliament of England, and of the Royal Society of London. The experiment, of which I am going to give you an account, was made in the presence of the Academy of this city. A live Torpedo was placed on a table. Round another table stood five persons insulated. Two brass wires, each thirteen feet long, were suspended to the ceiling by silken strings. One of these wires rested by one end on the wet napkin on which the fish lay; the other end was immersed in a basin full of water placed on the second table, on which stood four other basins likewise full of water. The first person put a finger of one hand in the basin in which the wire was immersed, and a finger of the other hand in the second basin. The second person put a finger of one hand in this last basin, and a finger of the other hand in the third; and so on successively, till the five persons communicated with one another by the water in the basins. In the last basin one end of the second wire was immersed; and with the other end Mr. Walsh touched the back of the Torpedo, when the five persons felt a commotion which differed in nothing from that of the Leyden experiment, except in the degree of force. Mr. Walsh, who was not in the circle of conduction, received no shock. This experiment was repeated several times, even with eight persons; and always with the same success. The action of the Torpedo is communicated by the same mediums as that of the electric fluid. The bodies which intercept the action of the one, intercept likewise the action of the other. The effects produced by the Torpedo resemble in every respect a weak electricity."'[21]

AND!

'Did not Sir Isaac Newton write in his *Principia*: In experimental philosophy, propositions collected from the phenomena of induction, are deemed (notwithstanding contrary hypotheses) either exactly or very nearly true, till other phenomena occur by which they may be rendered either more accurate, or liable to exception?[22] Because! Even

---

20 From a letter to Benjamin Franklin from John Walsh, 27 August 1772.

21 Extract of a Letter from the Sieur Seignette, Mayor of la Rochelle, and second perpetual Secretary of the Academy of that City, to the publisher of the French Gazette

22 From *The Mathematical Principles of Natural Philosophy* by Isaac Newton, published in 1726.

Felice Fontana, the strongest and most ardent disciple in the discipline of Albrecht von Haller, who was himself the fiercest of opponents to the conception of the electrical nature of animal spirits, changed his mind. Did Fontana not concur that in short, not only the mechanism of muscle motion is unknown, but we cannot even image anything capable of accounting for it? It seems that we are forced to make recourse to some other principle, perhaps to something analogous to electricity, if not to ordinary electricity itself. The electric Gymnotus and the torpedo make the thing at least possible, if not probable. One could believe that this principle follows the most ordinary laws of electricity. It might be even more modified in nerves than it is in the torpedo and the Gymnoti. Nerves would be the organs devoted to conducting his fluid, and possibly also to exciting it. But all remains to be done.'[23] 'We must first assure ourselves by firm experiments, whether the electrical principle has really its site in the contracting muscles; we must determine the laws that this fluid observes in the animal body; and after all it remains to be known what excites this principle and who it is excited.'[24]

Pleased with his contribution to the debate, poor Polidori sat back again; he had been on sitting, quite literally, on the edge of his seat, hunched over his haunches.

'True. True,' my Beloved said complimenting Dr Polidori. He then continued his argument from the point-of-view of Galvani. 'As several anatomists have thought that the electric fluid either enters into the composition of that very subtle fluid which is considered, and not without reason, to flow through the nerves, or it is that same nervous fluid, so he decided to carry out some experiments on the nerves with the electric fluid, in the hope that they could disclose the truth or at least contribute to throw some light on the obscurity of the phenomena of nerves.[25] Giovani prepared his frogs in the usual way: 'The frogs being cut transversally below the upper limbs, skinned and disembowelled, he flet only their inferior limbs joined together, with their long crural nerves inserted. These latter were wither left loose and free, or attached to the spinal cord, which in turn was either left intact in its vertebral canal or artificially extracted from it and partly or wholly separated. The phenomena he describe occurred only if the animals had been prepared for experimentation in the manner I have mentioned above; otherwise the contractions failed to take place.'[26]

---

23 From *Treatise on viper venom, on American poison, on cherry laurel, and on some other vegetable poisons* by Felice Fontana, published in 1781.

24 Ibid

25 From an unpublished draft by Luigi Galvani

26 Ibid

Then Lord Byron chimed in with his own critique, 'Did not Marcellow Malpighi know that the way our souls use the body in operating is ineffable. Yet it is certain that in the operations of growth, sensation, and motion the soul is forced to act in conformity with the machine on which it is acting. Just as a clock or a mill is moved in the same way be a pendulum of lead or stone, or by an animal, or a man; indeed, if an angel moved it, he would produce the same motion with changes of position as the animals or other agents do. Hence, even though he did not know how the angel operates, if on the other hand he did know the precise structure of the mill, he would understand this motion and action, and if the mill were out of order,he would try to repair the wheels or the damage to their structure without bothering to investigate how the angel moving them operated.'[27]

'How an angel operates?' my Beloved countered with slight mockery, 'Galvani himself formulated a handful of laws that function outside of how an angel operates. Law 1: The muscular contraction produced by nerve irritation is proportional both to the minimum parts of the nerve moved by the stimulus and to the force by which they are moved. Law 2: Independently on the irritating cause, the irritation is almost uniquely local, that is, it spreads very poorly— if any— beyond the place of application. Law 3: The communication, as well as the propagation to the muscle, of either the action of the nervous force or of the induced motion is dependent only on the nerve.[28] He would observe what could be considered a fourth law, though he did not state it thus, in Galvani's words, very little electric fluid which is far from giving any electric sign, is able to excite the contractions.

Dr Polidori piped in, 'Was not Galvani to have said, to be sure, that a direct proportion seemed to him to be maintained in the contractions, but only within certain limits. It has been found, for example, that if, after fixing a certain length of a nerve-conductor which is sufficient to bring about contractions, you shorten it, then the contractions do not diminish, but disappear. If, however, you lengthen it, the contractions in fact grow strong, but only up to a certain point, beyond which— however far you extend the nerve-conductor— the contractions are augmented imperceptibly, if at all. The same can be said about the other elements of the proportion I have set forth.'[29]

And with these words, this chapter of their Galvanising debate closed.

---

27 From Response of Doctor Marcellow Malpighi to the Letter by Mercello Malpighi, published posthumously.
28 From Luigi Galvani's manuscripts kept in the archives of the Academy of Sciences of Bologna.
29 From De viribus elecricitatis in motu musculari commentaries by Luigi Galvani.

* * *

Only to reopen again after the briefest of intermissions to pour new brandy.

Dr Polidori continued his liberal quoting, 'Was not Priestly to have seen abundant reason, since the publication of his former volume of *Observations on different kinds of air,* to applaud himself for the little delay he made in putting it to press; the consequences having been that, instead of the experiments being prosecuted by himself only, or a few other, the subject had now gained almost universal attention among philosophers, in every part of Europe,' poor Polidori paused to breathe, 'and this branch of science, of which nothing, in a manner was known till very lately indeed, now bids fair to be farther advanced than any other in the whole compass of natural philosophy.'[30]

'Ah, yes,' Lord Byron said, 'Was it not then possible to isolate "inflammable air" or hydrogen, "phlogisticated air" or nitrogen, "fixed air" otherwise now known as carbon dioxide, "swamp air" or methane" and "dephlogisticated air" or the wonderous oxygen? Is it not queer that remarkable advancements of scientists would rival the poets and philosophizers in the understanding of our world. No longer are we restricted to the laughably mythological Scriptures of the Jews and Christians.'

'Yes! Yes,' Dr Polidori exclaimed, continuing his argument, 'In the meantime, did not Galvani among others, diligently examine the above mentioned principles [i.e. the various airs] with the aim of finding their quality and quantity in the various fluid and solid parts of animals, an examination— as far as they would know— that nobody has done before.[31] Did not Galvani find that inflammable air was to be found present in all animal parts– both the solid and the fluid— and in particular the nerves? Was not this in flammable principle wholly or partly that fluid in the nerves called nervous fluid or animal spirits, which is the author of sense and motion? For either the nerves are of an idioelectric [i.e. non-conductive] nature, as many affirm, and for this reason they could not function as conductors, or else they are conductive; and how can it then happen that they retain the animal electric fluid within them so that it is not diffused and spread to adjacent parts, with, undoubtedly, a great diminution of muscular contractions? On the other hand this idoelectric substance of the nerves, which seems to have the function of preventing the electric nerve fluid from being dispersed with great consequent damage. Will not prevent this fluid coursing through the inner conducting

---

30 From *History and Present State of Electricity* by Joseph Priestly.
31 From Luigi Galvani's manuscripts kept in the archives of the Academy of Sciences of Bologna.

substance of the nerves, from leaving these same nerves when needed to produce contractions.'[32]

My Beloved asserted his own argument on the pedanticness of these arguments, 'We are trudging through the weeds too greatly. Let us dine on the meat of the argument we are having this evening by debating the war of not only words, but philosophies between Luigi Galvani and Alessandro Volta. I choose to speak for Galvani.'

'And I'll speak for Volta,' Lord Byron said, effectively cutting poor Polidori out of any further debate. But knowing the doctor as well as I do, only having known him less than a fortnight, silencing him will be a task of Herculean efforts rivalling the cleaning out of the Aegean stables. 'Do we know if Galvani and Volta ever have any direct interactions before or during or after the controversy?' Dr Polidori inquired, the Herculean task already falling defeated. My Beloved and our Little Lord and I knew the intent of his inquiry. He was putting either my Beloved's or Byron's feet to the proverbial flame.

'Well, dearest doctor,' my Beloved said, 'Volta tarried a few days in Bologna, where he visited the Institute of Sciences. Did not Sebastiano Canterzani, the secretary of the Academy of Sciences, remember the visit in a letter dated September 20, 1780, and addressed to Carlo Bianconi, the secretary of the Academy of Milan?'

'Perchance he did,' Dr Polidori said, truly doubting such a letter ever existed.

Then my Beloved quoted it in part, 'I am most obliged to You, illustrious Sir, for giving me the possibility of personally meeting Mr Alessandro Volta, whose celebrated name I knew before for his great discoveries in physics! The special esteem provided for similar people renders their company most satisfactory, in particular when they possess such a likable character and exquisite manners Don Alessandro. But he stayed in Bologna very briefly, only two days. I went with him to the Institute, where he spent several hours, and I introduced him to Mr Monti, Veratti, Metteucci, and some others of our professors.'[33]

Defeated, Poor Polidori, slumped back in his chair. Now, the adults in the room would continue their Galvanising debate.

'First off,' Lord Byron said, 'it must be stated first before any argument— or disagreement— can be made concerning the debate before Volta and Galavani that the former hailed Galvani's discovery of animal electricity as "one of those great and brilliant discoveries, which deserves to be considered defining an ear in the field of physical and

---

32 From *De viribus elecricitatis in motu musculari commentaries* by Luigi Galvani.
33 From a letter from S Canterzani to C Bianconi, Bologna, September 20, 1780.

medical science."[34] Is this not a comparison with Franklin's discovery of the electrical nature of lightning?' Did not Volta esteem and appreciate "his very fine experience" or for "the many nice experiment he made", even when Volta disagreed. Vehemently. This could not and should not be the nature of electricity that the Bolognese doctor "obsintately" called "animal".'

'It is the height of scientific rigor and method,' my Beloved added, 'that for every argument raised and for every answer submitted, they returned, time and time again, to experimentation to get the necessary elements to refute the other's criticisms. Did not Galvania write, in clear reference to Volta, "However I do not want to base my claims only on analogy arguments, and, as Mr Volta uses experiments to prove the truth of his theory and the falsity of mind, so it is fair that I purse a similar path".'[35]

'But first,' Lord Byron said, 'Galvani was charged with resurrected Tommaso Laghi's discredited neuro-electric hypothesis. Galvani must first, the argument held, overcome the objections raised some decades previous by Felice Fontana and Leopoldo Caldani, whom we have mentioned during our Galvanising debate.'

'Oh! Ho! Galvani would indeed argue in these objections are contradicted by the example and existence of tourmaline and of electric fish, which produce electricity even when completely immersed in water. Remember, Lord Byron, that water is in itself a conducting liquid. And Galvani argued that his own experiments, as well as Volta's, proved that "animal humidity does not prevent electrical excitation; on the contrary, it makes an easy way for electricity to obey the soul and, on its command, to move toward various places in order to put muscles in motion."[36] I would argue, Lord Byron, as Aldini and Galvani did before me, that the Hallerian theory of irritability is "not a well known" principle as Haller himself conceded, I challenge you to prove its existence within the framework of "established laws" as Galvani as so proven for animal electricity! Prove it or abandon your theory in favour of Galvani's!'

Lord Byron sat silent.

But then protested, 'Did not Volta's criticize the crucial experiments on muscular contractions without the use of metals gave doubtful and inconstant results?'

Oh! Ho!,' my Beloved answered, 'Galvani himself answered this criticism, "I can assure that I obtained the motions of the frog's legs not

---

34 From *Le opere di Alessandro Volta. Edizione nazionale sotto gli auspice della Reale Accademia dei Licnei e el Reale Istituto Lambardo di Scinze e Lettere* by Alessandro Volta
35 From *De viribus elecricitatis in motu musculari commentaries* by Luigi Galvani.
36 From *Memorie ed esperimenti inedita* by Luigi Galvani.

a few times, as Volta claims, but in many, many experience, so that in a hundred times the effect had not happened just once; and these experiments have been recently replicated in our Institute of Sciences in the presence of many learned scholars, and other people well, versed in this sort of things, and they never failed.' AND! 'To confirm the truth, I succeeded in obtaining the kind attention and assistance of several illustrious friends to my experiments; among them I think it suffices to cite the most learned secretary of our academy, Sebastiano Canterzani, to whom I never omitted to show any of my experiments, and to communicate any of my contjectures before publishing; but more than any other I could quote, You"— meaning Lazzaro Spallanzani— "who are such an excellent and absolute master in every scientific field, as in the difficult art of experiment, and who, for my good fortune, have been only a witness to this experiment, but an approving judge."'[37]

Lord Byron then challenged Galvani on his overuse of a literary style in his scientific works, which my Beloved countered by quoting them freely from the book that had rested upon his lap, "If a frog is held by one leg with the fingers so that the hook fastened in the spinal cord touches a silver plate and if the other leg calls down freely on the same plate, the muscles are immediately contracted at the instant that this leg makes contact with the plate. There upon the leg is raised and lifted up, but soon, however, it spontaneously relaxes and again falls down on the plate. As soon as contact is made, the leg is again lifted for the same reason and thus it continues alternately to be raised and lowered so that the great astonishment and pleasure of the observer, the leg seems to function like an electric pendulum."[38]

Lord Byron altered the argument back to Volta. 'I acknowledge that Volta had repeated some of Galvani's experiments but I argue that Volta himself had stated "the existence of a real and true animal electricity is evidently proved in the third part of the work you hold in your hands, dearest Percy, with many well combined and accurately described experiments." He acknowledged Galvani having "all the merit and paternity of this great and stupendous discovery!"[39] But this love affair with Galvani's experiments and scientific concludes would be short lived. There was no animal electricity, instead he introduced a new concept into physics: the electromotive power of metals!'

'In fact, Volta's criticism goes well beyond Galvani's first experiment. The criticism encompasses the very foundation of Galvani's theory of animal electricity, namely the analogy between the neuromuscular

37 From *Memorie sulla electricita... al celebre abate Lazzaro Spallanzani* by Luigy Galvani, published in 1797.
38 From *De viribus electricitatis in motu musculari commenarius* by Luigi Galvani, published in 1791.
39 From *Le opere di Alessandro Volta. Edizione nazionale sotto gli auspice della Reale Accademia dei Licnei e el Reale Istituto Lambardo di Scinze e Lettere* by Alessandro Volta.

system and the Leyden jar: "The most plausible and fascinating explanations, which seem in agreement with the fist general appearances, are rarely confirmed by a more rigorous examination of particular phenomenon; and when we try to extend a nice discovery, which has presented us, to great and magnificent consequences, we are often obliged to make a step backward and to renounce to great part of our conceived plans."[40]

'In a letter to Giovanni Aldini, whom we know to be Galvani's nephew, Volta argued he believed that: "It is on the nerves, and solely on them that electricity acts, both in the case of a mild artificial electricity and of animal electricity; it is not at all necessary that the electric fluid flows through the nerves to the muscles; even less so that there follows any discharge between nerve and muscle, or between the internal and external surface of the latter: in sum, the electric fluid is not the immediate cause, even if as a stimulus,., of muscular motions, but only mediate, occasional and remote cause, as his proper action consists in stimulating and exciting the nerves."[41]

'But,' my Beloved countered, 'while Volta may have rejected Galvani's explanation of muscle motion, based on the analogy between the muscle and the Leyden jar, Volta, who however still acknowledge Galvani with the great merit of having opened a new and important path: "There remain the materials of Galvani's edifice, namely the beautiful outcomes of his original experiments and the discoveries that followed; oh yes, there remain such precious materials for another fabric, more solid if not finer, which may be raised."'[42]

'But!' Lord Byron argued, 'Did not an esteemed publication, that had previously reviewed Galvani's work, report the news that "the most illustrious Prof Volta, by continuing the experiments on animal electricity— a subject which can now be considered his own— makes new discoveries everyday"?'

Poor Polidori, sitting on his hands, interjected, 'What was the path that led Volta in a few months to change his opinion from an enthusiastic acceptance of Galvani's theory of animal electricity to the rejection of the analogy between the muscle and the Leyden jar, and to the denial of the existence of animal electricity?'

Lord Byron offered an answer, 'In his but first letter to Tiberio Cavallo, Volta wrote, "I do not know whether Galvani has carried out other experiments, but hose which he has made public in his work are restricted in an excessively narrow circle; every time they consist in uncovering and isolating the nerves, and in establishing a communication between

---

40 Ibid
41 Ibid
42 Ibid

these nerves and the depending muscles through electrical conducting bodies. However, by varying this sort of experiences in multiple ways, I showed that both these conditions, to uncover and isolate the nerves and to simultaneously touch these and the muscles in order to produce the pretended discharge, are not at all necessary."[43]

Eagerly biding his time and biting his lip, My Beloved launched into his counter argument: 'Galvani needed to understand the role of a conducting arc in the phenomena of contractions, it was necessary, first of all, to assess the "natural muscular force" of the animal. If, indeed, the same type of ace produced contractions in one animal but not another, that could depend not on the characteristics of the arc, but on the "varying strength of the animals". Likewise, and that was the case pointed out by Volta, the variable efficacy of different arcs applied to the same animal could be due to the variation in the strength of the animal, and not to the difference in the arc.'

Lord Byron argued, 'Did not Galvani distinguish three degrees of "animal force"— maximum, medium, and minimum—?' Did he not say, 'It is not convenient to perform the experiments, especially those implying comparisons, in the third degree, that is the minimum degree of the said force, as the re-occurring of contractions through a new type of arc in this case may be not the effect of this arc; so that the conclusions of a more powerful activity of the given arc could be erroneous.'[44] Erroneous! Percy, erroneous!

My Beloved laughed, 'Here Galvani is clearly referring to Volta's experiments in which the special efficacy of bimetal arcs was particularly evident! But it is the choice of the type of animal, on which Galvini insisted, was one of the fundamental criteria of the experimental method developed by Lazzaro Spallanzani. Spallanzani, for example, in his research on blood circulation carried out in the 1770s, had used "preferably the water newt, as it seems very apt to manifest and clear up those phenomena thanks to the easy preparation of its vases, their great transparency, and the most vivid purple-red colour of its blood. The choice of this animal, like that of the frog by Galvani, had been particularly felicitous, so much so that Spallanzani commented: "In truth, from the examination of the newt I acquired so much physiological knowledge, that I doubt whether a different animal had conceded the same to another observer after the discovery of circulation"

'Volta did in fact attribute great importance to experimental conditions. He considered, for example the variability of the action exerted

---

43 Ibid
44 From *Dell'uo e dell'attivita dell'arco conduttore nelle contrazioni dei muscoli* by Luigi Galvani, publishing in 1794

by external stimuli on animal preparations, as Volta would write: "as this action depends on the varying strength and disposition of the same animal on it being more of less well prepared, recently or less recently on ambient temperature, etc." Moreover he distinguished, on the basis of his observations on the animals "electric vitality," "four degrees of stages of death." About the contractions obtained in a "living and intact" animal, Volta wrote: "As to the animal preparation, these experiments are easier to perform than those carried out in Mr Galvani's way, as no dissection of the animal is needed: and they much finer and more pleasant.[45]""

My Beloved laughed again as Lord Byron was contributing to his own side of the argument, 'Surely, Volta was surprised when he noticed the contractions could be excited in animals where were alive and prepared, or "lacerated" in various ways, and his surprise was followed by the felling that this was indeed an original observation, a discovery of his own. It was similar to what had happened to Galvani when he placed the conducting arc between the nervle and muscle of the prepared from "in the unusual manner"; Volta placed the bitmetal arc on the skin of the "alive and intact" animal, often armed with thin metal "shirts" or "dresses" and this because the ideal point of reference for interpreting the electrical phenomenon included in neuromuscular physiology.'

'What Galvani needed' my Beloved argued, 'was an general interpretation that could account for all the experiments and phenomena observed up to that point. The new theoretical conception proposed by Galvani in his *Trattato* did not just off a coherent explanation of the special efficacy of bimetal arcs in the production of muscular contractions but accounted for a number of observations that were difficult to explain on the basis of the initial model of the animal Leyden jar developed in *De viribus*.

He proposed the following "small machine": "Let's take a glass jar in the form of a flask, which is more convenient to build, and armed [i.e., covered with a metal coating] both internally and externally as usual; a conductor connected to the internal surface must exit from the flask's neck as long as one like, then it must be all plastered with some insulating matter like wax and be put into conact with the external armature. Let's now make little holes in different points of the plastering which relates to the conductor and then pour water or another conducting fluid on all the plastering so that the fluid enters the holes and gets into direct contact with the conductor. In this way it is sure that there is communi-

---

45 From *Le opere di Alessandro Volta. Edizione nazionale sotto gli auspice della Reale Accademia dei Licnei e el Reale Istituto Lambardo di Scinze e Lettere* by Alessandro Volta.

cation between the internal and external surfaces of the jar through the fluid."

'This "small machine", a perfected version of the animal Leyden jar could artificially reproduce the normal conditions of the electric flow within the nerve-muscle system. The flask represented the muscle fibre, while the conductor communicating with its internal and external surfaces presented the nerve, which was covered by an insulating but perforated sheath that allowed a moderate passage of electric fluid from the interior to the exterior of the muscle. This mechanism was designed to keep an electrical disequilibrium in the system, at the same time avoiding an excessive accumulation of electricity, which could produce "a serious danger of lesion and alteration" of both nerves and muscles.'

Eagerly biding his time and biting his lip, My Beloved launched into his counter argument: 'Galvani's further experiments allowed him to respond to Volta's objections also from a methodological point of view: "In truth, as it is firm and proved by many facts that the arc applied from the nerve to the muscle elicits the contractions, before admitting a new and equally efficient one which is applied to other parts or to the same part, namely to the same nerve, it seems necessary– in view of prudent laws of philosophising– that this new arc cannot refer to the fire one, i.e., that it cannot ever communicate with the muscles through any conducting body: but in this case it is certain that this communication is established through the humidity which extends itself from the nerve to the muscle; therefore to suppose that the above mentioned contractions are excited by the mere arc applied form one nerve to another, or from a part of the nerve to another part of the same nerve is contrary to the right law of philosophising."[46]

'These "right laws of philosophising"', My Beloved argued, 'implied that one should not invoke a new cause to explain new phenomena that culd be explained by known causes, were often referred to by both Galvani and Volta during their controversy on animal electricity.'

'With the publication of the *Tratto* and its *Supplemento* Galvani believed he had answered Volta's objections again this theory of animal electricity and refuted his opponent's ideas. Reversing the meaning of one of Volta's judgments, he thus claimed: "If things are as I said, if such electricity is truly and completely proper to the animal, and not common and external to it, what will it be of Mr Volta's opinion, who on the basis of the alleged experiments has pretended to completely exclude animal

---

[46] From *Dell'uo e dell'attivita dell'arco conduttore nelle contrazioni dei muscoli* by Luigi Galvani, publishing in 1794.

electricity, and to limit Galvani's discovery to the mere invention of the most exquisite electrometer in the animal?[47]'"

"Oh! Ho! My dearest Shelley,' Lord Byron crowed, 'the debate was far from over.'

My Beloved added to the argument, 'In publishing the *Tratto dell'arco coduttore,* Galvani hoped that "the experiments and arguments" he was adducing were such as to convince everybody of the existence of "an electricity proper to animal,' as he expressed himself in a letter addressed to Lazzaro Spallanzani. The choice of Spallanzani as an interlocutor was made with intent. First, he was one of my most found scientific scholars of the period. He had been studying a great vvariety of phenomena, from volcanoes to sea animals, from geological conformation of the territory to the "sense" of bats. Moreover, since 1769, he had been professor of natural history in Pavia, the University where Volta also works, where the criticism to Galvani and Volta's theory of metallic electricity were well received.

'I can site a comment Spallanzani made in a letter of October 1797 as evidence of the areful and objective view he held with regard to Galvani's work. Spallanzani remarked that the experiments on spark production in the torpedo referred to by the Bolognese doctor had indeed been carried out exclusively in the "electric gymnotus". In his response, he praised the "new pamphlet" and its author. Thess words would have sounded very sweet to Galvani's ears because in a letter dated August 1, 1794, he answered in this way:

"I give thanks to Your very Illustrious Lordship for the letter you sent me, which could not be more courteous and appreciated. Concerning the controversies and doubts on animal electricity, this letter produces a fulsome calmness in my soul, which was indeed rather restless. I was very much concerned that, with the possibility of many opposing opinions, this new branch of animal physics would remain without some of those advantages that hopefully sometimes it could produce. In hearing now your judgment, a judgement of complete certitude and authoritativeness, as favourable to the afore-said animal electricity, and to the expressed laws, I no longer have any doubt about the truth of the thing and of the usefulness that is desired for it."

Lord Byron countered, 'Galvani (together with Spallanzani and various of their colleaues) *may have* convinced *themselves* that the *Trattato dell'arco conduttore* would solve all doubts and put an end to any controversy, clarifying the problem of the existence of animal electricity and the mechanism of muscle contraction. This was not, however a

---

47 Ibid

unanimous opinion. Volta was quick to read the *Tratto* and used it to restate his views on the arguments raised by Galvani. Volta did that by inserting his comments in a letter sent to Piedmontese abbot Anton Maria Vassalli, perpetual secretary of the Turin Academy of Sciences. Galvani sometimes shows that he has not fully understood the meaning of Volta's theory of the electromotive powers of metals. For instance, in once passage he negates the possibility of an electric disequilibrium between heterogenous metals. This is because "being metal conductive bodies, the electricity of one part of the arc should necessarily be in a condition of equilibrium with the electricity of the other part.'

'Oh! Ho!' my Beloved answered, 'On the other hand, Volta did not fully apricate the new model of animal electric developed by Galvani in the *Tratto*. In the third letter to Vassalli, Volta opposes his concept of "circulation, i.e., of a continuous flow of electric fluid" between different conductors, to Galvani's theory based on the concept of "charge or un- balance, and consequent discharge in animal organisms!"'

'Oh! Ho!' Lord Byron countered, 'Far from admitting the need of an animal type of electricity in the circumstances of direct muscle-nerve contact, what Volta actually did was modify and extend his conception the electromotive power of metals. It sufficed to assume that electric- ity could be moved by contact of two dissimilar bodies, without them needed to be metals. "In this way the principle is generalized, that any time two different conductors are connected, an action arises, which pushes more or less the electric fluid: in such a way that, as far as the circuit is closed between three of them, whatever they are, with the pro- viso that they are different from each other, some current is constantly excited , either modest, or week or very weak.'"[48] In other words, a cur- rent could be produced not only by connecting tother different metals, between them or with the Galvanian frog, but also by the contact of all "humid" conductive bodies of different natures! The new theory of Volta appeared to be at the same time simple and comprehensive: with a sin- gle principle, it sufficed to account for all phenomena put on the stage by the various protagonists of the controversy of animal electricity.'

'I will admit' my Beloved said 'In their researches, both Galvani and Volta had become progressively aware of the importance of coating (or "arming") both nerves and muscles with laminas of different metals. This experimental arragment proved to be particularly important with weak frog preparations, that is, with preparations that did not show any contractions when tested in the ordinary way.'

---

48 From *Le opere di Alessandro Volta. Edizione nazionale sotto gli auspice della Reale Accademia dei Licnei e el Reale Istituto Lambardo di Scinze e Lettere* by Alessandro Volta.

'Volta made his victor lap,' Lord Bryon added, 'in a fourth letter to Vassalli: "There could perhaps be a possibility to straighten up this pretended animal electricity, that I declare as nonexistent, and that with many experiments I think to have knock down; I have substitutes it with the other principle that I have contrived, of a purely artificial electricity, i.e., a form of electricity moved by an extrinsic cause. It would be necessary that adversaries show the appearance of convulsions in frogs etc, with the making of conductor, all of the same species, by no way dissimilar the one from the other; this they would never be able to do so."[49]

'In then unpublished letters which are of great importance for the complete picture,' Lord Byron said, 'Volta wrote to Fransico Mocchetti, a doctor who had been a student at University: "This discovery makes it clear that the course of electric fluid in nerves most favourable to the excitation of motion in muscles is that made in the same direction in which the power of will acts and manifests itself on the muscles under its control. That is, by going down from head or trunk toward the branks. This could induce us to conjecture that the electric fluid is the one used by the soul in order to produce motions in Voluntary muscles" And! "To put an end, if the electric fluid has an influence on animal movements, it does have it under the domain of will. The will commands to the electric fluid, which is stationary in all bodies and in all the parts of the living animal, and particularly in the nerves of voluntary motion, which are perhaps more conductive than other parts. On the other hand, in dead animals, or in the excised parts, in which the action of will is cased, electric fluid remains equilibrated and quiet, as in any other Conductor whatsoever." AND! "What I have mentioned here suffices to make it clear that I do no exclude all forms of *Animal electricity*; on the contrary I ascribe to it the most noble part in the Economy, whereas I show to be inexistent the one put on the stage by Galvani, and supported by his adherents; one based on the supposed unbalance of electric fluid between nerves and muscles, or between interior and the exterior of muscles"[50]

Believing he had won the argument and the debate, Lord Byron stood and bowed. Repeatedly bowed. Obscenely bowed.

'While Galvani may have gone silent as a friar, he was not inactive!' My Beloved argued. 'Had he not gone in August 1795 "for leisure, together with some honest friends, to the beaches of the Adriatic Seas" first in Senigallia and afterward in Rimini? But Galvani would publish the results of these experiments in *Memorie sulla electrrcita animale* addressed to Sapallanzani. Oh! The horror to know when one shall die!

49 Ibid
50 Ibid

This was his last public document! For in one year, he would be dead. The legacy of this fundamental document cannot be underrepresented or underappreciated!

'Spallanzani judgment is my own! "For his novelty, for the importance of its doctrines, for the nobility and delicacy of its experiments, for the subtle analysis and the solid criterion accompanying them, for the felicity of the explanations of the most complex and abstruse phenomena, for the clarity and brilliance with which it is written, this work appears to me as one of the most beautiful and valuable of the eighteenth century Physics."[51]

'Galvani *sought* to remove the problem of mechanical stimulation in an experimental setup based on the use of small pieces of muscles tissues excised from the animal. One of those pieces was placed in contact with the nerve and the other with muscle of the leg remaining in situ. When the circuit was completed by manipulating with a small glass rod a third piece of muscle (or even a small piece of frog skin), contractions were produced despite the absence of any movement in the preparation. He concluded by saying: "Everybody sees therefore that the arc is here made up exclusively of animal substances. He sees, moreover, that any uncertainty or doubt is removed, together with any suspicion of mechanical stimulus, and, finally, proved at once that the circulation of electricity depends exclusively on the animal machine that is thus active."[52]

'Are you implying that,' Lord Byron said, 'with these experiments Galvani seems to answer Volta's objections purposefully and with the force of experiments?

'In these particular circumstances he was addressing the challenge contained in a note added by Volta to the second letter to Vassalli, where the physicist of Pavia claimed that a mechanical artifact could not be excluded even when Galvani did his nerve-muscle experiments with the greatest care, bringing the two tissues to a delicate contact rather than to a hit: "Let us conclude then that these experiments do not prove anything, because they leave the suspicion of a mechanical stimulus. In order to exclude a suspicion of this type, one should come to experiments in which the frog nerves and muscles do rest quietly, and are not touched or pressed in any other possible way."[53]

'Galvani's answer to Volta's initial objection against the experiment of the contact between nerve and muscle can be undoubtedly be considered detailed and timely. Galvani himself describes his new experi-

51 From a letter by L. Spallanzani to L. Galvani, Scandinao, October 25, 1797.
52 From *Memorie sulla electricita... al celebre abate Lazzaro Spallanzani* by Luigy Galvani, published in 1797.
53 From *Le opere di Alessandro Volta. Edizione nazionale sotto gli auspice della Reale Accademia dei Licnei e el Reale Istituto Lambardo di Scinze e Lettere* by Alessandro Volta.

ment thusly,' my Beloved said, lifting the books that had been resting open-faced on his lap, "I prepared the animal in the usual way; then I cut the one and the other of the sciatic nerves near their exit from the vertebral canal; afterwards, I divided, and separated a leg from the other, in such a way that any of them would remain with its corresponding nerve; in the following I bent the nerve of one in the shape of a small bow, and after that having lifted with the usual small glass rod the nerve of the other leg. I let its fall, the nerve should touch in two points the other nerve bent as a bow; and moreover, that the small mouth of the first nerve is one of the two points. I saw then the moving of the leg corresponding t the nerve that I let fall onto the nerve of the other; sometimes even both legs. The experiment succeeds while the two preparations are totally isolated one from the other, and have no reciprocal relation, except for the touching of the nerves."[54]

'Did,' my Beloved asked Lord Byron, 'did either Volta or the other adversaries of animal electricity propose any substantial objection capable of undermining the evidential value of the experiment as support of an electricity intrinsic to the animal? Volta could not even invoke the agency of mechanical artifact at the moment the circuit between the nerves was closed. The counterargument was expressed by Galvani himself, who anticipated this kind of objection, with these words: "But why then by hitting one of the same nerves on an arc much hard and rougher made of non-conductive materials, as those made up of sulphur of glass contractions are not produced? And still in this case the stimulus originating from the hitting should be much stronger?[55]

'Galvani,' my Beloved crowed, 'summarized his theory in a series of points:

    I.   That the electricity which induces muscle contractions is already singularly gathered and cumulated in muscle... in a condition of imbalance.

   II.   That this imbalance is the basis for the circulation of the electricity in the muscle itself.

  III. That this circulation consists of electricity leaving the muscle and returning to the same muscle by an inviolable law.

  IV. That this circulation occurs in the following way: The electricity leaves the muscle by the way of the nerve; it rushes to the place of that nerve to which it is attracted by the force of the armature, and arc; its comes out from the nerve in this same place, being drawn by the same forces; then it enters into the

---

54 From *Memorie sulla electricita... al celebre abate Lazzaro Spallanzani* by Luigy Galvani, published in 1797.
55 Ibid

arc and by means of it returns eventually with all the power of the muscle from which it left.

V.   That because of this tendency, and of the effort that electricity uses in order to come back to the muscle, it chooses always the shortest route to arrive there.

VI.   That nerves are the natural and specific conductors of that electricity.

VII. Finally, that the nerves exert this duty with their intimate and medullar substance."[56]

'Concerning the nature of the principle of life,' the doctor blurted out. Poor Polidori had been sitting on his hands, listening to this Galvanising debate between two equals. He sought to add to the argument in the spirit of debate between my Beloved and our little Lord, 'Dr Erasmus Darwin, who we all esteem, would record, "If two particles of iron lie near each other without motion, and afterwards approach each other; it is reasonable to conclude that something besides the iron particles is the cause of their approximation; this invisible something is termed magnetism. The contraction of a muscular fibre may be compared to the following electric experiment, which is here mentioned not as a philosophical analogy, but as an illustration or simile to facilitate the conception of a difficult subject.

' "The attractions of electricity or of magnetism do not apply philosophically to the illustration of the contraction of animal fibres, since the force of those attractions increases in some proportion inversely as the distance, but in muscular motion there appears no difference in velocity or strength during the beginning or end of the contraction, but what may be clearly ascribed to the varying mechanic advantage in the approximation of one bone to another. Nor can muscular motion be assimilated with greater plausibility to the attraction of cohesion or elasticity; for in bending a steel spring, as a small sword, a less force is required to bend it the first inch than the second; and the second than the third; the particles of steel on the convex side of the bent spring endeavouring to restore themselves more powerfully the further they are drawn from each other."

Poor Polidori beamed. He seemed absolutely delighted to be participating in the game of debate with my Beloved and our little Lord. He continued, 'The esteemed Dr Darwin, was no doubt aware that this may be explained another way, because he wrote, "By supposing the elasticity of the spring to depend more on the compression of the particles on the concave side than on the extension of them on the convex side; and by supposing the elasticity of the elastic gum to depend more

---

56 Ibid

on the resistance to the lateral compression of its particles than to the longitudinal extension of them. Nevertheless in muscular contraction, as above observed, there appears no difference in the velocity or force of it at its commencement or at its termination; from whence we must conclude that animal contraction is governed by laws of its own, and not by those of mechanics, chemistry, magnetism, or electricity.

' "On these accounts I do not think the experiments conclusive, which were lately published by Galvani, Volta, and others, to shew a similitude between the spirit of animation, which contracts the muscular fibres, and the electric fluid. Since the electric fluid may act only as a more potent stimulus exciting the muscular fibres into action, and not by supplying them with a new quantity of the spirit of life. Thus in a recent hemiplegia I have frequently observed, when the patient yawned and stretched himself, that the paralytic limbs moved also, though they were totally disobedient to the will. And when he was electrified by passing shocks from the affected hand to the affected foot, a motion of the paralytic limbs was also produced. Now as in the act of yawning the muscles of the paralytic limbs were excited into action by the stimulus of the irksomeness of a continued posture, and not by any additional quantity of the spirit of life; so we may conclude, that the passage of the electric fluid, which produced a similar effect, acted only as a stimulus, and not by supplying any addition of sensorial power.

' "If nevertheless this theory should ever become established, a stimulus must be called an eductor of vital ether; which stimulus may consist of sensation or volition, as in the electric eel, as well as in the appulses of external bodies; and by drawing off the charges of vital fluid may occasion the contraction or motions of the muscular fibres, and organs of sense.

' "For nothing can act, where it does not exist; for to act includes to exist; and therefore the particles of the muscular fibre (which in its state of relaxation are supposed not to touch) cannot affect each other without the influence of some intermediate agent; this agent is here termed the spirit of animation, or sensorial power, but may with equal propriety be termed the power, which causes contraction; or may be called by any other name, which the reader may choose to affix to it.

' "Thus in the common experiments, where the vitreous or resinous ether is accumulated by art, metallic bodies have been esteemed the best conductors, and next to these water, and all other moist bodies; but it was lately discovered, that dry charcoal, recently burnt, was a more perfect conductor than metals; and it appears from the experiments discovered by Galvani, which have thence the name of Galvanism, that animal flesh, and particularly perhaps the nerves of animals, both which are composed of much carbon and water, are the most perfect conductors yet discovered; that is, that they give the least resistance to the junction of the spontaneous electric atmospheres, which exist round metallic bodies, and which differ very little in respect to the proportions of their vitreous and resinous ingredients.'

Lord Byron interrupted his personal physician, 'O! my lovely companion, even Dr Darwin's own experiments preclude the need for electricity in simple creatures whom naturally reanimate. As the doctor himself wrote, "Some of the microscopic animals are said to remain dead for many days or weeks, when the fluid in which they existed is dried up, and quickly to recover life and motion by the fresh addition of water and warmth. Thus the chaos redivivum of Linnæus dwells in vinegar and in bookbinders paste: it revives by water after having been dried for years, and is both oviparous and viviparous. Thus the vermicelli'— (why did I hear and get stuck in my mind 'vermicelli'? I struggled to reconcile this error. There is no doubt in my mind that he said something-anything other than 'vermicelli'. While it may be true that *vermicelli* in Italian translates as 'little worm', I obviously misheard. As I sit in my bedchamber recording this debate into my journal, I ponder the origin of this mishearing and I believe I have found it![57])— 'or wheel animal, which is found in rain water that has stood some days in leaden gutters, or in hollows of lead on the tops of houses, or in the slime or sediment left by such water, though it discovers no sign of life except when in the water, yet it is capable of continuing alive for many months though kept in a dry state. In this state it is of a globulous shape, exceeds not the bigness of a grain of sand, and no signs of life appear; but being put into water, in the space of half an hour a languid motion begins, the globule turns itself about, lengthens itself by slow degrees, assumes the form of a lively maggot, and most commonly in a few minutes afterwards puts out its wheels, swimming vigorously through the water as if in search of food; or else, fixing itself by the tail, works the wheels in such a manner as to bring its food to its mouth." Therefore, my friend, natural reanimation is common, at least in less complex creatures.'

My Beloved interjected himself between the Lord and the Doctor pressing his own argument, 'Ho-ho! You strike down your own argu-

---

57 Dr Darwin writes, 'These microscopic animals are believed to possess a power of generating others like themselves by solitary reproduction without sex; and these gradually enlarging and improving for innumerable successive generations. Mr Ellis gives drawings of six kinds of *animalcula infusoria*, which increase by dividing across the middle into two distinct animals. Thus in PASTE COMPOSED OF FLOUR AND WATER, which has been suffered to become acescent, the animalcules called eels, *vibrio anguillula*, are seen in great abundance; their motions are rapid and strong; they are viviparous, and produce at intervals a numerous progeny: animals similar to these are also found in vinegar. These eels were probably at first as minute as other microscopic animalcules; but by frequent, perhaps hourly reproduction, have gradually become the large animals above described, possessing wonderful strength and activity.'

ment. I concede to you your facts, but! natural reanimation is *not* common in the *more* complex creature! I will give you points for mentioning "vermicelli" (again! with this error! My Beloved and I are so often in synchronization that we finish sentences and make similar errors!) What of reptilians or of mammalians?' I return you to John's argument of Dr Darwin who wrote, "Would it be too bold to imagine, that all warm-blooded animals have arisen from one living filament, which THE GREAT FIRST CAUSE endued with animality, with the power of acquiring new parts, attended with new propensities, directed by irritations, sensations, volitions, and associations; and thus possessing the faculty of continuing to improve by its own inherent activity, and of delivering down those improvements by generation to its posterity, world without end!"[58]

'THE FIRST GREAT CAUSE? Are you going to skew our argument into the Aquinasian? Shame! Shame! Here we are debating the philosophers Galvani and Volta and Darwin, esteemed natural philosophers and yet you, by-the-way-of Dr Darwin, bring in Thomas Aquinas into our purely scientific conversation. Surely, I will not allow the Five Ways of St. Thomas Aquinas to taint our electric debate, pun quite intended. If we are to continue our lines of argument, let me further the point of reanimation in more complex creations.'

'Did you not just argue "natural reanimation is common, at least in *less* complex creatures?"' my Beloved countered, 'and now you wish to argue natural reanimation in *more* complex creatures? My head is spinning with this turnabout.'

'Oh! no! my dearest Percy, you misunderstand me. My only desire to not to descend into religiosity. Our debate concerns the natural philosophers— nay! scientists— Luigi Galvani and Alessandro Volta and Erasmus Darwin and hopefully Galvani's nephew Giovanni Aldini.'

'Giovanni Aldini!' both my Beloved and poor Polidori parroted simultaneously.

'Quite. We need to bring our debate to the subject of George Foster if it is to continue at all. This is of the utmost importance!'

'Point well taken. Please, continue.'

'Thank you,' Lord Byron said, bowing is head slightly in acknowledgement of the permission, 'It is one thing to experiment on frog's legs or cattle heads, but certainly another when the subject of experimentation is a man. Man is far too complex and noble a creature for reanimation. Despite the scientific air we breathe in our modern age, there are certain natural philosophies that go a step too far. The British

---

58 From *Zoonomia; or The Laws of Organic Life. Vol. 1* and *The Temple of Nature; or, The Origin of Society* by Erasmus Darwin. M.D. F.R.S.

Parliament erred when they instituted the Murder Act of 1751, pro-claiming it is "an act for better preventing the horrid crime of murder that some further terror and peculiar mark of infamy be added to the punishment of death. It shall be in the power of any such judge or justice to appoint the body of any such criminal to be hung in chains: but that in no case whatsoever the body of any murderer shall be suffered to be buried; unless after such body shall have been dissected and anatomized as aforesaid." O! the indignity of dissection even on those executed for murder! The sanctity of the body and the sanctity of the grave is a nec-essary even for the condemned.

'George Forster in some accounts; George Foster in this one' the Lord read from his personal copy of the *Newgate Calendar* (subtitled *The Malefactors' Bloody Register*) which he, no doubt, travelled with, 'The conviction of this wretched man was founded entirely upon circum-stantial evidence. He was indicted on the 14th January, 1803, at the Old Bailey, for the wilful murder of his wife and child.'

Why is it said by the respectable that every respectable English household should possess a copy of the King James' Bible, Foxe's *Book of Martyrs*, the *Pilgrim's Progress*, and an edition of the *Newgate Cal-endar*? Why would its editors steadfastly compose a ghastly nursery rhyme encouraging devoted mothers to gift their cherished children a copy of the *Newgate Calendar* and be nourished at bedtime by reading the horrid and sordid accounts of perished criminals and their crimes?

> *The anxious Mother with a Parents Care,*
> *Presents our Labours to her future Heir*
> *"The Wise, the Brave, the temperate and the Just,*
> *Who love their neighbour, and in God who trust*
> *Safe through the Dang'rous paths of Life may Steer,*
> *Nor dread those Evils we exhibit Here".'*

The Lord's eyes darted over the horry backstory concerning the crimes committed by George Foster, the chimes of testimonies from witnesses, and the rhymes and reasonings of the prosecutors regarding the execution of the sentence. His eyes landed on the moment he wish-es to relate in his debate with my Beloved Percy and continues, 'This un-fortunate malefactor was executed pursuant to his sentence, January 18, 1803. At three minutes after eight he appeared on the platform before the debtor's door in the Old Bailey, and after passing a short time in prayer with Dr Ford, the ordinary of Newgate, the cap was pulled over his eyes, when the stage falling from under him, he was launched into eternity.

'When he ascended the platform his air was dejected in the extreme; and the sorrow manifested in his countenance depicted the inward workings of a heart conscious of the heinous crime be had committed, and the justness of his sentence.

'From the time of his condemnation to the moment of his dissolution, he had scarcely taken the smallest nourishment; which, operating with a tortured conscience, had so enfeebled him, that he was obliged to be supported from the prison to the gallows, being wholly incapable of ascending the staircase with out assistance. Previous to his decease, he fully confessed his having perpetrated the horrible crime for which he suffered: confessed that he had unhappily conceived a most inveterate hatred for his wife, that nothing could conquer, and determined to rid himself and the world of a being he loathed: acknowledged also, that he had taken her twice before to the Paddington canal, with the wicked intent of drowning her, but that his resolution had failed him, and she had returned unhurt; and even at the awful moment of his confession, and the assurance of his approaching dissolution, he seemed to regret more the loss of his infant, than the destruction of the woman he had sworn to cherish and protect. He was questioned, as far as decency would permit, if jealousy had worked him to the horrid act; but be made no reply, except saying, that 'he ought to die'; and dropped into a settled and fixed melancholy, which accompanied him to his last moments. He was a decent looking young man, and wore a brown great coat, buttoned over a red waistcoat, the same in which be was tried.

'He died very easy; and, after hanging the usual time, his body was cut down and conveyed to a house not far distant, where it was subjected to the galvanic process by Professor Aldini, under the inspection of Mr Keate, Mr Carpue and several other professional gentlemen. M. Aldini, who is the nephew of the discoverer of this most interesting science, showed the eminent and superior powers of galvanism to be far beyond any other stimulant in nature. On the first application of the process to the face, the jaws of the deceased criminal began to quiver, and the adjoining muscles were horribly contorted, and one eye was actually opened. In the subsequent part of the process the right hand was raised and clenched, and the legs and thighs were set in motion. Mr Pass, the beadle of the Surgeons' Company, who was officially present during this experiment, was so alarmed that he died of fright soon after his return home.

'Some of the uninformed bystanders thought that the wretched man was on the eve of being restored to life. This, however, was impossible, as several of his friends, who were under the scaffold, had violently pulled his legs, in order to put a more speedy termination to his sufferings. The experiment, in fact, was of a better use and tendency. Its object was to show the excitability of the human frame when this animal electricity was duly applied. In cases of drowning or suffocation it promised to be of the utmost use, by reviving the action of the lungs, and thereby rekindling the expiring spark of vitality. In cases of apoplexy, or disorders of the head, it offered also most encouraging prospects for the benefit of mankind.

'The professor, we understand, had made use of galvanism also in several cases of insanity, and with complete success. It was the opinion of the first medical men that this discovery, if rightly managed and duly prosecuted, could not fail to be of great, and perhaps as yet unforeseen, utility.'[59]

My mind's eye travelled back through time to a memory of when I was five. I stood in my childhood home, peaking around the corner of a doorframe. Behind me was the hallway leading to my bedchamber on the left and the apartment of my father on the right. In front of me was the grand parlour of William Godwin. How ladies and their gentlemen cherished invitations to Godwin's home on a Saturday. My father hosted many literary, scientific, and philosophical salons. Dinner was served promptly at eight, usually of four courses, but sometimes of seven, and rarely of anything more. These evenings were not intended for nourishment or merriment, but for enlightenment, though guests often left with all three. Esteemed and interesting persons were brought in to speak on any subject that struck my father's fancy this week or that week. Many critics would accuse my father of atheism, anarchism, anti-monarchism, feminism, utilitarianism, and radicalism inspired by the revolutionaries of France. My father was nothing if not outspoken.

This night, when I was five, my father had invited one Anthony Carlisle to speak. This student of the natural arts had eyewitnessed the very experiment Lord Byron spoke of in 1816. But in 1803, Mr Carlisle had presented himself to my father, William Godwin, with all of the pomp and pageantry these cocktail parties warranted. He wore his hair wild, his muttonchops long, his ascot neat, his suit pressed, and his shoes shined. To the guests assembled to hear him, in particular, speak, he told his harrowing tale: 'George Foster,' Mr Carlisle paused not for effect, but as unaccustomed to public speaking as he was, he required a moment to find the beginning which was at the end of poor George Foster's life, 'Galvanism is every day offering so many new objects to our research, that we have no hesitation in pronouncing it the most curious subject of inquiry that is now engaging the attention of the lovers of natural philosophy. The experiments lately performed in this town by

59 From an edition of *The Newgate Calendar*.

Professor Aldini, must be fresh in the memory of those who were gratified with a sight of these infinitely interesting phenomena; and by those who were not so fortunate, this short narration will be perused with interest, and may suggest a variety of new and untried objects of inquiry. The subject of the experiments was a malefactor executed at Newgate, on the morning of the 17th of January last. The body was exposed a whole hour, in a temperature of about 30°, after which it was delivered to the College of Surgeons, in pursuance of the usual sentence of the law, and was transferred to Professor Aldini, who with the assistance of Mr Keate, Mr Carpue, Mr Hutchins, Mr Cuthbertson, and other able men, subjected it to the following experiments, the galvanic power being in all of them supplied by three troughs, combined together, each of which contained forty plates of zinc, and as many of copper; the interposed fluid was diluted muriatic acid.

'1. One arc being applied to the mouth and another to the ear (wetted with a solution of common salt) the jaw immediately began to quiver, the adjoining muscles were horribly contorted, and the left eye actually opened.

2. On applying the arc to both ears, a motion of the head was manifested, all the muscles of the face became convulsed, and the lips and eye lids were evidently affected. The action was increased by making one extremity of the arc to communicate with the nostrils and the other with the ear.

'3. On applying the conductors to the ear and to the rectum, such violent muscular contractions were excited, as almost to give the appearance of re animation.

'4. Volatile alkali was first applied to the nostrils and mouth, but without the least sensible effect; but galvanism immediately excited violent action. This, however, was still more increased by uniting both of these stimuli; and applying them together.

'5. The fibres of the biceps flexor cubiti were laid bare, and one arc was applied to them, whilst the other remained in the ear. This produced violent convulsions of all the muscles of the arm.

'6. One arc remaining in the ear, and the other being applied to an incision in the wrist, among the small filaments of the nerves and cellular membrane, a very strong action of the muscles of the forearm and hand was perceived. In these two last experiments, the natural moisture of the part was sufficient to conduct the galvanic influence without the intervention of salt water.

'7. The short muscles of the thumb were dissected, and on applying the conductor to them, a forcible effort to clench the hand was induced.

'8. The effect of other powerful stimulants, caustic ammonia, concentrated sulphuric acid, and the mechanical stimulus of pricking the fibres with the point of the scalpel, were tried by way of comparison with galvanism, but without producing the smallest effect.

'9. The thorax and pericardium being opened, and the heart exposed *in situ*, the conducting are was applied to the ventricles, first upon its surface then in the substance of its fibres, then upon the carneæ columnæ, and the septum ventriculorum; and, lastly, in the course of the nerves by the coronary arteries, but without being followed by the slightest contraction or muscular motion.

'10. The arc was then conveyed to the right auricle and the appendix auricularis, and considerable contraction was immediately produced, even without the intervention of salt water. In the left auricle, however, scarcely any motion was excited.

'11. Conductors being applied from the spinal marrow to the fibres of the biceps flexor cubiti, the gluteus maximus, and the gastrocnemius, separately, no considerable action in the muscles of the arm and leg was produced.

'12. One of the conducting arcs being applied to the spinal marrow, and the other to the sciatic nerve, (which was exposed between the great trochanter and the tuberosity of the ischium, and dissected out from its sheath) no contraction whatever ensued in the muscles. But the conductor being removed from the nerve to the adjacent muscular fibres and cellular membrane, as strong an action was manifested as in the former experiments.

'13. By making the arc to communicate with the sciatic nerve, and the gastrocnemius muscle, a very great action was produced in the latter.

'14. Conductors being applied from the sciatic to the peroneal nerve, scarcely any motion was excited in the muscle.

'15. The sciatic nerve being divided about the middle of the thigh, and conductors being applied from the biceps flexor auris to the gastrocnemius, there ensued a violent contraction of both.

'Mr Carpue, giving account of the appearances on dissection, observes that the blood in the head was not extravasated, but several vessels were prodigiously swelled, and the lungs were entirely deprived of air; he also saw that there was a great inflammation of the intestines, and that the bladder was fully distended with urine.

'These are the principal circumstances of the interesting experiments which are here related; and the reader will readily concur in the leading inference which Professor Aldini deduces from them; namely, that the power of galvanism, as a stimulant, is stronger than any mechanical action whatever, and that hence it affords very powerful means of resuscitation in cases of suspended animation under common circumstances, perhaps superior to any that are usually employed. This consideration may serve to give this study additional interest to those who are not satisfied with any object of philosophical pursuit, without discovering n it an immediate prospect of benefit to mankind. The physiologist, however, will not fail to perceive the variety of curious questions for future inquiry, involved in the singular unsusceptibility of the ventricles of the heart to a stimulus which powerfully affects every other muscle with this influence, compared with that of nerve and medulla spinalis.

'From the circumstance of the rapid exhaustion of the power of the troughs, and the extent of active metallic surface requisite to produce the galvanic action in sufficient intensity to exhibit the above phenomena, the author infers the probability that the method of coating nerves with metallic surface, as first practised by Galvani, (on frogs and cold blooded animals) serves merely to conduct the fluid pre existent in the animal system; whereas, with Volta's galvanic batteries, the muscles are excited to action by the influence of the apparatus itself.'[60]

As I dropped my eaves on this (not quite a bedtime) story, I witnessed respectable women faint and distinguished men become green with nausea. My father found enthusiasm for this particular peculiar salon immediately extinguished. With *sal volatile*, Mr Carlisle revived many those reviled by the recitation of his eyewitness account. The witless found their mind's cloudy as they exited out of my family's front door into the streets to awaiting carriages. No a one would publicly disparage my father's literary, scientific, and philosophical salons lest a future invitation be rescinded.

Suddenly my grasp on this scene in my father's salon wrenched free from memory. My eyes slowly opened to find myself back in the parlour at the Villa Diodati dropping eaves on the previous scene of the electric debate between Lord Byron and my Beloved, but after my brief interlude in the past, the scene had continued on without my being conscious of the passage of time. My Beloved now stood before the fire where Lord Byron had told a mere fragment of a story and where Dr Polidori would no doubt soon tell own his substantial one. He held a handful of pages handwritten in this often-smudged scrawl. Was he at last contributing to Lord Byron's game of ghost stories.

---

60 From the Appendix in *General Views on the Application of Galvanism to Medical Purposes* by John Aldini, published by J. Callow, Princes-Street, and Burgess and Mill, Great Windmil-Street, 1819.

Chapter Six
Prometheus (Unbound)

Mary Wollstonecraft Godwin's Journal

21 June. Witching hour— 'I'm afraid this is not my contribution to the game of ghost stories, my Beloved said dashing my hopes upon the rocks of the sea. 'My mind has not been inspired by the ghostly and the ghastly, but the mythological. Upon these shelves,' he says indicating the bookshelves, 'I have found, not a French translation of German ghost stories, but a playscript written in its original Greek. The Greek tragic writers, in selecting as their subject any portion of their national history or mythology, employed in their treatment of it a certain arbitrary discretion. They by no means conceived themselves bound to adhere to the common interpretation or to imitate in story as in title their rivals and predecessors. Such a system would have amounted to a resignation of those claims to preference over their competitors which incited the composition. The Agamemnonian story was exhibited on the Athenian theatre with as many variations as dramas.

'I have presumed to employ a similar license. The "Prometheus Unbound" of Æschylus supposed the reconciliation of Jupiter with his victim as the price of the disclosure of the danger threatened to his empire by the consummation of his marriage with Thetis. Thetis, according to this view of the subject, was given in marriage to Peleus, and Prometheus, by the permission of Jupiter, delivered from his captivity by Hercules. Had I framed my story on this model, I should have done no more than have attempted to restore the lost drama of Æschylus; an ambition which, if my preference to this mode of treating the subject had incited me to cherish, the recollection of the high comparison such an attempt would challenge might well abate. But, in truth, I was averse from a catastrophe so feeble as that of reconciling the Champion with the Oppressor of mankind. The moral interest of the fable, which is so powerfully sustained by the sufferings and endurance of Prometheus, would be annihilated if we could conceive of him as unsaying his high language and quailing before his successful and perfidious adversary. The only imaginary being, resembling in any degree Prometheus, is Satan; and Prometheus is, in my judgment, a more poetical character than Satan, because, in addition to courage, and majesty, and firm and patient opposition to omnipotent force, he is susceptible of being described as exempt from the taints of ambition, envy, revenge, and a desire for personal aggrandisement, which, in the hero of Paradise Lost, interfere with the interest. The character of Satan engenders in the mind a pernicious casuistry which leads us to weigh his faults with his wrongs, and to excuse the former because the latter exceed all measure. In the minds of those who consider that magnificent fiction with a religious feeling it engenders something worse. But Prometheus is, as it were, the type of the highest perfection of moral and intellectual nature, impelled by the purest and the truest motives to the best and noblest ends.[61] Permit me the pleasure, if you have the leisure, to read of the few lines thus far written. First the character of Prometheus:'

> *Monarch of Gods and Dæmons, and all Spirits*
> *But One, who throng those bright and rolling worlds*
> *Which Thou and I alone of living things*
> *Behold with sleepless eyes! regard this Earth*
> *Made multitudinous with thy slaves, whom thou*
> *Requitest for knee-worship, prayer, and praise,*
> *And toil, and hecatombs of broken hearts,*
> *With fear and self-contempt and barren hope.*
> *Whilst me, who am thy foe, eyeless in hate,*
> *Hast thou made reign and triumph, to thy scorn,*
> *O'er mine own misery and thy vain revenge.*
> *Three thousand years of sleep-unsheltered hours,*
> *And moments aye divided by keen pangs*
> *Till they seemed years, torture and solitude,*
> *Scorn and despair,— these are mine empire:*
> *More glorious far than that which thou surveyest*
> *From thine unenvied throne, O, Mighty God!*
> *Almighty, had I deigned to share the shame*
> *Of thine ill tyranny, and hung not here*
> *Nailed to this wall of eagle-baffling mountain,*
> *Black, wintry, dead, unmeasured; without herb,*
> *Insect, or beast, or shape or sound of life.*
> *Ah me! alas, pain, pain ever, for ever!*
>
> *No change, no pause, no hope! Yet I endure.*
> *I ask the Earth, have not the mountains felt?*
> *I ask yon Heaven, the all-beholding Sun,*

---

61 From the preface to *Prometheus Unbound* by Percy Bysshe Shelley, published by C and Jo Ollier, 1820.

Has it not seen? The Sea, in storm or calm,
Heaven's ever-changing Shadow, spread below,
Have its deaf waves not heard my agony?
Ah me! alas, pain, pain ever, for ever!

The crawling glaciers pierce me with the spears
Of their moon-freezing crystals; the bright chains
Eat with their burning cold into my bones.
Heaven's winged hound, polluting from thy lips
His beak in poison not his own, tears up
My heart; and shapeless sights come wandering by,
The ghastly people of the realm of dream,
Mocking me: and the Earthquake-fiends are charged
To wrench the rivets from my quivering wounds
When the rocks split and close again behind:
While from their loud abysses howling throng
The genii of the storm, urging the rage
Of whirlwind, and afflict me with keen hail.
And yet to me welcome is day and night,
Whether one breaks the hoar-frost of the morn,
Or starry, dim, and slow, the other climbs
The leaden-colored east; for then they lead
The wingless, crawling hours, one among whom
— As some dark Priest hales the reluctant victim—
Shall drag thee, cruel King, to kiss the blood
From these pale feet, which then might trample thee
If they disdained not such a prostrate slave.
Disdain! Ah, no! I pity thee. What ruin
Will hunt thee undefended thro' the wide Heaven!
How will thy soul, cloven to its depth with terror,
Gape like a hell within! I speak in grief,
Not exultation, for I hate no more,
As then ere misery made me wise. The curse
Once breathed on thee I would recall. Ye Mountains,
Whose many-voiced Echoes, through the mist
Of cataracts, flung the thunder of that spell!
Ye icy Springs, stagnant with wrinkling frost,
Which vibrated to hear me, and then crept
Shuddering thro' India! Thou serenest Air
Thro' which the Sun walks burning without beams!
And ye swift Whirlwinds, who on poisèd wings
Hung mute and moveless o'er yon hushed abyss,

As thunder, louder than your own, made rock
The orbèd world! If then my words had power,
Though I am changed so that aught evil wish
Is dead within; although no memory be
Of what is hate, let them not lose it now!
What was that curse? for ye all heard me speak.[62]

Our little Lord guffawed mightily and slapped his knee in excitement and exaltation and said, 'O! Muse sing, O! Goddess sing of the spontaneous plagiarism of Mad Jack Byron's son George and his son's dearest friend Percy Bysshe Shelley, whom in midst of these swirling storms and swelling waters of Lake Geneva are both inspired by Calliope, the mother of Orpheus and Linus from the loins of King Oeagrus of Thrace, to produce works based upon Prometheus? The gifter of fire to mankind stands before us this dark and stormy night as a phantasm summoned by our interwoven minds.' He laughed again and shapped his knee again and stood to grasp my Beloved in a hearty and heathy embrace. 'How is it possible that we two friends find ourselves this very night holdings pages composed yesternight with no foreknowledge of the other's composition! If we were in the separate homes back in merry ol' England, warring poets might accuse the other of outright thievery and seek to murder the other professionally... or perchance personally. But how queer is the ghost of an idea that we both saw floating in the ether possessing the premise of poetic Prometheus. This literary ghost mingles with literal ghosts on the edge of human perception. But only a poet's eye can see these ghosts of ideas, so the layman is blind to such spectres. Our ghost, no doubt, floated through the Villia Diodati praying that one of the four of us writers would see it out of our peripheral vision and seize upon it. If none of us did, the idea would slip through the walls of his villa and continue on until another poetic soul saw it and recognized it for what it was: inspiration. And! we both saw that phantom and seized it independently of the other.

'Give me space. Give me space, dearest Percy,' and my Beloved yielded the floor to Lord Byron, 'and listen to my own interpretation of that literary ghost of an idea!'

Titan! to whose immortal eyes
The sufferings of mortality,
Seen in their sad reality,

---

62 From *Prometheus Unbound* by Percy Bysshe Shelley, published by C and Jo Ollier, 1820. "This is the only work not actually begun during the stay at the Villa Diodati in1816, though it is certainly conceivable the closet play had been conceived then. The first to describe its writing is Mary in a letter on 5 September 1818." – R.D.B.

Were not as things that gods despise;
What was thy pity's recompense?
A silent suffering, and intense;
The rock, the vulture, and the chain,
All that the proud can feel of pain,
The agony they do not show,
The suffocating sense of woe,
Which speaks but in its loneliness,
And then is jealous lest the sky
Should have a listener, nor will sigh
Until its voice is echoless.

Titan! to thee the strife was given
Between the suffering and the will,
Which torture where they cannot kill;
And the inexorable Heaven,
And the deaf tyranny of Fate,
The ruling principle of Hate,
Which for its pleasure doth create
The things it may annihilate,
Refused thee even the boon to die:
The wretched gift Eternity
Was thine— and thou hast borne it well.
All that the Thunderer wrung from thee
Was but the menace which flung back
On him the torments of thy rack;
The fate thou didst so well foresee,
But would not to appease him tell;
And in thy Silence was his Sentence,
And in his Soul a vain repentance,
And evil dread so ill dissembled,
That in his hand the lightnings trembled.

Thy Godlike crime was to be kind,
To render with thy precepts less
The sum of human wretchedness,
And strengthen Man with his own mind;
But baffled as thou wert from high,
Still in thy patient energy,
In the endurance, and repulse
Of thine impenetrable Spirit,
Which Earth and Heaven could not convulse,

A mighty lesson we inherit:
Thou art a symbol and a sign
To Mortals of their fate and force;
Like thee, Man is in part divine,
A troubled stream from a pure source;
And Man in portions can foresee
His own funereal destiny;
His wretchedness, and his resistance,
And his sad unallied existence:
To which his Spirit may oppose
Itself— an equal to all woes—
And a firm will, and a deep sense,
Which even in torture can descry
Its own concentered recompense,
Triumphant where it dares defy,
And making Death a Victory.[63]

23 June. Morning— Yesternight waned upon this talk, and even the witching hour had gone by, before we retired to rest. When I placed my head on my pillow, I did not sleep, nor could I be said to think. My imagination, unbidden, possessed and guided me, gifting the successive images that arose in my mind with a vividness far beyond the usual bounds of reverie. I saw— with shut eyes, but acute mental vision,— I saw the pale student of unhallowed arts kneeling beside the thing he had put together. I saw the hideous phantasm of a man stretched out, and then, on the working of some powerful engine, show signs of life, and stir with an uneasy, half vital motion. Frightful must it be; for supremely frightful would be the effect of any human endeavour to mock the stupendous mechanism of the Creator of the world. His success would terrify the artist; he would rush away from his odious handy-work, horror-stricken. He would hope that, left to itself, the slight spark of life which he had communicated would fade; that this thing, which had received such imperfect animation, would subside into dead matter; and he might sleep in the belief that the silence of the grave would quench for ever the transient existence of the hideous corpse which he had looked upon as the cradle of life. He sleeps; but he is awakened; he opens his eyes; behold the horrid thing stands at his bedside, opening his curtains, and looking on him with yellow, watery, but speculative eyes.

I opened mine in terror. The idea so possessed my mind, that a thrill of fear ran through me, and I wished to exchange the ghastly image of

---

63 From *Prisoner of Chillon, and Other Poems* by Lord Byron, published by John Murray, 1816

my fancy for the realities around. I see them still; the very room, the dark parquet, the closed shutters, with the moonlight struggling through, and the sense I had that the glassy lake and white high Alps were beyond. I could not so easily get rid of my hideous phantom; still it haunted me. I must try to think of something else. I recurred to my ghost story,— my tiresome unlucky ghost story! O! if I could only contrive one which would frighten my reader as I myself had been frightened that night!

Swift as light and as cheering was the idea that broke in upon me. 'I have found it! What terrified me will terrify others; and I need only describe the spectre which had haunted my midnight pillow.' On the morrow I announced that I had *thought of a story*. I began that day with the words, It was on a dreary night of November, making only a transcript of the grim terrors of my waking dream.

I opened mine in terror. The idea so possessed my mind, that a thrill of fear ran through me, and I wished to exchange the ghastly image of my fancy for the realities around. I see them still; the very room, the dark parquet, the closed shutters, with the moonlight struggling through, and the sense I had that the glassy lake and white high Alps were beyond. I could not so easily get rid of my hideous phantom; still it haunted me. I must try to think of something else. I recurred to my ghost story,— my tiresome unlucky ghost story! O! if I could only contrive one which would frighten my reader as I myself had been frightened that night!

Swift as light and as cheering was the idea that broke in upon me. "I have found it! What terrified me will terrify others; and I need only describe the spectre which had haunted my midnight pillow." On the morrow I announced that I had thought of a story. I began that day with the words, *It was on a dreary night of November*, making only a transcript of the grim terrors of my waking dream.

At first I thought but of a few pages— of a short tale; but Shelley urged me to develope the idea at greater length. I certainly did not owe the suggestion of one incident, nor scarcely of one train of feeling, to my husband, and yet but for his incitement, it would never have taken the form in which it was presented to the world.[64]

---

64 From the Introduction to the 1831 Edition of *Frankenstein; or, The Modern Prometheus*, published by Henry Colburn & Richard Bentley.

Chapter Seven
Frankenstein[65]
(The Birth of the Creature)

P.B. Shelley Writing In Mary Wollstonecraft Godwin's Journal

28 August. Lake Geneva— The event on which this fiction (which Mary has been chronicling in a second journal) is founded has been supposed, by Dr Darwin, and some of the physiological writers of Germany, as not of impossible occurrence. I shall not be supposed as according the remotest degree of serious faith to such an imagination; yet, in assuming it as the basis of a work of fancy, I have not considered myself as merely weaving a series of supernatural terrors. The event on which the interest of the story depends is exempt from the disadvantages of a mere tale of spectres or enchantment. It was recommended by the novelty of the situations which it developes; and, however impossible as a physical fact, affords a point of view to the imagination for the delineating of human passions more comprehensive and commanding than any which the ordinary relations of existing events can yield.

I have thus endeavoured to preserve the truth of the elementary principles of human nature, while I have not scrupled to innovate upon their combinations. The *Iliad*, the tragic poetry of Greece,— Shakespeare, in the *Tempest* and *Midsummer Night's Dream*,— and most especially Milton, in *Paradise Lost*, conform to this rule; and the most humble novelist, who seeks to confer or receive amusement from his labours, may, without presumption, apply to prose fiction a licence, or rather a rule, from the adoption of which so many exquisite combinations of human feeling have resulted in the highest specimens of poetry.

The circumstance on which my story rests was suggested in casual conversation. It was commenced, partly as a source of amusement, and partly as an expedient for exercising any untried resources of mind. Other motives were mingled with these, as the work proceeded. I am by no means indifferent to the manner in which whatever moral tendencies exist in the sentiments or characters it contains shall affect the reader; yet my chief concern in this respect has been limited to the avoiding of the

---

65 From *Frankenstein; or the Modern Prometheus* by Mary Wollstonecraft Shelley, published by Lackington, Hughes, Harding, Mavor & Jones, 1818

enervating effects of the novels of the present day, and to the exhibitions of the amiableness of domestic affection, and the excellence of universal virtue. The opinions which naturally spring from the character and situation of the hero are by no means to be conceived as existing always in my own conviction; nor is any inference justly to be drawn from the following pages as prejudicing any philosophical doctrine of whatever kind.

It is a subject also of additional interest to the author, that this story was begun in the majestic region where the scene is principally laid, and in society which cannot cease to be regretted. I passed the summer of 1816 in the environs of Geneva. The season was cold and rainy, and in the evenings we crowded around a blazing wood fire, and occasionally amused ourselves with some German stories of ghosts, which happened to fall into our hands. These tales excited in us a playful desire of imitation. Two other friends (a tale from the pen of one of whom would be far more acceptable to the public than any thing I can ever hope to produce) and myself agreed to write each a story, founded on some supernatural occurrence.

The weather, however, suddenly became serene; and my two friends left me on a journey among the Alps, and lost, in the magnificent scenes which they present, all memory of their ghostly visions. The following tale is the only one which has been completed.[66]

ᴛᴡᴏ ᴍᴏɴᴛʜꜱ ᴇᴀʀʟɪᴇʀ!

Mary Wollstonecraft Godwin's Journal

Chapter I

22 June. Small hours— I awoke from the dead of sleep. Curious phrase. Do the dead sleep in a dreamless slumber? Or do they dream of the Resurrection of the dead? Do Christians not believe we believe that *Jesus died and rose again, even so them also which sleep in Jesus will God bring with him*? I believe St. Austin said of this very passage, 'That the Scripture saith of those that are dead, that they are but asleep, because of the certain hope of a Resurrection, by which they shall speedily be awakened from the sleep of death, and raised out of their Sepulchres as out of their beds.' But I awoke to find myself not dead, but in the curious state of a women longing for the return of her lover having been parted.

I felt the weight of my Beloved next to me in bed, the candle on his side having long been snuffed out and his book having fallen to the

---

66 From the Introduction to the 1818 Edition of *Frankenstein; or, The Modern Prometheus,* published by Lackinton, Hughes, Harding, Mavor, and Jones, London.

floor. But in the corner of the bedchamber, sitting in an armchair was a nameless human-shaped form. Briefly— quite briefly— I thought maybe this was my Beloved having awoke in the night and now sits in the armchair. But then I remembered the weight of my Beloved next to me and came to the sudden realization that someone else... something else sat across from me in the darkness. Was this the poor doctor having violated the sanctity of my Beloved's bedchamber? The fire of my ire quickly lit, and I prepared myself to chastise him for his impudence. Then lightning flashed and I saw the hollowed face of the pale student of the unhallowed arts. In the brief moment my eyes captured his image, he looked forlorn.

I hurried to the hearth, the final embers slowly dying. Retrieving a spill from its holder, I lit it on an ember and immediately relit the candles on the mantle and on my bedside table. The form was my pale student of the unhallowed arts, but he was dressed not for scientific experimentation as if did ereyesterday, but for a gentleman's morning ride. He wore a smart, charcoal cutaway morning coat, a grey vest over a high stand collared shirt, and a puff tie. A governor's cane propped against his ankle high dress boot with the head resting on one knee, and his top hat sat upon the small table beside the chair. His shoulder-length blonde hair, having lost all its lustre, appeared flustered as if by a blustery day. His lips were thin, so thin as to be expressionless. His sharp cheekbones were shrunken; his sunken eyes brightened tolerably in the candlelight, that forlorn expression slowly melting away like candlewax. He was handsome, looking like he could have been a long-lost Shelley, the brother of my Beloved.

My pale student quietly— so quietly in fact that he uttered not a word— asked me to sit at the writing desk opposite him in the adjacent corner of the room. I did as he bid. I found my journal sitting where I left off with 'It was on a dreary night of November, making only a transcript of the grim terrors of my waking dream.' I had failed to record how I had burst into the kitchen the next morning, exclaiming, 'I have found it!'. My Beloved, poor Polidori, and our little Lord already sat for breakfast, with my helping of bacon and sausage still sizzling in the iron pan. 'Found what, my dove,' my love inquired. 'I found my ghost story!' I beamed. Then the doctor said, 'About time.' I nearly screamed in frustration. How I have grown tired of this supposedly grown man! My hands desired to wring his neck, for every morning for days he inquired if I had found my ghost story yet; every morning for days I had *not* found my ghost story yet; yet on the day that I find my ghost story, I find him unimpressed. Since that morning of exaltation, I have, in my exhaustion, been in mourning. How I longed for my pale student to be returned to me. But his voice had been eerily quiet— so eerily quiet that I had not yet written a single word in my journal. Back in the present, I opened my journal to an empty page. This queer clairvoyance did not in any way strike me as odd, but quite natural. Had I been of right mind, with the effects of sleep still not having worn off, I would have been frightened by this preternatural experience, but instead, I readied myself to transcribe the tale which he was to begin:

'I am by birth a Genevese,' my pale student said. He certainly had not travelled far to visit me at the Villa Diodati, itself positioned on the shore of Lake Geneva. I wonder where the estate lies. 'And my family is one of the most distinguished of that republic. My ancestors had been for many years counsellors and syndics; and my father had filled several public situations with honour and reputation. He was respected by all who knew him for his integrity and indefatigable attention to public business. He passed his younger days perpetually occupied by the affairs of his country; and it was not until the decline of life that he thought of marrying, and bestowing on the state sons who might carry his virtues and his name down to posterity.

'As the circumstances of his marriage illustrate his character, I cannot refrain from relating them. One of his most intimate friends was a merchant, who, from a flourishing state, fell, through numerous mischances, into poverty. This man, whose name was Beaumont, was of a proud and unbending disposition, and could not bear to live in poverty and oblivion in the same country where he had formerly been distinguished for his rank and magnificence. Having paid his debts, therefore, in the most honourable manner, he retreated with his daughter to the town of Lucerne, where he lived unknown and in wretchedness. My father loved Beaumont with the truest friendship, and was deeply grieved by his retreat in these unfortunate circumstances. He grieved also for the loss of his society, and resolved to seek him out and endeavour to persuade him to begin the world again through his credit and assistance.

'Beaumont had taken effectual measures to conceal himself; and it was ten months before my father discovered his abode. Overjoyed at this discovery, he hastened to the house, which was situated in a mean street, near the Reuss. But when he entered, misery and despair alone welcomed him. Beaumont had saved but a very small sum of money from the wreck of his fortunes; but it was sufficient to provide him with sustenance for some months, and in the mean time he hoped to procure some respectable employment in a merchant's house. The interval was consequently spent in inaction; his grief only became more deep and rankling, when he had leisure for reflection; and at length it took so fast hold of his mind, that at the end of three months he lay on a bed of sickness, incapable of any exertion.

'His daughter attended him with the greatest tenderness; but she saw with despair that their little fund was rapidly decreasing, and that there was no other prospect of support. But Caroline Beaumont possessed a mind of an uncommon mould; and her courage rose to support her in her adversity. She procured plain work; she plaited straw; and by various means contrived to earn a pittance scarcely sufficient to support life.

'Several months passed in this manner. Her father grew worse; her time was more entirely occupied in attending him; her means of subsistence decreased; and in the tenth month her father died in her arms, leaving her an orphan and a beggar. This last blow overcame her; and she knelt by Beaumont's coffin, weeping bitterly, when my father entered the chamber. He came like a protecting spirit to the poor girl, who committed herself to his care, and after the interment of his friend he conducted her to Geneva, and placed her under the protection of a relation. Two years after this event Caroline became his wife.

'When my father became a husband and a parent, he found his time so occupied by the duties of his new situation, that he relinquished many of his public employments, and devoted himself to the education of his children. Of these I was the eldest, and the destined successor to all his labours and utility. No creature could have more tender parents than mine. My improvement and health were their constant care, especially as I remained for several years their only child. But before I continue my narrative, I must record an incident which took place when I was four years of age.'

The tenor of my pale student of the unhallowed arts' voice was a baritone, low and weighty, bearing the sins of a lifetime on his timbre. His accent was proper though foreign, his diction clean, and his language educated. The weight of his grievous sin also hunched his shoulders. What sin could he have committed in the short span of his young life to create this darkness haunting his eyes? Was his mortal sin that of creating the hideous phantasm of a man I had seen stretched out, and then, on the working of some powerful engine, shown signs of life and stirred with an uneasy, half vital motion? Is the guilt-ridden story he had just begun a confession of this very sin? Is his penance before God to repent of his sin to me in a Rite of Reconciliation? I am a laywoman, not a priest who can bestow the assurance of pardon and the grace of absolution. Is this phantasm the ghost of a real student of the unhallowed arts having committed a very real sin of the resurrection of the dead; or is he a mere figment of an overactive imagination longing for the ghost story to share?

I should halt this expositional digression and allow him his own story in his own time.

'My father had a sister, whom he tenderly loved, and who had married early in life an Italian gentleman. Soon after her marriage, she had accompanied her husband into his native country, and for some years my father had very little communication with her. About the time I mentioned she died; and a few months afterwards he received a letter from her husband, acquainting him with his intention of marrying an Italian lady, and requesting my father to take charge of the infant Elizabeth, the only child of his deceased sister. "It is my wish," he said, "that you should consider her as your own daughter, and educate her thus. Her mother's fortune is secured to her, the documents of which I will commit to your keeping. Reflect upon this proposition; and decide whether you would prefer educating your niece yourself to her being brought up by a stepmother."

'My father did not hesitate, and immediately went to Italy, that he might accompany the little Elizabeth to her future home. I have often heard my mother say, that she was at that time the most beautiful child she had ever seen, and shewed signs even then of a gentle and affectionate disposition. These indications, and a desire to bind as closely as possible the ties of domestic love, determined my mother to consider Elizabeth as my future wife; a design which she never found reason to repent.

'From this time Elizabeth Lavenza became my playfellow, and, as we grew older, my friend. She was docile and good tempered, yet gay and playful as a summer insect. Although she was lively and animated, her feelings were strong and deep, and her disposition uncommonly affectionate. No one could better enjoy liberty, yet no one could submit with more grace than she did to constraint and caprice. Her imagination was luxuriant, yet her capability of application was great. Her person was the image of her mind; her hazel eyes, although as lively as a bird's, possessed an attractive softness. Her figure was light and airy; and, though capable of enduring great fatigue, she appeared the most fragile creature in the world. While I admired her understanding and fancy, I loved to tend on her, as I should on a favourite animal; and I never saw so much grace both of person and mind united to so little pretension.

'Every one adored Elizabeth.' As do I already! 'If the servants had any request to make, it was always through her intercession. We were strangers to any species of disunion and dispute; for although there was a great dissimilitude in our characters, there was an harmony in that very dissimilitude. I was more calm and philosophical than my companion; yet my temper was not so yielding. My application was of longer endurance;

but it was not so severe whilst it endured. I delighted in investigating the facts relative to the actual world; she busied herself in following the aërial creations of the poets. The world was to me a secret, which I desired to discover; to her it was a vacancy, which she sought to people with imaginations of her own.

'My brothers were considerably younger than myself; but I had a friend in one of my schoolfellows, who compensated for this deficiency. Henry Clerval was the son of a merchant of Geneva, an intimate friend of my father. He was a boy of singular talent and fancy. I remember, when he was nine years old, he wrote a fairy tale, which was the delight and amazement of all his companions. His favourite study consisted in books of chivalry and romance; and when very young, I can remember, that we used to act plays composed by him out of these favourite books, the principal characters of which were Orlando, Robin Hood, Amadis, and St. George.

'No youth could have passed more happily than mine. My parents were indulgent, and my companions amiable. Our studies were never forced; and by some means we always had an end placed in view, which excited us to ardour in the prosecution of them. It was by this method, and not by emulation, that we were urged to application.' Oh, how I can hear my father's own words: Refer them to reading, to conversation, to meditation; but teach them neither creeds nor catechisms, either moral or political... Speak the language of truth and reason to your child, and be under no apprehension for the result. Show him that what you recommend is valuable and desirable, and fear not but he will desire it. Convince his understanding, and enlist all his powers animal and intellectual in your service.[67]

'Elizabeth was not incited to apply herself to drawing, that her companions might not outstrip her; but through the desire of pleasing her aunt, by the representation of some favourite scene done by her own hand. We learned Latin and English, that we might read the writings in those languages; and so far from study being made odious to us through punishment, we loved application, and our amusements would have been the labours of other children. Perhaps we did not read so many books, or learn languages so quickly, as those who are disciplined according to the ordinary methods; but what we learned was impressed the more deeply on our memories.

'In this description of our domestic circle I include Henry Clerval; for he was constantly with us. He went to school with me, and generally passed the afternoon at our house; for being an only child, and destitute of companions at home, his father was well pleased that he should find

---

67 From *Politi cal Justic* by William Godwin.

associates at our house; and we were never completely happy when Clerval was absent.

'I feel pleasure in dwelling on the recollections of childhood, before misfortune had tainted my mind, and changed its bright visions of extensive usefulness into gloomy and narrow reflections upon self. But, in drawing the picture of my early days, I must not omit to record those events which led, by insensible steps to my after tale of misery: for when I would account to myself for the birth of that passion, which afterwards ruled my destiny, I find it arise, like a mountain river, from ignoble and almost forgotten sources; but, swelling as it proceeded, it became the torrent which, in its course, has swept away all my hopes and joys.

'Natural philosophy is the genius that has regulated my fate; I desire therefore, in this narration, to state those facts which led to my predilection for that science. When I was thirteen years of age, we all went on a party of pleasure to the baths near Thonon: the inclemency of the weather obliged us to remain a day confined to the inn. In this house I chanced to find a volume of the works of Cornelius Agrippa.' Ah! No doubt, the magician-alchemist and philosopher's *De Oculta Philosophlia libri III*! I hope and pray that my pale student recites no incantations said to invoke demonic beings. Being haunted by my pale student is certainly enough. 'I opened it with apathy; the theory which he attempts to demonstrate, and the wonderful facts which he relates, soon changed this feeling into enthusiasm. A new light seemed to dawn upon my mind; and, bounding with joy, I communicated my discovery to my father. I cannot help remarking here the many opportunities instructors possess of directing the attention of their pupils to useful knowledge, which they utterly neglect. My father looked carelessly at the title-page of my book, and said, "Ah! Cornelius Agrippa! My dear Victor, do not waste your time upon this; it is sad trash." Which is certainly is.

'If, instead of this remark, my father had taken the pains, to explain to me, that the principles of Agrippa had been entirely exploded, and that a modern system of science had been introduced, which possessed much greater powers than the ancient, because the powers of the latter were chimerical, while those of the former were real and practical; under such circumstances, I should certainly have thrown Agrippa aside, and, with my imagination warmed as it was, should probably have applied myself to the more rational theory of chemistry which has resulted from modern discoveries. It is even possible, that the train of my ideas would never have received the fatal impulse that led to my ruin.' Oh, how he suffers. Fatal impulses? Ruin? How I desire to be a comfort to the pale student, but he is as transient as a phantasm. 'But the cursory glance my father had taken of my volume by no means assured me that he was acquainted with its contents; and I continued to read with the greatest avidity.' Such oedipal hostility towards his father.

'When I returned home, my first care was to procure the whole works of this author, and afterwards of Paracelsus'–curious– 'and Albertus Magnus.' –Curiouser– While the teachings of these magician-alchemists may have been overthrown in the modern age, they have their place in natural philosophic history for their stress on experimentation and observation. 'I read and studied the wild fancies of these writers with delight; they appeared to me treasures known to few beside myself; and although I often wished to communicate these secret stores of knowledge to my father, yet his definite censure of my favourite Agrippa always withheld me. I disclosed my discoveries to Elizabeth, therefore, under a promise of strict secrecy; but she did not interest herself in the subject, and I was left by her to pursue my studies alone.

'It may appear very strange, that a disciple of Albertus Magnus should arise in the eighteenth century; but our family was not scientifical, and I had not attended any of the lectures given at the schools of Geneva. My dreams were therefore undisturbed by reality; and I entered with the greatest diligence into the search of the philosopher's stone and the elixir of life.'

What draws an man born into modernity to pursue such anachronisms. If my Beloved had overheard the pale student utter such absurdities, he would be readily dismissed out of hand... with the wave of a hand. But I am one to dismiss anyone of their studies, no matter how overthrown they may have been. How wondrous would it be to discover the 'alkahest,' that universal solvent known in great secrecy to dissolve anything or transmute lead into gold. Did not Eirenæus Philathese write, 'It is a Catholic and Universal Menstruum, and in a word, may be called *(Ignis-Aqua)* a firery water, an uncompounded and immortal *ens,,* which is penetrative, resolving all things into their first Liquid Matter, nor can anything resist its power, for it acteth without any reaction from the patient, nor doth it suffer from anything but its equal, by which it is brought into subjection; but after it hath dissolved all other things, it remaineth in its former nature, and is of the same virtue after a thousand operations as at the first'?[68] Did not *Encyclopædia Britanica* observe that 'the third method of making gold is by transmutation, or by turning all metals readily into pure gold, by melting them in fire, and calling a little quantity of a certain preparation into the fushed matter; upon which the feces retire, are volatized and burnt, and carried off, and the rest of the mass is turned into pure gold. That which works this change in the metals is called the philosopher's stone... Whether this third meth-

---

68 From *The Secret of the Immortal Liquor Called Alkahest, or Ignis-aqua* by Eirenæus Philalethes.

od is possible or not, it is difficult to say. We have so many testimonies of it from persons who on all other occasions speak truth that it is hard to say they are guilty of direct falsehood, even when they say that they have been masters of the secret.'[69] While my pale student's father would readily dismiss this encyclopædic entry as hogwash, did not Isaac Newton, the author of *Philosophiæ Naturalis Principia Mathematica*, also pursue the philosopher's stone and the elixir of life? How could my pale student be faulted for following in the alchemical footsteps of Isaac Newton? I do not!

'But the latter obtained my most undivided attention: wealth was an inferior object; but what glory would attend the discovery, if I could banish disease from the human frame, and render man invulnerable to any but a violent death!

'Nor were these my only visions. The raising of ghosts or devils was a promise liberally accorded by my favourite authors, the fulfilment of which I most eagerly sought; and if my incantations were always unsuccessful, I attributed the failure rather to my own inexperience and mistake, than to a want of skill or fidelity in my instructors.

'The natural phænomena that take place every day before our eyes did not escape my examinations. Distillation, and the wonderful effects of steam, processes of which my favourite authors were utterly ignorant, excited my astonishment; but my utmost wonder was engaged by some experiments on an air-pump, which I saw employed by a gentleman whom we were in the habit of visiting.

'The ignorance of the early philosophers on these and several other points served to decrease their credit with me: but I could not entirely throw them aside, before some other system should occupy their place in my mind.

'When I was about fifteen years old, we had retired to our house near Belrive,' –that is only a few miles removed for the Villa Diodati. How short a distance has my pale student journeyed to educate me– 'when we witnessed a most violent and terrible thunder-storm.' How I know this feeling intimately. Does a violent and terrible thunder-storm not rage outside my bedchamber's windows as my pale student visits me. 'It advanced from behind the mountains of Jura; and the thunder burst at once with frightful loudness from various quarters of the heavens. I remained, while the storm lasted, watching its progress with curiosity and delight. As I stood at the door, on a sudden I beheld a stream of fire issue from an old and beautiful oak, which stood about twenty yards from our house; and so soon as the dazzling light vanished, the oak had disappeared, and nothing remained but a blasted stump. When we visited

69 From 1797 *Encyclopædia Britanica* (Vol. 14)

it the next morning, we found the tree shattered in a singular manner. It was not splintered by the shock, but entirely reduced to thin ribbands of wood. I never beheld any thing so utterly destroyed.

'The catastrophe of this tree excited my extreme astonishment; and I eagerly inquired of my father the nature and origin of thunder and lightning. He replied, "Electricity;" describing at the same time the various effects of that power.' As my Beloved and our little Lord discussed electricity exciting frog's legs a few short days ago, they have made their debates of many subjects. I have heard John Abernethy's famous lecture oft quoted to me through obstinate opposition, because our friend and my Beloved's physician William Lawrence so publicly opposed this belief: The phaenomena of electricity and of life correspond. Electricity may be attached to, or inhere, in a wife; it may be suddenly dissipated, or have its powers annulled, or it may be removed by degrees or in portions, and the wire may remain less and less strongly electrified, in proportion as it is abstracte. So life inheres in vegetables and animals; it may sometimes be suddenly dissipated, or have its powers abolished, though in general it is lost by degrees, without any apparent change taking place in the structure; and in either case purification begins when life terminates.[70] 'He constructed a small electrical machine, and exhibited a few experiments; he made also a kite, with a wire and string, which drew down that fluid from the clouds.

'This last stroke completed the overthrow of Cornelius Agrippa, Albertus Magnus, and Paracelsus, who had so long reigned the lords of my imagination. But by some fatality I did not feel inclined to commence the study of any modern system; and this disinclination was influenced by the following circumstance.

'My father expressed a wish that I should attend a course of lectures upon natural philosophy, to which I cheerfully consented. Some accident prevented my attending these lectures until the course was nearly finished. The lecture, being therefore one of the last, was entirely incomprehensible to me. The professor discoursed with the greatest fluency of potassium and boron, of sulphates and oxyds, terms to which I could affix no idea.' How is my pale student so keenly aware of the contents of my travelling library? I am currently (no pun intended) reading Sir Humphry Davy's *A Discourse, Introductory to A Course of Lectures on Chemistry*? I too share my pale student of the unhallowed arts' optimism! 'And I became disgusted with the science of natural philosophy, although I still read Pliny and Buffon with delight, authors, in my estimation, of nearly equal interest and utility.

---

70 From "An Enquiry into the Probability and Rationality of Mr. Hunter's Theory of Life", a lecture by John Abernethy.

'My occupations at this age were principally the mathematics, and most of the branches of study appertaining to that science. I was busily employed in learning languages; Latin was already familiar to me, and I began to read some of the easiest Greek authors without the help of a lexicon. I also perfectly understood English and German. This is the list of my accomplishments at the age of seventeen; and you may conceive that my hours were fully employed in acquiring and maintaining a knowledge of this various literature.

'Another task also devolved upon me, when I became the instructor of my brothers. Ernest was six years younger than myself, and was my principal pupil. He had been afflicted with ill health from his infancy, through which Elizabeth and I had been his constant nurses: his disposition was gentle, but he was incapable of any severe application. William, the youngest of our family, was yet an infant, and the most beautiful little fellow in the world; his lively blue eyes, dimpled cheeks, and endearing manners, inspired the tenderest affection.

'Such was our domestic circle, from which care and pain seemed for ever banished. My father directed our studies, and my mother partook of our enjoyments. Neither of us possessed the slightest pre-eminence over the other; the voice of command was never heard amongst us; but mutual affection engaged us all to comply with and obey the slightest desire of each other.)

Chapter II

When I had attained the age of seventeen, my parents resolved that I should become a student at the university of Ingolstadt. I had hitherto attended the schools of Geneva; but my father thought it necessary, for the completion of my education, that I should be made acquainted with other customs than those of my native country. My departure was therefore fixed at an early date; but, before the day resolved upon could arrive, the first misfortune of my life occurred— an omen, as it were, of my future misery.' Oh! No! His story has only just begun, and he is already suffering misfortune. Omens? Future misery? If this was but the first, surely there will be a second misfortune of his life! And what a third? Or a fourth? What future misery was to come? I know of both misery and misfortune! With the birth of my dear boy, William, I struggled through the first nine days of his life despondent; I lived in constant fear that he too would succumb to a death in infancy as my first child had. But my William is alive! He thrives into infancy sleeping peacefully in this very room! The death of my firstborn was not, however, the first misfortune of my life; the death of my mother as a result of my own birth was the first misfortune of my life. I was only eleven days old when she succumbed to childbed fever and septic shock.

> 'My Dear Friend. The passage in your last kind letter that related to the subject of self-reproach was rather out of season. It has dwelt upon my mind ever since. My wife is now dead. She died this morning at eight o'clock. She grew worse before your letter arrived. Nobody has a greater call to reproach himself, except for want of kindness and attention in which I hope I have not been very deficient, than I have. But reproach would answer no good purpose, and I will not harbour it. I firmly believe that there does not exist her equal in the world. I know from experience we were formed to make each other happy. I have not the least expectation that I can now ever know happiness again. When you come to town, look at me, and talk to me, but do not-if you can help it-exhort me, or console me.
> —My father, William Godwin, to Thomas Holcroft

How could an all-loving God in Heaven insult me so?! He left a suckling babe motherless. But I digress. My pale student is telling me the story of the first misfortune in his life; my own is in this moment immaterial.

'Elizabeth had caught the scarlet fever' Oh no! Scarlatina? Oh! Would Hippocrates be surprised to know how many of the diseases he described still threaten humanity after two thousand years? He would have mourned that superstition and religiosity and ignorance have yet to fully acquiesce to the sciences. How many countless children and adults have been lost to such diseases as scarlatina? 'Her illness was *not* severe, and she quickly recovered.' Thank God! I was afeared she was in the greatest danger. But Victor's emphasis on the severity of the Elizabeth's illness gives a particular and peculiar weight to both pain and blame. What of Elizabeth's illness still haunts him so so many years later? 'During her confinement, many arguments had been urged to persuade my mother to refrain from attending upon her. She had, at first, yielded to our entreaties; but when she heard that her favourite was recovering, she could no longer debar herself from her society, and entered her chamber long before the danger of infection was past.' As any good mother would do her part to tend the health of this girl. A mother's instincts are primal (even towards a niece), an urge so deep seeded into the very soil of her being that it supersedes the most basic of instincts: her own survival. She thinks not of the consequences, though... 'The consequences of this imprudence were fatal. On the third day my mother sickened; her fever was very malignant, and the looks of her attendants prognosticated the worst event. On her death-bed the fortitude and benignity of this admirable woman did not desert her. She joined the hands of Elizabeth and myself.' As any good mother would share her heart to them. She joins the hands of the child of her flesh and the child of her choice, not to mourn but to rejoice! "'My children," she said, "my firmest hopes of future happiness were placed on the prospect of your union. This expectation will now be the consolation of your father. Elizabeth, my love, you must supply my place to your younger cousins. Alas! I regret that I am taken from you; and, happy and beloved as I have been, is it not hard to quit you all? But these are not thoughts befitting me; I will endeavour to resign myself cheerfully to death, and will indulge a hope of meeting you in another world."' As any good mother should depart this world. Where had Victor dug up these words? I am not naïve of the fact that this Victor Frankenstein is doubtless a figment of my overactive imagination and not a haunting incorporeal entity nor a daunting corporeal reality relating his life's story to me. Is Victor reaching back through my own memories into the past immemorial to retrieve the final words of my mother, Mary Wollstonecraft? I would be delighted if this were true. To know as an adult what an eleven-day-old babe was told by her dying mother. Did my dying mother possess the strength to hold me swaddled her in arms? Was my father present to catch me should her strength fail her, and I should fall? Oh, philosophers from the ancient to the modern surely have pondered why is it that adults remember nothing of the first few years of our lives. Perhaps our minds are so immature in our grasp of language and grammar that we as adults could never decipher the memories of what was spoken to us as children. I cannot imagine that an eleven-day-old has enough knowledge of their parent's language to remember the words accurately; the memory of my mother's final words would be as incomprehensible as a babbling child.

'She died calmly; and her countenance expressed affection even in death. I need not describe the feelings of those whose dearest ties are rent by that most irreparable evil, the void that presents itself to the soul, and the despair that is exhibited on the countenance. It is so long before the mind can persuade itself that she, whom we saw every day, and whose very existence appeared a part of our own, can have departed for ever— that the brightness of a beloved eye can have been extinguished, and the sound of a voice so familiar, and dear to the ear, can be hushed, never more to be heard. These are the reflections of the first days; but when the lapse of time proves the reality of the evil, then the actual bitterness of grief commences. Yet from whom has not that rude hand rent away some dear connexion; and why should I describe a sorrow which all have felt, and must feel? The time at length arrives, when grief is rather an indulgence than a necessity; and the smile that plays upon the lips, although it may be deemed a sacrilege, is not banished. My mother was dead, but we had still duties which we ought to perform; we must continue our course with the rest, and learn to think ourselves fortunate, whilst one remains whom the spoiler has not seized.' The death of a parent is an irreparable evil only surpassed by the death of a child. To lose a parent at the age of seventeen is a difficult struggle that leaves one's life in utter rubble. To know the deceased parent will never hold their grandchild in their loving arm; nor will they ever spoil that bugger rotten as every grandparent is wont to do. To lose a child as I had at age of seventeen is a unique endeavour that haunts one's life forever. My daughter haunted me with visons! Nightmares may scare; but visions of a dead child were incisions in my eyes! How I loathed waking because I the daughter I had cradled in my arms, suckling at my own breast, slowly evaporated into the ether of waking's reality. Sitting upright in bed, I would only hold her tearstained and empty swaddling clothes. The only solace I found was finding myself pregnant so soon again! I listened acutely for William to breathe or sigh in his sleep. Once I heard the cherished sound, I returned my focus back to my pale student.

'My journey to Ingolstadt, which had been deferred by these events, was now again determined upon. I obtained from my father a respite of some weeks. This period was spent sadly; my mother's death, and my speedy departure, depressed our spirits; but Elizabeth endeavoured to renew the spirit of cheerfulness in our little society. Since the death of her aunt, her mind had acquired new firmness and vigour. She determined to fulfil her duties with the greatest exactness; and she felt that that most imperious duty, of rendering her uncle and cousins happy, had devolved upon her. She consoled me, amused her uncle, instructed my brothers; and I never beheld her so enchanting as at this time, when she was continually endeavouring to contribute to the happiness of others, entirely forgetful of herself.' How Elizabeth has not only become a woman at such a tender age, but also a surrogate mother. Women are often called upon to rear the children of widowers, whose wives so often die in childbirth. Was not my own step-mother, Mary Jane Clairmont, called upon by marital vows to rear me after her marriage to my father? But my father's new wife was certainly not up to the task! I wrote my Beloved in a letter:

'I detest Mrs. Godwin; she plagues my father out of his life; and these— —Well, no matter. Why will Godwin not follow the obvious bent of his affections, and be reconciled to us? No; his prejudices, the world, and she— all these forbid it. What am I to do? trust to time, of course, for what else can I do. Good-night, my love; to-morrow I will seal this blessing on your lips. Press me, your own Mary, to your heart. Perhaps she will one day have a father; till then be everything to me, love; and, indeed, I will be a good girl, and never vex you. I will learn Greek and— — but when shall we meet when I may tell you all this, and you will so sweetly reward me? But good-night; I am wofully tired, and so sleepy. One kiss—well, that is enough— to-morrow!'[71]

'The day of my departure at length arrived. I had taken leave of all my friends, excepting Clerval, who spent the last evening with us. He bitterly lamented that he was unable to accompany me: but his father could not be persuaded to part with him, intending that he should become a partner with him in business, in compliance with his favourite theory, that learning was superfluous in the commerce of ordinary life. Henry had a refined mind; he had no desire to be idle, and was well pleased to become his father's partner, but he believed that a man might be a very good trader, and yet possess a cultivated understanding.' Fathers and their steely will! Do not the desires of education, enlightenment, and love not factor into decisions when it concerns their offspring? Of course not. Even into adulthood, they treat us as children.

'We sat late, listening to his complaints, and making many little arrangements for the future. The next morning early I departed. Tears gushed from the eyes of Elizabeth; they proceeded partly from sorrow at my departure, and partly because she reflected that the same journey was to have taken place three months before, when a mother's blessing would have accompanied me.

'I threw myself into the chaise that was to convey me away, and indulged in the most melancholy reflections. I, who had ever been surrounded by amiable companions, continually engaged in endeavouring to bestow mutual pleasure, I was now alone. In the university, whither I was going, I must form my own friends, and be my own protector. My life had hitherto been remarkably secluded and domestic; and this had given me invincible repugnance to new countenances. I loved my brothers, Elizabeth, and Clerval; these were "old familiar faces;"' Oh! I know this poem. *Where are they gone, the old familiar faces?/ I had a mother, but she died, and left me,/ Died prematurely in a day of horrors—/ All, all are gone, the old familiar faces!*[72] Victor continued, 'But I believed myself totally unfitted for the company of strangers. Such were my reflections as I commenced my journey; but as I proceeded, my spirits and hopes

---

71 From a letter from Mary Wollstonecraft Godwin to Percy Bysshe Shelley on 25 October 1814.
72 From the June 1798 poem, 'The Old Familiar Faces' by Charles Lamb.

rose. I ardently desired the acquisition of knowledge. I had often, when at home, thought it hard to remain during my youth cooped up in one place, and had longed to enter the world, and take my station among other human beings. Now my desires were complied with, and it would, indeed, have been folly to repent.

'I had sufficient leisure for these and many other reflections during my journey to Ingolstadt, which was long and fatiguing. At length the high white steeple of the town met my eyes. I alighted, and was conducted to my solitary apartment, to spend the evening as I pleased.

'The next morning I delivered my letters of introduction, and paid a visit to some of the principal professors, and among others to Mr Krempe, professor of natural philosophy. He received me with politeness, and asked me several questions concerning my progress in the different branches of science appertaining to natural philosophy. I mentioned, it is true, with fear and trembling, the only authors I had ever read upon those subjects.' Oh no! My dearest Victor do not mention them! Had you not learned from your father how the modern world had abandoned them. Albertus Magnus! Paracelsus! You will be run out of town by a mob of professors and undergraduants carrying torches and pitchforks. 'The professor stared: "Have you," he said, "really spent your time in studying such nonsense?"' Oh!

'I replied in the affirmative. "Every minute," continued Mr Krempe with warmth, "every instant that you have wasted on those books is utterly and entirely lost. You have burdened your memory with exploded systems, and useless names. Good God! in what desert land have you lived, where no one was kind enough to inform you that these fancies, which you have so greedily imbibed, are a thousand years old, and as musty as they are ancient? I little expected in this enlightened and scientific age to find a disciple of Albertus Magnus and Paracelsus. My dear Sir, you must begin your studies entirely anew."

'So saying, he stept aside, and wrote down a list of several books treating of natural philosophy, which he desired me to procure, and dismissed me, after mentioning that in the beginning of the following week he intended to commence a course of lectures upon natural philosophy in its general relations, and that Mr Waldman, a fellow-professor, would lecture upon chemistry the alternate days that he missed.'

'I returned home, not disappointed, for I had long considered those authors useless whom the professor had so strongly reprobated; but I did not feel much inclined to study the books which I procured at his recommendation.' Oh, no, my dearest, Victor. No! The joy of a new venture in education of immeasurable. Getting a new bibliography to explore is a wondrous adventure. Even the scribes of the Bible can write

wisdom the Apostle Paul advices: *When I was a child, I spake as a child,*
I understood as a child, I thought as a child: but when I became a man, I
put away childish things.[73] Mr Krempe was a little squat man, with a gruff
voice and repulsive countenance.' Oh, for shame, Victor! Do not fall
into the pseudoscience of physiognomy. First alchemy. Now physiognomy! Your studies have been as useless as Mr Krempe has adviced. Do
not believe that there is so intimate a relation between the dispositions
of the mind and the features of the countenance is a fact which cannot
be questioned.[74] 'The teacher, therefore, did not prepossess me in favour
of his doctrine. Besides, I had a contempt for the uses of modern natural
philosophy. It was very different, when the masters of the science sought
immortality and power; such views, although futile, were grand: but now
the scene was changed. The ambition of the inquirer seemed to limit
itself to the annihilation of those visions on which my interest in science
was chiefly founded. I was required to exchange chimeras of boundless
grandeur for realities of little worth.

'Such were my reflections during the first two or three days spent
almost in solitude. But as the ensuing week commenced, I thought of the
information which Mr Krempe had given me concerning the lectures.
And although I could not consent to go and hear that little conceited fellow deliver sentences out of a pulpit, I recollected what he had said of Mr
Waldman, whom I had never seen, as he had hitherto been out of town.

'Partly from curiosity, and partly from idleness, I went into the lec-
turing room, which Mr Waldman entered shortly after. This professor
was very unlike his colleague. He appeared about fifty years of age, but
with an aspect expressive of the greatest benevolence; a few gray hairs
covered his temples, but those at the back of his head were nearly black.
His person was short, but remarkably erect; and his voice the sweetest
I had ever heard. ' Not physiognomy again! I am growly weary of your
wary intellect. Let us hope that your schooling widens your mind. 'He
began his lecture by a recapitulation of the history of chemistry and the
various improvements made by different men of learning, pronouncing
with fervour the names of the most distinguished discoverers. He then
took a cursory view of the present state of the science, and explained
many of its elementary terms. After having made a few preparatory experiments, he concluded with a panegyric upon modern chemistry, the
terms of which I shall never forget:—

' "The ancient teachers of this science," said he, "promised impossi-
bilities, and performed nothing. The modern masters promise very little;
they know that metals cannot be transmuted, and that the elixir of life is

73 From 1 Corinthians 13:11
74 From the 1797 Encyclopædia Britanica.

a chimera. But these philosophers, whose hands seem only made to dabble in dirt, and their eyes to pour over the microscope or crucible, have indeed performed miracles. They penetrate into the recesses of nature, and shew how she works in her hiding places. They ascend into the heavens; they have discovered how the blood circulates, and the nature of the air we breathe. They have acquired new and almost unlimited powers; they can command the thunders of heaven, mimic the earthquake, and even mock the invisible world with its own shadows.'"

I would have adored this Mr Waldman as would my father and my Beloved. Was not the grand parlour of William Godwin a bastion of learning? How ladies and their gentlemen cherished invitations to Godwin's home on a Saturday. My father hosted many literary, scientific, and philosophical salons. Dinner was served promptly at eight, usually of four courses, but sometimes of seven, and rarely of anything more. These evenings were not intended for nourishment or merriment, but for enlightenment, though guests often left with all three. Esteemed and interesting persons were brought in to speak on any subject that struck my father's fancy this week or that week. Many critics would accuse my father of atheism, anarchism, anti-monarchism, feminism, utilitarianism, and radicalism inspired by the revolutionaries of France. My father was nothing if not outspoken. And my Beloved as well. He devoured the lectures held in my father's parlour and scoured the globe for papers and letters on this new discovery or this new discovery. Did not my Beloved and our little Lord spend a fateful evening debating galvanism? And if not for this singular debate my pale student of the unhallowed arts would not have visited me.

'I departed highly pleased with the professor and his lecture, and paid him a visit the same evening. His manners in private were even more mild and attractive than in public; for there was a certain dignity in his mien during his lecture, which in his own house was replaced by the greatest affability and kindness. He heard with attention my little narration concerning my studies, and smiled at the names of Cornelius Agrippa, and Paracelsus, but without the contempt that Mr Krempe had exhibited.' Curious! 'He said, that "these were men to whose indefatigable zeal modern philosophers were indebted for most of the foundations of their knowledge. They had left to us, as an easier task, to give new names, and arrange in connected classifications, the facts which they in a great degree had been the instruments of bringing to light. The labours of men of genius, however erroneously directed, scarcely ever fail in ultimately turning to the solid advantage of mankind." Curiouser! 'I listened to his statement, which was delivered without any presumption or affectation; and then added, that his lecture had removed my prejudices against modern chemists; and I, at the same time, requested his advice concerning the books I ought to procure.

' "I am happy," said Mr Waldman, "to have gained a disciple; and if your application equals your ability, I have no doubt of your success. Chemistry is that branch of natural philosophy in which the greatest improvements have been and may be made; it is on that account that I have made it my peculiar study; but at the same time I have not neglected the other branches of science. A man would make but a very sorry chemist, if he attended to that department of human knowledge alone. If your wish is to become really a man of science, and not merely a petty experimentalist, I should advise you to apply to every branch of natural philosophy, including mathematics."

'He then took me into his laboratory, and explained to me the uses of his various machines; instructing me as to what I ought to procure, and promising me the use of his own, when I should have advanced far enough in the science not to derange their mechanism. He also gave me the list of books which I had requested; and I took my leave.

'Thus ended a day memorable to me; it decided my future destiny.

Chapter III

From this day natural philosophy, and particularly chemistry, in the most comprehensive sense of the term, became nearly my sole occupation. I read with ardour those works, so full of genius and discrimination, which modern inquirers have written on these subjects. I attended the lectures, and cultivated the acquaintance, of the men of science of the university.' Good! Wondrous is learning. How often did I stand in my childhood home, peaking around the corner of a door-frame. Behind me was the hallway leading to my bedchamber on the left and the apartment of my father on the right. In front of me was the grand parlour of William Godwin, where many a lecture was made after a glorious dinner party. I was, more often than not, shooed away to bed because the lecture would be to advanced or heady for a child. But, more often than not, I crept from my bed to witness and absorb these lectures. My father knew, of course he did, that I was dropping eaves, but seeing that I was not shooed away a second or even third time implies his acceptance of my disobedience. 'And I found even in Mr Krempe a great deal of sound sense and real information, combined, it is true, with a repulsive physiognomy and manners, but not on that account the less valuable. In Mr Waldman I found a true friend. His gentleness was never tinged by dogmatism; and his instructions were given with an air of frankness and good nature, that banished every idea of pedantry. It was, perhaps, the amiable character of this man that inclined me more to that branch of natural philosophy which he professed, than an intrinsic love for the science itself. But this state of mind had place only in the first steps towards knowledge: the more fully I entered into the science, the more exclusively I pursued it for its own sake. That application, which at first had been a matter of duty and resolution, now became so ardent and eager, that the stars often disappeared in the light of morning whilst I was yet engaged in my laboratory.

'As I applied so closely, it may be easily conceived that I improved rapidly. My ardour was indeed the astonishment of the students; and my proficiency, that of the masters. Professor Krempe often asked me, with a sly smile, how Cornelius Agrippa went on? whilst Mr Waldman expressed the most heart-felt exultation in my progress.'

A sly smile. Mr Krempe would have concerned me more if his digs were genuine. I have encountered too many professors, lecturers, and supposed experts in their field, who dismissed alternate views of their dogmatic believes as blasphemous. And their dismissal of women was as pointed as clergymen. Where is it written in any of scientific words of Nicolaus Copernicus, Galileo Galilei, Johannes Kepler, René Descartes, William Harvey, Isaac Newton, Tycho Brahe, Andreas Vesalius, Robert Boyle, Antonie van Leeuwenhoek, and Evangelista Torricelli: *Let your women keep silence: for it is not permitted unto them to speak; but they are commanded to be under obedience, as also saith the law.*[75] No! Only in the words of religious scripture do you find such decrees. Yet, too often, women are summarily dismissed for the crime of being born without a penis. Sorry for this digression. Let us return to my pale student.

'Two years passed in this manner, during which I paid no visit to Geneva, but was engaged, heart and soul, in the pursuit of some discoveries, which I hoped to make. None but those who have experienced them can conceive of the enticements of science. In other studies you go as far as others have gone before you, and there is nothing more to know; but in a scientific pursuit there is continual food for discovery and wonder. A mind of moderate capacity, which closely pursues one study, must infallibly arrive at great proficiency in that study; and I, who continually sought the attainment of one object of pursuit, and was solely wrapt up in this, improved so rapidly, that, at the end of two years, I made some discoveries in the improvement of some chemical instruments, which procured me great esteem and admiration at the university.'

Hear! Hear! I could not have written it better myself. But perchance I have written it myself. I am not foolish enough to believe that my phantasm is nothing more than my eager imagination made

---

75 From 1 Corinthians 14:34

manifest. How weary had I grown of poor Polidori's relentless teasing *every* morning when I did not have a ghost story to enter into Lord Byron's game. For far too long I tried far too hard to conceive of a ghost story, but the spark of inspiration did not come. Only when I was too weary from a long evening of debate between my Beloved and our little Lord and poor Polidori on galvanism, was my mind finally primed to conceive of a ghost story to enter into our little game. While it is far too early to tell this story to my fellow prisoners in the Villa Diodati, Polidori has shifted his teasing from when would I get an idea for a ghost story to when would I share my ghost idea. He is an infuriating small man.

'When I had arrived at this point, and had become as well acquainted with the theory and practice of natural philosophy as depended on the lessons of any of the professors at Ingolstadt, my residence there being no longer conducive to my improvements, I thought of returning to my friends and my native town, when an incident happened that protracted my stay.

'One of the phænonema which had peculiarly attracted my attention was the structure of the human frame, and, indeed, any animal endued with life. Whence, I often asked myself, did the principle of life proceed? It was a bold question, and one which has ever been considered as a mystery.' This word. This confounded word. When the clergyman encountered a question that their particular translation of the Holy Bible or their peculiar variation of Christianity cannot answer, they answer with this word and the conversation is ended. Natural philosophers, at the very least, seek an answer, but when one cannot be readily found, they likewise answer with this word and the conversation is ended. Infuriating!

'Yet with how many things are we upon the brink of becoming acquainted, if cowardice or carelessness did not restrain our inquiries. I revolved these circumstances in my mind, and determined thenceforth to apply myself more particularly to those branches of natural philosophy which relate to physiology. Unless I had been animated by an almost supernatural enthusiasm, my application to this study would have been irksome, and almost intolerable. To examine the causes of life, we must first have recourse to death. I became acquainted with the science of anatomy: but this was not sufficient; I must also observe the natural decay and corruption of the human body. In my education my father had taken the greatest precautions that my mind should be impressed with no supernatural horrors.' Alphonse Frankenstein sounds very similar to William Godwin. Which he would, of course, seeing that William Godwin is my father and Victor Frankenstein is me, at least while immersed in this harrowing tale. As a writer, our protagonist is ourselves, no matter the deviation from ourselves. If the deviation is slight, we will trumpet the similarity. If the deviation is too great, we will dismiss the character as a mere creation and not anything like ourselves. As Thomas, Duke of Norfolk opined to Thomas Cromwell: 'a man cannot have his cake and eat his cake.' But to date, Victor is very much me. I cannot wait to see when he deviates from my own psyche.

'I do not ever remember to have trembled at a tale of superstition, or to have feared the apparition of a spirit. Darkness had no effect upon my fancy; and a church-yard was to me merely the receptacle of bodies deprived of life, which, from being the seat of beauty and strength, had become food for the worm. Now I was led to examine the cause and progress of this decay, and forced to spend days and nights in vaults and charnel houses. My attention was fixed upon every object the most insupportable to the delicacy of the human feelings. I saw how the fine form of man was degraded and wasted; I beheld the corruption of death succeed to the blooming cheek of life; I saw how the worm inherited the wonders of the eye and brain. I paused, examining and analysing all the minutiæ of causation, as exemplified in the change from life to death, and death to life, until from the midst of this darkness a sudden light broke in upon me— a light so brilliant and wondrous, yet so simple, that while I became dizzy with the immensity of the prospect which it illustrated, I was surprised that among so many men of genius, who had directed their inquiries towards the same science, that I alone should be reserved to discover so astonishing a secret.' My pale student makes me long to stalk the cemeteries, vaults, and charnel houses too. How would William Godwin or my Beloved react if a mere woman examined the dead as my dear Victor did? How will Lord Byron or poor Polidori react when I write read these very words as part of our little game of ghost stories? How unseemly it would be for a woman to have written these words. This will be seen as an 'aggravation of that which is the prevailing fault of the novel; but if our authoress can forget the gentleness of her sex, it is no reason why we should; and we shall therefore dismiss the novel without further comment.'[76]

'Remember, I am not recording the vision of a madman. The sun does not more certainly shine in the heavens, than that which I now affirm is true. Some miracle might have produced it, yet the stages of the discovery were distinct and probable. After days and nights of incredible labour and fatigue, I succeeded in discovering the cause of generation and life; nay, more, I became myself capable of bestowing animation upon lifeless matter.'

---

76 From *The British Critic. New Series.* 9: 432–438. April 1818

'The astonishment which I had at first experienced on this discovery soon gave place to delight and rapture. After so much time spent in painful labour, to arrive at once at the summit of my desires, was the most gratifying consummation of my toils. But this discovery was so great and overwhelming, that all the steps by which I had been progressively led to it were obliterated, and I beheld only the result. What had been the study and desire of the wisest men since the creation of the world, was now within my grasp. Not that, like a magic scene, it all opened upon me at once: the information I had obtained was of a nature rather to direct my endeavours so soon as I should point them towards the object of my search, than to exhibit that object already accomplished. I was like the Arabian who had been buried with the dead, and found a passage to life aided only by one glimmering, and seemingly ineffectual light.' No! Do not dismiss Elizabeth so! I know this tale from *One Thousand and One Nights* well. You are not trapped by a *dead wife*! Elizabeth has not died like Sinbad's on the island of pepper-growers. She still lives! You are not bound to their most vile, lewd custom that if the wife dies first, to bury the husband alive with her and in like manner the wife, if the husband dies first; so that neither may enjoy life after losing his or her mate. You must not cry out:

> ' "Almighty Allah never made it lawful to bury the quick with the dead! I am a stranger, not one of your kind; and I cannot abear your custom, and had I known it I never would have wedded among you!" They heard me not and paid no heed to my words, but laying hold of me, bound me by force and let me down into the cavern, with a large gugglet of sweet water and seven cakes of bread, according to their custom... When they left me in the cavern with my dead wife and, closing the mouth of the pit, went their ways, I looked about me and found myself in a vast cave full of dead bodies, that exhaled a fulsome and loathsome smell and the air was heavy with the groans of the dying.'[77]

My pales student unfazed by my silent cry continued, 'I see by your eagerness and the wonder and hope which your eyes express, my dearest Mary, that you expect to be informed of the secret with which I am acquainted; that cannot be. Listen patiently until the end of my story, and you will easily perceive why I am reserved upon that subject. I will not lead you on, unguarded and ardent as I then was, to your destruction and infallible misery. Learn from me, if not by my precepts, at least by my example, how dangerous is the acquirement of knowledge, and how

---

77 From *One Thousand and One Nights*, translated by Richard F. Burton, 1885

much happier that man is who believes his native town to be the world, than he who aspires to become greater than his nature will allow.' My greatest fear was that my pale student would take this secret to his own grave. But it is best for the writer of fictional works to keep this knowledge 'secret', therefore withholding it from the reader, lest the science one day be disproven, or God forbid, the reader seeks to recreate our fictional science, no matter how thorough our research may have been. I would greatly fear newspaper headlines screaming that readers of my novel were inspired to stalk cemeteries, vaults, and charnel houses and to purchase the requisite equipment from laboratories and attempt a recreation of Victor's experiments. So, he keeps the secret from me so I can withhold the secret from my readers.

'When I found so astonishing a power placed within my hands, I hesitated a long time concerning the manner in which I should employ it. Although I possessed the capacity of bestowing animation, yet to prepare a frame for the reception of it, with all its intricacies of fibres, muscles, and veins, still remained a work of inconceivable difficulty and labour. I doubted at first whether I should attempt the creation of a being like myself or one of simpler organization; but my imagination was too much exalted by my first success to permit me to doubt of my ability to give life to an animal as complex and wonderful as man. The materials at present within my command hardly appeared adequate to so arduous an undertaking; but I doubted not that I should ultimately succeed. I prepared myself for a multitude of reverses; my operations might be incessantly baffled, and at last my work be imperfect: yet, when I considered the improvement which every day takes place in science and mechanics, I was encouraged to hope my present attempts would at least lay the foundations of future success. Nor could I consider the magnitude and complexity of my plan as any argument of its impracticability. It was with these feelings that I began the creation of a human being. As the minuteness of the parts formed a great hindrance to my speed, I resolved, contrary to my first intention, to make the being of a gigantic stature; that is to say, about eight feet in height, and proportionably large.' My! How would he find bones of such proportion in the vaults and charnel houses around the vicinity of Ingolstadt. Surely the men of that region are similarly proportioned to the men of Britian where the average height of an English solider being five foot five. How could he assemble such height in such a creature! Oh! Victor would not limit himself to human cadavers! Will he seek out the slaughterhouses for meat and bones of cattle and horses? What of the exotic species of rhinoceroses and elephants and the great cats of the zoos! What manner of abomination does Victor desire to as his creation? After having formed this determination, and having spent some months in successfully collecting and arranging my materials, I began.' Surely, he must have had difficulty in finding the requisite human parts for the experiment. Did not resurrectionist, those grotesque body snatchers who stole corpses from graveyards, not struggle in the finding the bodies to supply the market? Where would students of human anatomy find the cadavers required for their studies. The fashionable decline in capital punishment, which is a great advancement of the modern age, likewise contributed to the scarcity of human cadavers.

'No one can conceive the variety of feelings which bore me onwards, like a hurricane, in the first enthusiasm of success. Life and death appeared to me ideal bounds, which I should first break through, and pour a torrent of light into our dark world. A new species would bless me as its creator and source; many happy and excellent natures would owe their being to me. No father could claim the gratitude of his child so completely as I should deserve their's. Pursuing these reflections, I thought, that if I could bestow animation upon lifeless matter, I might in process of time (although I now found it impossible) renew life where death had apparently devoted the body to corruption.' I desired to cry out to my pale student as he relates his story to me concerning his foolishness and hubris. 'A new species?' We are not living in Ancient Greece where natural creatures were an amalgamation of man and beast: the minotaur of man and bull, the centaur of man and horse, the griffon of lion and eagle, the chimera of lion and goat and snake, the pegasus of horse and bird, the sphynx of woman and lion and eagle, the harpies of woman and bird, *etc. ad nauseum.* This 'new species' is a comedy of errors!

'These thoughts supported my spirits, while I pursued my undertaking with unremitting ardour. My cheek had grown pale with study, and my person had become emaciated with confinement. Sometimes, on the very brink of certainty, I failed; yet still I clung to the hope which the next day or the next hour might realize. One secret which I alone possessed was the hope to which I had dedicated myself; and the moon gazed on my midnight labours, while, with unrelaxed and breathless eagerness, I pursued nature to her hiding places. Who shall conceive the horrors of my secret toil, as I dabbled among the unhallowed damps of the grave, or tortured the living animal to animate the lifeless clay?'

Oho, my dear Victor. There is your hubris. The Jewish magicians who created Golems saw Adam as but the first: With regard to Adam the first man, his torso was fashioned from clay taken from Babylonia, and his head was fashioned from clay taken from Eretz Yisrael, the most important land, and his limbs were fashioned from clay taken from the rest of the lands in the world. With regard to his buttocks, Rav Aha says: They were fashioned from clay taken from Akra De'agma, on the outskirts of

Babylonia.[78] And here my dearest Victor is plotting and planning to create a new Adam, not created in the likeness of the Judaeo-Christian God, but himself! You are taking pieces from this vault and that charnel house, this farm and that slaughterhouse in cruel blasphemy of the creation of the first man.

'My limbs now tremble, and my eyes swim with the remembrance; but then a resistless, and almost frantic impulse, urged me forward; I seemed to have lost all soul or sensation but for this one pursuit. It was indeed but a passing trance, that only made me feel with renewed acuteness so soon as, the unnatural stimulus ceasing to operate, I had returned to my old habits. I collected bones from charnel houses; and disturbed, with profane fingers, the tremendous secrets of the human frame. In a solitary chamber, or rather cell, at the top of the house, and separated from all the other apartments by a gallery and staircase, I kept my workshop of filthy creation; my eyeballs were starting from their sockets in attending to the details of my employment. The dissecting room and the slaughter-house furnished many of my materials; and often did my human nature turn with loathing from my occupation, whilst, still urged on by an eagerness which perpetually increased, I brought my work near to a conclusion.

'The summer months passed while I was thus engaged, heart and soul, in one pursuit. It was a most beautiful season; never did the fields bestow a more plentiful harvest, or the vines yield a more luxuriant vintage: but my eyes were insensible to the charms of nature. And the same feelings which made me neglect the scenes around me caused me also to forget those friends who were so many miles absent, and whom I had not seen for so long a time. I knew my silence disquieted them; and I well remembered the words of my father: "I know that while you are pleased with yourself, you will think of us with affection, and we shall hear regularly from you. You must pardon me, if I regard any interruption in your correspondence as a proof that your other duties are equally neglected."

'I knew well therefore what would be my father's feelings; but I could not tear my thoughts from my employment, loathsome in itself, but which had taken an irresistible hold of my imagination. I wished, as it were, to procrastinate all that related to my feelings of affection until the great object, which swallowed up every habit of my nature, should be completed.

'I then thought that my father would be unjust if he ascribed my neglect to vice, or faultiness on my part; but I am now convinced that he was justified in conceiving that I should not be altogether free from blame. A human being in perfection ought always to preserve a calm

---

78 From Sanhedrin 38b, one of ten tractates of Seder Nezikin (a section of the Talmud that deals with damages, i.e. civil and criminal proceedings)

and peaceful mind, and never to allow passion or a transitory desire to disturb his tranquillity. I do not think that the pursuit of knowledge is an exception to this rule. If the study to which you apply yourself has a tendency to weaken your affections, and to destroy your taste for those simple pleasures in which no alloy can possibly mix, then that study is certainly unlawful, that is to say, not befitting the human mind. If this rule were always observed; if no man allowed any pursuit whatsoever to interfere with the tranquillity of his domestic affections, Greece had not been enslaved.' 'Cæsar would have spared his country; America would have been discovered more gradually; and the empires of Mexico and Peru had not been destroyed.' Oh, how the words of Lord Byron linger in my mind. He recently complete is third canto in his 'Child Harold's Pilgrimage', but in his second he lamented the Greeks' *trembling beneath the scourge of Turkish hand/ From birth till death enslaved; in word, in deed, unmanned.*

'But I forget that I am moralizing in the most interesting part of my tale; and your looks remind me to proceed.

'My father made no reproach in his letters; and only took notice of my silence by inquiring into my occupations more particularly than before. Winter, spring, and summer, passed away during my labours; but I did not watch the blossom or the expanding leaves— sights which before always yielded me supreme delight, so deeply was I engrossed in my occupation. The leaves of that year had withered before my work drew near to a close; and now every day shewed me more plainly how well I had succeeded. But my enthusiasm was checked by my anxiety, and I appeared rather like one doomed by slavery to toil in the mines, or any other unwholesome trade, than an artist occupied by his favourite employment. Every night I was oppressed by a slow fever, and I became nervous to a most painful degree.' I longed to add my own words to his but could not bring myself to speak: 'the fall of a leaf startled me, and I shunned my fellow-creatures as if I had been guilty of a crime. Sometimes I grew alarmed at the wreck I perceived that I had become; the energy of my purpose alone sustained me: my labours would soon end, and I believed that exercise and amusement would then drive away incipient disease'. In my silence, my pale student continued, 'A disease that I regretted the more because I had hitherto enjoyed most excellent health, and had always boasted of the firmness of my nerves. But I believed that exercise and amusement would soon drive away such symptoms; and I promised myself both of these, when my creation should be complete.'

Chapter IV

I awakened when a thundercrack thundered and cracked so violent my first fear was Napoleon had returned to wage war on Lake Geneva. Had he not been defeated by Duke Wellington at Waterloo? Had he not been a second time exiled, this time on the island of Saint Helena? Did he escape Saint Helena as easily as he had his first exile on Elba? Oh! The thunder shook walls of the Villa Diodati as if rained on by cannon fire. Droplets of rain struck the windowpanes as if rained on by musket fire. I shook. My Beloved slept. I almost wept.

I found the door to our chamber was ajar. Had my pale student of the unhallowed arts abandoned our nightly conversation in fear of sheer violence of the storm? I wrapped my robe securely and fastened around the waist and crept out of the chamber so not to disturb my slumbering Beloved. When I stepped into the hallway, I found myself no longer in hallways of the Villa Diodati. I did not see Lord Byron's apartment, nor the doctor's, nor Claire's where they should be found. Did I find myself in a dream? Can one have consciousness of being in a dream? Seldom if ever do I come to the realisation I am in a dream. And if so, what recourse does one have but to allow the dream to continue. Does one fight the dream? Does one allow the dream to overwhelm them? Does one not control the dream? Or does one fight to awake? My conversation with my pale student was quite lucid. I could not have possibly dreamt them; my pale student could not be merely a dream, because the transcriptions are in my journal in each morning. And! This night I had awoken so clearly and experienced the thunderstorm so severely, that I could not possibly be dreaming.

I found myself not in the Villa Diodati, but a castle I had visited briefly while on our six weeks' tour through a part of France, Switzerland, Germany, and Holland with my Beloved and my dearest Claire. I had encountered the dark haunted forests and narrow valleys surrounding the castle that were as much shrouded in legendary mystery as they were a darkness that hung like London fog. Was this where my pale student of the unhallowed arts had acquired his name? Were my inner thoughts and memories affecting our conversations?

My Beloved wished to tarry at the castle because he personally knew several members of the '*Kreis der Empfindsamen*', a literary circle from Darmstadt, who used the castle for their readings. Did they believe they were a Hellfire Club reciting their poems as if spells to summon the Great Dragon himself, that old serpent, called the Devil, and Satan, who deceives the whole world? At the Castle Frankenstein, we encountered students from the University of Strasbourg, of which Johann Konrad Dippel was an infamous alumnus. We learned from them of Dippel's discovery of the 'Elixir of Life', as evidenced by his *Maladies and Remedies of the Life of the Flesh*. He made this dark, viscous, tar-like, and putrid oil through the destructive distillation of bones. How could rotting death ever be an 'elixir of life'? The students spoke quiet highly of the Pietist theologian, physician, and alchemist, though they admitted that one Emanuel Swedenborg, both once a devoted disciple and then staunch critic had dismissed him as 'bound to no principles, but was in general opposed to all, whoever they may be, of whatever principle or faith ... becoming angry with any one for contradicting him.' How Swedenborg had fallen from once being enamoured to then being repulsed by 'a most vile devil... who attempted wicked things.' But the students hailed the glorious alchemist (though locals remembered him as notorious graverobber), who experimented in anatomy and supposedly transferred the souls from one cadaver to another with a funnel, as an exorcist and a saint! Did he not, they claimed, create an alchemic potion concocted from boiled animal bones and their flesh to supplant the *Rituale Romanum*, and therefore the Vatican, in the exorcising of demons?

After the mysterious, almost dreamlike transition of stepping foot over the threshold of the hold, I went from being in my bedchamber at the Villa Diodati to the halls of the castle Frankenstein. The walls of the medieval castle did little protect from the thunderous storm raging outside. If it had been daylight, I could have peered out one of the windows, over the sheer cliff, and down into the hauntingly forested valley far below. I made my way upwards toward the tower that had been so utterly collapsed that it was exposed to the elements. Not alchemical elements mind you, but the natural elements. The students who had two years previous pointed up towards this very tower, telling us of nitro-glycerine experiments that destroyed it; though my Beloved doubted whether or not it was an anachronism. When nitro-glycerine was first discovered, we could not deduce; surely this discovery was not made by Johann Konrad Dippel! In the ruins of the tower, I found my pale student of the unhallowed arts sitting in an armchair near an extinguished fireplace with a ruined chimney. Behind him stood the very same powerful engine I saw in my awaking dream but now fully destroyed; the metal spilt open from explosions within. The walls of the tower had been charred black by a raging inferno. I did not see the hideous phantasm of a man stretched out as I had seen before. Oh! The violence of the thunderstorm that had awaken me from a dreamless slumber was so much more explosive above the ruined tower. The raindrops buffeted our shoulders; the wind whipped against our faces like painful slaps. Even though the torrential rain drenched us in a deluge not seen by man since the days of Noah, the pale student offered me a chair opposite it. I took out my journal fearful that the previous conversation with my pale student would be obliterated by the weather, but the rain did not wet the pages nor ruin the ink. *Thanks be to God!* Where did this come from? I could not have possibly heard it during the Roman Mass. I shook off the saying as my nervous shivering shook off the rain.

Victor continued his tale: 'It was on a dreary night of November, that I beheld the accomplishment of my toils.' November! Did my pale student not say that winter, spring, and summer had passed away during his 'labours'! March. April. May. June. July. August. September. October. And now November have passed away. Oh! 'Labours!' This is the word my pale student chose! He gestated on his 'labours' for nine months! This is most telling.

'With an anxiety that almost amounted to agony, I collected the instruments of life around me, that I might infuse a spark of being'— Curious phrase this. Reminds me of the phrase *flavilla viae*, or when translated literally into English, 'the spark of vitality. Of course, Erasmus Darwin was describing the passing of vitality from parent to offspring in plants. But 'spark of being' is quite the interesting turn of phrase.— 'into the lifeless thing that lay at my feet. It was already one in the morning; the rain pattered dismally against the panes, and my candle was nearly burnt out, when, by the glimmer of the half-extinguished light, I saw the dull yellow eye of the creature open; it breathed hard, and a convulsive motion agitated its limbs.' The poor creature is jaundiced. Dear God! Curse God! I remember intimately giving birth at only six months gestation. I was not ready. I was not prepared. The yellow pallor of my daughter who was too live only nine short days is so vivid in my memory that I wish to cry out again:

> 'My dearest Hogg my baby is dead— will you come to see me as soon as you can. I wish to see you— It was perfectly well when I went to bed— I awoke in the night to give it suck it appeared to be sleeping so quietly that I would not awake it. It was dead then, but we did not find that out till morning— from its appearance it evidently died of convulsions— Will you come— you are so calm a creature & Shelley is afraid of a fever from the milk— for I am no longer a mother now.'[79]

'How can I describe my emotions at this catastrophe, or how delineate the wretch whom with such infinite pains and care I had endeavoured

---

79 From a letter 6 March, 1815 to Thomas Jefferson Hogg

to form? His limbs were in proportion, and I had selected his features as beautiful. Beautiful!— Great God! His yellow skin scarcely covered the work of muscles and arteries beneath; his hair was of a lustrous black, and flowing; his teeth of a pearly whiteness; but these luxuriances only formed a more horrid contrast with his watery eyes, that seemed almost of the same colour as the dun white sockets in which they were set, his shrivelled complexion, and straight black lips.'

Beautiful and repulsive all in one Creation. Can a mother look down at her child newly born, twisted and distorted by a malignant pregnancy and not feel even a sliver of maternal love for her child? Does she not desire to put the abomination to her breast to suckle the life-giving nourishment of her breast? The father, who did not carry the growing child in his own body, feeding it nourishment through the afterbirth as the womb grows bone and knits the fibres of the foetal flesh, will seek to snatch the child away from its mother's breast to cast the deformed newborn off a cliff into the battering waves of the sea. Having lost my own sickly jaundiced child at only nine days, this is beyond my comprehension.

'The different accidents of life are not so changeable as the feelings of human nature. I had worked hard for nearly two years, for the sole purpose of infusing life into an inanimate body. For this I had deprived myself of rest and health. I had desired it with an ardour that far exceeded moderation; but now that I had finished, the beauty of the dream vanished, and breathless horror and disgust filled my heart.'

My pale student has created an offspring without the contribution of a woman! Now unnatural is this phenomenon. He has sewn disparate parts from the bodies he desperately stole from the grave, bought from the laboratories, and acquired from the slaughterhouses. And yet my pale student is disgusted by its unnatural appearance. So typical of men. He did not carry this creation in his womb feeling the kicks of the foetus and seeing his belly grow with each passing day. He did not experience the discomfort the child causes, disrupting sleep and disturbing common everyday activities. And yet the mother caresses her belly with eager anticipation of the birth and the coming years of rearing the child into adulthood. The father is physically disconnected from the pregnancy. True, he may rest his head on the growing belly to feel the child kick and therefore feel some connection to the child, but this feeling is fleeting. His own eager preparations for the coming of the child are purely financial. He wants the best possible future for his child, but a father's mind is preoccupied with how he will provide for the child, and this involves money and perchance the growing of his station in life. The nurturing of the growing baby and the education of the child is left into the service of the mother, or if the family is afflu-ent enough, a nurse. If a man experiences an unnatural growing in his body is not the result cancerous? Such swelling is nearly always fatal. My pale student did not grow his Creation his womb, but assembled it on a slab.

'Unable to endure the aspect of the being I had created, I rushed out of the room, and continued a long time traversing my bed-chamber, una-ble to compose my mind to sleep. At length lassitude succeeded to the tu-mult I had before endured; and I threw myself on the bed in my clothes, endeavouring to seek a few moments of forgetfulness. But it was in vain: I slept indeed, but I was disturbed by the wildest dreams. I thought I saw Elizabeth, in the bloom of health, walking in the streets of Ingolstadt. De-lighted and surprised, I embraced her; but as I imprinted the first kiss on her lips, they became lurid with the hue of death; her features appeared to change, and I thought that I held the corpse of my dead mother in my arms; a shroud enveloped her form, and I saw the grave-worms crawling in the folds of the flannel.'

Shall I attempt to analyse this dream or if this even be a dream? Ancient man saw dreams as messages from the gods, but did not Ar-istotle believe them merely a psychosomatic phenomenon? Given the absence of external sensory stimulation, our eyes are closed and unable to see, he posits that sleep is akin to hallucinations, 'that the faculty by which, in waking hours, we are subject to illusion when affected by disease, is identical with that which produces illusory effects in sleep.'[80] This dream– nay! hallucination– may rest the blame for the death of his mother at the hands of Elizabeth. Did not the disease first come into the Frankenstein home through his cousin! On her death-bed, Caro-line decreed that Elizabeth must supply Caroline's place to her younger cousins. Did Victor believe that Elizabeth, his mother's 'favourite', pre-sumed to replace his mother or did he believe his mother was forcing him into an incestuous marriage with his own cousin? These abomina-tions of marriages were reserved for royalty! Or did Victor believe— fie! It would be folly to continue further down the rabbit-hole of dream interpretation. We could awaken any number of interpretations and drown ourselves in speculation. It is best to leave the sleeping world to the sleeping.

'I started from my sleep with horror; a cold dew covered my fore-head, my teeth chattered, and every limb became convulsed; when, by the dim and yellow light of the moon, as it forced its way through the window-shutters, I beheld the wretch— the miserable monster whom I had created. He held up the curtain of the bed; and his eyes, if eyes they

---

80 From *On Dreams* by Aristotle, translated by J. I. Beare

may be called, were fixed on me. His jaws opened, and he muttered some inarticulate sounds, while a grin wrinkled his cheeks. He might have spoken, but I did not hear; one hand was stretched out, seemingly to detain me, but I escaped, and rushed down stairs.' No! My dear Victor! No! Your Creation is but a babbling babe reaching out for a parent's love. He may not purse his lips longing to nurse upon his mother's breast, but he longs for the connection that any child desires of a parent. You see his height and his weight, and see a man, but no man is this. His speech is inarticulate because he is an infant. Any other parent would delight if a grin wrinkled the cheeks of their child. But Victor is not just any parent. 'I took refuge in the court-yard belonging to the house which I inhabited; where I remained during the rest of the night, walking up and down in the greatest agitation, listening attentively, catching and fearing each sound as if it were to announce the approach of the demoniacal corpse to which I had so miserably given life.' The endless hubris of a man. This is why men were not gifted by the gods to grow life within their bellies. A man is an external creature with his sexual organs hanging limp and flaccid on the outside of his body; only when the fires of desire stir within a man does that serpentine organ show signs of life. A woman in an internal creature, the workings of her body a mystery. A man concerns himself with the external world while a woman concerns herself with her children she has grown internally. This is the natural order. One that my pale student of the unhallowed arts has torn assunder.

At this moment, I know not why I endeavoured to gain from Frankenstein the particulars of his creatures formation: but on this point he was impenetrable.

'Are you mad, my dear?' said Victor; 'or whither does your senseless curiosity lead you? Would you also create for yourself and the world a demoniacal enemy? Peace, peace! learn my miseries, and do not seek to increase your own.' He then continued his tale as if I had not interrupted nor irritated him so greatly.

'Oh! no mortal could support the horror of that countenance. A mummy again endued with animation could not be so hideous as that wretch. I had gazed on him while unfinished; he was ugly then; but when those muscles and joints were rendered capable of motion, it became a thing such as even Dante could not have conceived.

'I passed the night wretchedly. Sometimes my pulse beat so quickly and hardly, that I felt the palpitation of every artery; at others, I nearly sank to the ground through languor and extreme weakness. Mingled with this horror, I felt the bitterness of disappointment: dreams that had been my food and pleasant rest for so long a space, were now become a hell to me; and the change was so rapid, the overthrow so complete!

'Morning, dismal and wet, at length dawned, and discovered to my sleepless and aching eyes the church of Ingolstadt, its white steeple and clock, which indicated the sixth hour.' Victor is speaking as if he is not in Castle Frankenstein, but in Ingolsdtadt. Are these surroundings I see around me a dreamlike illusion? Victor did not create his creation here in the ruined castle, but in his private apartment in Ingolstadt. ' The porter opened the gates of the court, which had that night been my asylum, and I issued into the streets, pacing them with quick steps, as if I sought to avoid the wretch whom I feared every turning of the street would present to my view. I did not dare return to the apartment which I inhabited, but felt impelled to hurry on, although wetted by the rain, which poured from a black and comfortless sky.

'I continued walking in this manner for some time, endeavouring, by bodily exercise, to ease the load that weighed upon my mind. I traversed the streets, without any clear conception of where I was, or what I was doing. My heart palpitated in the sickness of fear; and I hurried on with irregular steps, not daring to look about me:

> 'Like one who, on a lonely road,
>   Doth walk in fear and dread,
>   And, having once turn'd round, walks on,
>   And turns no more his head;
> Because he knows a frightful fiend
>   Doth close behind him tread.

'Continuing thus, I came at length opposite to the inn at which the various diligences and carriages usually stopped. Here I paused, I knew not why; but I remained some minutes with my eyes fixed on a coach that was coming towards me from the other end of the street. As it drew nearer, I observed that it was the Swiss diligence: it stopped just where I was standing; and, on the door being opened, I perceived Henry Clerval, who, on seeing me, instantly sprung out. "My dear Frankenstein,"— ah! The pale student finally utters his family name but has put the words onto the lips of her most cherished friend. And it is the very name of the castle which I and my Beloved visited during our six weeks tour through a part of France, Switzerland, Germany, and Holland. It is most curious that I would envisage my surroundings as the Castle Frankenstein despite never hearing his family name spoken aloud until this very moment. Curious and curiouser— 'exclaimed he, "how glad I am to see you! how fortunate that you should be here at the very moment of my alighting!"

'Nothing could equal my delight on seeing Clerval; his presence brought back to my thoughts my father, Elizabeth, and all those scenes of home so dear to my recollection. I grasped his hand, and in a moment forgot my horror and misfortune; I felt suddenly, and for the first time during many months, calm and serene joy. I welcomed my friend, therefore, in the most cordial manner, and we walked towards my college. Clerval continued talking for some time about our mutual friends, and his own good fortune in being permitted to come to Ingolstadt. "You may easily believe," said he, "how great was the difficulty to persuade my father that it was not absolutely necessary for a merchant not to understand any thing except book-keeping; and, indeed, I believe I left him incredulous to the last, for his constant answer to my unwearied entreaties was the same as that of the Dutch schoolmaster in the *Vicar of Wakefield*: 'You see me, young man; I never learned Greek, and I don't find that I ever missed it. I have had a Doctor's cap and gown without Greek: I have ten thousand florins a year without Greek, I eat heartily without Greek In short, I don't know Greek, and I do not believe there is any use in it.' But his affection for me at length overcame his dislike of learning, and he has permitted me to undertake a voyage of discovery to the land of knowledge."

' "It gives me the greatest delight to see you; but tell me how you left my father, brothers, and Elizabeth."

' "Very well, and very happy, only a little uneasy that they hear from you so seldom. By the bye, I mean to lecture you a little upon their account myself.— But, my dear Frankenstein," continued he, stopping short, and gazing full in my face, "I did not before remark how very ill you appear; so thin and pale; you look as if you had been watching for several nights."

' "You have guessed right; I have lately been so deeply engaged in one occupation, that I have not allowed myself sufficient rest, as you see: but I hope, I sincerely hope, that all these employments are now at an end, and that I am at length free."

'I trembled excessively; I could not endure to think of, and far less to allude to the occurrences of the preceding night. I walked with a quick pace, and we soon arrived at my college. I then reflected, and the thought made me shiver, that the creature whom I had left in my apartment might still be there, alive, and walking about. I dreaded to behold this monster; but I feared still more that Henry should see him. Entreating him therefore to remain a few minutes at the bottom of the stairs, I darted up towards my own room. My hand was already on the lock of the door before

I recollected myself. I then paused; and a cold shivering came over me. I threw the door forcibly open, as children are accustomed to do when they expect a spectre to stand in waiting for them on the other side; but nothing appeared. I stepped fearfully in: the apartment was empty; and my bedroom was also freed from its hideous guest. I could hardly believe that so great a good-fortune could have befallen me; but when I became assured that my enemy had indeed fled, I clapped my hands for joy, and ran down to Clerval.

'We ascended into my room, and the servant presently brought breakfast; but I was unable to contain myself. It was not joy only that possessed me; I felt my flesh tingle with excess of sensitiveness, and my pulse beat rapidly. I was unable to remain for a single instant in the same place; I jumped over the chairs, clapped my hands, and laughed aloud. Clerval at first attributed my unusual spirits to joy on his arrival; but when he observed me more attentively, he saw a wildness in my eyes for which he could not account; and my loud, unrestrained, heartless laughter, frightened and astonished him.

' "My dear Victor," cried he, "what, for God's sake, is the matter? Do not laugh in that manner. How ill you are! What is the cause of all this?"

' "Do not ask me," cried I, putting my hands before my eyes, for I thought I saw the dreaded spectre glide into the room; "*he* can tell.— Oh, save me! save me!" I imagined that the monster seized me; I struggled furiously, and fell down in a fit.

'Poor Clerval! what must have been his feelings? A meeting, which he anticipated with such joy, so strangely turned to bitterness. But I was not the witness of his grief; for I was lifeless, and did not recover my senses for a long, long time.

'This was the commencement of a nervous fever, which confined me for several months. During all that time Henry was my only nurse. I afterwards learned that, knowing my father's advanced age, and unfitness for so long a journey, and how wretched my sickness would make Elizabeth, he spared them this grief by concealing the extent of my disorder. He knew that I could not have a more kind and attentive nurse than himself; and, firm in the hope he felt of my recovery, he did not doubt that, instead of doing harm, he performed the kindest action that he could towards them.

'But I was in reality very ill; and surely nothing but the unbounded and unremitting attentions of my friend could have restored me to life. The form of the monster on whom I had bestowed existence was for ever before my eyes, and I raved incessantly concerning him. Doubtless my words surprised Henry: he at first believed them to be the wanderings of my disturbed imagination; but the pertinacity with which I continually recurred to the same subject persuaded him that my disorder indeed owed its origin to some uncommon and terrible event.

'By very slow degrees, and with frequent relapses, that alarmed and grieved my friend, I recovered. I remember the first time I became capable of observing outward objects with any kind of pleasure, I perceived that the fallen leaves had disappeared, and that the young buds were shooting forth from the trees that shaded my window. It was a divine spring; and the season contributed greatly to my convalescence. I felt also sentiments of joy and affection revive in my bosom; my gloom disappeared, and in a short time I became as cheerful as before I was attacked by the fatal passion.

' "Dearest Clerval," exclaimed I, "how kind, how very good you are to me. This whole winter, instead of being spent in study, as you promised yourself, has been consumed in my sick room. How shall I ever repay you? I feel the greatest remorse for the disappointment of which I have been the occasion; but you will forgive me."

' "You will repay me entirely, if you do not discompose yourself, but get well as fast as you can; and since you appear in such good spirits, I may speak to you on one subject, may I not?"

'I trembled. One subject! what could it be? Could he allude to an object on whom I dared not even think?

' "Compose yourself," said Clerval, who observed my change of colour, "I will not mention it, if it agitates you; but your father and cousin would be very happy if they received a letter from you in your own hand-writing. They hardly know how ill you have been, and are uneasy at your long silence."

' "Is that all? my dear Henry. How could you suppose that my first thought would not fly towards those dear, dear friends whom I love, and who are so deserving of my love."

' "If this is your present temper, my friend, you will perhaps be glad to see a letter that has been lying here some days for you: it is from your cousin, I believe."

When I awoke the next morning, I found myself wearing yesternight's clothes. Yesternight's clothing, my hair, and myside of the bed were drenched as if I had in reality been in that deluge at the ruined tower of Castle Frankenstein. My rational mind struggled to dismiss the sogginess as night sweats... of a Biblical magnitude.

Chapter Eight
The Prisoner of Chillon[81]

P.B. Shelley Writing a Letter to Thomas Love Peacock

Montalègre, near Colgoni,
July 12

It is nearly a fortnight since I have returned from Vevai. This journey has been on every account delightful, but most especially, because then I first knew the divine beauty of Rousseau's imagination, as it exhibits itself in Julie. It is inconceivable what an enchantment the scene itself lends to those delineations, from which its own most touching charm arises. But I will give you an abstract of our voyage, which lasted eight days, and if you have a map of Switzerland, you can follow me.

G.G.B., M., C., and I[82] left Montalègre at half past two on the 23d of June. J. disappeared for the first of twice this summer. Perhaps with Countess P. or Princess Something. No one knows; no one cares. The care we did have was the sullenly wet, ungenial summer gave such a strange birth to a suddenly pleasant, genial week; one in which us four all escaped our prison at the Villa Diodati. The lake was calm, and after three hours of rowing we arrived at Hermance, a beautiful little village, containing a ruined tower, built, the villagers say, by Julius Cæsar. There were three other towers similar to it, which the Genevese destroyed for their own fortifications in 1560. We got into the tower by a kind of window. The walls are immensely solid, and the stone of which it is built so hard, that it yet retained the mark of chisels. The boatmen said, that this tower was once three times higher than it is now. There are two staircases in the thickness of the walls, one of which is entirely demolished, and the other half ruined, and only accessible by a ladder. The town itself, now an inconsiderable village inhabited by a few fishermen, was built by a Queen of Burgundy, and reduced to its present state by the inhabitants of Berne, who burnt and ravaged every thing they could find.

Leaving Hermance, we arrived at sunset at the village of Nerni. After looking at our lodgings, which were gloomy and dirty, we walked out by the side of the lake. It was beautiful to see the vast expanse of these purple and misty waters broken by the craggy islets near to its slant and "beached margin." There were many fish sporting in the lake, and multi-

---

81 From *Prisoner of Chillon, and Other Poems* by Lord Byron, published by John Murray, 1816
82 George Gordin Byron, Lord; Mary Wollstonecraft Godwin; Claire Clairmont

tudes were collected close to the rocks to catch the flies which inhabited them.

On returning to the village, we sat on a wall beside the lake, looking at some children who were playing at a game like ninepins. The children here appeared in an extraordinary way deformed and diseased. Most of them were crooked, and with enlarged throats; but one little boy had such exquisite grace in his mien and motions, as I never before saw equalled in a child. His countenance was beautiful for the expression with which it overflowed. There was a mixture of pride and gentleness in his eyes and lips, the indications of sensibility, which his education will probably pervert to misery or seduce to crime; but there was more of gentleness than of pride, and it seemed that the pride was tamed from its original wildness by the habitual exercise of milder feelings. My companion gave him a piece of money, which he took without speaking, with a sweet smile of easy thankfulness, and then with an unembarrassed air turned to his play. All this might scarcely be; but the imagination surely could not forbear to breathe into the most inanimate forms some likeness of its own visions, on such a serene and glowing evening, in this remote and romantic village, beside the calm lake that bore us hither.

On returning to our inn, we found that the servant had arranged our rooms, and deprived them of the greater portion of their former disconsolate appearance. They reminded my companion of Greece: it was five years, he said, since he had slept in such beds. The influence of the recollections excited by this circumstance on our conversation gradually faded, and I retired to rest with no unpleasant sensations, thinking of our journey tomorrow, and of the pleasure of recounting the little adventures of it when we return.

The next morning we passed Yvoire, a scattered village with an ancient castle, whose houses are interspersed with trees, and which stands at a little distance from Nerni, on the promontory which bounds a deep bay, some miles in extent. So soon as we arrived at this promontory, the lake began to assume an aspect of wilder magnificence. The mountains of Savoy, whose summits were bright with snow, descended in broken slopes to the lake: on high, the rocks were dark with pine forests, which become deeper and more immense, until the ice and snow mingle with the points of naked rock that pierce the blue air; but below, groves of walnut, chesnut, and oak, with openings of lawny fields, attested the milder climate.

As soon as we had passed the opposite promontory, we saw the river Drance, which descends from between a chasm in the mountains, and makes a plain near the lake, intersected by its divided streams. Thousands of besolets, beautiful water-birds, like sea-gulls, but smaller, with purple on their backs, take their station on the shallows, where its waters mingle with the lake. As we approached Evian, the mountains descended more precipitously to the lake, and masses of intermingled wood and rock overhung its shining spire.

We arrived at this town about seven o'clock, after a day which involved more rapid changes of atmosphere than I ever recollect to have observed before. The morning was cold and wet; then an easterly wind, and the clouds hard and high; then thunder showers, and wind shifting to every quarter; then a warm blast from the south, and summer clouds hanging over the peaks, with bright blue sky between. About half an hour after we had arrived at Evian, a few flashes of lightning came from a dark cloud, directly over head, and continued after the cloud had dispersed. *'Diespiter, per pura tonantes egit equos:'* a phenomenon which certainly had no influence on me, corresponding with that which it produced on Horace.

The appearance of the inhabitants of Evian is more wretched, diseased and poor, than I ever recollect to have seen. The contrast indeed between the subjects of the King of Sardinia and the citizens of the independent republics of Switzerland, affords a powerful illustration of the blighting mischiefs of despotism, within the space of a few miles. They have mineral waters here, eaux savonneuses, they call them. In the evening we had some difficulty about our passports, but so soon as the syndic heard my companion's rank and name, he apologized for the circumstance. The inn was good. During our voyage, on the distant height of a hill, covered with pine-forests, we saw a ruined castle, which reminded me of those on the Rhine.

We left Evian on the following morning, with a wind of such violence as to permit but one sail to be carried. The waves also were exceedingly high, and our boat so heavily laden, that there appeared to be some danger. We arrived however safe at Mellerie, after passing with great speed mighty forests which overhung the lake, and lawns of exquisite verdure, and mountains with bare and icy points, which rose immediately from the summit of the rocks, whose bases were echoing to the waves.

We here heard that the Empress Maria Louisa had slept at Mellerie, before the present inn was built, and when the accommodations were those of the most wretched village, in remembrance of St. Preux. How beautiful it is to find that the common sentiments of human nature can attach themselves to those who are the most removed from its duties and its enjoyments, when Genius pleads for their admission at the gate of Power. To own them was becoming in the Empress, and confirms the affectionate praise contained in the regret of a great and enlightened nation. A Bourbon dared not even to have remembered Rousseau. She owed this power to that democracy which her husband's dynasty outraged, and of which it was however in some sort the representative among the nations of the earth. This little incident shews at once how unfit and how impossible it is for the ancient system of opinions, or for any power built upon a conspiracy to revive them, permanently to subsist among mankind. We dined there, and had some honey, the best I have ever tasted, the very essence of the mountain flowers, and as fragrant. Probably the village derives its name from this production. Mellerie is the well known scene of St. Preux's visionary exile; but Mellerie is indeed inchanted ground, were Rousseau no magician. Groves of pine, chesnut, and walnut overshadow it; magnificent and unbounded forests to which England affords no parallel. In the midst of these woods are dells of lawny expanse, inconceivably verdant, adorned with a thousand of the rarest flowers and odorous with thyme.

The lake appeared somewhat calmer as we left Mellerie, sailing close to the banks, whose magnificence augmented with the turn of every promontory. But we congratulated ourselves too soon: the wind gradually increased in violence, until it blew tremendously; and as it came from the remotest extremity of the lake, produced waves of a frightful height, and covered the whole surface with a chaos of foam. One of our boatmen, who was a dreadfully stupid fellow, persisted in holding the sail at a time when the boat was on the point of being driven under water by the hurricane. On discovering his error, he let it entirely go, and the boat for a moment refused to obey the helm; in addition, the rudder was so broken as to render the management of it very difficult; one wave fell in, and then another. My companion, an excellent swimmer, took off his coat, I did the same, and we sat with our arms crossed, every instant expecting to be swamped. The sail was however again held, the boat obeyed the helm, and still in imminent peril from the immensity of the waves, we arrived in a few minutes at a sheltered port, in the village of St. Gingoux.

I felt in this near prospect of death a mixture of sensations, among which terror entered, though but subordinately. My feelings would have been less painful had I been alone; but I know that my companion would have attempted to save me, and I was overcome with humiliation, when I thought that his life might have been risked to preserve mine. When we arrived at St. Gingoux, the inhabitants, who stood on the shore, unaccustomed to see a vessel as frail as ours, and fearing to venture at all on such a sea, exchanged looks of wonder and congratulation with our boatmen, who, as well as ourselves, were well pleased to set foot on shore.

St. Gingoux is even more beautiful than Mellerie; the mountains are higher, and their loftiest points of elevation descend more abruptly to the lake. On high, the aerial summits still cherish great depths of snow in their ravines, and in the paths of their unseen torrents. One of the highest of these is called Roche de St. Julien, beneath whose pinnacles the forests become deeper and more extensive; the chesnut gives a peculiarity to the scene, which is most beautiful, and will make a picture in my memory, distinct from all other mountain scenes which I have ever before visited.

As we arrived here early, we took a voiture to visit the mouth of the Rhone. We went between the mountains and the lake, under groves of mighty chesnut trees, beside perpetual streams, which are nourished by the snows above, and form stalactites on the rocks, over which they fall. We saw an immense chesnut tree, which had been overthrown by the hurricane of the morning. The place where the Rhone joins the lake was marked by a line of tremendous breakers; the river is as rapid as when it leaves the lake, but is muddy and dark. We went about a league farther on the road to La Valais, and stopped at a castle called La Tour de Bouverie, which seems to be the frontier of Switzerland and Savoy, as we were asked for our passports, on the supposition of our proceeding to Italy.

On one side of the road was the immense Roche de St. Julien, which overhung it; through the gateway of the castle we saw the snowy mountains of La Valais, clothed in clouds, and on the other side was the willowy plain of the Rhone, in a character of striking contrast with the rest of the scene, bounded by the dark mountains that overhang Clarens, Vevai, and the lake that rolls between. In the midst of the plain rises a little isolated hill, on which the white spire of a church peeps from among the tufted chesnut woods. We returned to St. Gingoux before sunset, and I passed the evening in reading Julie.

As my companion rises late, I had time before breakfast, on the ensuing morning, to hunt the waterfalls of the river that fall into the lake at St. Gingoux. The stream is indeed, from the declivity over which it falls, only a succession of waterfalls, which roar over the rocks with a perpetual sound, and suspend their unceasing spray on the leaves and flowers that overhang and adorn its savage banks. The path that conducted along this river sometimes avoided the precipices of its shores, by leading through meadows; sometimes threaded the base of the perpendicular and caverned rocks. I gathered in these meadows a nosegay of such flowers as I never saw in England, and which I thought more beautiful for that rarity.

On my return, after breakfast, we sailed for Clarens, determining first to see the three mouths of the Rhone, and then the castle of Chillon; the day was fine, and the water calm. We passed from the blue waters of the lake over the stream of the Rhone, which is rapid even at a great distance from its confluence with the lake; the turbid waters mixed with those of the lake, but mixed with them unwillingly. I read Julie all day; an overflowing, as it now seems, surrounded by the scenes which it has so wonderfully peopled, of sublimest genius, and more than human sensibility. Mellerie, the Castle of Chillon, Clarens, the mountains of La Valais and Savoy, present themselves to the imagination as monuments of things that were once familiar, and of beings that were once dear to it. They were created indeed by one mind, but a mind so powerfully bright as to cast a shade of falsehood on the records that are called reality.

We passed on to the Castle of Chillon, and visited its dungeons and towers. These prisons are excavated below the lake; the principal dungeon is supported by seven columns, whose branching capitals support the roof. Close to the very walls, the lake is 800 feet deep; iron rings are fastened to these columns, and on them were engraven a multitude of names, partly those of visitors, and partly doubtless of the prisoners, of whom now no memory remains, and who thus beguiled a solitude which they have long ceased to feel. One date was as ancient as 1670. At the commencement of the Reformation, and indeed long after that period, this dungeon was the receptacle of those who shook, or who denied the system of idolatry, from the effects of which mankind is even now slowly emerging.

Close to this long and lofty dungeon was a narrow cell, and beyond it one larger and far more lofty and dark, supported upon two unornamented arches. Across one of these arches was a beam, now black and rotten, on which prisoners were hung in secret. I never saw a monument more terrible of that cold and inhuman tyranny, which it has been the delight of man to exercise over man. It was indeed one of those many tremendous fulfilments which render the *"pernicies humani generis"* of the great Tacitus, so solemn and irrefragable a prophecy. The gendarme, who conducted us over this castle, told us that there was an opening to the lake, by means of a secret spring, connected with which the whole dungeon might be filled with water before the prisoners could possibly escape![83]

But what was the story of their most famous prisoner? The gendarme, a little old man, his eyes wise, his hair wild, his back hunched, served as the custodian of the castle and its guide. He launched into his spiel as soon as we dropped coins into his outstretched, withered hand, which snapped shut like a steal-trap. His tour had grown a little long in the tooth for me, as I wished to continue our tour of the lake, but G.G.B. was enthused by the old man's stories of the castle, of whom I was only barely amused. The gendarme waxed historical and philosophical on the Prisoner of Chillon. Afterwords, when the words and

---

83 From the *History of a Six Weeks Tour Through a Part of France, Germany, Switzerland, and Holland* by Mary Shelley, published by T. Hookham, Jun. Old Bond Street, and C. and J. Ollier, Welback Street, 1817

the words and – oh God!– the words were uttered, we ascended from the dungeon having had this story bludgeoned into our skulls like a war-mallet. My brains oozed from my ears from the pummelling of such verbosity. But my companion on the other hand seemed moved by this news. So enthused was he that was already writing a new poem in his head:

> *Eternal Spirit of the chainless Mind!*
> *Brightest in dungeons, Liberty! thou art:*
> *For there thy habitation is the heart—*
> *The heart which love of thee alone can bind;*
> *And when thy sons to fetters are consigned—*
> *To fetters, and the damp vault's dayless gloom,*
> *Their country conquers with their martyrdom,*
> *And Freedom's fame finds wings on every wind.*
> *Chillon! thy prison is a holy place,*
> *And thy sad floor an altar— for 'twas trod,*
> *Until his very steps have left a trace*
> *Worn, as if thy cold pavement were a sod,*
> *By Bonnivard!— May none those marks efface!*
> *For they appeal from tyranny to God.*

We proceeded with a contrary wind to Clarens, against a heavy swell. I never felt more strongly than on landing at Clarens, that the spirit of old times had deserted its once cherished habitation. A thousand times, thought I, have Julia and St. Preux walked on this terraced road, looking towards these mountains which I now behold; nay, treading on the ground where I now tread. From the window of our lodging our landlady pointed out "le bosquet de Julie." At least the inhabitants of this village are impressed with an idea, that the persons of that romance had actual existence. In the evening we walked thither. It is indeed Julia's wood. The hay was making under the trees; the trees themselves were aged, but vigorous, and interspersed with younger ones, which are destined to be their successors, and in future years, when we are dead, to afford a shade to future worshippers of nature, who love the memory of that tenderness and peace of which this was the imaginary abode. We walked forward among the vineyards, whose narrow terraces overlook this affecting scene. Why did the cold maxims of the world compel me at this moment to repress the tears of melancholy transport which it would have been so sweet to indulge, immeasurably, even until the darkness of night had swallowed up the objects which excited them?

I forgot to remark, what indeed my companion remarked to me, that our danger from the storm took place precisely in the spot where Julie and her lover were nearly overset, and where St. Preux was tempted to plunge with her into the lake.

On the following day we went to see the castle of Clarens, a square strong house, with very few windows, surrounded by a double terrace that overlooks the valley, or rather the plain of Clarens. The road which conducted to it wound up the steep ascent through woods of walnut and chesnut. We gathered roses on the terrace, in the feeling that they might be the posterity of some planted by Julia's hand. We sent their dead and withered leaves to the absent.

We went again to "the bosquet de Julie," and found that the precise spot was now utterly obliterated, and a heap of stones marked the place where the little chapel had once stood. Whilst we were execrating the author of this brutal folly, our guide informed us that the land belonged to the convent of St. Bernard, and that this outrage had been committed by their orders. I knew before, that if avarice could harden the hearts of men, a system of prescriptive religion has an influence far more inimical to natural sensibility. I know that an isolated man is sometimes restrained by shame from outraging the venerable feelings arising out of the memory of genius, which once made nature even lovelier than itself; but associated man holds it as the very sacrament of his union to forswear all delicacy, all benevolence, all remorse, all that is true, or tender, or sublime.

We sailed from Clarens to Vevai. Vevai is a town more beautiful in its simplicity than any I have ever seen. Its market-place, a spacious square interspersed with trees, looks directly upon the mountains of Savoy and La Valais, the lake, and the valley of the Rhone. It was at Vevai that Rousseau conceived the design of Julie.

From Vevai we came to Ouchy, a village near Lausanne. The coasts of the Pays de Vaud, though full of villages and vineyards, present an aspect of tranquillity and peculiar beauty which well compensates for the solitude which I am accustomed to admire. The hills are very high and rocky, crowned and interspersed with woods. Water-falls echo from the cliffs, and shine afar. In one place we saw the traces of two rocks of immense size, which had fallen from the mountain behind. One of these lodged in a room where a young woman was sleeping, without injuring her. The vineyards were utterly destroyed in its path, and the earth torn up.

The rain detained us two days at Ouchy. We however visited Lausanne, and saw Gibbon's house. We were shewn the decayed summer-house where he finished his History, and the old acacias on the terrace, from which he saw Mont Blanc, after having written the last sentence. There is something grand and even touching in the regret which he expresses at the completion of his task. It was conceived amid the ruins of the Capitol. The sudden departure of his cherished and accustomed toil must have left him, like the death of a dear friend, sad and solitary.

My companion gathered some acacia leaves to preserve in remembrance of him. I refrained from doing so, fearing to outrage the greater and more sacred name of Rousseau; the contemplation of whose imperishable creations had left no vacancy in my heart for mortal things. Gibbon had a cold and unimpassioned spirit. I never felt more inclination to rail at the prejudices which cling to such a thing, than now that Julie and Clarens, Lausanne and the Roman Empire, compelled me to a contrast between Rousseau and Gibbon.

When we returned, in the only interval of sunshine during the day, I walked on the pier which the lake was lashing with its waves. A rainbow spanned the lake, or rather rested one extremity of its arch upon the water, and the other at the foot of the mountains of Savoy. Some white houses, I know not if they were those of Mellerie, shone through the yellow fire.

On Saturday the 30th of June we quitted Ouchy, and after two days of pleasant sailing arrived on Sunday evening at Montalègre.[84]

Mary Wollstonecraft Godwin's Journal

2 July. Lake Geneva— Lord Byron presents 'The Prisoner of Chillon' to the group.

> *My hair is grey, but not with years,*
> *Nor grew it white*
> *In a single night,*
> *As men's have grown from sudden fears:*
> *My limbs are bowed, though not with toil,*
> *But rusted with a vile repose,*
> *For they have been a dungeon's spoil,*
> *And mine has been the fate of those*
> *To whom the goodly earth and air*
> *Are banned,* and barred—forbidden *fare;*
> *But this was for my father's faith*
> *I suffered chains and courted death*
> *That father perished at the stake*
> *For tenets he would not forsake;*

84 From the *History of a Six Weeks Tour Through a Part of France, Germany, Switzerland, and Holland* by Mary Shelley, published by T. Hookham, Jun. Old Bond Street, and C. and J. Ollier, Welback Street, 1817

And for the same his lineal race
In darkness found a dwelling place;
We were seven—who now are one,
Six in youth, and one in age,
Finished as they had begun,
Proud of Persecution's rage;
One in fire, and two in field,
Their belief with blood have sealed,
Dying as their father died,
For the God their foes denied;—
Three were in a dungeon cast,
Of whom this wreck is left the last.

II.

There are seven pillars of Gothic mould,
In Chillon's dungeons deep and old,
There are seven columns, massy and grey,
Dim with a dull imprisoned ray,
A sunbeam which hath lost its way,
And through the crevice and the cleft
Of the thick wall is fallen and left;
Creeping o'er the floor so damp,
Like a marsh's meteor lamp:
And in each pillar there is a ring,
And in each ring there is a chain;
That iron is a cankering thing,
For in these limbs its teeth remain,
With marks that will not wear away,
Till I have done with this new day,
Which now is painful to these eyes,
Which have not seen the sun so rise
For years—I cannot count them o'er,
I lost their long and heavy score
When my last brother drooped and died,
And I lay living by his side.

III.

They chained us each to a column stone,
And we were three—yet, each alone;
We could not move a single pace,
We could not see each other's face,
But with that pale and livid light

That made us strangers in our sight:
And thus together—yet apart,
Fettered in hand, but joined in heart,
'Twas still some solace in the dearth
Of the pure elements of earth,
To hearken to each other's speech,
And each turn comforter to each
With some new hope, or legend old,
Or song heroically bold;
But even these at length grew cold.
Our voices took a dreary tone,
An echo of the dungeon stone,
A grating sound, not full and free,
As they of yore were wont to be:
It might be fancy—but to me
They never sounded like our own.

IV.

I was the eldest of the three,
And to uphold and cheer the rest
I ought to do—and did my best—
And each did well in his degree.
The youngest, whom my father loved,
Because our mother's brow was given
To him, with eyes as blue as heaven—
For him my soul was sorely moved:
And truly might it be distressed
To see such bird in such a nest;
For he was beautiful as day—
(When day was beautiful to me
As to young eagles, being free)—
A polar day, which will not see
A sunset till its summer's gone,
Its sleepless summer of long light,
The snow-clad offspring of the sun:
And thus he was as pure and bright,
And in his natural spirit gay,
With tears for nought but others' ills,
And then they flowed like mountain rills,
Unless he could assuage the woe
Which he abhorred to view below.

V.

The other was as pure of mind,
But formed to combat with his kind;
Strong in his frame, and of a mood
Which 'gainst the world in war had stood,
And perished in the foremost rank
With joy:—but not in chains to pine:
His spirit withered with their clank,
I saw it silently decline—
And so perchance in sooth did mine:
But yet I forced it on to cheer
Those relics of a home so dear.
He was a hunter of the hills,
Had followed there the deer and wolf;
To him this dungeon was a gulf,
And fettered feet the worst of ills.

VI.

Lake Leman lies by Chillon's walls:
A thousand feet in depth below
Its massy waters meet and flow;
Thus much the fathom-line was sent
From Chillon's snow-white battlement,
Which round about the wave inthralls:
A double dungeon wall and wave
Have made—and like a living grave.
Below the surface of the lake
The dark vault lies wherein we lay:
We heard it ripple night and day;
Sounding o'er our heads it knocked;
And I have felt the winter's spray
Wash through the bars when winds were high
And wanton in the happy sky;
And then the very rock hath rocked,
And I have felt it shake, unshocked,
Because I could have smiled to see
The death that would have set me free.

VII.

I said my nearer brother pined,
I said his mighty heart declined,
He loathed and put away his food;

It was not that 'twas coarse and rude,
For we were used to hunter's fare,
And for the like had little care:
The milk drawn from the mountain goat
Was changed for water from the moat,
Our bread was such as captives' tears
Have moistened many a thousand years,
Since man first pent his fellow men
Like brutes within an iron den;
But what were these to us or him?
These wasted not his heart or limb;
My brother's soul was of that mould
Which in a palace had grown cold,
Had his free breathing been denied
The range of the steep mountain's side;
But why delay the truth?—he died.
I saw, and could not hold his head,
Nor reach his dying hand—nor dead,—
Though hard I strove, but strove in vain,
To rend and gnash my bonds in twain.
He died—and they unlocked his chain,
And scooped for him a shallow grave
Even from the cold earth of our cave.
I begged them, as a boon, to lay
His corse in dust whereon the day
Might shine—it was a foolish thought,
But then within my brain it wrought,
That even in death his freeborn breast
In such a dungeon could not rest.
I might have spared my idle prayer—
They coldly laughed—and laid him there:
The flat and turfless earth above
The being we so much did love;
His empty chain above it leant,
Such Murder's fitting monument!

VIII.

But he, the favourite and the flower,
Most cherished since his natal hour,
His mother's image in fair face,
The infant love of all his race,
His martyred father's dearest thought,

My latest care, for whom I sought
To hoard my life, that his might be
Less wretched now, and one day free;
He, too, who yet had held untired
A spirit natural or inspired—
He, too, was struck, and day by day
Was withered on the stalk away.
Oh, God! it is a fearful thing
To see the human soul take wing
In any shape, in any mood:
I've seen it rushing forth in blood,
I've seen it on the breaking ocean
Strive with a swoln convulsive motion,
I've seen the sick and ghastly bed
Of Sin delirious with its dread:
But these were horrors—this was woe
Unmixed with such—but sure and slow:
He faded, and so calm and meek,
So softly worn, so sweetly weak,
So tearless, yet so tender—kind,
And grieved for those he left behind;
With all the while a cheek whose bloom
Was as a mockery of the tomb,
Whose tints as gently sunk away
As a departing rainbow's ray;
An eye of most transparent light,
That almost made the dungeon bright;
And not a word of murmur—not
A groan o'er his untimely lot,—
A little talk of better days,
A little hope my own to raise,
For I was sunk in silence—lost
In this last loss, of all the most;
And then the sighs he would suppress
Of fainting Nature's feebleness,
More slowly drawn, grew less and less:
I listened, but I could not hear;
I called, for I was wild with fear;
I knew 'twas hopeless, but my dread
Would not be thus admonished;
I called, and thought I heard a sound—
I burst my chain with one strong bound,

And rushed to him:—I found him not,
I only stirred in this black spot,
I only lived, I only drew
The accursed breath of dungeon-dew;
The last, the sole, the dearest link
Between me and the eternal brink,
Which bound me to my failing race,
Was broken in this fatal place.
One on the earth, and one beneath—
My brothers—both had ceased to breathe:
I took that hand which lay so still,
Alas! my own was full as chill;
I had not strength to stir, or strive,
But felt that I was still alive—
A frantic feeling, when we know
That what we love shall ne'er be so.
I know not why
I could not die,
I had no earthly hope—but faith,
And that forbade a selfish death.

IX.

What next befell me then and there
I know not well—I never knew—
First came the loss of light, and air,
And then of darkness too:
I had no thought, no feeling—none—
Among the stones I stood a stone,
And was, scarce conscious what I wist,
As shrubless crags within the mist;
For all was blank, and bleak, and grey;
It was not night—it was not day;
It was not even the dungeon-light,
So hateful to my heavy sight,
But vacancy absorbing space,
And fixedness—without a place;
There were no stars—no earth—no time—
No check—no change—no good—no crime—
But silence, and a stirless breath
Which neither was of life nor death;
A sea of stagnant idleness,
Blind, boundless, mute, and motionless!

X.

A light broke in upon my brain,—
It was the carol of a bird;
It ceased, and then it came again,
The sweetest song ear ever heard,
And mine was thankful till my eyes
Ran over with the glad surprise,
And they that moment could not see
I was the mate of misery;
But then by dull degrees came back
My senses to their wonted track;
I saw the dungeon walls and floor
Close slowly round me as before,
I saw the glimmer of the sun
Creeping as it before had done,
But through the crevice where it came
That bird was perched, as fond and tame,
And tamer than upon the tree;
A lovely bird, with azure wings,
And song that said a thousand things,
And seemed to say them all for me!
I never saw its like before,
I ne'er shall see its likeness more:
It seemed like me to want a mate,
But was not half so desolate,
And it was come to love me when
None lived to love me so again,
And cheering from my dungeon's brink,
Had brought me back to feel and think.
I know not if it late were free,
Or broke its cage to perch on mine,
But knowing well captivity,
Sweet bird! I could not wish for thine!
Or if it were, in wingéd guise,
A visitant from Paradise;
For—Heaven forgive that thought! the while
Which made me both to weep and smile—
I sometimes deemed that it might be
My brother's soul come down to me;
But then at last away it flew,
And then 'twas mortal well I knew,
For he would never thus have flown—

And left me twice so doubly lone,—
Lone—as the corse within its shroud,
Lone—as a solitary cloud,
A single cloud on a sunny day,
While all the rest of heaven is clear,
A frown upon the atmosphere,
That hath no business to appear
When skies are blue, and earth is gay.

XI.

A kind of change came in my fate,
My keepers grew compassionate;
I know not what had made them so,
They were inured to sights of woe,
But so it was:—my broken chain
With links unfastened did remain,
And it was liberty to stride
Along my cell from side to side,
And up and down, and then athwart,
And tread it over every part;
And round the pillars one by one,
Returning where my walk begun,
Avoiding only, as I trod,
My brothers' graves without a sod;
For if I thought with heedless tread
My step profaned their lowly bed,
My breath came gaspingly and thick,
And my crushed heart felt blind and sick.

XII.

I made a footing in the wall,
It was not therefrom to escape,
For I had buried one and all,
Who loved me in a human shape;
And the whole earth would henceforth be
A wider prison unto me:
No child—no sire—no kin had I,
No partner in my misery;
I thought of this, and I was glad,
For thought of them had made me mad;
But I was curious to ascend
To my barred windows, and to bend

Once more, upon the mountains high,
The quiet of a loving eye.

XIII.

I saw them—and they were the same,
They were not changed like me in frame;
I saw their thousand years of snow
On high—their wide long lake below,
And the blue Rhone in fullest flow;
I heard the torrents leap and gush
O'er channelled rock and broken bush;
I saw the white-walled distant town,
And whiter sails go skimming down;
And then there was a little isle,
Which in my very face did smile,
The only one in view;
A small green isle, it seemed no more,
Scarce broader than my dungeon floor,
But in it there were three tall trees,
And o'er it blew the mountain breeze,
And by it there were waters flowing,
And on it there were young flowers growing,
Of gentle breath and hue.
The fish swam by the castle wall,
And they seemed joyous each and all;
The eagle rode the rising blast,
Methought he never flew so fast
As then to me he seemed to fly;
And then new tears came in my eye,
And I felt troubled—and would fain
I had not left my recent chain;
And when I did descend again,
The darkness of my dim abode
Fell on me as a heavy load;
It was as is a new-dug grave,
Closing o'er one we sought to save,—
And yet my glance, too much opprest,
Had almost need of such a rest.

XIV.

It might be months, or years, or days—
I kept no count, I took no note—

I had no hope my eyes to raise,
And clear them of their dreary mote;
At last men came to set me free;
I asked not why, and recked not where;
It was at length the same to me,
Fettered or fetterless to be,
I learned to love despair.
And thus when they appeared at last,
And all my bonds aside were cast,
These heavy walls to me had grown
A hermitage—and all my own!
And half I felt as they were come
To tear me from a second home:
With spiders I had friendship made,
And watched them in their sullen trade,
Had seen the mice by moonlight play,
And why should I feel less than they?
We were all inmates of one place,
And I, the monarch of each race,
Had power to kill—yet, strange to tell!
In quiet we had learned to dwell;
My very chains and I grew friends,
So much a long communion tends
To make us what we are:—even I
Regained my freedom with a sigh.

Chapter Nine
Ernestus Berchtold;
or, The Modern Oedipus — Part Two[85]

Dr. Polidor's Letter to His Publisher' 1819

The tale here presented to the public is the one I began at Coligny, when *Frankenstein* was planned, and when a noble author having determined to descend from his lofty range, gave up a few hours to a tale of terror, and wrote the fragment published at the end of Mazeppa. Though I cannot boast of the horrible imagination of the one, or the elegant classical style of the latter, still I hope the reader will not throw mine away, because it is not equal to these. Whether the use I have made of supernatural agency, and the colouring I have given to the mind of *Ernestus Berchtold*, are original or not, I leave to the more erudite in novels and romances to declare. I am not conscious of having seen any where a prototype of either; yet I fear that whatever is original, is not always pleasing. Nor is this my only apprehension. A tale that rests upon improbabilities, must generally disgust a rational mind; I am therefore afraid that, though I have thrown the superior agency into the back ground as much as was in my power, still, that many readers will think the same moral, and the same colouring, might have been given to characters acting under the ordinary agencies of life; I believe it, but I had agreed to write a supernatural tale, and that does not allow of a completely every-day narrative.[86]

Mary Wollstonecraft Godwin's Journal

1 July. — Lord Byron's personal physician and my personal annoyance stood before the four of us in earnest with pages of his manuscript in hand. Sweat dripped from his brow as his clammy hands grip the pages with a surprisingly light touch. Torrential rain buffeted and violent lightning flashed through the high windows and apocalyptic thunder crashed in a fearsome overture preluding the doctor's

---

85 Published by John William Polidori as *Ernestus Berchtold; or, The Modern Oedipus: A Tale* in 1819, publisher unknown.'Parts one, three, and four are included in the appendix located by the end of this book. I feel part two is the most self-contained section to include in the main text. I feel it would too greatly detract from the 'Playing a Game of Ghost Stories' to include the entire novella-length work here.' – R.D.B.
86 From the Introduction to *Ernestus Berchtold; or, The Modern Oedipus: A Tale*.

ghost story. Winds whipped across the panes of glass, rattling not only the panes but also the doctor's nerves. Poor Polidori, his hands trembled first with tremors, then with shakes, and finally and fatefully with quakes. The pages of his manuscript fell from his quivering hands just as a tree branch breaks through a pane in the window. Shards and slivers of glass rained onto the stone tiles. The storm twirled into a whirlwind that scattered the pages of poor Polidori's contribution to Lord Byron's game. Suddenly and sullenly panicked, John dropped to his knees, quite in distress, to collect the pages. Many were lost under chairs and tables and the piano, some slid under the door into the hallway beyond. An unknown number burnt to cinder having being blown into the hearth. Poor Polidori lunged towards the hearth and plunged his hands into the flames hoping beyond all hope to rescue the burning pages before they curl into ash. The doctor saw and seized a fateful stack that appeared the most intact. Were the pages collected into his still shaking and quaking hands the beginning of his tale or the end or somewhere in the middle? I'm afraid the poor Polidori didn't even know.

I cast a glance at Lord Byron perchance he was thinking of heckling poor Polidori, but the expression of the Lord's face gave me the impression that no such improper commentary would issue force from his lips. I was thankful for this small mercy afforded to poor Polidori by Lord Byron. One night, after being engaged in marital sport, as we lay in bed, I admonished my Beloved not to make a scene when it came to Dr Polidori's reading of his 'feverishly' written work (not my words, but John's). I, myself, possessed no desire in my heart to fluster the Doctor during the recitation of his story. I could see his heart fluttering in his throat, his temples damp, and his throat parched. He sipped on a glass of wine sitting on the table nearest the hearth. Wine slapped over the rim of the glass, so violent were his shaking— nay! quaking— Then in earnest, Dr Polidori began reading from *Ernestus Berchtold*, his contribution to Lord Byron's game of ghost stories:

'You have visited our alpine scenes and have undoubtedly been witness to the approach of one of those dreadful visitations of angry nature, which sometimes occur in the pent-up valleys.' By the pained expression on poor Polidori's face, this place in his story did not mark the beginning. Was its placement somewhere in the middle or was this at the end? I'm afraid only the doctor could answer the question. But he soldiered on. 'The black speck gathers upon the mountain's brow; amidst the silence and dead stillness of the air, it seems as if all were resting, in hopes of gaining strength to resist the desolating fury of the powers let loose against them. Only the lowing of the cattle, which, with its hollow lengthened sound, seems to give unheeded notice of the dread storm's approach, echoes upon the air, awed by the very stillness. Yet the sun shines brilliantly on the scene, doubled in the unrippled surface of the lake that seems proudly to bear the beauteous image, as if it were conscious how soon that smiling scene would be changed.— So passed the years, in which day succeeded day in unperceived succession, in which I lived under the same roof, partook innocently of the same joys and sorrows as Louisa. There was yet a weight upon my heart I could not explain; my dreams always terminated unhappily, and sleep, that refuge common to all misery, was to me like the waking hours of others. Immediately after our arrival, my sister was visited with a threatening appeal from our mother, who bade her depart with me once more to our native wilds, and never return. We could not understand the decrees of fate, lulled by the peace and apparent happiness around us, we were unconscious of what was in future,— we remained,— and I am what you see— a spectre amongst the living.

'Encouraged by Louisa, I again returned to my studies. All the morning engaged in the library of my benefactor, I followed them under his direction, chiefly reading the modern poets and historians, with whom I had little acquaintance. Louisa would often come, and, sitting by my side, read the same passages, and discuss the merits of a particular image, often directing my taste, and pointing out many beauties I had not before perceived, even in my favourite authors. You see those volumes; they are those we read together; they now form my whole library, but you cannot know the pleasure there is contained in a single one of those pages. I read them, and every word again sounds upon my ear, as if she spoke it. I turn round and am undeceived, Louisa is not by my side, though her voice seems speaking as when we were innocent.

'In the evening we assembled in the saloon of the palace. Doni was distinguished from his countrymen by a state of affluence, which was apparently boundless, but which was the more extraordinary in this respect, that it did not excite the envy of his neighbours. His riches indeed seemed less for his own use than for that of his friends. He was of a noble family, but being the offspring of a younger branch, he had been early inured to hardships. Disdaining the mean idle life he was obliged to lead, in subservience to the will of a proud relation, he had left Milan at an early age, and had travelled into the East. He never, however, spoke of his journey, and always seemed anxious to direct the conversation into another channel, whenever it turned upon subjects in any manner connected with it. He had returned rich, no one knew whence; but there were whisperings abroad, that he had not gained his riches by commerce; though no one could trace where his riches lay; yet as his gold was poured forth with so liberal a hand, his wealth was deemed almost infinite. He had been strikingly handsome, and was extremely intelligent; but grief had weighed down his energies, and sorrow had broken his faculties. After his return he had married. Beauty was the mere casket, the riches were within; his wife was described as having possessed a mind, that without laying aside all that appealing delicacy and weakness, which binds woman to man; had all those powers and accomplishments, which unfortunately in her sex have generally been the panders to vice; but which, with her, were the handmaids to virtue. Her presence was commanding, but her voice was persuasive; its tones struck the heart and produced those emotions, which all remember, none can express, the feeling, as if we had been always virtuous, and were worthy of listening to the voice of a being superior to ourselves. The poor followed her steps, not with their usual boisterous cry for charity, but in silence; they seemed to watch the glance of her eye, as if the sympathy which shone there, had made them even forget their ragged miseries. Louisa was her counterpart, when I heard any one describing what her mother had been, it seemed that I could read the whole upon her daughter's face, and methought I could often perceive the speaker reading on the same page. Doni had loved her; nay more, had adored her, but she had married him by the persuasion of her parents, while her heart was engaged to another far away; he had returned, they saw one another, and fled together; Doni pursued them, fired at the carriage which was escaping and blood fell upon the road;— they did not stop. Doni then entirely lost all command of himself, he fell in the road, calling for mercy and relief from that curse, which had already begun to blast him. He had never recovered the shock; had retired from all those gaieties in which he had been once engaged, and devoted himself to the education of his children. For their sake he had, however, again entered into society, but in a very different style from his former magnificence. These are the circumstances which I heard of his history, from those friends with whom I spoke in the course of the two first years of my stay at Milan; besides this, I also found the reports of his supernatural powers to be believed: and whenever I enquired concerning them, the speaker always looked round the room, before he ventured to speak, and would then only answer in whispers.

'I have mentioned our evening assembly in the saloon of the palace; thither all distinguished by rank or science came— all visitors were alike welcome. There, no ceremony, which is but the vain-pointing of selfishness to its sacrifices, incommoded those, who, invited by the society they found there, chose to take a chair in this circle. Louisa's father always held the reins of conversation in his own hands, and instead of letting it fall upon the common place subjects of fashion, he turned the minds of his company to disquisitions that gave to each an opportunity of showing his information or judgement. At times, the existence and powers of the Deity were canvassed,— at times, the reality of beings intermediate between God and man; their qualities, and the facts related concerning them, came under consideration. Other evenings heard discussions upon the nature of virtue, whether it really were definite and felt, as is beauty, in every breast, or whether it were not merely an object of policy and self-convenience. The father and son generally took opposite sides, and under one or the other, each individual of the company enlisted himself, accordingly as it happened that he were either in a humour to be pleased with the general dispensation of providence throughout the day to himself, or was smarting under what he conceived to be an undeserved infliction of the evil spirit.

'Olivieri made it a point to bewilder every one. He was a little older than myself; his head, though not perfect, had much beauty; a fine forehead, black hair, a dark, though small eye, united to a Grecian contour, formed, if not a pleasing, a striking physiognomy. I soon found that he had read much. His body also had been exercised; though not graceful, he was active, and hardly any excelled him in a certain quickness of adaptation, both of mind and body, to any thing required. His opinions were paradoxical and singular. In religion he outwardly professed Catholicism, and strongly opposed those scribbling philosophers, who by sarcasm, attempt to overturn the religion of ages, though at the same time he allowed the absurdity and falsehood of the prevailing doctrines. This did not appear to arise from a spirit of opposition, but, if the motives he gave were true, from a chain of thought that did honour to his heart, not head. He asserted that Catholicism was the only religion affording to the poor and to the sick of heart, a balm for their evils. Calvinism, deism and atheism, were by him called the professions of the northern nations, cold as their native rocks. Professions to which enthusiasm, and the feeling of a certain refuge, so heart-soothing in Catholicism, were unknown. He maintained that it was not for individuals, who had the advantage of education and imagination, to shelter them from the overwhelming force of mental miseries, and unlooked for misfortunes, to attempt under a real, though vain pretence of the love of truth, to deprive the poor and uneducated millions forming the mass of mankind, of the consolation always offered by this religion, which instead of shunning the poor, gladly seeks their miserable hovel, in the hope of administering present comfort and future hope. Indeed he was inconsistent in his principles. He had not mingled much in general life, but while at Padua, where he had been sent to study, he had sought the acquaintance of all. From the knowledge of man he had there acquired, whether it were that he had constantly met with mean and weak companions, or that conscious of his own bad qualities, he had thence estimated the value of man's professions, he always seemed to view the human character in a darker hue than was warranted by truth, and to have formed his mind into a general contempt for mankind as a mass, and a determination, if ever an occasion offered, of rising at their expence, considering them but as tools to work with. His manners were at first always engaging, and rather pleasing, but this seemed irksome to him, and he gave way to an imperious, assuming air in conversation, which soon disgusted his friends. His ideas of a life after death seemed strangely childish, he did not believe in an immortality, yet he had so strong a love of fame, that there was no reputation he did not covet. He sometimes formed visions of a throne raised upon the blood of his countrymen spilt in civil war; at times, of the fame of a benefactor to debtors and galley slaves. He sought at the same time for the applause of the philosophers and the drunkard, the divine, and the libertine. Things, of which, even at the moment of action he was ashamed, were often done by him in the view of proving himself capable of excelling even in vice. It was hard to say, whether he owed a certain frankness and easiness of attachment, to his weakness, or to seeds sown in his breast by nature. But whether it were from his incapability of constantly acting up to his system, or to the overpowering force of nature, it was strange to hear him express himself a follower of a doctrine that has proved the leech of human blood, and at the same time refuse to tread upon a worm. The evil was, his riches induced the young to pander for him, the old to flatter him, on account of his specious talents and handsome appearance. He was a student, a gambler, and a libertine.

This man became my companion, his father often pointed me out to him, as the model for his conduct, and when he had to reproach him for the losses at the Ridotto, or when Olivieri sought an excuse in the plea of youth, for the ruin his libertinism had brought on many families, he would speak of me as an example of strength, resisting all the temptations of vice. I was a reed when the storm came, Olivieri had watched me at the meetings in the saloon, I was generally a mere listener, but my curiosity was alive, though silent; my mind had an insatiable thirst for knowledge. I was a catholic, Berchtold had educated me in doctrines, without teaching me the foundation upon which they were built; he thought it impiety to question them. The conversation to which I was now present, seemed to rest upon the entire conviction, that all I believed was false. Yet this was not satisfactory. I heard arguments adduced in support of one assertion which seemed irresistible; but what was my surprise, on another evening to hear the same person adduce more than plausibilities in favour of the contrary hypothesis. I at last was bewildered, I was unwilling to believe the human mind incapable of truth, the more I examined, the more difficulty I found in the attainment of it. I heard the deist and the atheist contend; following but one of the chains of argument, I was convinced; looking at them together, I saw the lustre of truth equally on both; I knew not which to choose. I was a sceptic in fact, not in name. Night after night upon my sleepless couch, I called upon the God, whose existence I doubted, to visit me, as if God heeded the belief of an individual, as if the happiness of an infinite being like him depended on a man's faith in his existence. Olivieri perceived the state of my mind, I asked his assistance, he laughed at my attempt at knowledge, and bewildered me still more; I was restless, and seemed at length to be deprived of all motive for action. No superior being to smile upon our efforts, to whom we may show our gratitude, and whose approbation we may obtain; no virtue, but artificial trammels set up under its name, to lure the unwary into the toils of the wittiest knave. I wished I had never left those mountains, amidst which, I had thought, I felt the breath of a superior being, though he was clothed by my imagination in terrors. Nothing above man, and that man the sport of chance, of his own caprice. Yet within my breast it seemed as if aspirings dwelt which seemed to have been born with me. Were they but a mockery? I grew melancholy, whole days confined to my room, I meditated till my brain became a wilderness of various thoughts so entangled I knew not how to extricate myself.

'My sister, fearing I was ill, would often sit by me, would bring Louisa, and they would together listen to my doubts. Julia seemed to be as much affected by them as myself, she listened with avidity, and echoed my own ideas. Not so Louisa, she talked of revelation, of a beneficent Deity, who had for a while left man in ignorance, to prove to him his own weakness, but had at last revealed himself, and announced a better state. While she spoke, she seemed like the first vision of the Wengern Alp destined again to save me, and set me free from these bewilderings, the first step towards vice. She soothed my mind, her lips quelled doubt into the peaceful certainty attendant upon Christianity. I no more paid any attention to the conversation of the evening, but set myself down by Louisa, and listened to her, while she was engaged in some work, which, though it employs the hands, leaves the mind at liberty. I sat by her, asking for some errand, some office, in doing which I might do her bidding; she was evidently gratified by my attentions, she would blush at my approach and smile; she would make room for me by her side. Oftentimes I gazed in silence upon her, and often our eyes met. Her breath at moments played upon my cheek, and sometimes her hand by accident touched mine. She would bid me read poetry to her, and often love was the subject of the poet's lay; my voice trembled, I dared not look upon her, for fear she should perceive the emotion upon my face. I loved her, but it was not a common love. I did not rest upon the hope of gaining her, she appeared a being superior to myself, of whom I was unworthy, yet it seemed, as if her smile were necessary to induce me to exert myself, and was a reward sufficient for the greatest deeds. She would sing to me, she would walk with me in the garden; but you must imagine, I cannot paint the charm, the magic, in her conversation. I have not described her person, for I could not, her mind was more heavenly than her eye, its expressions more delicately varying than the bloom on her cheek; there was meekness attendant upon power, softness upon strength.

'If she had not left me for a moment, I might have been spared much guilt; but the sickness of a near relation was a call she could not resist. I had often followed her, when masked, she attended upon the sick in the hospitals. It is an Italian custom: often have I, disguised in the covering gown of the Misericordia, stood by her, whom it was impossible not to recognize. The dying called for her, though they knew her not; they soon distinguished her powerful tones which pierced through the bond of grief around the most withered heart, and poured upon it those precious consolations afforded by her religion. Her manner, her voice, her gestures, seemed at such moments to be those of a being who was conscious of the truth of what it announced; not from the testimony of man, but from having witnessed the presence of the very Deity. The loud groan, the stifled sigh, were silenced in her presence; pain seemed to have no power; conscience no sting. She left me to visit her relation. For some days I felt lost; I knew not to whom to apply; my sister seemed always occupied; she spoke with me; but I was sorry to find she had imbibed those doctrines so easily eradicated, as I thought, from my own mind. I observed Olivieri paid her particular attention, and often conversed with her. He at last perceived how restless I was; he seized the opportunity, determined to gain an object, which I did not think him capable of attempting. During my stay at Milan, I had hardly ever been out in the evening, for, as it is not customary for unmarried females to go into society, I should have lost the pleasure of sitting by Louisa. Now I had no inducement to remain at home. Olivieri persuaded me to accompany him to the theatre of La Scala. I was induced by the splendour of the scenery, the beautiful dancers, the exquisite singing, to return. I was led into the boxes of our friends, and behind the scenes. I found my companion was every where well received. The dancers and actresses crowded around him: their conversation was lively and various. Gradually, the freedom in their discourse, which had at first disgusted me, grew indifferent; then pleasing by the wit sometimes shown even upon such subjects. One of these women, to whom Olivieri introduced me, was a mistress in her art, and well understood the artifices by which the young and unwary are misled: she was beautiful, and though her eye was never free from a certain look of confidence, the characteristic of this class, she could soften its expression, and cause it, in the presence of him she intended to inveigle, to send forth such glances as it was impossible to resist. By Olivieri's desire she attached herself to me, and I gradually took pleasure in her company; I saw her neglect the attentions of the first nobles in Milan to gain mine; in the midst of the rapturous applause of the whole theatre, she would turn her eye upon me to see if I approved; she seemed to sacrifice herself for me. When the opera was over, she would take my arm and lead me to the saloon of the theatre, where all were engaged in gambling. Sitting at a window, she drew me into conversation, gradually she approached the table; we at first stood merely as spectators; at last she tempted me to try my fortune: I consented, laid down my stake, it was soon increased to an enormous amount, for I was successful: I threw it into her lap, and we parted. For several nights I was equally fortunate; but at length I lost. I was so profusely supplied with money by the kind friend who called me son, that I did not at first heed my losses. I had given all I gained to the syren, who still urged me on: I lost every franc I had. She then supplied me; I was ashamed to take it of her, though it was what I myself had gained; but I hoped my luck would change; I lost the whole. She then began to exert her more baneful powers, she led me from folly to vice, in search of what she assured me was an antidote to memory; I joined the libertine and the desperate. I was ashamed of letting Doni know that he, whom he had pointed out as a model of virtue to his son, had sunk into the lowest debauchery. Louisa's image often—often was before me; but how dare I name her in conjunction with my vices. She had thrice been a ministering angel, guiding my steps, but then I was innocent. I dared not now rest upon the thought; and often I threw myself deeper into the sinks of vice, in hopes that such reflections would not pursue me thither.

The syren, instigated by Olivieri, led me into every excess; while he plied me again with insinuations against religion, and sneers upon my credulous conscience that pictured a future state. I was now glad to seek refuge in unbelief; and I strove to lose myself in those thoughts which I had before fled, and from which I had been saved by my protecting angel. He also excited me to gamble, lent me money himself when I had none, and gathered round me every incentive to vice. He had been mortified at his father's holding me up as a pattern of strength against temptation; he was revenged, he exposed my weakness. I had hardly resisted the first approaches of vice, and had, in a short time, sunk below the lowest frequenters of its haunts.

'One night I was desperate, every thing of value that I had was gone. Olivieri himself had been unsuccessful; and I knew not where to seek for the money I wanted to satisfy my creditors. I rushed out from the house, and found myself in the Piazza del Duomo. My brain was hot, my hair dishevelled; I rushed along, not knowing what I was about. I knew not where to apply. To destroy at once Doni's opinion of my virtue by telling him my situation, seemed worse than my present feeling. I stood still holding my head with my hand; I lifted my eyes from the ground on which they had been fixed. It was night, there was no light save from the glimmering stars and the newly risen moon, upon the dark canopy of heaven. The white façade of the Duomo raised its huge mass in contrast with the night; shining even upon its dark veil, it seemed to awe the mind by its indistinct mass, which, weighing on the earth, forced itself upon the eye when all else was lost in the shading darkness. All was still and sunk to rest; I alone seemed waking midst sleep; in anguish, midst repose. I stood, I know not why, for some time gazing upon the marble statues and forms which gained a certain charm from the moon's silvering light. The mats, spread like a curtain before the doors, being raised by the dying breeze, struck with a measured impulse the wall: unconsciously I entered. Save where the light of the moon fell upon the heavy columns, vesting them with the faint hues of the coloured glass that adorned the windows, it was all darkness that seemed sensible to the touch. I walked towards the high altar. There is a subterranean chapel dedicated to St. Borromeo, which receives its light through the flooring of the dome. The silver lamps, hung over the shrine, sent up a column of light to the very roof. I descended the stairs, and found myself within the chapel. The lamps were almost failing, and the silver walls darkened by the torch of the devotees absorbed the little light they emitted. I approached the shrine; the dried corpse of the saint, arrayed in his pontificals, seemed, by its repose, to invite me to seek peace where he possessed it. His eye, which once might also have known anguish, was now sunk in the socket, and presented but a mass of blackened mould in the corner of its former throne. I gazed upon it until I thought I saw it move; methought there was a smile upon its lips, as if it mocked my thoughts of peace. I repose with him, a benefactor to the poor, a saint! A laugh was almost playing upon my lips, when the words, half stifled with emotion, "intercede my patron, intercede for Berchtold," sounded on my ear.— I turned; a female figure, I had not observed, was kneeling near the wall in earnest prayer. I approached, "who prays for Berchtold? your prayer is mocked." Alarmed, she raised her head; it was— you know whom I would say— it was Louisa. She looked upon my face convulsed with the violence of my emotions, upon my dishevelled hair. "Is it you? Ernestus," she said, rising, "are you come to pray; heaven has then heard even me, and has not left you. Break not my heart." I could not utter more. She took my arm, we passed through the long nave; I dared not look around, methought some other form would burst upon my eyes in spite of the circling darkness, and blast me. A carriage was waiting at a little distance; she had left the gay dance to pray for me. I had handed her into her carriage, and was going; "Berchtold," she said, "will you leave me?" She wished me, the wretch, to be still near her. I jumped into the carriage, and blessed the darkness that hid my face; we spoke no more. Every one had retired at Doni's. She took my hand when leaving me, and pressing it in her's, whilst she gazed upon my face; she bade me think— she would have said more; a tear fell from her unwilling eye, and she hastily turned away.

'I returned to my room, I had not entered it for many days. Louisa knew my guilt; sleep would not refresh me, my thoughts revelled in a maddening breast. Whither could I turn for refuge from their power? Religion I had cast from me, as a foul fiend's mock; Louisa! rest upon purity, I dared not; then my native mountains rushed upon my sight, I seemed bounding along the crags, Berchtold smiled upon my innocence, I laughed aloud— innocence? it was but the want of temptation. I threw myself upon my bed, and though not asleep, I became so stupified by the very excess of pain, that even the phantoms of conscience no longer passed with distinctness before me. The night seemed to hang suspended over my head, as if in pity it would hide me from the day, so slow was its progress; morning at last returned, but with it were the same thoughts as had visited me during the night.

'It was hardly day before I heard some one at my door, I opened it, it was Doni. I turned away my head ashamed to look upon him, he did not reproach me, telling me that he knew my present way of life needed a more abundant supply of money, than he had given me, he bade me to apply to him for any sum I wanted. I could not speak, I had expected he would have attempted to show me my vices in all their native horror; he pressed his offer upon me; ashamed to tell him the whole amount of my folly, I at last named a sum not half sufficient to satisfy my creditors, but I thought it would stop the mouths of the most clamorous, and that in the mean time, by economizing my allowance, I might clear the rest. He asked me repeatedly, if it was the entire sum I owed; I answered yes; he left me, and in a few minutes returned, with gold to the amount required; "take it" he said, "it is no loss to me, but your wonted happiness I see is fled, that grieves me. Believe one who is older than yourself, Vice is not the path of happiness." I was silent. I intended immediately to pay my debts as far as I could, and at once to free myself from the life of a gambler, and a libertine.

'My sister came to see me in my room, for I was ashamed of appearing at the breakfast table. I observed that the colour in her cheeks was gone, that she no longer was the open-hearted girl I remembered; attributing this however to the effect of my own follies upon her mind, I said nothing. She remained with me some time, but I no longer felt that pleasure I had always known in her company upon former occasions. We seemed both afraid of touching upon any thing relating to ourselves, and both evidently with minds deeply occupied about other important objects, talked of the most trivial circumstances.

'When night came, I issued forth, determined to pay my debts, as far as was in my power; I entered the saloon of the theatre; there were only the banker and the punters arrived; they had arranged every thing for the faro table, and immediately they saw me, they began talking of the various successes of the last night. They told me how Olivieri had regained every thing at the very close of the evening. One or two gradually stepped in; amongst them was my friend, he was in high spirits; I took him aside, and told him that I was weary of this kind of life, and was determined to pay every one as far as I had it in my power. He would not let me finish, he laughed at my intentions, and told me, that as our good luck was now returned, it would be a folly to throw it away, that as I acknowledged myself incapable of paying the whole, it would be as well to owe a greater as a lesser sum.

'His companions soon perceived the subject of our conversation, and joined us. They all ridiculed my intention, and I was persuaded to venture once more. I at first lost, but suddenly the rouleaus poured upon me; one more stake, and I had regained even all my enormous losses; it was soon too late to retire, I almost lost all I had that morning received from Doni. It was now quite useless to think of retreating, I fell again into my former life, with more than double energy. I was at times surprised to find that great sums were paid to several of my creditors, I could not learn by whom; I imagined it was by Olivieri's father; this did not stop me. My vicissitudes were great, but I could never entirely extricate myself, so that I was always either lured by hope or urged by despair.

'I need not describe to you the progress of my other vices; debauched women, men of whom one is ashamed, and wine, are generally the attendants upon gambling. I could not seek the house of Doni, nor of virtue; I threw myself into every haunt of desperate characters like myself, and learnt to boast alike of the smile of the prostitute, or of the tear of the debauched virgin; when losing, I stupified my mind with wine, and was glad to fall from my chair, provided memory failed with my senses. Noted cheats, and men proscribed from society for their low dissoluteness, often seized upon my arm on the Corso, as if I were one of their equals, and I dared not repel their familiarity, for I was in their power. Once Louisa saw me in this situation, she never again rode out on the Corso; I had the maddened impudence to bow to her. I at last became mad, and once, was induced to aid in depriving a young novice of all his wealth, by means of false dice. I could not however stand by and see his horrible despair, he had beggared a wife and two lovely babes. I had just then been lucky, I confessed my participation to him, and gave him the whole amount of his loss; it became known, and I was laughed at; but for once I could withstand ridicule.

'At the Doni palace in the mean time, the same outward appearance was preserved; there were still the same evening assemblies, but they were less frequented, for Olivieri was almost always with me. He was apparently afraid I should escape him; he was constantly stifling all thoughts that arose in my breast, tending towards a return to virtue. He never left me but when I was deeply engaged in play or debauch; then he constantly went I knew not whither. I have since found it out, and that discovery has not been the least of those pangs my guilt has brought upon me. I entered so little into society, that I heard nothing of what was passing there. I was, however, one day standing on the Corso with Olivieri, speaking to some ladies who had drawn up their carriage close to a shop, when the conversation turning upon the number of foreigners, who were moving about in consequence of the peace which had just been concluded, a lady turning, asked me if I had seen the stranger who excited so much the curiosity of all circles. Upon my saying I had not, she began expatiating upon his singular character, rested upon his powers of fascination, and told me that all the ladies were in love with him. I did not pay much attention to this, thinking it but the foolish prattle of a young girl. She however continued; she wondered that I had not seen him, as he was a constant attendant upon Louisa, she having engrossed the whole of his attention, much to the mortification of all Milan.

'Now I was roused. I let go Olivieri's arm, and wandered about alone. I dared not hope that Louisa could resist one whom all seemed to admire. The whole weight of my guilt fell heavily upon my recollection, and one after another all my vices presented themselves, arrayed against me. I did not return that day to any of my usual haunts. Towards evening, I found myself, fatigued with wandering, at the gate of the Doni palace. I know not what inspired me, it seemed as if I wished to gain the certainty of my fate. My steps, which till now had been slow and measured, suddenly quickened. I found myself at the entrance of the saloon; all was silent; the red purple glare of sunset pierced the windows. I stood for a moment still; a sigh burst upon my ear— I entered— Louisa was sitting looking upon the setting sun. It was her sigh. She did not turn: "Is it you, my father?" I did not speak, she turned her head, her face was pale, but a blush mantled her cheek at the sight of me; her eyes were sunk and dim, but they brightened at my presence. She spoke my name, she rose, and with faultering steps attempted to reach a door leading to her apartments. I murmured audibly, but with a stifled voice: "She flies, she flies, she hates me!" She turned. "Oh no: I do not Ernestus, do no believe it." She fell upon the floor; approached, knelt by her side, but dared not touch her. I attempted it, my hand retreated; there seemed to be pollution in my touch; I dared not. The cool air played upon her face, and the chill of the marble floor gradually recovered her; she opened her eyes; I was not near her; I could see the marks of a suffering mind upon her face; her cheek now had no colour, save that reflected from the red light of the illumined west. Her tresses were disordered and neglected; her eyes sunk deep in their socket, how changed from the vision of the Wengern Alp! Her subdued voice could hardly articulate when she again assured me with earnestness that she did not hate me, that she forgave me. Tears flowed down my cheeks, and I did not try to stop them. She looked upon me: "It is too late," she said, smiling with the smile of a broken heart; "it is too late, Berchtold; I wish that I could weep, but my eyes are dried up." The sounds of approaching footsteps were heard; she rose with difficult; trembling, I offered my arm, she took it. I thought she would have spurned it. I could hardly support my own weight. I saw her to her door, and threw myself upon the staircase hear it; but I soon heard strange voices in the saloon; the thought of its being his voice, who, I had heard, was my rival, at once made me start. I rose, retired for a moment to my room, and then entered.

The apartment was now lit up. The company were in greater numbers than I have ever seem before. My rival, I said to myself, is them so attractive. No one observed my entry; they all seemed engaged around one man. It was my rival; I never saw so singular a figure. His bust and head here handsome, and bore the sings of strength. His black hair was in ringlets; his face was pale with a blueish tint that diminished even the colour of a naturally pale eye. His hands were joined with their palms tuned towards the ground; his eyelids almost covered his eyes, which turned upon the floor, while his head erect, bore in its general expression the marks of contempt. He was speaking with elegance upon the fallen glories of some sunken nation; when he had ended, and the conversation had became more general, he raised his eyes, and affecting surprize, he seemed ashamed of having attracted so much notice, though he did not blush, for the hue of his features seemed invariable. He retreated to a corner of the room, left vacant by the pressure of the company towards the sport he had just occupied. He there bent down his head, as if abstracted in thought; but looking under his eye-brows, he was evidently engaged in remarking the effect he had made upon the company. He again gradually go a circle round him, and again was apparently carried away by the great powers of his mind, and held forth upon some subject, and then once more retreated. I was tired of watching such acting, and look round for my sister. She was at that moment entering; she immediately addressed Doni, who seemed alarmed, and wet out. I approached— Louisa was il and could not appear. Julia looked upon me as if she knew it had been my presence which had thus affected her friend; I could not bear that look: "Do not reproach me, I feed all the shame of my crimes." "I reproach you!" she answered, "You mock me, I! it is not for one like me to do it." She turned away, I did not understand her; I asked her why she rested upon one like her. "Oh! do not ask me, my shame must not be spoken." The noble stranger approached, and broke off our conversation by asking after Louisa. I could not stand by him, but joined some of my former acquaintances; for though my heart was breaking, I dared not leave the room, determined to watch minutely every action of him I fancied my rival.

'I entered into conversation, and forced myself to enquire about this stranger, who thus engaged the attention of all. There was a certain affectation of mystery about hi, which induced all to seek him, in hopes of penetrating the veil he threw round his actions/ I met with one who had know him intimately in his own country. From whom I learnt several traits of his character; it appeared that this German was much distinguished amongst his countrymen for his talents,— that he was generally esteemed a hater of all the vanities of the world, but that he passed many hours at his toilette; that he was deemed broken-hearted from having been cross in love; but that he was incapable of feeling that passion, being wrapt in selfishness, that made his sacrifice every thing around him to the whim of the moment: that he was deemed irresistible, and that no woman upon whom he fixed his eye could withstand the fascination of his tongue, but that he had never dared to tempt any woman, who was not the most abandoned character; that even they were never addressed with boldness, but were always made to compromise themselves by some folly with him in public, before he would give them the least marked sign of attention; that in fine he was a confirmed coward with women. In society he was playing off a strange coquetry with the whole world, affecting to be modest and diffident, whilst he protruded himself into notice. He was, however, rich, handsome, and noble by birth, I was an orphan dependent upon charity. He was every where received with great attention, no where with greater than in Doni's palace.

'Perceiving that Louisa's father did not return, I became alarmed, and anxious to gain some information, I sought for him. He was walking with hasty steps before her door. Upon seeing me, he was turning away, but moved by my broken voice, he stopped looked upon me, and addressed me, "You saved my son, Berchtold, but my daughter, my beloved daughter dies; it is however, useless to speak to you, leave me, go to you room, Louisa's better" Every thing seemed confused to me, I could not believe that I was the cause of Louisa's illness, I could not believe that she could love such an outcast as myself. I was several times in the course of the night by her door, listening for some sound that should assure me of her existence. I fell asleep at last upon the sofa in my room, and I saw her in my dream as when she first appeared before me, glowing in health, buoyant with spirits; suddenly I thought she ran towards me, but ere she reached me, she faded like a flower, and fell to the ground. I awoke, all was still, but my heart beat violently. I seemed as if this were the fulfilment of my former drams, my vices were the evils, the warning voice of my mother commanded my sister to fly, for thy were doomed to be the death of all I loved.

'Morning came, my first enquires were concerning Louisa; she was very ill, and in a state of great weakness. Doni was not yet rise, and was apparently quite overcome. During the whole day, I was not one moment at rest; I wandered from one room to another, and sent every instant to enquire concerning my protector's daughter. I stood by the door watching all who came from her room, and begged them to tell me every change they observed. Towards evening a packet was put into my hands; it contained receipts from every one of my creditors. There was no explanatory paper. Imagining it to be the gift of Doni, I determined to thank him; I went to his room; I found him lying upon his couch very much fatigued and exhausted; he was courting repose, but it was in vain; anxiety was painted upon his face, and grief seemed to stamp him with its chilling furrows. My first question was concerning his daughter. I then showed him the packet, and had begun to thank him, when he interrupted me. "Young man, thank not one, who wished that you should first have paid the price of your vices before he freed you from your embarrassments. I had resistered my daughter's entreaties, till last night, she offered to give up her allowance, every thing, to free you; I refused, but I could no long do so, to a child I thought dying." I was thunderstruck, the packet fell from my hand; I thought I should have fallen through shame; but he spoke again, "Would that your apparent shame were the least security against your follies, but I believe you to be incurable." He motioned me away; I fell at his feet, and called Heaven to witness that I would never again partake of vicious pleasure. He raised me from the ground, pressed me to his bosom, and with a blessing told me, that if I kept this promise, he might yet be happy; he bade me leave him to his hopes, again embraced me, and I left him.

'For the first time during the last many weary months, I felt something like repose in my mind. I seemed as if the vow I had made to heaven might be relied on, and as if I again might know the consolation of a conscience at rest. That night I slept quietly and soundly, for Louisa was announced to be much better, and my heart felt a little repose. I was but to give me strength to bear worse than I had yet endured.

'Next morning Louisa saw me, she was upon the bed of sickness, but she had partly recovered the show my abrupt entry had caused her. I shall never forget the moment I entered. I had expected she would have received me with marks of horror; she smiled; oh, no! she did not hate me. I sat by her, she allowed me to take her thin cold hand within my own; it chilled my heart with its touch. There was a clear whiteness that overspread her face, where it was not tinged by the hectic flush, her eye shone with a glassy brilliancy that seemed not mortal, it was the glance of death mocking my senses thought a beauteous vizour, for there were the seeds of death sown deep through broken heart. She spoke but a little, what she did utter, however, were words of kindness, and they were all her weakness allowed her to say. She often turned her brilliant eyes upon me, and the soft smile upon her lip, I thought was excited by the gentle whisperings of hope, that I was snatch for ever from vice. The latter part of the morning was passed near her in a silence that was not mute, for there is a language which, though no addressed to the ear, still speaks the thought within. Her physician came and advised me to retire. I bade her farewell; an anxious look accompanied the words, "where are you going?" but when intimated my determination of staying at home, I cannot describe to you the joy expressed upon her face as she repeated my farewell.

'I had been so little at home, that I knew nothing of what had lately happened. I was, therefore, much surprised, when, upon desiring a servant, towards night, to see if Doni was in his apartment, he refused, saying he had not courage. Upon making enquiries, I found that their mater's supernatural powers had been much talked of lately amongst the servants; for during the latter days unusual noises had been heard in his room, and every morning, all his things had been found in a strange confusion while he was apparently so exhausted, that it was evident had had no rest during the night. Thinking of all the very explicable from the state of anxiety in which he had been kept, I tried to convince the servant, he appeared firm in his belief, and refused to carry my message.

'Louisa seemed rapidly to recover strength. As we were in the very middle of summer it was thought proper by her physicians that she should be removed to a cooler situation than the neighbourhood of a great city. We accordingly retired to the banks of the Lago Maggiore. The palace close to the lake weas refreshed by the cooling breeze that passed over the water's vast expanse, and the playful fountains that sported with their noisy showers in the apartments towards the land, promised to shield the invalid from the noxious effects of an Italian sun; while the magnificent scenery of the varying basin before our view, seemed to promise relaxation to the mind. We arrived late at night, and immediately retired to our beds. I arose betimes, and issuing forth ascended the numerous terraces, which, one above another, seemed like the work of some enchanter. When viewed from the water's edge, garden seemed to be hanging above garden, as if man had acquired the power of piling nature's gift even into the air. I did not heed this, for my native mountains were in sight; I did not gaze upon the rich islands, which seemed dwellings springing from the lake; I gazed upon Monte Rosa, which, high above the neighbouring hills, asserted the glory of its alpine birth. Though all around seemed burnt by the sun's ray, it marked his power and bore its unvarying white vest, in defiance of his frown, upon its aged limbs. While yet engaged looking upon its high summit, with all the crowded images of infancy offered by my memory, my sister passed me. She seemed lately to have lost all of her spirits, she did not appear to be attracted by the beautiful scene near us, or the sublimity of the alpine ridge beyond. She was gazing upon the ground, I joined her, she started, and with a trembling voice asked me, "Why I was come?" I answered here; at that moment I saw Olivieri turn the corner of the alley and approach; but immediately he saw me he retired, and I at the same time perceived that my sister was violently agitated. I looked at her, and begged of her to tell me what I was to imagine; she hastily replied, "Nothing, nothing;" and her colour, which had deserted her at the sight of Olivieri returned with greater rapidity than it had fled the moment before. I insisted upon an explanation; she said she was unwell, weak, and made other excuses of the same nature. I now remembered her agitation a few evenings before, when we were interrupted by the Count Wilhelm. I threatened, if she would not satisfy me, to seek an explanation from Olivieri. She fell upon her knees before me, begged me not, assured me that it concerning a third person. I was moved, I had the weakness to promise that I would seek no farther.

'I had not seen my friend till this moment, since the payment of my debts; he had never been home, and I had not sought him. He had not accompanied us, and I had not been aware that he was expected. I re-entered the house, hoping to find him; but no one had seen him, and he did not appear at breakfast.

'Louisa made her appearance at that meal. You may imagine my pleasure at again seeing her out of her sick chamber. She made room for me by her side. I accompanied her into the orange-walk near the house while she enjoyed the beauty of the scene. She looked at the Alps, then at me, it seemed as if the recollection of our first meeting passed though the minds of both. Involuntarily I opened the bosom of my vest and showed her the scarf, which I had constantly worn since that day. She smiled. "I did not think of this at that time" she said, "I did not know your name, but when the fame of Berchtold, Ernestus Berchtold, was echoed by the wild rocks to the voice of every peasant, I sighed and wished he might be the chamois hunter of the Wengern Alp. It was I set the saviour of my brother's life to battle. I sent the hero to aid in the rescue of his country; it was in vain, yet I was conscious of a feeling of pride whenever I thought of it." She spoke of my former life, and passed in silence over that part, when every moment had been spent in shame. I cannot describe my sensations to you. The feeling of how little I deserved such praise, mingling with the pleasure of hearing it from Louisa's lips, embittered what else would have been the proudest moment of my life. Her father joined us, and seemed pleased at seeing us together; he seated himself upon the other side of his daughter, and we spent the whole morning together in conversation, till the sun becoming too powerful, Louisa was obliged to retire for shelter and repose, and we separated.

'Day passed after day, and Louisa's health seemed rapidly to recover; but my sister evidently became more and more restless. She generally avoided, and very seldom sought our society. I knew not what to understand; determined however to force her to an explanation, I one evening, finding her alone, induced to her to walk out with me. We wandered, without perceiving it, into the garden. She seemed determined upon silence. Wrapt in thought, the sun's red disk fast sinking in the west, the bird's evening carol, the varied light of the heavens reflected from the soft silky cloudes over the purling surface of the late, the cooling breeze which played upon her feverish cheek, were all unnoticed. Yet she was wont, in all that feeling of nature's charms which accompanies youth, to gaze upon that orb, and figuring it as the image of that Providence she adored, and all was unheeded. There was a seat upon the river's side, which, shaded by the plants that crept entangled round the branches of a noble chestnut, formed a bower, whence all the beauties of the rich nature round could be view. I attempted in vain to enter upon the subject of what was causing this apparent misery in her breast; she was abstracted, and answered merely by monosyllables. I at last ceased to press her, and we both sunk into silence.

'The spreading clematis of the bower hid us completely from the path near us, while its open leaves allowed us to see distinctly all that passed in the avenue. There was a wall of cypress which ran along one side of the gravel walk, fully exposed at his moment to the sun's rays. I saw at last approaching from the bottom, the Count our protector; he seemed in earnest conversation with some one, but I could perceive no one near him; yet his lips and hands certainly moved as if he spoke. As he gradually approached, I could even distinguish sounds. I motioned Julia to observe him; she did so and soon pointed to the hedge. I could not at first see to what she directed my attention; but at last I perceived the outline of a figure, through the shape of whose body the very leaves were visible; something in the manner that I have seen in the summer, a current of heated air, accurately defined by the wavering outline of the things between which and our sight it stands., only that this was even more sensible to vision. I could not distinguish its voice, but I at last caught some of the words of Doni. I had hardly time to make these observations, when the Count seemed to start, and the figure vapour went.

'We did not move; we for some time seemed rooted to our seats; at last Doni disappeared amidst the trees, and we looked at each other. It was then true that we heard at the lake of Thun, our protector had communication with a spirit. My sister seized the subject of conversation with avidity. We related to one another several slight circumstances, which had come to our knowledge, many incidents which we could not explain. The reluctance of the servants to approach the chambers of the Count all pressed upon our minds. The immense wealth, which seemed inexhaustible, must, it appeared to us, be connected with this untenanting spirit. We resolved not to mention the circumstance we had just witnessed to any one. But it was not effaced from our own memory. We returned to the house and saw our protector there as usual, but his face was, or I imagined it to be, pale; his eyes wandered, and then seemed to fix their angry glance at times upon us; but whether there were imagination or reality, I could not decide. I went to bed, but not to sleep, the thoughts of having seen an unembodied being, the tales of my foster-mother, of power, of wealth, arising from the communication with beings of another world, arose before me. Obtaining such a power, it seemed as if I might learn things hidden in the earth's deepest recesses, the ocean's depth; I even thought, that by such a power, I might tear away the veil which the first Cause had thrown over itself. Nor did these visions disappear with the morning's light, they were as distinct in the sun's brightness, as in the night's obscurity. I arose determined to speak on the subject with the

Count. He met me with an affectionate embrace; I took his hand, had the words upon my lips, when, meeting his eye, I saw expressed therein such anxious fear, such meaning, that the words fell into inarticulate sounds; instantly his eye was as usuals; nothing but brilliancy was there. We went to felth Louisa from her apartment, and descended to the breakfast table.

'Louisa seemed to take a great pleasure in my society, and sought in every way to bring me near her; she seemed afraid of trusting me to myself in my first steps towards retracing the paths of virtue. She again resumed the subject which had formed the topic of conversation, before her fatal departure to visit her sick relation. She painted to me the charms of religion, which taught us to look up to the infinite power above us, not as to an object of terror and fear, but of love and hope. Her mind, without losing the least of that delicacy which is the magic charm that spreads its influence round the footsteps of woman, was energetic and clear. Her simplicity was not misled by the winding, intricate sophisms of the deist and unbeliever; her belief was built upon persuasion, which though it had at first depended upon faith, had not scorned the bulwarks of reason. The earnestness with which she spoke, did not make her appear bold or presuming; for the mild look in her dark eye seemed looking to heaven to beg for inspiration from him, whose cause her lips were pleading. She would often lead me towards the chapel, and without affectation, would kneel down by my side motioning me to imitate her, and bending devoutly before her maker, would pray for me. I did not think myself; but gazing upon that veiled eye, which did not seem to think itself worthy of looking towards the throne of God, while petitioning for strength against mortal weakness, a prayer would involuntarily rise from my heart for her. I did not feel the time long when near her, though it was even spent in prayer; to have communication with the Almighty in union with her, seemed to be an additional bond against those numberless ties which bound me to her. From the first moment that I had seen her, she seemed to visit this earth as my protecting angel; now it appeared as if such a being had led me to the throne of him of whose commands she was the bearer. I did not notice the lapse of months; and autumn had already vested the scene around with its checquered hues, ere this happiness was interrupted; I had even forgotten all my imaginations concerning the being attendant upon Doni. It seemed as if misfortune could no longer visit me; such is human foresight.

'I have already mentioned to you the singularity of my sister's conduct; it grew more and more remarkable. She never came down in the morning, but, confined to her room, she spent the hours in solitude: when she did appear, it was to retire to a corner, where, enveloping herself in her shawl, she apparently brooded over some thoughts that destroyed her peace. Her appearance was completely changed; her auburn hair, which once floated in ringlets of soft varying light upon her shoulders, was now entangled and neglected; her cheeks, on which was wont to play a hue more delicate than that of the white rose, were pale and sickly; her eyes no longer shone with sparkling lustre, they were now heavy and inflamed from the want of sleep. I often saw the silent tears fall from her eye; but it was in vain to question her; she wept bitterly at every enquiry I made, and seemed agitated to the most violent excess whenever Olivieri's name was mentioned. I was bewildered by the enquiries of Doni and Louisa, who constantly expressed their anxiety concerning her.

'We were assembled together at the breakfast table as usual one morning, and were conversing about Julia, who had made her appearance the evening before at the supper table, which she had not done for a long time, when a servant came to tell us that her maid had applied several times in the course of the last hour for admission to her room, but that she could obtain no answer. Louisa offered to see if she could obtain admission; in vain, we went together; all, all was silent. We burst open the door, there was no one, every thing seemed in disorder, the bed had not been slept in the last night; upon the floor there were many pieces of paper torn into fragments; and upon the table there was a note addressed to myself. I took it trembling, I was afraid she had committed some desperate act. I could not open it, but gave it into Doni's hands; he read it:

'My shame can no longer be hidden; I fly then to hide myself; curse not your sister, my own feelings are sufficiently bitter to satisfy even the injured honour of Berchtold.— Your degraded Julia.

'I sunk upon the bed; Olivieri immediately pressed himself to my mind as the seducer of y sister. I could not speak, and my friends were silent, they looked upon me with pity. I dared not inform them of my suspicions, they would bring the old man's grey hairs to their grave, and would cut off the feeble thread of life with Louisa. She bore up against the shock; and while the tear trembled in her eye, she sat down by me, and strove to sooth, no console me, for that she knew was impossible.

'Servants were sent in every direction. I searched all the neighbourhood. I determined instantly to go to Milan, and make enquiries directly to Olivieri, concerning the fate of my sister. I made a plausible excuse for my departure, and soon reached the Corso, Doni' palace. The servants had no seen him for some time. I forced himself to seek him in the laces which had been my former resort. My late companions hailed my approach; but I turned from them in disgust. Olivieri had no where been heard of lately. Distracted by my suspicions, which now seemed to wear the semblance of certainty, after several days spent in the vain search, I returned to the Lake.

'We soon fixed ourself again at Milan. It was now impossible to keep his son's absence a secret from Doni. He learnt it, but did not seem to imagine any connection between the flight of my sister and his son's conduct. Perceiving this, I did not intimate to him my horrible doubts, but left him in entire ignorance. In the mean time I made the most minute enquiries concerning both; but could learn nothing;

'Louisa's health in the mean time gradually recovered; but she never lost the hectic flush upon her cheek; she gained strength, but the seeds of death were hidden, not destroyed. During her gradual recovery, I was always with her; and if you can picture the happy hours of one sitting by a being he loves— adores, at the same time, that his imagination paints her to him as a spirit of heaven, you may imagine my happiness, when sitting by Louisa, whose smile, whose glance told me she loved. She had gained me fame; had saved my life, my honour; had restored to me the hopes of a future state, the belief in a kind God. I know no your belief, your principles; you may sneer at the feeling which dictates my ranking the two last with the former; but, young man! Believe one who has experienced the whole of fate's wanton inflictions;— he who can still rest upon futurity, confident in the goodness of his maker, may find a refuge in the greatest misery; he who cannot, may indeed despair, he has but the present, and that may indeed be dreadful.

'Louisa's image was always with me. I loved her, but so did every one; I could not for that reason hope to gain her. I was an orphan, how often has the thought of that sunk my buoyant hope, which still would revive. I had no rank. Count Wilhelm had again renewed his addresses. It seemed dishonourable in me to continue any long near her, endeavouring to gain her affections; it seemed as if the debt of gratitude I owed to Doni forbade my attempting to gain his daughter. The count had rank and wealth. I could no hope that her father should prefer me, degraded by vice, my birth perhaps tainted with dishonour, to one whose name was a spell upon all Europe. I had determined to leave Milan, and to please the necessity of further enquiries for my sister. Doni approved of my intentions, and in a few days I was set off. I had been preparing for my departure, and had been talking to the servant about the trifles necessary for a solitary journey; it was not yet the hour for the company to assemble, and lost in sorrow I was slowly approaching the saloon, when those notes which had sung hope to me in prison, sounded on the air. They were falling upon the breeze broken, and in a melancholy tone; though the air was lively, it seemed as if Louisa was sought to sing of hope, while her heart could not echo back the strain. I had not heard the song since I sunk into vice. The sound was silences, I entered; Louisa was leaning upon her harp, the head was fallen upon her hand. There was no light, and the lowering clouds hid the little daylight that might have been afforded by the setting sun. I could just distinguish her form, almost lost in the obscurity, suddenly she moved, struck her harp in wild notes, and sung the words of a broken heart. I could not hear more; Louisa's name feel from my lips; "Sing not so, Louisa, if you have not happiness, who shall possess it?" she sunk upon a chair, and I approached. "You leave me to morrow," she said, "I shall no longer have any one to cheer me, any one, whom I can"— She stopped and hesitated. I stood breathless by her side. "I shall, I will return." "You will find me a corpse, I feel no power of life within me, it seems as if my soul still clung to life that it might converse with you, when you are gone." I took her hand; I bade her, if she loved me, not to speak in words that pierced my heart. "Love you," she answered, "you cannot know what I feel towards you, I am myself ashamed that any can divide my heart with God, but you— " I fell upon my knees. I will not go, I cannot, Louisa has confessed her love, she loves the orphan Berchtold, if that words could express the least part of what I feel, I would speak. I love you, let my silence speak the rest. I felt her feeble hand press mine, she had fainted, her weak health had not given her strength to listen. We had not heard the storm which had burst over our heads, I had not seen the flashes of heaven's anger, which had unobserved spread its lurid light around us. I lifted her in my arms, carried her to her chamber, and observed her to her maid. She recovered.

'I was alone; the thunders echoed still in the distance, and the horizon was lit by the forked lightning. But in my breast the convulsions were no subsiding. At the first moment it seemed as if happiness indeed were mine; but Doni's imagine came quickly across my mind, and all I owed him seemed to be imagined as so many reproaches for my having stolen the affections of my benefactor's daughter. The company assembled, but I could not joie them. The tumult in my breast was too powerful to allow me to participate in the light frivolity of a drawing room. I retired to my chamber, and was soon lost in mediation upon that fatality, which made the very circumstance on which I had rested as the bourne of all my hopes, a cause of anguish and reproach. I determined to see the Count immediately after the company had retired. No malefactor, who is listening in expectation of hearing the lengthened toll, warning him of the executioner's approach, ever counted the moments with greater anxiety than mine. The clock stuck, and each brazen sound seemed to vibrate thought my body, as if it bore grief upon its sound. At last the carriages began to depart, and I entered the apartment of my friend. I had never dared to call him father, it seemed to my mind too sacred a title to be profaned by me; he was Louisa's father.

'I had been some time in his apartment before he entered. He came, his face was full of anxiety. "My daughter," he said "I fear is going to relapse, something has agitated her strongly, and she will not tell even her father what it is. Berchtold," he continued, "you have never before seen a father in the agony that I endure, my daughter's life sinks visibly before me, and I cannot discover the cause. You have therefore no conception of the pain it brings." I knew not what to say. "Olivieri too is I know not where, perchance in the haunt of the lowest vice, perhaps acting again the hero, as when with you. You are not my child, yet you now form my only comfort, my only hope." I could not hear more;— he praise me! Who had, like the snake stinging the child enchanted by the beauty of its scales, robbed him of his treasure, insidiously won his daughter's love; I interrupted him. "I am a wretch, not worthy of your affection, your daughter love me. I have dared to tell her she was my only hope; spurn me from you, I expect it; but do not blame her." I fell upon my knees. "Do not blame her for loving such a wretch as me, she pitied me and my daring devotion changed pity into love." My head was hid within my ahdns, I expected to be cursed by him I looked up to as a father. He raised me from the ground, "Ernestus, this is nobly spoken, I will not reproach you with your former vices, Louisa shall be security to me, that you will always prove what you now show yourself." I was amazed; I embraced him, but could not speak. Louisa was to be mine,— my guide, my wife. At that moment of happiness seemed to be descending from heaven to be our handmaid, while in fact despair and horror seemed to be preparing their flight from the lowest abyss to wait upon our nuptials.

'Next morning I was admitted to Louisa's chamger; I told her that her father had consent to our union. A gleam of Joy cross her pale face, she said she was happy, but those words were in a broken and weak voice. I heeded it not, so great was my joy, I sat with hcr, she listened to my plans of happiness, and smiled; it seemed as if she were conscious of their being but to be imagined. I was at last called away by my own servant, who putting a letter in my hand, told me that he had found it thrown in at the door. It was my sister's hand writing; fearful of agitating Louisa, I hastily put it into my bosom, and making an excuse left her. When in my chamber, I opened the note. The lines were few:

' "A mother appeals for her child to your charity, she has but a short time to live, but her child has not a break heart. Julia."

'Berchhold had been written, but a tear had effaced the characters. There was the name of an obscure street in the most retired part of Milan.

'I immediately repaired thither, and soon found myself in an abode of misery I cannot describe. It was upon the highest story, the roof in several parts let in the hot ray of the sun, and the window was not glazed, but stuffed with dirty rags. It could not be called a shelter, for the floor bore on its black soft texture the marks of every cloud that had passed over it. In one corner there was a bedstead, over which was spread a blanket, that seemed not to have been removed for many years, it was no black and thick with dirt. A broken dish and rags, which I but too well recognized as the remnants of my sister's dress, were the only things upon the floor. I heard a difficult breathing, which proceeded from the bed. I approached, and found my sister. She was pale and squalid, her hair entangled and loose, covered her face and bosom, and her clasped hands hung from the bed. She was apparently asleep, and her child was grasping her breast with its little hand, trying in vain to obtain sustenance from its fevered mother. I stood for some time gazing upon her; finding she slept soundly, I descended the creaking stairs, and sending some person of the house for clothes and food, I waited till they returned and carried them up with me. The noise I made awakened her, she shrunk from me; "I did not call you for myself, but this child's cry pierced my heart,— do, do not therefore curse me, if I have even brought you to witness your sister's infamy. I could not die and leave my child sinking unaided upon my putrid corpse." I spoke findly to her, she looked upon me and said, "Ernestus", with an incredulous voice, and burst into tears. I soothed her, spoke to her of her child, induced her to take a little nourishment, and saw her feed her little bade. She looked at its eager eye and face will feeding, at moments hugged it to her bosom, while a stifled laugh escaped her; she did not seem to notice me, and I spoke not. At last she fell exhausted upon the bed. I gave her the clothes I had brought, she did not heed m.e

'I hastened to Doni, related what I had seen; he ordered every thing to be got ready at he palace, and procuring a litter he accompanied me to the abode of my wretched Julia. At sight of him, she hid her face, and would not speak. I had her conveyed to the little with her child, and we arrived at the palace. The physician of the family being sent for, announced to us, that from the state of exhaustion, into which she had fallen, there were but a few hours remaining of her life. I watched by her all night, she did not speak; I took Louisa for my model, and spoke to her of those hopes which had seemed on her lips to have the power of soothing sickness, and to still the fears of death. She was moved by what I said, for her cold hand pressed mine. I put questions to her with regard to her seducer; she was silent; but a convulsive motion seemed to seize her whole features. I urged her no more. She seemed to revive a little in the morning; auguring well from it, I began to speak to her of her child, talked to her of its health, said it should be named Ernestus, and promised that I would be its father. She raised her fallen head, and looking with tears in her eyes, blessed me, but hardly had the words fallen from her lips, when shuddering, she said, "my blessing! That, that's a curse." I took her to my breast, she shrunk from me, "you know not whom you embrace." "It is my sister whom I hold in my hands," I cried, she burst into loud sobs, and fell again, upon her pillow. "You shall hear," she replied, "what a sister!" She prepared to relate to me the whole of her late history; I advised her to repose awhile first. "Well, well, I shall have the less time to feel the blush of shame, and to hear your reproaches. 'Tis better so. She fell asleep after uttering these words, but she was restless, her face was convulsed, and the twitching of her arms began to give the signs of the rapid approach death.

'I seized this moment of apparent rest to enquire for Louisa. She was much better; we had kept our discovery of Julia a secret, fearful of agitating her too much; I determined therefore to see her, lest, making some enquiry concerning me, she might hear now I was engaged. I entered her room, and staid with her for some time; she spoke of her love, and added, that all that she thought wanting was the presence of her brother and Julia. I could not answer, but rose, and again went to my unconscious sister. She was disturbed in her sleep, and was calling upon Louisa's name; she seemed to reproach her for not seeing her; but then she appeared to meditate and said; "true, true, I am an outcast". She awoke, looked wildly around, met my eye. She was lost some time in thought, and then addressed me; "I know what you are waiting for but ere I unfold the whole of my shame, give me your solemn promise that you will grant your sister her last dying request." I gave it her. "You will then never mention to either of my former friends what I narrate, and you will let me die, certain that you will never injure him that ruined me, for still, still I love him." I assured her, that I would leave it to heave to punish hi, for I was conscious it was Olivieri, Louisa's brother. It was him, the account that I had given of his bravery in the Swiss war, the description I had made of his daring feats had gained an entire possession of her imagination. When, therefore, she met him at Milan, his beauty, his specious manner and apparent knowledge had completed her fascination. I myself, when bewildered by doubts, had sapped the foundation of her religious principles; and Olivieri, who was not blind to her partiality, had fanned the spark of scepticism, till he had destroyed all belief in virtue and a future state. I lost myself at the gambling table; and my conduct was but an additional proof in her mind, that the present was all that belong to man. Before we left Milan, the seducer accomplished his criminal purpose. Though however, she had become a convert to his theories, she could not divest herself of all feeling of shame, much less could she entirely drive from her heart those doctrines which Berchtold had instilled at that age when the first impressions become part of our very nature; they hung around her, and haunted her day and night; she had sought for courage to apply to Louisa or myself in her difficulties, but had not dared.

'Her mind being in this state, she described the effect upon it, at the sight of that being almost lost amidst the ambient air in conversation with Doni, as wonderful. Her mind had immediately recovered its elasticity, for she hoped, if she could obtain communication with such a being, to be able to find some certainty amidst the horrid doubts that revelled in her mind, and to procure the means of hiding her shame, or daring to face the day, but means of its power. Determined to learn the spell which could raise a transparent, all pervading being, she resolved to watch without remission, the conduction of the Count; she learnt nothing for some time. He apparently differed in no habit from the others around. But the impression in her mind was not effaced: at last it appeared to her that upon certain days, the Count never touched animal food, and she found by observation that this happened on every combination of seven in the days of the month. Upon enquiry amongst the servants, she found that upon the morning of those days, the room of Doni was always in the greatest confusion, and she herself remarked, that upon the evening proceeding, he seemed always more anxious, and the day after more fatigued than usual.

'Julia resolved to watch the Count upon the next seventh night; she found that it was possible to look into his room through the wainscot of a closet for wood that opened into the passage leading to his apartment. The night name, meat had been avoided, all were gone to their rooms, only the footsteps of the domestics arranging every thing for rest, sounded on her ear; she described herself, as having listened apparently for hours; though only minutes elapsed, while these sounds continued. At last, all was silent; she said, that not even the vine leaves overspreading her casement were heard to rustle; for every breeze was hushed, all was so quiet, that the ear seemed to feel as it were the silence. She was awed, her heart beat quick, she held her breath; at that moment she thought a slow step sounded along the corridor; alarmed she knew not why, she seized her lamp, and was upon the point of rushing out, when the door slowly opened, and a figure clad in a white robe entered; its dark black eye was fixed; its grey locks seemed as if no breath of air could move their weight; no sign of life, save the moving feet belonged to it, for the face was pale, the lips blueish. It approached with an unvarying step; it was Doni! Its hand took her's within its cold grasp, its eye shone, as if a tear had passed over it, its lips quivered as if it wished to speak, or thought it spoke. She stood still, motionless; while it approached, it seemed as if she had strength for any thing, but when it turned to go, the lamp fell from her hand, and she fell upon the floor. It was morn, ere her wildered senses returned, it was too late. Doni never noticed in any way the event of that night. She was bewildered, she knew not what to think, it seemed from his unchanged conduct towards her, that he was unconscious of the event. Yet she asserted that she could not have mistaken the features of him who had visited her in that awful manner; her imagination laboured, her judgment laid down the balance and became as dead. Her phantasy painted to her mind pictures of splendour and of power, more brilliant than those of the Arab tale-teller, or God creating Bramin. But more than all, it represented to her the means of ensuring Olivieri's love, which she could no longer flatter herself she possessed it; he had not seen her, but for a moment, since she had left Milan dishonoured, and then it was but to laugh at her fears, which she was but too conscious were not in vain.

'Day followed day towards the seventh. At times she caught Doni's eye fixed upon her, as if it sought to read her mind; but she thought this might be imagination, yet it seemed to her if her intentions were divined, and that from some cause or other, they could not be opposed, else why all this silence? That fatal night came. Julia, determined to brace very thing, went down that evening, which she had not lately done to supper. Her agitation was great, but she forced herself to conceal it. She was conscious of the Count's eyes were fixed upon her's, yet she dared not to look up and meet his. She rose to depart, he came to her room; she determined, frightened by the awful silence of her protection, to give up her intentions. She threw herself upon her bed, but sleep abandoned her, or if it for the moment came, it presented such brilliant visions to her eyes, that nothing mortal was to be compared to it, She seemed to have spirits instead of pages to attend her, genii instead of servants. It seemed as if at their bidding the very earth would heave and show within its entrails, all its richest treasures. Olivieri appeared joined with her in this state of power. She roused herself. The clock with its solemn peal seemed trembling to intrude upon the solemn night. One might have thought nature was dead, for not even the owl shrieked, and the darkness and nocturnal sleep that weighed on the earth, seemed no longer the type of the eternal rest of the world, but its fulfilment, all appeared sunk into such undisturbed repose. Julia alone seemed living, she looked in the creation like the Arab in the sandy plain, animate amidst inanimation, organized amidst unorganized matter. Even she must have appeared as if she were some sort of spirit of another more restless sphere, for her hurrying glance, the fearful resolution breathing in her face, must have made her bear the stamp of something more than mortality. She seized her lamp, started, then advanced, and laughed with that laugh that plays upon the lips, when the heart ceases to beat through violence of feeling.

'At least she reached the gallery of her protector's room; she opened with a trembling hand, the door of the adjoining closet, and entered. The dread silence still continued, it was only broken by the loud breathing of her heaving bosom. She sat down upon the pile of wood in the corner of the closet. She could not find courage to pursue her undertaking; at last a deep groan made her start; terrified she leant against the wall; as she gradually recovered herself, she raised her eyes, and looked through the crevice that opened to her sight the Count's room. I could not learn what she saw, she however informed me that she discovered the means of raising a superior being; but that startled at his appearance, she sunk to the ground. She found herself, when recovered, upon her bed, but no one was near her. She determined to put her power into effect the ensuing night. She would not join the family at breakfast, but remained in her all day. She did attempt to raise a spirit, but what was her horror, when the walls of her apartment echoed but scoffs and mockings, they seemed to say that she needed not a greater price than the gratification of her passions, and that they would not give her more; that she was theirs already, and that to command them could only be obtained by one not already damned. Unappalled she repeated her call, but it was in vain, all sunk to quiet. Desperate, for her shame could no longer be hidden, she formed at once the resolution of leaving the house and seeking her seducer. She got out, and entering a boat, managed by skulking along the banks of the lake throughout the day, ot arrive in the night at Sesto Calende; she thence easily obtained a conveyance, and reached Milan.

'She had sought refuge at a small in, and sending to Olivieri, he came to her, but it was only make fully known to her the horrors of the situation. It appears he treated her with brutality, thought she did not say so. He staid with her but a few minutes, and left her for ever. He offered her no assistance, seemed seven to have implied that if unwilling to return to her brother, she might live by exposing her shame to all, and boldly seeking whom she might inveigle. He left her with only the small sum remaining from what she had taken with her, and immediately left Milan to go she knew not where. She had thence retired to the room where I had found her, and had there managed to support life, and was delivered of her child. Her money however failed her, and at least, her poor neighbours, tireds of assisting her who could no longer pay them, having refused to aide her any more, she had struggled with the pains of hunger for two days in solitude, hoping for relief from death. But her milk had failed, and her child's voice had pierced its mother's heart; she could nor resist such an appeal; she arose, wrote a few lines to me, and staggering, in the morning, while all were at rest, to the gate of the palace, had thrown them under the gate. Form thence she had hardly found strength sufficient to reach her miserable couch, when fatigued, she sunk into a kind of stupor from which my approach had roused her.

'This is the substance of what my sister told me. Her narration was broken, and many were the pauses she was forced to make to recover strength. Her feeble breathe hardly seemed sufficient to allow her to end her tale. Night came, and she was delirious. She screamed for Olivieri, called on him to come and see her die. She held my hands, and looking on my asked me my name, denied it could be men, for I could not be more kind than Olivieri; but why rest upon such a scene? She died in the morning without a return of reason, but still calling, in the last moment, upon her lover.

'My sister was dead. Her tale had unfolded to me the causes whence her misconduct arose. I was the source of all, my colouring of Olivieri's good qualities, my exposing her to the sources of doubt int those doctrines our sainted foster-father had taught us, my example in the career of vice were the causes of her fault— her death. It was yet but the second victim to my fate; there were two others waiting; I sat by the dead body reflecting upon the horrible fatality that had caused my virtues and my vices to prove alike mortal to the two beings who for many years had been my only companions I possessed in nature, the only sympathizers in my joys and sorrows. If the pangs of conscience could be depicted, I would, for your sake, young man, painting its truest colours, the horror I then felt, the pangs I now feel; but the attempt would be vain. I had loved my sister will all my affection two isolated beings naturally feel towards each other. She had been to me as the darker part of myself, which always needed protection and defence. To me she had been the holder of all my secrets, the partaker of all my sorrows; when an outcast, she had received me; when a wretch, she had not spurned me.

'No one was with me when she died. The servant of Louisa found me many hours after her decease, extended upon her corpse. She came from her mistress to seek me. I rose; I knew not how to conceal my anguish of my mind. Louisa soon discovered it, and obtained from me the knowledge of my sister's illness and death. She did not enquire further; she perceived I was not willing she should know the rest, and was silent. I was astonished to see how firmly she bore the shock, she exerted herself to find some means of allaying my grief, but she did not know that it was conscience that work within. I left her, and her pretended strength was gone. She had forced herself to assume an apparent calm to assuage my grief, but could not command her own.

'My sister was interred privately. Doni and myself, were the only mourners, and a tablet, with merely the name of Julie Berchtold, marked the spot where my sister lay. Her child was put to nurse. I gave him his mother's and my own name, that I might still have a bond between us. Every day I went to see the little orphan, and taking him from the fearful nurse, I gaze upon his infantile face, while a bitter tear fell from the eye of him who had been the cause of his birth being loaded with infamy and shame. While I looked upon him he would smile, but that smile brought to my mind my sister's, it was melancholy playing of the lips, that seemed to mock at the pleasure that excited it; the eyes was not lit up with the same feeling, but still appeared absorbed in its continued grief.'

We cheered poor Polidori and we hear-heared. For a writer to put words to the page is an act of bravery. The blank page staring at all writers when we begin a story or poem is the most frightening beast of all. Many would rather undertake Hercules' Nine Labours than write a story or God-forbid a poem. What are we trying to say? Where does one begin? When does one begin? How does one begin? Why does one begin? Who are we to begin? All writers put ourselves into our work so completely that any criticism of our story is an evisceration of our very bowels. To criticize a writer's story is a cruelty akin to complaining about a child to his parent. We desire constructive criticism not destructive cynicism. If an author asks of her reader, whether family, friend, or a fellow traveller on this journey of creativity, we will bloody the pages with constructive criticism. For the author who wielded the quill of creativity and the friend who wields the quill of criticism both desire the work to be the best it can be. This early criticism must murder the story so that author can resurrect the story into its final glorious form. If Dr Polidori requests and requires such criticism, I will freely give it in the spirit of the Muses who inspire us all. Now, do not misunderstand me, we all have our opinions, some sharper than others. I'm convinced Lord Byron itched to criticize the verbose prose of his personal physician; the Lord, no doubt, wondered if the ink was laid on the page has heavy handed as the words, but his lips were sewn shut. I knew by the looks on each of faces of our party, having heard Dr Polidori's recitation of his 'Modern Oedipus' that our opinions of this work would be taken to our graves. And you, Constant Reader, your opinions are you own.

Chapter Ten
Frankenstein[87]
(The Abandonment of the Creature)

Chapter I

July. Back at Lake Geneva.— After a hearty breakfast, I lounged in the parlour deliriously rereading my transcriptions from my encounter with my pale student of the unhallowed arts in Castle Frankenstein. After our eight-day tour of Lake Geneva, our party had returned to the Villa Diodati just as the inclement weather also returns from its eight-day tour of who knows where. But last night and into the morning, the storms promised not only rain, but in the small hours threatened snow. The date is the first of July in the Year of Our Lord Eighteen Hundred and Sixteen and the first snowfall is cascading large fluffy snowflakes past the parlour window. The fire is roaring in the hearty to such a degree that I feel immersed in Dante's Inferno. Hellfire and brimstone from the hearth and only a few feet away outside the window, I feel the promise of Lake Geneva freezing over into a crude imitation of Cocytus, the Ninth Circle of Hell. Will I and my Beloved and our Little Lord and poor Polidori and dearest Claire become trapped in the frozen lake like the traitors. How I remember the words of the Florentine poet:

> "'Vexilla Regis prodeunt Inferni'
> *Towards us; therefore look in front of thee,"*
> *My Master said, "if thou discernest him."*
>
> *As, when there breathes a heavy fog, or when*
> *Our hemisphere is darkening into night,*
> *Appears far off a mill the wind is turning,*
>
> *Methought that such a building then I saw;*
> *And, for the wind, I drew myself behind*
> *My Guide, because there was no other shelter.*

---

87 From *Frankenstein; or the Modern Prometheus* by Mary Wollstonecraft Shelley, published by Lackington, Hughes, Harding, Mavor & Jones, 1818

Now was I, and with fear in verse I put it,
There where the shades were wholly covered up,
And glimmered through like unto straws in glass.

Some prone are lying, others stand erect,
This with the head, and that one with the soles;
Another, bow-like, face to feet inverts.

When in advance so far we had proceeded,
That it my Master pleased to show to me
The creature who once had the beauteous semblance,

He from before me moved and made me stop,
Saying: "Behold Dis, and behold the place
Where thou with fortitude must arm thyself."[88]

I turned away from poetic digressions and the coming wintry squall to my journal. The effects of my reading of the experiences of the Creation of the Creature and my pale student's subsequent abandonment of his very Creation lingered more as a memory of clear waking than a memory of a mere dream. I can still hear the thunder; I can still feel the rumble; I can still see the lightning burned into my eyes when I blink; I can still taste and smell the electricity in the air. My hair is still damp. My nerves shivered. Then there can a clear rapping upon the entry door. Claire called out that she would answer; then moments later she appeared in parlour holding two envelopes having arrived by post. 'Strange', Claire said, 'these letters must have addressed to be previous guest of the Villa Diodati; or perhaps posted in anticipation of a future guest?' I inquired to whom the letters were addressed, and Claire answered, '*To* V. Frankenstein.' I leapt from my chair like a Burmese tiger pouncing upon its prey and snatched the envelope from poor little Claire's dainty hand. Startled, she cowered, then threatened to bolt from the parlour as if I had been a Burmese tiger raring to strike. I tore the envelope open with a fury of claws. The letters were indeed addressed to my pale student of the unhallowed arts. They were written by his cousin, Elizabeth and his father, Alphonse. Curious that my psychosomatic phantasm would choose to communication his tale through physical letters. But having seen inspiration strike my Beloved and our little Lord in queer ways, I will trust my pale student to tell his tell in any manner he so choses. I read the letter out loud in the quiet of

---

88 From *The Divine Comedy – The Inferno* (Canto XXXIV) by Dante Alighieri, translated by Henry Wadsworth Longfellow

the parlour as if my pale student was sitting by the hearth surrounded by books.

To V. Frankenstein

My Dear Cousin,

I cannot describe to you the uneasiness we have all felt concerning your health. We cannot help imagining that your friend Clerval conceals the extent of your disorder: for it is now several months since we have seen your hand-writing; and all this time you have been obliged to dictate your letters to Henry. Surely, Victor, you must have been exceedingly ill; and this makes us all very wretched, as much so nearly as after the death of your dear mother. My uncle was almost persuaded that you were indeed dangerously ill, and could hardly be restrained from undertaking a journey to Ingolstadt. Clerval always writes that you are getting better; I eagerly hope that you will confirm this intelligence soon in your own hand-writing; for indeed, indeed, Victor, we are all very miserable on this account. Relieve us from this fear, and we shall be the happiest creatures in the world. Your father's health is now so vigorous, that he appears ten years younger since last winter. Ernest also is so much improved, that you would hardly know him: he is now nearly sixteen, and has lost that sickly appearance which he had some years ago; he is grown quite robust and active.

My uncle and I conversed a long time last night about what profession Ernest should follow. His constant illness when young has deprived him of the habits of application; and now that he enjoys good health, he is continually in the open air, climbing the hills, or rowing on the lake. I therefore proposed that he should be a farmer; which you know, Cousin, is a favourite scheme of mine. A farmer's is a very healthy happy life; and the least hurtful, or rather the most beneficial profession of any. My uncle had an idea of his being educated as an advocate, that through his interest he might become a judge. But, besides that he is not at all fitted for such an occupation, it is certainly more creditable to cultivate the earth for the sustenance of man, than to be the confidant, and sometimes the accomplice, of his vices; which is the profession of a lawyer. I said, that the employments of a prosperous farmer, if they were not a more honourable, they were at least a happier species of occupation than that of a judge, whose misfortune it was always to meddle with the dark side of human nature. My uncle smiled, and said, that I ought to be an advocate myself, which put an end to the conversation on that subject.

And now I must tell you a little story that will please, and perhaps amuse you. Do you not remember Justine Martin? Probably you do not; I will relate her history, therefore, in a few words. Madame Martin, her mother, was a widow with four children, of whom Justine was the third. This girl had always been the favourite of her father; but, through a strange perversity, her mother could not endure her, and, after the death of Monsieur Martin, treated her very ill. My aunt observed this; and, when Justine was twelve years of age, prevailed on her mother to allow her to live at her house. The republican institutions of our country have produced simpler and happier manners than those which prevail in the great monarchies that surround it. Hence there is less distinction between the several classes of its inhabitants; and the lower orders being neither so poor nor so despised, their manners are more refined and moral. A servant in Geneva does not mean the same thing as a servant in France and England.

This is the same sentiment as my Beloved. My Beloved observed in a letter dated June 1, 1816, merely a month ago while on our journey to visit Lord Byron at the Villa Diodati, where we would hopefully spent our summer lounging, hiking, and touring the lake by boat, that 'There is more equality of classes here than in England. This occasions a greater freedom and refinement of manners among the lower orders than we meet with in our own country. I fancy the haughty English ladies are greatly disgusted with this consequence of republican institutions, for the Genevese servants complain very much of their scolding, an exercise of the tongue, I believe, perfectly unknown here. The peasants of Switzerland may not however emulate the vivacity and grace of the French. They are more cleanly, but they are slow and inapt. I know a girl of twenty, who although she had lived all her life among vineyards, could not inform me during what month the vintage took place, and I discovered she was utterly ignorant of the order in which the months succeed to one another. She would not have been surprised if I had talked of the burning sun and delicious fruits of December, or of the frosts of July. Yet she is by no means deficient in understanding.'[89] Are own memories are creeping into Victor's tale— nay! Elizabeth's letter— again?

Justine, thus received in our family, learned the duties of a servant; a condition which, in our fortunate country, does not include the idea of ignorance, and a sacrifice of the dignity of a human being.

After what I have said, I dare say you well remember the heroine of my little tale: for Justine was a great favourite of your's; and I recollect you once remarked, that if you were in an ill-humour, one glance from Justine could dissipate it, for the same reason that Ariosto gives concerning the beauty of Angelica— she looked so frank-hearted and happy. My

---

89 From the *History of a Six Weeks Tour Through a Part of France, Germany, Switzerland, and Holland* by Mary Shelley, published by T. Hookham, Jun. Old Bond Street, and C. and J. Ollier, Welback Street, 1817

aunt conceived a great attachment for her, by which she was induced to give her an education superior to that which she had at first intended. This benefit was fully repaid; Justine was the most grateful little creature in the world: I do not mean that she made any professions, I never heard one pass her lips; but you could see by her eyes that she almost adored her protectress. Although her disposition was gay, and in many respects inconsiderate, yet she paid the greatest attention to every gesture of my aunt. She thought her the model of all excellence, and endeavoured to imitate her phraseology and manners, so that even now she often reminds me of her.

When my dearest aunt died, every one was too much occupied in their own grief to notice poor Justine, who had attended her during her illness with the most anxious affection. Poor Justine was very ill; but other trials were reserved for her.

One by one, her brothers and sister died; and her mother, with the exception of her neglected daughter, was left childless. The conscience of the woman was troubled; she began to think that the deaths of her favourites was a judgment from heaven to chastise her partiality. She was a Roman Catholic; and I believe her confessor confirmed the idea which she had conceived. Accordingly, a few months after your departure for Ingolstadt, Justine was called home by her repentant mother. Poor girl! she wept when she quitted our house: she was much altered since the death of my aunt; grief had given softness and a winning mildness to her manners, which had before been remarkable for vivacity. Nor was her residence at her mother's house of a nature to restore her gaiety. The poor woman was very vacillating in her repentance. She sometimes begged Justine to forgive her unkindness, but much oftener accused her of having caused the deaths of her brothers and sister. Perpetual fretting at length threw Madame Martin into a decline, which at first increased her irritability, but she is now at peace for ever. She died on the first approach of cold weather, at the beginning of this last winter. Justine has returned to us; and I assure you I love her tenderly. She is very clever and gentle, and extremely pretty; as I mentioned before, her mien and her expressions continually remind me of my dear aunt.

I must say also a few words to you, my dear cousin, of little darling William. I wish you could see him; he is very tall of his age, with sweet laughing blue eyes, dark eye-lashes, and curling hair. When he smiles, two little dimples appear on each cheek, which are rosy with health. He has already had one or two little *wives*, but Louisa Biron is his favourite, a pretty little girl of five years of age.

My! How William Frankenstein reminds me of my own William, my babbling little 'Willmouse'. Again and again and again my own life creeps into Victor's tale. My own William is a mere six months old, but how I can imagine him having one or two little wives when he reaches the age of schooling. How delightful. I cannot help but to think that the name 'Louisa Biron' could be prescient, a form of prophecy, that my own William will encounter a girl named 'Louisa Biron' at some point in his schooling. Would this girl be his first childhood 'wife' or perchance this is the name of a woman he will encounter at university. I hope I look back on the journal with found remembering. Maybe I will gift these pages, torn from my journal, to the young woman on their wedding day!

Now, dear Victor, I dare say you wish to be indulged in a little gossip concerning the good people of Geneva. The pretty Miss Mansfield has already received the congratulatory visits on her approaching marriage with a young Englishman, John Melbourne, Esq. Her ugly sister, Manon, married Mr Duvillard, the rich banker, last autumn. Your favourite schoolfellow, Louis Manoir, has suffered several misfortunes since the departure of Clerval from Geneva. But he has already recovered his spirits, and is reported to be on the point of marrying a very lively pretty Frenchwoman, Madame Tavernier. She is a widow, and much older than Manoir; but she is very much admired, and a favourite with every body.

I have written myself into good spirits, dear cousin; yet I cannot conclude without again anxiously inquiring concerning your health. Dear Victor, if you are not very ill, write yourself, and make your father and all of us happy; or— — I cannot bear to think of the other side of the question; my tears already flow. Adieu, my dearest cousin.

Elizabeth Lavenza
Geneva, March 19th 1795

Having read the letter, I looked up and the thunderclouds must have grown so dark and dreary that noon now appeared midnight. The thunderstorm raged as violently as those I experienced above the Castle Frankenstein yesterweek. In the armchair set next to the hearth, where my Beloved preferred to sit, including during his galvanising debate with Lord Byron, sat not my Beloved, but the pale student of the unhallowed arts. Had he heard my reading of the letter under my breath? Perhaps, I read a little too loudly for the reading had caught his attention. I apologized most furiously for having betrayed him by reading a letter clearly addressed to him. I recognized in myself that I still believed the pale student to be a figment of my overactive imagination and not a person. But here and now he appeared more a person than a dream. He exclaimed when I read her letter:

' "Dear, dear Elizabeth! I will write instantly, and relieve them from the anxiety they must feel." I wrote, and this exertion greatly fatigued me; but my convalescence had commenced, and proceeded regularly. In another fortnight I was able to leave my chamber.' I wonder how much time has passed since that 'deary night in November' when his Creation was born without the necessity of a womb. Four months? Perhaps five? And still he makes little reference to his Creation. Does he ponder his Creation's hereabouts or his happenings. Four months is a long time for a creature with the mentality of a child to experience this cruel world created by an equally cruel God. And speak of the cruel world, did not Marcion of Sinope, an early Church Father turned Heretic, believe that the God of the Old Testament, the Demiurge, was far too severely just with all His precise and preposterous Laws written through the Torah of Moses? Did he not believe that Jesus the Christ was the Son of the Good God and not as Christians suppose the Son of the God of the Old Testament? Victor is behaving like the Demiurge with no concern for his Creation. Does not the God of the Old Testament command: *Remember, O Lord, the children of Edom in the day of Jerusalem; who said, Rase it, rase it, even to the foundation thereof. O daughter of Babylon, who art to be destroyed; happy shall he be, that rewardeth thee as thou hast served us. Happy shall he be, that taketh and dasheth thy little ones against the stones.*[90] I am growing in dislike and distrust and disgust for my pale student when it concerns his Creation created by the unhallowed arts!

'One of my first duties on my recovery was to introduce Clerval to the several professors of the university. In doing this, I underwent a kind of rough usage, ill befitting the wounds that my mind had sustained. Ever since the fatal night, the end of my labours, and the beginning of my misfortunes, I had conceived a violent antipathy even to the name of natural philosophy. When I was otherwise quite restored to health, the sight of a chemical instrument would renew all the agony of my nervous symptoms. Henry saw this, and had removed all my apparatus from my view.'

Curious and curiouser. In my waking dream of the laboratory at Castle Frankenstein where he breathed life into his Creation through unrelatable means, I did not think to imagine what his apartment in Ingolstadt with its queer apparatuses collected by a desperate student from disparate laboratories around Ingolstadt and the bloody and rotting and now putrid body parts collected from charnel houses and slaughterhouses. My pale student makes little mention having repaired his apartment to a natural state before falling deep into his coma. If his dearest Henry saw nothing out of the ordinary, can the readiest explanation be that all of this the product of a deeply disturbed imagination?

---

90 From Psalm 137:7-9

Or did he choose to omit this fact from his telling. And if he did choose to omit this fact, what else is he withholding from me!

'He had also changed my apartment; for he perceived that I had acquired a dislike for the room which had previously been my laboratory. But these cares of Clerval were made of no avail when I visited the professors. Mr Waldman inflicted torture when he praised, with kindness and warmth, the astonishing progress I had made in the sciences. He soon perceived that I disliked the subject; but, not guessing the real cause, he attributed my feelings to modesty, and changed the subject from my improvement to the science itself, with a desire, as I evidently saw, of drawing me out. What could I do? He meant to please, and he tormented me. I felt as if he had placed carefully, one by one, in my view those instruments which were to be afterwards used in putting me to a slow and cruel death. I writhed under his words, yet dared not exhibit the pain I felt. Clerval, whose eyes and feelings were always quick in discerning the sensations of others, declined the subject, alleging, in excuse, his total ignorance; and the conversation took a more general turn. I thanked my friend from my heart, but I did not speak. I saw plainly that he was surprised, but he never attempted to draw my secret from me; and although I loved him with a mixture of affection and reverence that knew no bounds, yet I could never persuade myself to confide to him that event which was so often present to my recollection, but which I feared the detail to another would only impress more deeply.

'Mr Krempe was not equally docile; and in my condition at that time, of almost insupportable sensitiveness, his harsh blunt encomiums gave me even more pain than the benevolent approbation of Mr Waldman. "Damn the fellow!" cried he; "why, Mr Clerval, I assure you he has outstript us all. Aye, stare if you please; but it is nevertheless true. A youngster who, but a few years ago, believed Cornelius Agrippa as firmly as the gospel, has now set himself at the head of the university; and if he is not soon pulled down, we shall all be out of countenance.— Aye, aye," continued he, observing my face expressive of suffering, "Mr Frankenstein is modest; an excellent quality in a young man. Young men should be diffident of themselves, you know, Mr Clerval; I was myself when young: but that wears out in a very short time."

'Mr Krempe had now commenced an eulogy on himself, which happily turned the conversation from a subject that was so annoying to me.

'Clerval was no natural philosopher. His imagination was too vivid for the minutiæ of science. Languages were his principal study; and he sought, by acquiring their elements, to open a field for self-instruction on his return to Geneva. Persian, Arabic, and Hebrew, gained his attention, after he had made himself perfectly master of Greek and Latin. For my

own part, idleness had ever been irksome to me; and now that I wished
to fly from reflection, and hated my former studies, I felt great relief in
being the fellow-pupil with my friend, and found not only instruction but
consolation in the works of the orientalists. Their melancholy is soothing, and their joy elevating to a degree I never experienced in studying
the authors of any other country. When you read their writings, life appears to consist in a warm sun and garden of roses,— in the smiles and
frowns of a fair enemy, and the fire that consumes your own heart. How
different from the manly and heroical poetry of Greece and Rome.

'Summer passed away in these occupations, and my return to Geneva was fixed for the latter end of autumn; but being delayed by several
accidents, winter and snow arrived, the roads were deemed impassable,
and my journey was retarded until the ensuing spring. I felt this delay
very bitterly; for I longed to see my native town, and my beloved friends.
My return had only been delayed so long from an unwillingness to leave
Clerval in a strange place, before he had become acquainted with any of
its inhabitants. The winter, however, was spent cheerfully; and although
the spring was uncommonly late, when it came, its beauty compensated
for its dilatoriness.

'The month of May had already commenced.' Damn this Victor
Frankenstein straight to Hell. I no longer wish to be haunted by him.
How long has his Creation wandered alone through the cruel world
without a parent to guide his education. Not a single thought is given.
This abandonment of his Creation has my intestines twisted into knots.
The pain I feel for his Creation is a mother's pain. But a father? Ha!
A father often cares not for his offspring. Lord Byron has abandoned
all children: The Honourable Augusta Ada Bryon, his only legitimate
child, and Elizabeth Medora Leigh, born of an incestuous relation with
his half-sister. His daughters know not the love of a father. And of that
child growing in the womb of my dearest sister Claire, he cares nothing, and it is not yet born. He is greatly inconvenienced by the mere
presence of dearest Claire. Lord Byron only concerns himself physical
aspects of the intimate acts and nothing for its consequences. And Victor has taken up our little Lord's mantle.

'And I expected the letter daily which was to fix the date of my departure, when Henry proposed a pedestrian tour in the environs of Ingolstadt that I might bid a personal farewell to the country I had so long
inhabited. I acceded with pleasure to this proposition: I was fond of exercise, and Clerval had always been my favourite companion in the rambles
of this nature that I had taken among the scenes of my native country.

'We passed a fortnight in these perambulations: my health and spirits
had long been restored, and they gained additional strength from the

salubrious air I breathed, the natural incidents of our progress, and the conversation of my friend. Study had before secluded me from the intercourse of my fellow-creatures, and rendered me unsocial; but Clerval called forth the better feelings of my heart; he again taught me to love the aspect of nature, and the cheerful faces of children. Excellent friend! how sincerely did you love me, and endeavour to elevate my mind, until it was on a level with your own. A selfish pursuit had cramped and narrowed me, until your gentleness and affection warmed and opened my senses; I became the same happy creature who, a few years ago, loving and beloved by all, had no sorrow or care. When happy, inanimate nature had the power of bestowing on me the most delightful sensations. A serene sky and verdant fields filled me with ecstacy. The present season was indeed divine; the flowers of spring bloomed in the hedges, while those of summer were already in bud: I was undisturbed by thoughts which during the preceding year had pressed upon me, notwithstanding my endeavours to throw them off, with an invincible burden.

'Henry rejoiced in my gaiety, and sincerely sympathized in my feelings: he exerted himself to amuse me, while he expressed the sensations that filled his soul. The resources of his mind on this occasion were truly astonishing: his conversation was full of imagination; and very often, in imitation of the Persian and Arabic writers, he invented tales of wonderful fancy and passion. At other times he repeated my favourite poems, or drew me out into arguments, which he supported with great ingenuity.

'We returned to our college on a Sunday afternoon: the peasants were dancing, and every one we met appeared gay and happy. My own spirits were high, and I bounded along with feelings of unbridled joy and hilarity.'

The pale student looked down at his hands and then up at me. He requested of me; he required of me to read the second letter. I observed the address '*To* V. Frankenstein' was written in a man's handwriting and Victor exclaimed that it must be from his father! I pealed open the envelope and revealed the letter that had, in fact, been written by his father! I prepared to hand him the letter, but he waved his hand away, so I read it aloud it aloud to him as I had the first:

Chapter II

'My Dear Victor,

You have probably waited impatiently for a letter to fix the date of your return to us; and I was at first tempted to write only a few lines, merely mentioning the day on which I should expect you. But that would be a cruel kindness, and I dare not do it. What would be your surprise, my son, when you expected a happy and gay welcome, to behold, on the contrary, tears and wretchedness? And how, Victor, can I relate our misfortune? Absence cannot have rendered you callous to our joys and griefs; and how shall I inflict pain on an absent child? I wish to prepare you for the woeful news, but I know it is impossible; even now your eye skims over the page, to seek the words which are to convey to you the horrible tidings.

'William is dead!— that sweet child, whose smiles delighted and warmed my heart, who was so gentle, yet so gay! Victor, he is murdered!'

I burst into tears when I read the words, weeping wildly. In the moment, I failed to connect my own unchristened daughter's infantile death to these very words and my sudden sullen sadness. But now writing these words into my journal, I do realize that not only am I weeping for my own unchristened daughter, but as a daughter having lost my mother due to my own childbirth. If my own birth had not been so laboured and difficult, the placenta that nourished me for nine months would have been discharged intact, but the afterbirth did not discharge intact. The childbed fever caused by my birth took my mother's life. How cursed are the Wollstonecrafts?

How cursed are the Frankensteins? I wept for Victor; I wept for his father, I wept for William. I struggled to look up for the page, becoming stained with my teardrops. Oh! no! I cannot allow the ink to become smudged. If this letter is ruined, then how will Victor know the conclusion? In a moment of sheer will, I looked over at Victor to see all life go out of my pale student. If he had been pale of complexion due to the burden of his creation of the Creature, now he was pale due to pain of having lost his younger brother. But what of Alphonse Frankenstein's own pain? He has lost a son! There is no pain equal to this! No man or woman becomes a father or mother and looks down at their child, believing they will outlive their own creation. But I do not intend to dismiss Victor's own pain, for now news comes by post that your cherished brother is murdered. Victor's legs weakened and his arm went wimp. His head rolled back onto his spine. He laboured to take a breath and when he exhaled the breath was nothing more than a wheeze. After several long moments for me and an eternity for him, he begged me to continue, and I did:

'I will not attempt to console you; but will simply relate the circumstances of the transaction.' Nor will I attempt to console my pale student. I too can only relate the circumstances of the transaction as written in his father's letter. How can this father, the patriarch of the Frankensteins, steel himself to relate the 'circumstances of the transaction' of his own son's murder in a mere letter to his surviving son? Were the tearstains and smudged ink of my cause or the father's in the penning of the letter? I did not attempt to answer my own question because I steeled myself to continue reading to my poor pale student:

'Last Thursday (May 7th) I, my niece, and your two brothers, went to walk in Plainpalais.' I know this location and the incident that occurred there well! My Beloved and I learned of the 'incident' during our *Six Weeks' Tour*:

> To the south of the town of Gevena is the promenade of the Genevese, a grassy plain planted with a few trees, and called Plainpalais. Here a small obelisk is erected to the glory of Rousseau, and here (such is the mutability of human life) the magistrates, the successors of those who exiled him from his native country, were shot by the populace during that revolution, which his writings mainly contributed to mature, and which, notwithstanding the temporary bloodshed and injustice with which it was polluted, has produced enduring benefits to mankind, which all the chicanery of statesmen, nor even the great conspiracy of kings, can entirely render vain. From respect to the memory of their predecessors, none of the present magistrates ever walk in Plainpalais.[91]

The evening was warm and serene, and we prolonged our walk farther than usual. It was already dusk before we thought of returning; and then we discovered that William and Ernest, who had gone on before, were not to be found. We accordingly rested on a seat until they should return. Presently Ernest came, and inquired if we had seen his brother: he said, that they had been playing together, that William had run away to hide himself, and that he vainly sought for him, and afterwards waited for him a long time, but that he did not return.

This account rather alarmed us, and we continued to search for him until night fell, when Elizabeth conjectured that he might have returned to the house. He was not there. We returned again, with torches; for I could not rest, when I thought that my sweet boy had lost himself, and was exposed to all the damps and dews of night: Elizabeth also suffered extreme anguish. About five in the morning I discovered my lovely boy, whom the night before I had seen blooming and active in health, stretched on the grass livid and motionless: the print of the murderer's finger was on his neck.' To lose a small child to illness is one nightmare for a parent, but to lose a small child to murder is an unwakeable nightmare! I look to my own William sleeping peacefully in his bassinette

---

91 From the *History of a Six Weeks Tour Through a Part of France, Germany, Switzerland, and Holland* by Mary Shelley, published by T. Hookham, Jun. Old Bond Street, and C. and J. Ollier, Welback Street, 1817

and my nerves are aflame with shudders. Gooseflesh prickles on my arms. Tear threaten to overwhelm my eyes. I cannot stomach to look upon my pale student and I continue my recitation of the letter:

'He was conveyed home, and the anguish that was visible in my countenance betrayed the secret to Elizabeth. She was very earnest to see the corpse. At first I attempted to prevent her; but she persisted, and entering the room where it lay, hastily examined the neck of the victim, and clasping her hands exclaimed, 'O God! I have murdered my darling infant!'

'She fainted, and was restored with extreme difficulty. When she again lived, it was only to weep and sigh. She told me, that that same evening William had teazed her to let him wear a very valuable miniature that she possessed of your mother. This picture is gone, and was doubtless the temptation which urged the murderer to the deed. We have no trace of him at present, although our exertions to discover him are unremitted; but they will not restore my beloved William.

'Come, dearest Victor; you alone can console Elizabeth. She weeps continually, and accuses herself unjustly as the cause of his death; her words pierce my heart. We are all unhappy; but will not that be an additional motive for you, my son, to return and be our comforter? Your dear mother! Alas, Victor! I now say, Thank God she did not live to witness the cruel, miserable death of her youngest darling!

'Come, Victor; not brooding thoughts of vengeance against the assassin, but with feelings of peace and gentleness, that will heal, instead of festering the wounds of our minds. Enter the house of mourning, my friend, but with kindness and affection for those who love you, and not with hatred for your enemies.

Your affectionate and afflicted father,
'Alphonse Frankenstein
'Geneva, May 12th, 1795'

I, who had watched Victor's countenance as I read this letter, was surprised to observe the despair that succeed to the joy he at first expressed on receiving news from his friends. I threw the letter on the table, and he covered his face with his hands.

'My dear Frankenstein,' exclaimed Henry, when he perceived him weep with bitterness. I heard this Henry Clerval speak audibly as he addressed his dear friend, though I saw him not. Was he standing in the parlour of the Villa Diodati with Victor and me, or his own study of oriental languages? Or both? I found myself no longer merely being a transcriber of the tale Victor was telling me; I was now a voyeur as this very scene played out. I tried desperately to force my eyes to capture

Henry's ghostly visage but could not. He was an invisible phantasm. 'Are you always to be unhappy? My dear friend, what has happened?' Was Henry's disembodied voice a mere figment of my overactive imagination? Or do authors of great fiction often hear the voices of imaginary characters speaking quite audibly? I heard Henry quite clearly; I heard and saw Victor with even more reality! Should I commit myself to in Bethlem Royal Hospital upon my return to London? I do not know!

My pale student motioned to Henry to take up the letter, while he walked up and down the parlour in the Villa Diodati in the extremest agitation. Tears no doubt gushed from their eyes as they all had heard the account of his misfortune.

'I can offer you no consolation, my friend,' said Henry again most audibly to my ears; 'your disaster is irreparable. What do you intend to do?'

'To go instantly to Geneva: come with me, Henry, to order the horses.'

'Poor William!' Clerval said clearly endeavouring to raise Victor's spirits; he did not do this by common topics of consolation, but by exhibiting the truest sympathy, 'that dear child; he now sleeps with his angel mother. His friends mourn and weep, but he is at rest: he does not now feel the murderer's grasp; a sod covers his gentle form, and he knows no pain. He can no longer be a fit subject for pity; the survivors are the greatest sufferers, and for them time is the only consolation. Those maxims of the Stoics, that death was no evil, and that the mind of man ought to be superior to despair on the eternal absence of a beloved object, ought not to be urged. Even Cato wept over the dead body of his brother.'

My pale student took back his armchair. My voyeurship of this all too brief scene ended abruptly as it had played to its conclusion. Victor resumed his tale as he had before my quite queer recitation of the mysterious letters upended our routine. I picked up my pen again to continue my transcription of this harrowing, horrifying tale: 'Soon we hurried through the streets; the words impressed themselves on my mind, and I remembered them afterwards in solitude. But now, as soon as the horses arrived, I hurried into a cabriole, and bade farewell to my friend.

'My journey, dearest Mary, was very melancholy. At first I wished to hurry on, for I longed to console and sympathize with my loved and sorrowing friends; but when I drew near my native town, I slackened my progress. I could hardly sustain the multitude of feelings that crowded into my mind. I passed through scenes familiar to my youth, but which I had not seen for nearly six years. How altered every thing might be during that time? One sudden and desolating change had taken place; but a thousand little circumstances might have by degrees worked other alterations which, although they were done more tranquilly, might not be the less decisive. Fear overcame me; I dared not advance, dreading a thousand nameless evils that made me tremble, although I was unable to define them.

'I remained two days at Lausanne, in this painful state of mind. I contemplated the lake: the waters were placid; all around was calm, and the snowy mountains, "the palaces of nature," were not changed. By degrees the calm and heavenly scene restored me, and I continued my journey towards Geneva.'

'The palaces of Nature.' Such a curious turn of phrase for my pale student to utter. On our eight-day excursion across the lake, Lord Byron confided to me in private, he did not wish Percy to know, that he was composing a third canto to 'Childe Harold's Pilgrimage'. I was delighted to know that he had picked up the poem having gestated for four long years since the publication of the first and second. The poem had not yet been completed and therefore not ready for recitation in the parlour of the Villa Diodati, but he handed me some pages, not the first and not the last, but somewhere in the middle, and asked me to give him my criticism. Not that there would be much to criticize, but an author is overeager to hear constructive feedback of his labours. Amongst the stanzas gifted to me that night was this particular one:

> But these recede. Above me are the Alps,
> The palaces of Nature, whose vast walls
> Have pinnacled in clouds their snowy scalps,
> And throned Eternity in icy halls
> Of cold sublimity, where forms and falls
> The avalanche—the thunderbolt of snow!
> All that expands the spirit, yet appals,
> Gathers around these summits, as to show
> How Earth may pierce to Heaven,
> Yet leave vain man below.[92]

'The road ran by the side of the lake, which became narrower as I approached my native town. I discovered more distinctly the black sides of Jura, and the bright summit of Mont Blânc; I wept like a child: "Dear mountains! my own beautiful lake! how do you welcome your wanderer? Your summits are clear; the sky and lake are blue and placid. Is this to prognosticate peace, or to mock at my unhappiness?"

'I fear, dearest Mary, that I shall render myself tedious by dwelling on these preliminary circumstances; but they were days of comparative

92 From *Childe Harold's Pilgrimage, a Romaunt* by Lord Byron, published by John Murray, 1816

happiness, and I think of them with pleasure. My country, my beloved country! who but a native can tell the delight I took in again beholding thy streams, thy mountains, and, more than all, thy lovely lake.

'Yet, as I drew nearer home, grief and fear again overcame me. Night also closed around; and when I could hardly see the dark mountains, I felt still more gloomily. The picture appeared a vast and dim scene of evil, and I foresaw obscurely that I was destined to become the most wretched of human beings. Alas! I prophesied truly, and failed only in one single circumstance, that in all the misery I imagined and dreaded, I did not conceive the hundredth part of the anguish I was destined to endure.

'It was completely dark when I arrived in the environs of Geneva; the gates of the town were already shut; and I was obliged to pass the night at Secheron, a village half a league to the east of the city.' I and my Beloved and dearest Claire encountered a similar encounter. On the first of June, as we neared beginning our summer with Lord Byron, we learned too 'that he town is surrounded by a wall, the three gates of which are shut exactly at ten o'clock, when no bribery (as in France) can open them.'[93] My pale student continued, while I was scribbling my digression, 'The sky was serene; and, as I was unable to rest, I resolved to visit the spot where my poor William had been murdered. As I could not pass through the town, I was obliged to cross the lake in a boat to arrive at Plainpalais. During this short voyage I saw the lightnings playing on the summit of Mont Blânc in the most beautiful figures. The storm appeared to approach rapidly; and, on landing, I ascended a low hill, that I might observe its progress. It advanced; the heavens were clouded, and I soon felt the rain coming slowly in large drops, but its violence quickly increased.

'I quitted my seat, and walked on, although the darkness and storm increased every minute, and the thunder burst with a terrific crash over my head. It was echoed from Salêve, the Juras, and the Alps of Savoy; vivid flashes of lightning dazzled my eyes, illuminating the lake, making it appear like a vast sheet of fire; then for an instant every thing seemed of a pitchy darkness, until the eye recovered itself from the preceding flash.' And if, like an actor waiting offstage for the hearing of their cue, a thunderstorm burst over Lake Geneva and buffeted the windows with wind and rain. 'The storm, as is often the case in Switzerland, appeared at once in various parts of the heavens. The most violent storm hung exactly north of the town, over that part of the lake which lies between the promontory of Belrive and the village of Copêt. Another storm en-

---

93 From the *History of a Six Weeks Tour Through a Part of France, Germany, Switzerland, and Holland* by Mary Shelley, published by T. Hookham, Jun. Old Bond Street, and C. and J. Ollier, Welback Street, 1817

lightened Jura with faint flashes; and another darkened and sometimes disclosed the Môle, a peaked mountain to the east of the lake.

'While I watched the storm, so beautiful yet terrific, I wandered on with a hasty step. This noble war in the sky elevated my spirits; I clasped my hands, and exclaimed aloud, "William, dear angel! this is thy funeral, this thy dirge!" As I said these words, I perceived in the gloom a figure which stole from behind a clump of trees near me; I stood fixed, gazing intently: I could not be mistaken. A flash of lightning illuminated the object, and discovered its shape plainly to me; its gigantic stature, and the deformity of its aspect, more hideous than belongs to humanity, instantly informed me that it was the wretch, the filthy dæmon to whom I had given life.' His Creation has returned. What wondrous news! 'What did he there? Could he be (I shuddered at the conception) the murderer of my brother? No sooner did that idea cross my imagination, than I became convinced of its truth; my teeth chattered, and I was forced to lean against a tree for support.'

'No! How can you be so certain', I said out loud. For the first time, I interrupted my pale student to the unhallowed arts, the very unhallowed arts that created his Creation, what he calls his Creature. 'The letter from your father was dated and posted on May the Twelfth and no doubt took a handful of days to reach your apartment in Ingolstadt. And! You yourself said that you tarried a tid bit on your journey home. Had your Creation lingered in the vicinity of the Plainpalais for all this time? No murderer no matter how mad lingers for so long. True, a murderer may linger awhile to bear witness to the aftermath of his deeds, but to linger, exposed to the elements for so long reeks of a lunatic or the innocent. Do you so dismiss your Creation as a lunatic? You assembled him. You breathed life into its amalgamation of body parts from charnel houses and slaughterhouses. And yet, you are so quick to lay the blame on your own Creation. Is it not just as logical that your Creation had learned of the murder, heard the child's surname, and sought the location out in hopes of finding you? His Creator.'

Dismissing my words as if I never uttered them, he continued, 'The figure passed me quickly, and I lost it in the gloom. Nothing in human shape could have destroyed that fair child. *He* was the murderer! I could not doubt it. The mere presence of the idea was an irresistible proof of the fact. I thought of pursuing the devil; but it would have been in vain, for another flash discovered him to me hanging among the rocks of the nearly perpendicular ascent of Mont Salêve, a hill that bounds Plainpalais on the south. He soon reached the summit, and disappeared.

'I remained motionless. The thunder ceased; but the rain still continued, and the scene was enveloped in an impenetrable darkness. I revolved in my mind the events which I had until now sought to forget: the whole train of my progress towards the creation; the appearance of the work of my own hands alive at my bed side; its departure. Two years had now nearly elapsed since the night on which he first received life; and was this his first crime?'

Did his Creation linger all this time in the vicinity of Ingolstadt? Where had his Creation been in the interim? Did his Creation learn of his Creator's surname? Did his Creation discover the homeland of his Creator? Question upon questions upon questions stir in my mind. A walk from Ingolstadt to Geneva would be perhaps a month in length, depending on the weather and weariness. Victor admitted he tarried a day here or there on his own carriage journey. Or is Victor correct? And his Creation had learned his surname and his homeland and sought to murder a cherished loved one. No! I cannot bear to think these thoughts. True, his Creation had been abandoned by his Creator mere moments after awaking, but nothing my pale student has said in the telling of this tale will lead me to the conclusion that his Creation murdered William Frankenstein in the coldest of blood. Does not a human heart beat within his chest, or did Victor implant the heart of a bull in his massive chest?

'Alas! I had turned loose into the world a depraved wretch, whose delight was in carnage and misery; had he not murdered my brother?

'No one can conceive the anguish I suffered during the remainder of the night, which I spent, cold and wet, in the open air. But I did not feel the inconvenience of the weather; my imagination was busy in scenes of evil and despair. I considered the being whom I had cast among mankind, and endowed with the will and power to effect purposes of horror, such as the deed which he had now done, nearly in the light of my own vampire, my own spirit let loose from the grave, and forced to destroy all that was dear to me.

'Day dawned; and I directed my steps towards the town. The gates were open; and I hastened to my father's house. My first thought was to discover what I knew of the murderer, and cause instant pursuit to be made. But I paused when I reflected on the story that I had to tell. A being whom I myself had formed, and endued with life, had met me at midnight among the precipices of an inaccessible mountain. I remembered also the nervous fever with which I had been seized just at the time that I dated my creation, and which would give an air of delirium to a tale otherwise so utterly improbable. I well knew that if any other had communicated such a relation to me, I should have looked upon it as the ravings of insanity. Besides, the strange nature of the animal would elude all pursuit, even if I were so far credited as to persuade my relatives to commence it. Besides, of what use would be pursuit? Who could arrest a creature capable of scaling the overhanging sides of Mont Salêve? These reflections determined me, and I resolved to remain silent.

'It was about five in the morning when I entered my father's house. I told the servants not to disturb the family, and went into the library to attend their usual hour of rising.

'Six years had elapsed, passed as a dream but for one indelible trace, and I stood in the same place where I had last embraced my father before my departure for Ingolstadt. Beloved and respectable parent! He still remained to me. I gazed on the picture of my mother, which stood over the mantle-piece. It was an historical subject, painted at my father's desire, and represented Caroline Beaumont in an agony of despair, kneeling by the coffin of her dead father.

'Her garb was rustic, and her cheek pale; but there was an air of dignity and beauty, that hardly permitted the sentiment of pity. Below this picture was a miniature of William; and my tears flowed when I looked upon it. While I was thus engaged, Ernest entered: he had heard me arrive, and hastened to welcome me. He expressed a sorrowful delight to see me: "Welcome, my dearest Victor," said he. "Ah! I wish you had come three months ago, and then you would have found us all joyous and delighted. But we are now unhappy; and, I am afraid, tears instead of smiles will be your welcome. Our father looks so sorrowful: this dreadful event seems to have revived in his mind his grief on the death of Mamma. Poor Elizabeth also is quite inconsolable." Ernest began to weep as he said these words.' As do I. The scene in which my pale student paints, like the painting of his dear, sweet Mother kneeling beside the coffin her dead father, is likewise inconsolable. I am also in the agony of despair.

' "Do not," said I, "welcome me thus; try to be more calm, that I may not be absolutely miserable the moment I enter my father's house after so long an absence. But, tell me, how does my father support his misfortunes? and how is my poor Elizabeth?"

' "She indeed requires consolation; she accused herself of having caused the death of my brother, and that made her very wretched. But since the murderer has been discovered—" Wait! What? The murderer discovered! Good God! How can that be?

Then Victor repeated my own words, ' "The murderer discovered! Good God! how can that be? who could attempt to pursue him? It is impossible; one might as well try to overtake the winds, or confine a mountain-stream with a straw."

' "I do not know what you mean; but we were all very unhappy when she was discovered. No one would believe it at first; and even now Elizabeth will not be convinced, notwithstanding all the evidence. Indeed, who would credit that Justine Martin, who was so amiable, and fond of all the family, could all at once become so extremely wicked?"

I know little of this poor girl, other than the brief words my pale student has spoken of her in his telling of his tale. Victor, of course he does, knows this girl more intimately as she has served his family for many years. As I know nothing of her, I can pass no judgments until I learn more of her situation.

' "Justine Martin! Poor, poor girl, is she the accused? But it is wrongfully; every one knows that; no one believes it, surely, Ernest?"

' "No one did at first; but several circumstances came out, that have almost forced conviction upon us: and her own behaviour has been so confused, as to add to the evidence of facts a weight that, I fear, leaves no hope for doubt. But she will be tried to-day, and you will then hear all."

'He related that, the morning on which the murder of poor William had been discovered, Justine had been taken ill, and confined to her bed; and, after several days, one of the servants, happening to examine the apparel she had worn on the night of the murder, had discovered in her pocket the picture of my mother, which had been judged to be the temptation of the murderer. The servant instantly shewed it to one of the others, who, without saying a word to any of the family, went to a magistrate; and, upon their deposition, Justine was apprehended. On being charged with the fact, the poor girl confirmed the suspicion in a great measure by her extreme confusion of manner.

'This was a strange tale, but it did not shake my faith; and I replied earnestly, "You are all mistaken; I know the murderer. Justine, poor, good Justine, is innocent."'

My pale student exposes his own prejudices against his Creation, the very Creation he abandoned mere moments after gifting it with life. It took mankind's Creator far longer to abandon His Creation. The Holy Scripture does not provide a perceptible timeline from Adam's creation from the dust of the earth and Eve's creation from his rib to their consuming of the fruit of the Tree of the Knowledge of Good and Evil. But God's abandonment of man did not come in mere moments after Adam's creation, but perhaps many years. And why was man cast out of the Garden of Eden? Not being he was evil, but merely because he now possessed the knowledge of *both* Good *and* Evil. My pale student of the unhallowed is so ready to dismiss his Creation as inherently evil. Why does he not see any good in his Creation. Here he is presented with evidence that jurisprudence finds accepting and he is completely dismissive of it.

'At that instant my father entered. I saw unhappiness deeply impressed on his countenance, but he endeavoured to welcome me cheerfully; and, after we had exchanged our mournful greeting, would have introduced some other topic than that of our disaster, had not Ernest exclaimed, "Good God, Papa! Victor says that he knows who was the murderer of poor William."

' "We do also, unfortunately," replied my father; "for indeed I had rather have been for ever ignorant than have discovered so much depravity and ingratitude in one I valued so highly."

' "My dear father, you are mistaken; Justine is innocent."

' "If she is, God forbid that she should suffer as guilty. She is to be tried to-day, and I hope, I sincerely hope, that she will be acquitted."

'This speech calmed me. I was firmly convinced in my own mind that Justine, and indeed every human being, was guiltless of this murder.' All humankind is guiltless of this murder? Oh, Victor. It is quite telling that you do not count your Creation among humankind? You sought to be the Creator of your own race of men but now cannot bear having created his own race of men. Your hubris knows no bounds. 'I had no fear, therefore, that any circumstantial evidence could be brought forward strong enough to convict her; and, in this assurance, I calmed myself, expecting the trial with eagerness, but without prognosticating an evil result.

'We were soon joined by Elizabeth. Time had made great alterations in her form since I had last beheld her. Six years before she had been a pretty, good-humoured girl, whom every one loved and caressed. She was now a woman in stature and expression of countenance, which was uncommonly lovely. An open and capacious forehead gave indications of a good understanding, joined to great frankness of disposition. Her eyes were hazel, and expressive of mildness, now through recent affliction allied to sadness. Her hair was of a rich, dark auburn, her complexion fair, and her figure slight and graceful. She welcomed me with the greatest affection. "Your arrival, my dear cousin," said she, "fills me with hope. You perhaps will find some means to justify my poor guiltless Justine.'

Elizabeth believes in the innocence of her servant and friend because of the nature of the feminine creature. Victor believes in the guilt of his Creation due to nature of the masculine creature. I do not regret the choosing of my words here. If the Christianity can lay the blame of Original Sin upon a single woman, Eve, then I can be afforded the same luxury by laying the hubris of mankind upon a single man, Victor Frankenstein!

'Alas! who is safe, if she be convicted of crime? I rely on her innocence as certainly as I do upon my own. Our misfortune is doubly hard to us; we have not only lost that lovely darling boy, but this poor girl, whom I sincerely love, is to be torn away by even a worse fate. If she is condemned, I never shall know joy more. But she will not, I am sure she will not; and then I shall be happy again, even after the sad death of my little William."

' "She is innocent, my Elizabeth," said I, "and that shall be proved; fear nothing, but let your spirits be cheered by the assurance of her acquittal."

' "How kind you are! every one else believes in her guilt, and that made me wretched; for I knew that it was impossible: and to see every one else prejudiced in so deadly a manner, rendered me hopeless and despairing." She wept.

' "Sweet niece," said my father, "dry your tears. If she is, as you believe, innocent, rely on the justice of our judges, and the activity with which I shall prevent the slightest shadow of partiality."'

Chapter III

2 July. Morning— 'We passed a few sad hours, until eleven o'clock, when the trial was to commence. My father and the rest of the family being obliged to attend as witnesses, I accompanied them to the court. During the whole of this wretched mockery of justice, I suffered living torture. It was to be decided, whether the result of my curiosity and lawless devices would cause the death of two of my fellow-beings: one a smiling babe, full of innocence and joy; the other far more dreadfully murdered, with every aggravation of infamy that could make the murder memorable in horror. Justine also was a girl of merit, and possessed qualities which promised to render her life happy: now all was to be obliterated in an ignominious grave; and I the cause! A thousand times rather would I have confessed myself guilty of the crime ascribed to Justine; but I was absent when it was committed, and such a declaration would have been considered as the ravings of a madman, and would not have exculpated her who suffered through me.'

What is the source of this guilt? The innerworkings of the mind remain a mystery to the natural philosophers. Confined to terms like mad and lunacy, these words do not capture the true depth and breadth of the mind that exists below consciousness. This is where Victor's guilt lies, under layers upon layers of the conscious mind. I believe the Creation is the source of this guilt. If Victor had not be playing God in his laboratory and was instead at home with his family, none of this horror would have occurred. And there is a part of the innerworkings of my mind that cannot shake the shocking belief that Victor's Creation has a part to play is this sadness.

The appearance of Justine was calm. She was dressed in mourning; and her countenance, always engaging, was rendered, by the solemnity

of her feelings, exquisitely beautiful. Yet she appeared confident in innocence, and did not tremble, although gazed on and execrated by thousands; for all the kindness which her beauty might otherwise have excited, was obliterated in the minds of the spectators by the imagination of
the enormity she was supposed to have committed. She was tranquil, yet
her tranquillity was evidently constrained; and as her confusion had before been adduced as a proof of her guilt, she worked up her mind to an
appearance of courage. When she entered the court, she threw her eyes
round it, and quickly discovered where we were seated. A tear seemed
to dim her eye when she saw us; but she quickly recovered herself, and a
look of sorrowful affection seemed to attest her utter guiltlessness.

'The trial began; and after the advocate against her had stated the
charge, several witnesses were called. Several strange facts combined
against her, which might have staggered any one who had not such proof
of her innocence as I had. She had been out the whole of the night on
which the murder had been committed, and towards morning had been
perceived by a market-woman not far from the spot where the body of
the murdered child had been afterwards found. The woman asked her
what she did there; but she looked very strangely, and only returned
a confused and unintelligible answer. She returned to the house about
eight o'clock; and when one inquired where she had passed the night,
she replied, that she had been looking for the child, and demanded earnestly, if any thing had been heard concerning him. When shewn the
body, she fell into violent hysterics, and kept her bed for several days.
The picture was then produced, which the servant had found in her
pocket; and when Elizabeth, in a faltering voice, proved that it was the
same which, an hour before the child had been missed, she had placed
round his neck, a murmur of horror and indignation filled the court.

'Justine was called on for her defence. As the trial had proceeded,
her countenance had altered. Surprise, horror, and misery, were strongly expressed. Sometimes she struggled with her tears; but when she was
desired to plead, she collected her powers, and spoke in an audible although variable voice:—

' "God knows," she said, "how entirely I am innocent. But I do not
pretend that my protestations should acquit me: I rest my innocence
on a plain and simple explanation of the facts which have been adduced
against me; and I hope the character I have always borne will incline my
judges to a favourable interpretation, where any circumstance appears
doubtful or suspicious."

'She then related that, by the permission of Elizabeth, she had passed
the evening of the night on which the murder had been committed, at
the house of an aunt at Chêne, a village situated at about a league from

Geneva. On her return, at about nine o'clock, she met a man, who asked her if she had seen any thing of the child who was lost. She was alarmed by this account, and passed several hours in looking for him, when the gates of Geneva were shut, and she was forced to remain several hours of the night in a barn belonging to a cottage, being unwilling to call up the inhabitants, to whom she was well known. Unable to rest or sleep, she quitted her asylum early, that she might again endeavour to find my brother.' — why, oh, why do I wish her to have said, 'Most of the night she spent here watching; towards morning she believed that she slept for a few minutes; some steps disturbed her, and she awoke. It was dawn, and she quitted her asylum, that she might again endeavour to find my brother.' What a difference a few words make in her defence to aid in her acquittal— 'If she had gone near the spot where his body lay, it was without her knowledge. That she had been bewildered when questioned by the market-woman, was not surprising, since she had passed a sleepless night, and the fate of poor William was yet uncertain. Concerning the picture she could give no account.

‘ "I know," continued the unhappy victim, "how heavily and fatally this one circumstance weighs against me, but I have no power of explaining it; and when I have expressed my utter ignorance, I am only left to conjecture concerning the probabilities by which it might have been placed in my pocket. But here also I am checked. I believe that I have no enemy on earth, and none surely would have been so wicked as to destroy me wantonly. Did the murderer place it there? I know of no opportunity afforded him for so doing; or if I had, why should he have stolen the jewel, to part with it again so soon?'

Why am I seeing a scene and hearing words in my mind that are not the scene that Victor's words are relating? I hear a deep, rumbling, unnatural voice in my head say, 'While I was overcome by these feelings, I left the spot where I had committed the murder, and was seeking a more secluded hiding-place, when I perceived a woman passing near me. She was young, not indeed so beautiful as her whose portrait I held, but of an agreeable aspect, and blooming in the loveliness of youth and health. Here, I thought, is one of those whose smiles are bestowed on all but me; she shall not escape: thanks to the lessons of Felix, and the sanguinary laws of man, I have learned how to work mischief. I approached her unperceived, and placed the portrait securely in one of the folds of her dress.' Who... or what is the source of this voice speaking within the layers and layers of my conscious mind?

‘ "I commit my cause to the justice of my judges, yet I see no room for hope. I beg permission to have a few witnesses examined concerning my character; and if their testimony shall not overweigh my supposed guilt, I must be condemned, although I would pledge my salvation on my innocence."

'Several witnesses were called, who had known her for many years, and they spoke well of her; but fear, and hatred of the crime of which they supposed her guilty, rendered them timorous, and unwilling to come forward. Elizabeth saw even this last resource, her excellent dispositions and irreproachable conduct, about to fail the accused, when, although violently agitated, she desired permission to address the court.'

How infuriating that she must ask permission of the court to address the court! Women are not allowed to testify in the western countries whose source of jurisprudence is based on the Ancient Greeks and Romans. My own mother, Mary Wollstonecraft, fought this quite legal silencing of women throughout her far too brief life! We must no longer suffer this silencing in silence. The suffrage movement just succeed!

' "I am," said she, "the cousin of the unhappy child who was murdered, or rather his sister, for I was educated by and have lived with his parents ever since and even long before his birth. It may therefore be judged indecent in me to come forward on this occasion; but when I see a fellow-creature about to perish through the cowardice of her pretended friends, I wish to be allowed to speak, that I may say what I know of her character. I am well acquainted with the accused. I have lived in the same house with her, at one time for five, and at another for nearly two years. During all that period she appeared to me the most amiable and benevolent of human creatures. She nursed Madame Frankenstein, my aunt, in her last illness with the greatest affection and care; and afterwards attended her own mother during a tedious illness, in a manner that excited the admiration of all who knew her. After which she again lived in my uncle's house, where she was beloved by all the family. She was warmly attached to the child who is now dead, and acted towards him like a most affectionate mother. For my own part, I do not hesitate to say, that, notwithstanding all the evidence produced against her, I believe and rely on her perfect innocence. She had no temptation for such an action: as to the bauble on which the chief proof rests, if she had earnestly desired it, I should have willingly given it to her; so much do I esteem and value her."

Why am I obsessing on choice words? '*My* aunt'? '*My* uncle?' Is there a deep oedipal connect between Elizabeth and Alphonse that fuels her antipathy towards Justine? Get out of your own head, Mary. Get out of your own way!

'Excellent Elizabeth! A murmur of approbation was heard; but it was excited by her generous interference, and not in favour of poor Justine, on whom the public indignation was turned with renewed violence, charging her with the blackest ingratitude. She herself wept as Elizabeth spoke, but she did not answer. My own agitation and anguish was extreme during the whole trial. I believed in her innocence; I knew it. Could the dæmon, who had (I did not for a minute doubt) murdered my brother, also in his hellish sport have betrayed the innocent to death and ignominy.' Victor has had the same premonition that I have had! Has he heard the low, haunting voice of his Creation, too? 'I could not sustain the horror of my situation; and when I perceived that the popular voice, and the countenances of the judges, had already condemned my unhappy victim, I rushed out of the court in agony. The tortures of the accused did not equal mine; she was sustained by innocence, but the fangs of remorse tore my bosom, and would not forego their hold.

'I passed a night of unmingled wretchedness. In the morning I went to the court; my lips and throat were parched. I dared not ask the fatal question; but I was known, and the officer guessed the cause of my visit. The ballots had been thrown; they were all black, and Justine was condemned.

'I cannot pretend to describe what I then felt. I had before experienced sensations of horror; and I have endeavoured to bestow upon them adequate expressions, but words cannot convey an idea of the heart-sickening despair that I then endured. The person to whom I addressed myself added, that Justine had already confessed her guilt. "That evidence," he observed, "was hardly required in so glaring a case, but I am glad of it; and, indeed, none of our judges like to condemn a criminal upon circumstantial evidence, be it ever so decisive."

'When I returned home, Elizabeth eagerly demanded the result.

' "My cousin," replied I, "it is decided as you may have expected; all judges had rather that ten innocent should suffer, than that one guilty should escape." ' — what is this nonsense that Victor speaks? Did not Benjiman Franklin, the American statesman say concerning Blackstone's Ratio, 'it is better one-hundred guilty Persons should escape than that one innocent Person should suffer'? Did not the French revolutionize the legal system proclaiming 'As every man is presumed innocent until he has been declared guilty, if it should be considered necessary to arrest him, any undue harshness that is not required to secure his person must be severely curbed by law'[94] — ' "But she has confessed."

'This was a dire blow to poor Elizabeth, who had relied with firmness upon Justine's innocence. "Alas!" said she, "how shall I ever again believe in human benevolence? Justine, whom I loved and esteemed as my sister, how could she put on those smiles of innocence only to betray; her mild

---

94 From Article IX of the Declaration of the Rings of Man and of the Citizen, written in 1789.

eyes seemed incapable of any severity or ill-humour, and yet she has committed a murder."

'Soon after we heard that the poor victim had expressed a wish to see my cousin. My father wished her not to go; but said, that he left it to her own judgment and feelings to decide. "Yes," said Elizabeth, "I will go, although she is guilty; and you, Victor, shall accompany me: I cannot go alone." The idea of this visit was torture to me, yet I could not refuse.

'We entered the gloomy prison-chamber, and beheld Justine sitting on some straw at the further end; her hands were manacled, and her head rested on her knees. She rose on seeing us enter; and when we were left alone with her, she threw herself at the feet of Elizabeth, weeping bitterly. My cousin wept also.

' "Oh, Justine!" said she, "why did you rob me of my last consolation. I relied on your innocence; and although I was then very wretched, I was not so miserable as I am now."

' "And do you also believe that I am so very, very wicked? Do you also join with my enemies to crush me?" Her voice was suffocated with sobs.

' "Rise, my poor girl," said Elizabeth, "why do you kneel, if you are innocent? I am not one of your enemies; I believed you guiltless, notwithstanding every evidence, until I heard that you had yourself declared your guilt. That report, you say, is false; and be assured, dear Justine, that nothing can shake my confidence in you for a moment, but your own confession."

' "I did confess; but I confessed a lie. I confessed, that I might obtain absolution; but now that falsehood lies heavier at my heart than all my other sins. The God of heaven forgive me! Ever since I was condemned, my confessor has besieged me; he threatened and menaced, until I almost began to think that I was the monster that he said I was. He threatened excommunication and hell fire in my last moments, if I continued obdurate.'

How I loathe the Catholic Church that this sword of Damocles they hang over heads of their sycophants called excommunication. To be denied Communion with the Lord is its very construction! And Catholics still cleave to the cannibalistic intent of the Transubstantiation of bread and wine into the literal Body and Blood of Jesus the Christ. The natural philosophies will never prove this religoius fallacy to be true on a molecular level based on John Dalton's atomic theory. Transubstantiation may be found true on a superstitious level! There is no doubt in my mind, but the sciences will ultimately prevail over superstition!

' "Dear lady, I had none to support me; all looked on me as a wretch doomed to ignominy and perdition. What could I do? In an evil hour I subscribed to a lie; and now only am I truly miserable."

'She paused, weeping, and then continued— "I thought with horror, my sweet lady, that you should believe your Justine, whom your blessed aunt had so highly honoured, and whom you loved, was a creature capable of a crime which none but the devil himself could have perpetrated. Dear William! dearest blessed child! I soon shall see you again in heaven, where we shall all be happy; and that consoles me, going as I am to suffer ignominy and death."

' "Oh, Justine! forgive me for having for one moment distrusted you. Why did you confess? But do not mourn, my dear girl; I will every where proclaim your innocence, and force belief. Yet you must die; you, my playfellow, my companion, my more than sister. I never can survive so horrible a misfortune."

' "Dear, sweet Elizabeth, do not weep. You ought to raise me with thoughts of a better life, and elevate me from the petty cares of this world of injustice and strife. Do not you, excellent friend, drive me to despair."

' "I will try to comfort you; but this, I fear, is an evil too deep and poignant to admit of consolation, for there is no hope. Yet heaven bless thee, my dearest Justine, with resignation, and a confidence elevated beyond this world. Oh! how I hate its shews and mockeries! when one creature is murdered, another is immediately deprived of life in a slow torturing manner; then the executioners, their hands yet reeking with the blood of innocence, believe that they have done a great deed. They call this *retribution*."'

Why do the words of Cesare Beccaria ring in my ears? 'The war of a nation against a citizen ... It appears absurd to me that the laws, which are the expression of the public will and which detest and punish homicide, commit murder themselves, and in order to dissuade citizens from assassination, commit public assassination.'[95] Why do the words of Jean-Jacques Rouseeau likewise ring in my ears? 'There is no man so bad that he cannot be made good for something. No man should be put to death, even as an example, if he can be left to live without danger to society.'[96]

' "Hateful name! When that word is pronounced, I know greater and more horrid punishments are going to be inflicted than the gloomiest tyrant has ever invented to satiate his utmost revenge. Yet this is not consolation for you, my Justine, unless indeed that you may glory in escaping from so miserable a den. Alas! I would I were in peace with my aunt and

---

95 From *On Crimes and Punishments* by Cesare Beccaria, published in 1764.
96 From *The Social Contract* by Jean-Jacques Rousseau, published in 1762.

my lovely William, escaped from a world which is hateful to me, and the visages of men which I abhor."

'Justine smiled languidly. "This, dear lady, is despair, and not resignation. I must not learn the lesson that you would teach me. Talk of something else, something that will bring peace, and not increase of misery."

'During this conversation I had retired to a corner of the prison-room, where I could conceal the horrid anguish that possessed me. Despair! Who dared talk of that? The poor victim, who on the morrow was to pass the dreary boundary between life and death, felt not as I did, such deep and bitter agony. I gnashed my teeth, and ground them together, uttering a groan that came from my inmost soul. Justine started. When she saw who it was, she approached me, and said, "Dear Sir, you are very kind to visit me; you, I hope, do not believe that I am guilty."

'I could not answer. "No, Justine," said Elizabeth; "he is more convinced of your innocence than I was; for even when he heard that you had confessed, he did not credit it."

' "I truly thank him. In these last moments I feel the sincerest gratitude towards those who think of me with kindness. How sweet is the affection of others to such a wretch as I am! It removes more than half my misfortune; and I feel as if I could die in peace, now that my innocence is acknowledged by you, dear lady, and your cousin."

'Thus the poor sufferer tried to comfort others and herself. She indeed gained the resignation she desired. But I, the true murderer, felt the never-dying worm alive in my bosom, which allowed of no hope or consolation. Elizabeth also wept, and was unhappy; but her's also was the misery of innocence, which, like a cloud that passes over the fair moon, for a while hides, but cannot tarnish its brightness. Anguish and despair had penetrated into the core of my heart; I bore a hell within me, which nothing could extinguish. We staid several hours with Justine; and it was with great difficulty that Elizabeth could tear herself away. "I wish," cried she, "that I were to die with you; I cannot live in this world of misery."

'Justine assumed an air of cheerfulness, while she with difficulty repressed her bitter tears. She embraced Elizabeth, and said, in a voice of half-suppressed emotion, "Farewell, sweet lady, dearest Elizabeth, my beloved and only friend; may heaven in its bounty bless and preserve you; may this be the last misfortune that you will ever suffer. Live, and be happy, and make others so."

My mind heard the next words that Victor spoke, but my own mind revised the words into something else... something more. I needed the consolation that this revision brought to my mind, lest the suffering of Justine be insufferable to me.

'And on the morrow Justine died. Elizabeth's heart-rending elo-
quence failed to move the judges from their settled conviction in the
criminality of the saintly sufferer. My passionate and indignant appeals
were lost upon them. And when I received their cold answers, and heard
the harsh unfeeling reasoning of these men, my purposed avowal died
away on my lips. Thus I might proclaim myself a madman, but not revoke
the sentence passed upon my wretched victim. She perished on the scaffold as a murderess!

'From the tortures of my own heart, I turned to contemplate the deep
and voiceless grief of my Elizabeth. This also was my doing! And my father's woe, and the desolation of that late so smiling home—all was the
work of my thrice-accursed hands! Ye weep, unhappy ones; but these are
not your last tears! Again shall you raise the funeral wail, and the sound
of your lamentations shall again and again be heard! Frankenstein, your
son, your kinsman, your early, much-loved friend; he who would spend
each vital drop of blood for your sakes—who has no thought nor sense of
joy, except as it is mirrored also in your dear countenances—who would
fill the air with blessings, and spend his life in serving you—he bids you
weep—to shed countless tears; happy beyond his hopes, if thus inexorable fate be satisfied, and if the destruction pause before the peace of the
grave have succeeded to your sad torments!

'Thus spoke my prophetic soul, as, torn by remorse, horror, and despair, I beheld those I loved spend vain sorrow upon the graves of William and Justine, the first hapless victims to my unhallowed arts.'

Chapter IV

Nothing is more painful to the human mind, than, after the feelings
have been worked up by a quick succession of events, the dead
calmness of inaction and certainty which follows, and deprives the
soul both of hope and fear. Justine died; she rested; and I was alive. The
blood flowed freely in my veins, but a weight of despair and remorse
pressed on my heart, which nothing could remove. Sleep fled from my
eyes; I wandered like an evil spirit, for I had committed deeds of mischief beyond description horrible, and more, much more, (I persuaded
myself) was yet behind. Yet my heart overflowed with kindness, and the
love of virtue. I had begun life with benevolent intentions, and thirsted
for the moment when I should put them in practice, and make myself
useful to my fellow-beings. Now all was blasted: instead of that serenity
of conscience, which allowed me to look back upon the past with self-sat-
isfaction, and from thence to gather promise of new hopes, I was seized
by remorse and the sense of guilt, which hurried me away to a hell of
intense tortures, such as no language can describe.

'This state of mind preyed upon my health, which had entirely recovered from the first shock it had sustained. I shunned the face of man; all sound of joy or complacency was torture to me; solitude was my only consolation— deep, dark, death-like solitude.

'My father observed with pain the alteration perceptible in my disposition and habits, and endeavoured to reason with me on the folly of giving way to immoderate grief. "Do you think, Victor," said he, "that I do not suffer also? No one could love a child more than I loved your brother;" (tears came into his eyes as he spoke); "but is it not a duty to the survivors, that we should refrain from augmenting their unhappiness by an appearance of immoderate grief? It is also a duty owed to yourself; for excessive sorrow prevents improvement or enjoyment, or even the discharge of daily usefulness, without which no man is fit for society."

'This advice, although good, was totally inapplicable to my case; I should have been the first to hide my grief, and console my friends, if remorse had not mingled its bitterness with my other sensations. Now I could only answer my father with a look of despair, and endeavour to hide myself from his view.

'About this time we retired to our house at Belrive. This change was particularly agreeable to me. The shutting of the gates regularly at ten o'clock, and the impossibility of remaining on the lake after that hour, had rendered our residence within the walls of Geneva very irksome to me. I was now free. Often, after the rest of the family had retired for the night, I took the boat, and passed many hours upon the water. Sometimes, with my sails set, I was carried by the wind; and sometimes, after rowing into the middle of the lake, I left the boat to pursue its own course, and gave way to my own miserable reflections. I was often tempted, when all was at peace around me, and I the only unquiet thing that wandered restless in a scene so beautiful and heavenly, if I except some bat, or the frogs, whose harsh and interrupted croaking was heard only when I approached the shore— often, I say, I was tempted to plunge into the silent lake, that the waters might close over me and my calamities for ever.'

No! Victor! That is the solution permanent to a problem temporary. I know better than most the loss of a child! While Victor did carry the life of his brother in his heart, he did not carry the life of his brother in his womb as I had my nameless, unbaptized daughter. There is a certain pain, a longing that aches in my belly like an amputated solider who still feels the unscratchable tickle of an itch in the phantom limb. I still feel the ghostly kicks of my daughter in my belly and her phantom suckling at my breast! It is a pain that will prove to be eternal.

'But I was restrained, when I thought of the heroic and suffering Elizabeth, whom I tenderly loved, and whose existence was bound up in mine. I thought also of my father, and surviving brother: should I by my base desertion leave them exposed and unprotected to the malice of the fiend whom I had let loose among them?'

But the pain that I do not possess is the pain that your Creation may be the cause of death. I cast a glance at my sweet William sleeping in his bassinette and I wonder and ponder what I would do, if at some point during his life I sit in a courtroom with my child accused of murder... or worse. To know that that evil had grown in my womb; that I had nourished that evil with my own blood and milk would be a torture unimaginable! And if this Creation is guilty as Victor believes? Inconsolable would I be.

'At these moments I wept bitterly, and wished that peace would revisit my mind only that I might afford them consolation and happiness. But that could not be. Remorse extinguished every hope. I had been the author of unalterable evils; and I lived in daily fear, lest the monster whom I had created should perpetrate some new wickedness. I had an obscure feeling that all was not over, and that he would still commit some signal crime, which by its enormity should almost efface the recollection of the past. There was always scope for fear, so long as any thing I loved remained behind. My abhorrence of this fiend cannot be conceived. When I thought of him, I gnashed my teeth, my eyes became inflamed, and I ardently wished to extinguish that life which I had so thoughtlessly bestowed. When I reflected on his crimes and malice, my hatred and revenge burst all bounds of moderation. I would have made a pilgrimage to the highest peak of the Andes, could I, when there, have precipitated him to their base. I wished to see him again, that I might wreak the utmost extent of anger on his head, and avenge the deaths of William and Justine.

'Our house was the house of mourning. My father's health was deeply shaken by the horror of the recent events. Elizabeth was sad and desponding; she no longer took delight in her ordinary occupations; all pleasure seemed to her sacrilege toward the dead; eternal woe and tears she then thought was the just tribute she should pay to innocence so blasted and destroyed. She was no longer that happy creature, who in earlier youth wandered with me on the banks of the lake, and talked with ecstacy of our future prospects. She had become grave, and often conversed of the inconstancy of fortune, and the instability of human life.

' "When I reflect, my dear cousin," said she, "on the miserable death of Justine Martin, I no longer see the world and its works as they before appeared to me. Before, I looked upon the accounts of vice and injustice, that I read in books or heard from others, as tales of ancient days, or imaginary evils; at least they were remote, and more familiar to reason than to the imagination; but now misery has come home, and men appear to me as monsters thirsting for each other's blood. Yet I am certainly unjust. Every body believed that poor girl to be guilty; and if she could have committed the crime for which she suffered, assuredly she would have been the most depraved of human creatures. For the sake of a few jewels, to have murdered the son of her benefactor and friend, a child whom she had nursed from its birth, and appeared to love as if it had been her own! I could not consent to the death of any human being; but certainly I should have thought such a creature unfit to remain in the society of men. Yet she was innocent. I know, I feel she was innocent; you are of the same opinion, and that confirms me. Alas! Victor, when falsehood can look so like the truth, who can assure themselves of certain happiness? I feel as if I were walking on the edge of a precipice, towards which thousands are crowding, and endeavouring to plunge me into the abyss. William and Justine were assassinated, and the murderer escapes; he walks about the world free, and perhaps respected. But even if I were condemned to suffer on the scaffold for the same crimes, I would not change places with such a wretch."

'I listened to this discourse with the extremest agony.' As did I, my pale student of the unhallowed arts. ' I, not in deed, but in effect, was the true murderer. Elizabeth read my anguish in my countenance, and kindly taking my hand said, "My dearest cousin, you must calm yourself. These events have affected me, God knows how deeply; but I am not so wretched as you are. There is an expression of despair, and sometimes of revenge, in your countenance, that makes me tremble. Be calm, my dear Victor; I would sacrifice my life to your peace. We surely shall be happy: quiet in our native country, and not mingling in the world, what can disturb our tranquillity?"

'She shed tears as she said this'— as did I, my pale student of the unhallowed arts — 'distrusting the very solace that she gave; but at the same time she smiled, that she might chase away the fiend that lurked in my heart. My father, who saw in the unhappiness that was painted in my face only an exaggeration of that sorrow which I might naturally feel, thought that an amusement suited to my taste would be the best means of restoring to me my wonted serenity. It was from this cause that he had removed to the country; and, induced by the same motive, he now proposed that we should all make an excursion to the valley of Chamounix.'

Would I read, in another lifetime, in a handbook for travellers stern warnings that 'these retired wilds, amidst the most sublime scenery in nature. And at the foot of the loftiest mountain of Europe, where thousands have made their pilgrimage. Unlike other places, merely fashionable, and crowded by idlers, no extent of participation can lessen the sublime emotions and impressions made by the scenery of the vale of

Chamouny. The route form Geneva is so much frequented by strangers in this season, that it is beset by all sorts of vagabonds, who plant themselves in the way openly as beggars, or covertly as dealers in mineral specimens, guides to thing which do not require their aid, dealers in echoes, by firing small cannon where its reverberation may be heard two or three times. These idle nuisances should be discountenanced.'[97]

'I had been there before, but Elizabeth and Ernest never had; and both had often expressed an earnest desire to see the scenery of this place, which had been described to them as so wonderful and sublime. Accordingly we departed from Geneva on this tour about the middle of the month of August, nearly two months after the death of Justine.

'The weather was uncommonly fine; and if mine had been a sorrow to be chased away by any fleeting circumstance, this excursion would certainly have had the effect intended by my father. As it was, I was somewhat interested in the scene; it sometimes lulled, although it could not extinguish my grief.

'During the first day we travelled in a carriage. In the morning we had seen the mountains at a distance, towards which we gradually advanced. We perceived that the valley through which we wound, and which was formed by the river Arve, whose course we followed, closed in upon us by degrees; and when the sun had set, we beheld immense mountains and precipices overhanging us on every side, and heard the sound of the river raging among rocks, and the dashing of water-falls around.

'The next day we pursued our journey upon mules. And as we ascended still higher, the valley assumed a more magnificent and astonishing character. Ruined castles hanging on the precipices of piny mountains; the impetuous Arve, and cottages every here and there peeping forth from among the trees, formed a scene of singular beauty. But it was augmented and rendered sublime by the mighty Alps, whose white and shining pyramids and domes towered above all, as belonging to another earth, the habitations of another race of beings.

'We passed the bridge of Pelissier, where the ravine, which the river forms, opened before us, and we began to ascend the mountain that overhangs it.'

Again, I recall observations mad during a residence in Switzerland and Auvergne that I have not myself made of the Pont Pelissier, a bridge over the Arve 'crosses this river a little below the sot where it issues from one of the most striking chasms or gorges in the Alps. On the eastern side are slate rocks of amazing height, nearly perpendicular, their summits, and feet ornaments with pine-trees; and, on the western side, there is a granitic mountain over which, the road is carried. The river Arve, a

97 From *Handbook for Travellers in Switzerland* by John Murray, published in 1838.

large and impetuous torrent, rushes between these two ranges of rocks, and towering over the whole, the snows of Mount Blânc are seen in dazzling whiteness, which, contrasted with the dark blue of the sky, almost overpowers the sight.'[98]

'Soon after we entered the valley of Chamounix. This valley is more wonderful and sublime, but not so beautiful and picturesque as that of Servox, through which we had just passed. The high and snowy mountains were its immediate boundaries; but we saw no more ruined castles and fertile fields. Immense glaciers approached the road; we heard the rumbling thunder of the falling avalanche, and marked the smoke of its passage. Mont Blânc, the supreme and magnificent Mont Blânc, raised itself from the surrounding *aiguilles*, and its tremendous *dome* overlooked the valley.

'During this journey, I sometimes joined Elizabeth, and exerted myself to point out to her the various beauties of the scene. I often suffered my mule to lag behind, and indulged in the misery of reflection. At other times I spurred on the animal before my companions, that I might forget them, the world, and, more than all, myself. When at a distance, I alighted, and threw myself on the grass, weighed down by horror and despair. At eight in the evening I arrived at Chamounix. My father and Elizabeth were very much fatigued; Ernest, who accompanied us, was delighted, and in high spirits: the only circumstance that detracted from his pleasure was the south wind, and the rain it seemed to promise for the next day.

'We retired early to our apartments, but not to sleep; at least I did not. I remained many hours at the window, watching the pallid lightning that played above Mont Blânc, and listening to the rushing of the Arve, which ran below my window.'

Chapter V

The next day, contrary to the prognostications of our guides, was fine, although clouded. We visited the source of the Arveiron, and rode about the valley until evening. These sublime and magnificent scenes afforded me the greatest consolation that I was capable of receiving. They elevated me from all littleness of feeling; and although they did not remove my grief, they subdued and tranquillized it. In some degree, also, they diverted my mind from the thoughts over which it had brooded for the last month. I returned in the evening, fatigued, but less unhappy, and conversed with my family with more cheerfulness than

98 From *Travels, Comprising Observations Made During a Residence in the Tarentaise and Various Parts of the Grecians and Pennine Alps, and in Switzerland and Auvergne, in the years 1820, 1821, and 1822* by Robert Bakewell, published in 1823.

had been my custom for some time. My father was pleased, and Elizabeth overjoyed. "My dear cousin," said she, "you see what happiness you diffuse when you are happy; do not relapse again!"

The following morning the rain poured down in torrents, and thick mists hid the summits of the mountains. I rose early, but felt unusually melancholy. The rain depressed me; my old feelings recurred, and I was miserable. I knew how disappointed my father would be at this sudden change, and I wished to avoid him until I had recovered myself so far as to be enabled to conceal those feelings that overpowered me. I knew that they would remain that day at the inn; and as I had ever inured myself to rain, moisture, and cold, I resolved to go alone to the summit of Montanvert.'

My mind returned to travelogues, which are all the rage in modern literature (I should know, I and my Beloved wish to publish one: 'On the other side of the valley of the Arveiron rises the immense glacier of Montanvert, fifty miles in extent, occupying a chasm among mountains of inconceivable heigh, and of forms so point and abrupt that they seem to piece the sky. From this glacier we saw as we sat on a rock, close to one of the streams of the Arveiron, Masses of ice detach themselves from on high, and rush with a loud dull noise into the vale. The violence of their fall turned them into powder, which flowed over the rocks in imitation of waterfalls, whose ravines they usurped and filled.'[99]

'I remembered the effect that the view of the tremendous and ever-moving glacier had produced upon my mind when I first saw it. It had then filled me with a sublime ecstacy that gave wings to the soul, and allowed it to soar from the obscure world to light and joy. The sight of the awful and majestic in nature had indeed always the effect of solemnizing my mind, and causing me to forget the passing cares of life. I determined to go alone, for I was well acquainted with the path, and the presence of another would destroy the solitary grandeur of the scene.'

How I wish to see Montanvert with my own eyes! I must endeavour to persuade my Beloved to undertake an excursion to the glacier! The journey will prove excellent material for our own travelogue.

'The ascent is precipitous, but the path is cut into continual and short windings, which enable you to surmount the perpendicularity of the mountain. It is a scene terrifically desolate. In a thousand spots the traces of the winter avalanche may be perceived, where trees lie broken and strewed on the ground; some entirely destroyed, others bent, leaning upon the jutting rocks of the mountain, or transversely upon other trees. The path, as you ascend higher, is intersected by ravines of snow, down which stones continually roll from above; one of them is particu-

---

99 From *Handbook for Travellers in Switzerland* by John Murray, published in 1838.

larly dangerous, as the slightest sound, such as even speaking in a loud voice, produces a concussion of air sufficient to draw destruction upon the head of the speaker. The pines are not tall or luxuriant, but they are sombre, and add an air of severity to the scene. I looked on the valley beneath; vast mists were rising from the rivers which ran through it, and curling in thick wreaths around the opposite mountains, whose summits were hid in the uniform clouds, while rain poured from the dark sky, and added to the melancholy impression I received from the objects around me.'

Curious how my pale student of the unhallowed arts describes this setting to me in such exquisite detail, when I, the source of his existence, have not yet laid my eyes upon the sights! Curiouser and curiouer!

'Alas! why does man boast of sensibilities superior to those apparent in the brute; it only renders them more necessary beings. If our impulses were confined to hunger, thirst, and desire, we might be nearly free; but now we are moved by every wind that blows, and a chance word or scene that that word may convey to us.

> 'We rest; a dream has power to poison sleep.
> We rise; one wand'ring thought pollutes the day.
> We feel, conceive, or reason; laugh, or weep,
> Embrace fond woe, or cast our cares away;
> It is the same: for, be it joy or sorrow,
> The path of its departure still is free.
> Man's yesterday may ne'er be like his morrow;
>
> Nought may endure but mutability!'

Where have I heard these words spoken by my dearest Victor? I know the source! But I know not how Victor comes to possess the knowledge of these words? They come from the most innermost recesses of my own mind. These words are words that I heard upon their composition by my Beloved and only published by Baldwin, Cradock, and Joy in London this very year. Curiously, they have found themselves on the lips of a phantasm relating events that take their place decades previous to my own. My dearest, Journal, shall I reprint the poem in its entirety? For posterity's sake, I shall.

> We are as clouds that veil the midnight moon;
> How restlessly they speed, and gleam, and quiver,
> Streaking the darkness radiantly!—yet soon
> Night closes round, and they are lost forever:

Or like forgotten lyres, whose dissonant strings
Give various response to each varying blast,
To whose frail frame no second motion brings
One mood or modulation like the last.

We rest.—A dream has power to poison sleep;
We rise.—One wandering thought pollutes the day;
We feel, conceive or reason, laugh or weep;
Embrace fond woe, or cast our cares away:

It is the same!—For, be it joy or sorrow,
The path of its departure still is free:
Man's yesterday may ne'er be like his morrow;
Nought may endure but mutability![100]

'It was nearly noon when I arrived at the top of the ascent. For some time I sat upon the rock that overlooks the sea of ice. A mist covered both that and the surrounding mountains. Presently a breeze dissipated the cloud, and I descended upon the glacier. The surface is very uneven, rising like the waves of a troubled sea, descending low, and interspersed by rifts that sink deep. The field of ice is almost a league in width, but I spent nearly two hours in crossing it. The opposite mountain is a bare perpendicular rock. From the side where I now stood Montanvert was exactly opposite, at the distance of a league; and above it rose Mont Blânc, in awful majesty. I remained in a recess of the rock, gazing on this wonderful and stupendous scene. The sea, or rather the vast river of ice, wound among its dependent mountains, whose aërial summits hung over its recesses. Their icy and glittering peaks shone in the sunlight over the clouds. My heart, which was before sorrowful, now swelled with something like joy; I exclaimed— "Wandering spirits, if indeed ye wander, and do not rest in your narrow beds, allow me this faint happiness, or take me, as your companion, away from the joys of life."

'As I said this, I suddenly beheld the figure of a man, at some distance, advancing towards me with superhuman speed. He bounded over the crevices in the ice, among which I had walked with caution; his stature also, as he approached, seemed to exceed that of man. I was troubled: a mist came over my eyes, and I felt a faintness seize me; but I was quickly restored by the cold gale of the mountains. I perceived, as the shape came nearer, (sight tremendous and abhorred!) that it was the wretch whom I had created. I trembled with rage and horror, resolving to wait his approach, and then close with him in mortal combat.

---

100 From *Alastor, or The Spirit of Solitude: And Other Poems* by Percy Bysshe Shelley in 1816.

He approached; his countenance bespoke bitter anguish, combined with disdain and malignity, while its unearthly ugliness rendered it almost too horrible for human eyes. But I scarcely observed this; anger— nay! rage— and hatred had at first deprived me of utterance, and I recovered only to overwhelm him with words expressive of furious detestation and contempt.

' "Devil!" I exclaimed, "do you dare approach me? and do not you fear the fierce vengeance of my arm wreaked on your miserable head? Begone, vile insect! or rather stay, that I may trample you to dust! and, oh, that I could, with the extinction of your miserable existence, restore those victims whom you have so diabolically murdered!"

' "I expected this reception," said the dæmon. "All men hate the wretched; how then must I be hated, who am miserable beyond all living things! Yet you, my creator, detest and spurn me, thy creature, to whom thou art bound by ties only dissoluble by the annihilation of one of us. You purpose to kill me. How dare you sport thus with life? Do your duty towards me, and I will do mine towards you and the rest of mankind. If you will comply with my conditions, I will leave them and you at peace; but if you refuse, I will glut the maw of death, until it be satiated with the blood of your remaining friends."

' "Abhorred monster! fiend that thou art! the tortures of hell are too mild a vengeance for thy crimes. Wretched devil! you reproach me with your creation; come on then, that I may extinguish the spark which I so negligently bestowed."

'My rage was without bounds; I sprang on him, impelled by all the feelings which can arm one being against the existence of another.

'He easily eluded me, and said,

' "Be calm! I entreat you to hear me, before you give vent to your hatred on my devoted head. Have I not suffered enough, that you seek to increase my misery? Life, although it may only be an accumulation of anguish, is dear to me, and I will defend it. Remember, thou hast made me more powerful than thyself; my height is superior to thine; my joints more supple. But I will not be tempted to set myself in opposition to thee. I am thy creature, and I will be even mild and docile to my natural lord and king, if thou wilt also perform thy part, the which thou owest me. Oh, Frankenstein, be not equitable to every other, and trample upon me alone, to whom thy justice, and even thy clemency and affection, is most due. Remember, that I am thy creature: I ought to be thy Adam; but I am rather the fallen angel, whom thou drivest from joy for no misdeed. Every where I see bliss, from which I alone am irrevocably excluded. I was benevolent and good; misery made me a fiend. Make me happy, and I shall again be virtuous.'"

How and by what source did this Creation come to be so articulate? By what means did a creature born from a deceased— and perchance diseased— brain retain or regain its intellect! Curiouser and curiouser. I feel myself physically and literally leaning into this tale of Victor's. I can only hope and pray that I can hear the Creation's own tale.

' "Begone! I will not hear you. There can be no community between you and me; we are enemies. Begone, or let us try our strength in a fight, in which one must fall."

' "How can I move thee? Will no entreaties cause thee to turn a favourable eye upon thy creature, who implores thy goodness and compassion? Believe me, Frankenstein: I was benevolent; my soul glowed with love and humanity: but am I not alone, miserably alone? You, my creator, abhor me; what hope can I gather from your fellow-creatures, who owe me nothing? they spurn and hate me. The desert mountains and dreary glaciers are my refuge. I have wandered here many days; the caves of ice, which I only do not fear, are a dwelling to me, and the only one which man does not grudge. These bleak skies I hail, for they are kinder to me than your fellow-beings. If the multitude of mankind knew of my existence, they would do as you do, and arm themselves for my destruction. Shall I not then hate them who abhor me? I will keep no terms with my enemies. I am miserable, and they shall share my wretchedness. Yet it is in your power to recompense me, and deliver them from an evil which it only remains for you to make so great, that not only you and your family, but thousands of others, shall be swallowed up in the whirlwinds of its rage. Let your compassion be moved, and do not disdain me. Listen to my tale.'

Hazzah! My hopes and prayers have been answered so quickly. But how will Victor relate the tale of his Creation to me? Will it be a tale within a tale? Or perchance I can hope and pray again that the Creation itself visits me in as equal a phantasmagorical conversation as I may presently having with my pale student of the unhallowed arts. Hopes and prayers.

'When you have heard that, abandon or commiserate me, as you shall judge that I deserve. But hear me. The guilty are allowed, by human laws, bloody as they may be, to speak in their own defence before they are condemned. Listen to me, Frankenstein. You accuse me of murder; and yet you would, with a satisfied conscience, destroy your own creature. Oh, praise the eternal justice of man! Yet I ask you not to spare me: listen to me; and then, if you can, and if you will, destroy the work of your hands."

' "Why do you call to my remembrance circumstances of which I shudder to reflect, that I have been the miserable origin and author?

Cursed be the day, abhorred devil, in which you first saw light! Cursed (although I curse myself) be the hands that formed you! You have made me wretched beyond expression. You have left me no power to consider whether I am just to you, or not. Begone! relieve me from the sight of your detested form."

' "Thus I relieve thee, my creator," he said, and placed his hated hands before my eyes, which I flung from me with violence; "thus I take from thee a sight which you abhor. Still thou canst listen to me, and grant me thy compassion. By the virtues that I once possessed, I demand this from you. Hear my tale; it is long and strange, and the temperature of this place is not fitting to your fine sensations; come to the hut upon the mountain. The sun is yet high in the heavens; before it descends to hide itself behind yon snowy precipices, and illuminate another world, you will have heard my story, and can decide. On you it rests, whether I quit for ever the neighbourhood of man, and lead a harmless life, or become the scourge of your fellow-creatures, and the author of your own speedy ruin."

'As he said this, he led the way across the ice: I followed. My heart was full, and I did not answer him; but, as I proceeded, I weighed the various arguments that he had used, and determined at least to listen to his tale. I was partly urged by curiosity, and compassion confirmed my resolution. I had hitherto supposed him to be the murderer of my brother, and I eagerly sought a confirmation or denial of this opinion. For the first time, also, I felt what the duties of a creator towards his creature were, and that I ought to render him happy before I complained of his wickedness. These motives urged me to comply with his demand. We crossed the ice, therefore, and ascended the opposite rock. The air was cold, and the rain again began to descend: we entered the hut, the fiend with an air of exultation, I with a heavy heart, and depressed spirits.'

I no longer wish to be haunted by my pale student of the unhallowed arts. I am done with him! His soul is as rotten and worm infested as an apple left on the windowsill to fester in the sun. My pale student of the unhallowed arts, whom I longed to know more about from our first chance encounter during that thunderstorm-and-lightning-fuelled nightmare after a spirited and galvanising debate, was shown to me to be nothing more than failed student with a hollow heart.

But I do wish to know what the story of his Creation is. How did he become so esteemingly articulate and so seemingly wise? What manner of education did this Creation have? Was he 'born' with the innate knowledge of language which having survived death was born again in this new form through the alchemical and forbidden processes created by my pale student of the unhallowed arts.

THESE ARE ANSWERS I MUST KNOW!

To Be Continued in...

How a Game of Ghost Stories Gives
A Strange Birth To
Frankenstein

Includes the Full Texts of:
Mary Shelley's "Frankenstein
or, The Modern Prometheus"
Dr. John Polidori's "The Vampyre"
& the Continuation of Robert Dwight Brown's "Playing a Game of Ghost Stories"

ISBN: 978-1-931608-72-5

About the Author

To the popular imagination, paranoid schizophrenics hear the Devil instructing us to commit murder, or we crowd mental institutions believing we are Jesus Christ Himself. My mental condition has coloured my creativity in a variety of different ways. Many writers will often encounter their "characters" actively participating in the stories they are writing. This "inner-voice" instructing the writing process can be unsettling to nascent writers. For an author with my condition, the voices are audible and very, very communicative.

My voices, however, are not those of the characters I am writing, but of pseudonymous co-writers, actively and audibly participating in the writing process. Each of my books has a very different and unique co-writer. Ophelia T'Wat, the co-writer of *The Marquis de Sade's Wettest Midummer Night's Dream Conceivable*, is a 21 year-old college student who is stripping her way through college. The co-author of Satan's Study Bible: The Four Gospels is far more a nefarious personality, Satan himself, but instead of instructing me to murder, he wanted nothing more than a Study Bible written from his own point-of-view. Satan's Preacher Man manifested more as a dreamlike past life experience. And finally, the granddaddy of them all, God and His Only Begotten Son Jesus Christ spoke to me audibly and through dreams instructing and inspiring The Holy Bible Trilogy and its Next Testament.

But can a novelist, who was diagnosed schizophrenic as a teenager, actually hear the Voice of God tell him to continue the Word of God? As a dutiful Catholic, I sought the intersession of a priest for exorcism from demonic forces. He instructed me to see a psychiatrist to alleviate my hallucinations. I am caught in a spiritual conundrum, would I rather be a Prophet of God or crazy?

Over decades of constant psychoanalysis, I have come to peace with my rather unique creativity. I have embraced the quirks that come with my writer's voice, or voices as it were. I hope you, the Reader, can appreciate and enjoy my collaborations with my voices.

This is a major contributing factor to both the Pale Student of the Unhallowed Arts and his Creation/Creature haunting Mary as a hallucinogenic phantasm. Authors often describe to lay readers that their characters 'speak' to them, specifically telling the author what they are going to say and do. Readers are aghast at the idea that a creation of the author's brain can override the author's own intentions with 'their' story. But it is not the author's story, it is the characters. The Pale Student and the Creation/Creature may be products of Mary's imagination, but they are a real to the author (and reader) as if they were flesh and blood. It is a shocking experience for the nascent author when their characters 'speak' to them, often saying, 'No! This is my story now. I shall relate it the way I wish!.'

If writing is as schizophrenic an experience as I allege, then what about an author who is a diagnosed schizophrenic? When I said earlier that 'pseudonymous co-writers, actively and audibly participat[e] in the writing process', I was not exaggerating. I, more often than not, hear my characters speaking to me over my left shoulder while I type on a MacBook. It *is* like they are a co-writer looking over my shoulder saying, 'No. No. Say this.'

To me my characters are co-writers ,and I have, in the past, given them co-writing credits, like I did with Abigail K.C. Sterling, the co-author of *Alistair Strange & the Fan Friction*. She deserves the credit as much, if not more so, than I do.

Acknowledgement on the Galvanising Debate Chapter

While obtaining the texts of *Frankenstein*, *The Burial*, *The Vampyre*, and other works collected in this collection were as simple as copying-and-pasting from the Internet (particularly Project Gutenberg), one chapter, in particular, needed to be an original story. The chapter on the galvanizing debate is so important to this collection because it was the very debate that inspired Mary Shelley's nightmare of the 'pale student of the unhallowed arts'. But this chapter would require intense research, and this research led me to a singular work: *Shocking Frogs: Galvani, Volta, and the electric origins of neuroscience* by Marco Piccolino and Marco Bresadola, with translation by Nicholas Wade. This $130 university-grade textbook required great investment, both financial and intellectual. I am indebted to this work. When the authors quote substantial quotations from Galvani, Volta, and others, I draw upon those quotations for Lord Byron's and Percy Shelley's arguments in their debate. Elsewhere, where they draw upon simpler quotations within the text, I admit to using the words and phrasings of Piccolino and Bresadola, not out of an attempt to plagiarize or diminish their work, but to communicate the scientific arguments between Shelley and Byron effectively. (I use the Adobe Caslon font to distinguish their words from either mine or those written in the late 17th or early 18th centuries). Part of the mission statement for this collection is to let the original work, whether *The Vampire*, *Ernestus Berchtold*, or *Frankenstein* stand on their own merits. And I wish to do the same with *Shocking Frogs*. If you have a spare $130, please purchase this textbook. It is well worth the read.